# The Caseroom

## KATE HUNTER

Cover illustration: Ciara O'Connor

Published by:
Fledgling Press Ltd,
First published 2017

www.fledglingpress.co.uk

Printed and bound by:
MBM Print SCS Ltd, Glasgow.

ISBN 9781905916221

# Acknowledgements

A big thank-you to Cathy, Becca and Adrian for reading drafts and for their suggestions and encouragement. Loving thanks to Phil for, well, being Phil, and to Jane for being Jane. And special thanks to my son Justyn and big sisters, Hazel and Maureen, for their quiet faith in me.

Thanks to Professor Siân Reynolds for climbing to her attic to retrieve her research files; to the staff of the National Library of Scotland and The British Library; to New Writing South for awarding me a free read with The Literary Consultancy (TLC); to the TLC and Lesley McDowell for their encouragement; and to Clare and Paul of Fledgling Press for truly appreciating my work. Thanks also to Ciara O'Connor of ECA for her cover illustration and Graeme Clarke for his graphic design.

*To my father, who took me to the library when I was wee*

# Part I    A frock at the frame: 1891–96

## 1891: Into the caseroom

# -1-

Wakening, she raised her head and peered through darkness to where dirty yellow light from a streetlamp smudged window panes, sink and stove. Going on six by her reckoning. Waiting for bells to strike the hour, she shut her eyes and opened her ears to rhythmic snuffles from her mother, dead to the world by her side; to creak of springs as her sister shifted in her bed in the corner; from ben the bedroom, a gasp as her father trawled for breath; a loud snort, then silence. Not a cheep from her brothers.

Hands clasped to her breast as though in prayer, she clamped elbows to ribs to contain a tingle in her veins that put her in mind of herself as a bairn on gala day, except that that bairn's blood would not have had this peppering of fear in it. So how come it was there? What this day held in store gave true cause for excitement, aye, for apprehension, aye. But fear? What was there to be feart of? In answer, her brother Rab's face, white-lipped and seething, came to mind. Last night when, silenced by a sharp word from their father, Rab had gritted his teeth, she'd felt triumphant. But even as she'd felt it she'd had an inkling that such a triumph would not withstand the light of day.

She'd not lain long before metal rang on stone in a nearby street. Keeping an ear pinned to the bedroom, she listened to hooves clip-clop closer. Rattle of milk churns. Must be gone six. She slipped from under blankets and squatted at the chanty, beam end pressed to cold rim to muffle the tinkle, a common enough sound of a night but one that at this hour, with day nearing, might act like a hooter to rouse folk. In two ticks she was dressed in clothes left ready over the back of a chair: drawers, light summer vest, stockings, faded grey and black striped dress, fresh-laundered, navy smock. Boots? No. She set them down by the door ready till she'd got porridge and dinner pieces made.

The strike of a match, hiss of gas, scrape of pot sounded deafening to her, but no-one roused. Set to soak overnight, the oatmeal porridge was ready by the time she'd sliced bread, spread lard, smeared on potted haugh and wrapped six pieces. After putting a package in her smock pocket, she ate a few spoonfuls of porridge straight from the pot, blowing to cool it, watching tenement windows across the street come to life as dawn light rinsed out dark.

Too early to leave yet, but she wanted to be off. She'd walk a long way round, stop at a bakers to buy a roll straight from the oven, sit on a step or crate to eat it. Though a trace of night's chill would be in the air, this September was mild as anything. She looked up. A wee strip of dulled silver sky above roofs was tinged with pink and blue. No sign of rain clouds.

First, though, the best bit, the bit she'd been leaving till last. From a corner of a shelf she took down the setting stick and box of rules her father had presented to her. Used tools, aye, but, still, good tools. Last night she'd held them in her lap to finger them, but Rab's glower had made her think better of loosening the screw on the stick to move the measure, opening the box's neat clasp to take out the stack of wee brass rules. Studiously ignoring her brother, she'd set her tools down safe with the hair clasp you'd easily take for real tortoiseshell and her wooden pencil case with a diamond of ebony inlay, sleek and fine despite being chipped.

Thump. Tinkle. Thought of Rab's glower had her fumble and drop her rule box. She braced. At least it sounded as though the clasp had held. Holding her breath, she crouched to run a hand across the floor, ear cocked. A murmur. A groan. Was that a shuffle? Her father and brothers were rousing. That dark wedge by the chair leg? Aye. Sure enough, the clasp had held tight, the rules had not spilt and she had the box safe in her pocket.

She'd run fingers through her hair, given her plait a quick tuck and tidy and coiled it under her navy hat, was into her boots and had a hand on the doorknob when creaking floorboards made her freeze.

A hand clasped her shoulder.

'Don't do it,' Rab hissed in her ear.

Sensing a trace of pleading in his command, she hesitated.

'You're in the wrong,' he growled.

'No ah'm not,' she growled back, shoving his hand from her.

On the stair, she heard him come after. It was early yet for neighbours to be off to work, the stair was clear, and she was at the door, nearly out in the street, when he barged in front to block her way.

'You're set to bring shame on this family. On your father, on your brothers, on me.'

Rab's doleful tone was nigh-on weighing her down with all this shame, but when he prodded his chest and squeaked 'on me' the weight fell away and, close to laughter, 'Who do you think you are?' came out of her mouth.

Rab grabbed her upper arms. His claws dug in. 'Me? Ah'm a man at the frame, doing a man's work. And you? You mean to be a frock at the frame? Better you'd never been born.'

That took the breath out of her. She went limp. She'd felt spit land on her cheek and she needed to be rid of it. As she tugged to raise a hand she looked into Rab's eyes. Though he was six years her elder, he wasn't so many inches taller. Seeing as he'd not stopped to put his specs on, his pale blue eyes looked frail, putting her in mind of a newborn's opened for the first time. They had sleep in the corners and rapid blinks weakened their glare. Again, she nearly laughed, but before the laugh was out it was stifled by a yen to comfort him, to pat his arm and say, 'It'll be fine, Rab. Go back up and get your breakfast. It's made ready.'

A clomp of boots had Rab keek over her shoulder. They were blocking the way of a neighbour off to work, and as Rab gave him a nervous smile and a clipped 'mornin', his grip on her loosened. Blood brought to the boil by that smile, that 'mornin', as if it was in the normal run of things for a brother to be bruising his sister's arms and telling her she'd be better off unborn, she wrenched free, skirted round him and stomped off.

First of the city's works' hooters sounding, folk were trickling out of stair doors, so there were a fair few heads to turn when Rab bawled after her, 'You and your ilk will be swept from the caseroom. Just you mark mah words.'

# -2-

Nothing in her thirteen years had prepared her for this, not the chorus of works hooters and great clomp of boots of a morning, not the oily tang of her father and brothers' overalls of an evening, not even the stream of printers sweeping by as she stood at the work's gates with her mother of a Saturday payday. All these were as known to her as the cracked lilt of her mother's voice and sweet-sour smell of her flesh. Still, after she'd done as she was told and waited a good long while by the timekeeper's cubbyhole at the entrance, back to the wall as folk streamed by, the commotion of Ballantyne's Pauls print works fair stoondit her.

Chin tucked to keep from gawping, she followed the overseer through the bindery. A wobble to his walk had her wanting to titter at the thought of his legs not being a matching pair, as if he'd reached for them and, bleary-eyed, pulled them on like odd stockings. But she was on her own, no classroom chum by her side to nudge and share a giggle with. Out of the corner of her eye she took in a row of women sitting at a long table, saw how their hands danced a jig as they snatched and flicked at paper being swept along on a roller belt. An empty space among them had her wanting, just then, to be shown, or, better still, beckoned, to that spot, to be joining them and not following the wobbly overseer straight by. Though she didn't recognise any of the women, they were not strangers to her. They were the likes of school chums she'd recently parted company with and lassies and wifeys from her streets. A few looked to be nearly as old as her mum, but many were ages with her, or just a bit older. Fifteen. Sixteen. Ah could slip into place among them without so much as a by-your-leave, she thought. The odd eyebrow would rise, but that you could ignore while you worked out the pecking order.

When one of the women looked her way then leant in to whisper to her chum, and the other looked over and smiled, or smirked, she lifted her chin to look straight over their heads to where lone men stood like charioteers at machines that yanked and jabbed at paper stacks and, beyond them, to men who, hunched over desks, poked and prodded at books. Turning her eyes back to the empty space among the women, she faltered, thinking twice about what she'd set herself to do. Earlier that morning she'd done just the same. After rounding the corner when she'd wrenched free of her brother, she'd stopped a moment, heart thudding, pulled by a longing to slip back into wonted family ways – morning's thick, low voices; warmth of bodies round the stove – before she'd steeled herself to merge with a swelling stream of workers heading for Causewayside.

The overseer had stopped to look over his shoulder. His mouth was moving but what came out of it couldn't be heard for the din. He flicked his head in annoyance. She speeded up. Leaving behind that empty space on the bench felt like tugging her eyes from fruit slices as she left the bakers with a plain loaf and her mum's change in her pocket.

All this time her ears had been taking in a chorus of rattles and clanks and, riding above them, the bindery lassies' blether, and she'd paid no mind to a rising tide of clatter, so that when the overseer opened a small door in the far wall a great belch of din had her stop short like a beast leaning back on its haunches as it's tugged into a pen.

'Casters,' the overseer mouthed over his shoulder as, at a quick hobble, he skirted round two muckle machines, all jerking limbs and levers, that fairly shook the floor. Where, in the bindery, a pitched glass roof let in a shower of soft grey beams, the small casting room's inky light came from slits of windows high on one black wall and a greenish glow from lamps fixed to another. As she passed a clarty-overalled man leaning in to tap at a juddering machine and a fresh-overalled apprentice craning over his shoulder, a wee tremor ran down her back to dislodge eyes that had stuck to it like ticks. Half-turning, she caught the apprentice eyeing her, and, seeing as she'd no reason to suppose he'd been taken with her striking beauty, she turned to face him and give him a taste of what her wee brother William called her fierce face, as in 'ye've got yer fierce face on.'

'When you're quite done with yer gawping.' Holding yet another door open, the overseer barked so loud his words carried.

And, letting go of the breath she didn't know she'd been holding as she heaved the casting room door shut behind her, she entered the caseroom.

'Wheesht,' she whispered to herself, blinking up at a canopy of powdery mauve light. Like the bindery, the caseroom was a long hall, only narrower. Like the bindery, its light came from a pitched glass roof. But where the bindery rattled and clanked, and the casting room pounded and clattered, the caseroom's taps and tinkles rode on an intent hush. And where the bindery smelled of glue and turpentine and hot rubber, and the casting room reeked of dirty grease and singed metal, the caseroom's smells were sawdust, mothballs, oiled wood and ink.

'Stone.' The overseer slapped the first of a column of squat tables that dotted the central aisle. 'Forme.' He tapped a mental frame that lay on the stone. By clasping in her smock pocket her setting stick and box of rules, she stopped herself from following suit, denying her hands their itch to be fingering the caseroom's furnishings and objects.

'Frames.' He punched the side of one of a rank of tall wooden cabinets with sloping tops that stretched down either side of the aisle. Each, she saw, was crowned with the top of a bare head, men's wiry bristles or balding pates on one side, women's bobs and buns on the other. Realising she still had her hat on, she snatched it off, though when the overseer stopped by a stocky woman with a fat knob of rich chestnut hair and, without staying the restless jigging of her hands, the woman took a sidelong glance, she wished she'd kept it on to cover her sandy wisps. The woman's glance, she thought, measured her and found her too slight a thing.

'New learner lassie. Get her started will ye, Fanny?'

'Right you are.'

'Just do as you're told and ye might do us,' the overseer grunted as he wobbled off.

And so, she stood like a bairn warned to mind its manners as the woman, Fanny, paying her no heed, read and spelled out from the top sheet of a wedge of papers propped atop her frame – 'Mrs Field took her boy in her arms. Cap *M*, *r*, *s*, nut space, cap *F*, *i*' – while her fingers plucked metal slivers from wee compartments in a big, shallow drawer and placed them in her setting stick. That her hands kept up with her mouth was amazing to behold.

'You'll catch flies.' A hint of a smile in deep-set eyes showed this woman knew it was wonder that kept Iza's mouth open.

'Have you got a name?'

'Aye.'

'Let's have it then.'

'Iza Ross.'

The woman cupped a hand to her ear.

'Iza Ross,' Iza said louder.

'Fanny Begg,' she announced. 'Now, Iza Ross, watch and learn. 'Manuscript' – with a horny, blackened fingernail she tapped the stack of papers – 'made up of folios' – her fingers fluttered pages – 'and, here, case full of type, or, as we say in the trade, sorts' – her hand swept over the drawer and, dipping into one of its wee compartments, index finger and thumb lifted slivers and let them trickle back – 'to be placed in your setting stick, starting at the right end, that's to say the left end, the right end being the wrong end of the stick'. Fanny Begg's head bobbed from left to right. 'And when you've filled your stick, you dump your lines to the galley,' she said, tapping a metal tray. 'Right, what was it again?'

Iza gawped at her.

'Your handle?'

'Iza Ross.'

'Well, Iza Ross, let's get you set to work.'

Without wishing to, Iza mimicked Fanny Begg's brisk sweeping at stray hairs with the back of a hand as she followed her back down the aisle. Glances to the left caught men's eyes weighing her up and, to the right, the odd fleeting smile from a woman, but most were too caught up in their work to pay her any mind. At the far end of the caseroom Fanny Begg stopped at an unoccupied frame and Iza watched and listened while this imposing woman eased a case from its slot, set it down on the frame's sloping top, plucked out a sort, an *m*, and named its parts: face, serif, beard, shoulder, feet, nick.

'Learn the lay of the case.' Fanny Begg swept a hand over the compartments. Then, seeing Iza's puzzlement, she explained 'Which go where.'

Even in the relative quiet of the caseroom you had to raise your voice to be heard. This, Iza had learnt. So she raised it, and was abashed to hear her 'Which what?' come out loud and gruff, as though she'd caught the overseer's bark.

Fanny Begg's eyes flashed. 'Sorts,' she snapped. 'Most are letters of the alphabet and numbers you'll be familiar with. Then there's foreign letters. And ligatures, two characters joined up, like *f* and *l* for the likes of flummoxed.'

Iza winced, aware that her face was a picture of the word.

'Over here.' Fanny Begg beckoned her a few paces to where a lanky man in a brown flannel jacket over an apron that draped his shins leant in to tap with a mallet and pronged metal stick at a slab of woven metal.

'John Adams,' Fanny said. 'Stonehand.'

Whistling a sweet tune Iza knew to be one of her dad's favourites, John Adams glanced up as he dropped a shoulder to lever his stick and tap at an angle. Like her dad he was a lean, wiry man, and, like her dad's, his face was gaunt and grey.

'If you can catch a few drips of John's knowledge of composing type you'll know a lot more than some ah could mention.'

Iza caught the scunnered glance Fanny Begg threw at a man working at a nearby frame. She'd already got a glimpse of that man. She'd been aware of him sniffing in her direction. She didn't think he'd recognised her, but she had certainly recognised his fat purple nose and slobbery mouth. She turned her back on him.

John Adams squinted up at Fanny.

'John's cloth-eared, like most in here,' Fanny said before raising her voice to say, 'Got a bit more time for frocks at the frame than some round here, eh John?', clearly aiming it at the other man's ears.

Though Fanny Begg said it lightly, still, her 'frocks at the frame' shook Iza. Like dry bread stuck in her gullet, the phrase repeated on her. Repeated in Rab's voice, at that.

'What's that?' John Adams cocked an ear.

'Just telling the lassie to pay you no mind, ye daft old codger.'

'Aye right. Give her a year or so in here and she'll be as daft as me,' he said, greeting Iza with a wee crease of his eyes and dip of his head.

Like a sip of water, John Adams' gesture helped Iza swallow and steady her nerves. It helped her take her place at her frame.

'The morn's morn you'll be set to earning your living reading out copy.' Fanny Begg gave her an enquiring look. Again, Iza felt herself being weighed up and, as before, she could not quite gauge this woman's measure of her, except Fanny Begg seemed to be giving her the benefit of the doubt because now she lowered her voice, leant in close and, nodding across the aisle, mouthed 'Mind out for the likes of George bloody-frocks-at-the-frame Seggie,' before leaving Iza to it.

As Iza Ross hung her hat on a hook, her upper arms hurt.

She could still feel her brother's bruising clench, still feel his spit on her face. Though none was there, she wiped her cheek with the back of a hand and muttered, 'It's not mah fault.' Then, catching herself girn like a bairn, she chided herself and stepped onto a platform that brought her elbows level with her case. On tiptoe, she looked down the length of the caseroom. The lassie at the frame in front keeked round and smiled. Iza smiled back. She looked up to where weak sunlight filtered through grimy glass. She listened. Near at hand, tap-tap of mallet on metal. In the aisle, rattle of a trolley. A rasping cough, answered by another. From through the wall the casters' infernal clatter. From further off, waves of rolling, rumbling thuds. Now, she shut her ears and, all itching fingers, took her setting stick and rules from her pocket and set them down on her frame.

## – 3 –

Iza had already run into George Seggie. A few weeks back she'd come home to find her father, James Ross, perched in his armchair by a guttering fire. Tang of Briar's Balsam in the air, steaming bowl clutched to his knee, old towel draped over his head, he was rattling and whistling like a dented kettle on the boil. Iza had come in starving hungry, but before she could take a bite her mum had sent her off for messages. First, though, she was to go to Typo Hall to collect the benefit.

'You'll have to scoot. It's gone one and they shut at half past.'

Her dad poked his out head out from under the towel to mutter that they wouldn't like it, a lassie being sent.

'Well they'll have to lump it. Mah kidneys are killing me and ah'm not about to hike them up the High Street.' Vi Ross stuck a scuffed buff card in one of Iza's hands and a message bag in the other and, with a 'Mind you don't lose the card and don't break the eggs,' shooed her out the door. Hungry as she was, she wasn't sorry to be off. These days, her dad's condition made a cold place of home. Even on hot days, or when of a chill evening the fire was well stoked, his sickness seemed to soak up warmth.

This was an autumn day of churning grey skies and drizzle that dissolved people, tenements and, behind and above them, Salisbury Crags and Arthur's Seat, in a thick grey broth. Card clasped in her pocket, Iza belted down the Pleasance and up St Mary's Street, skirting wifeys and bairns and carts and crates. In the High Street, she got stuck behind three gents who'd stopped to parley and nearly got a swipe when a stout one wearing the stupidest red and yellow tartan breeks swung his walking stick. She sheered round him to pant up to a sweetshop window for a quick suck of her gums at sight of a tower of macaroon. Next to the sweetshop, an iron stopper held a heavy dark green door slightly ajar. A brass nameplate said Argyll Hall, but she knew it was what her father called Typo Hall. When he'd pointed it out to her one day and she'd thought Typo Hall was a sort of hall he didn't know the right name for, he'd laughed at her in a nice way.

After keeking into two or three rooms off a long, dark corridor, she found the Edinburgh Typographical Society, or, rather, she came upon two men of her father's age sitting behind a long desk, one with a cashbox by him, the other a ledger. A third man, holding a newspaper up to grey light, stood tapping the stem of an unlit pipe on brown teeth. His mouth slobbered and his nose put Iza in mind of a big bruised raspberry.

Halted just inside the door, pinching her shoulder in to keep it clear of greasy brown bunnets hanging on a coat stand, she hinged a leg to tap a toe on the floor. The room smelt thick with men: that familiar reek of wet wool jackets and two-day-old mince on a hot summer's day. The union men had seen her, she knew, but they weren't letting on. The two at the desk busied themselves with their cashbox and ledger while the other, taking his pipe from his mouth, read from his newspaper as though he were addressing a congregation.

'Eight-hour day, no loss of pay. Under a banner emblazoned with this, the latest war cry of that agitator of the labouring classes, Mr James Connolly, last night addressed a gathering in Oddfellows Hall, Forrest Road. A collection for the masons of the city who struck work yesterday in a demand for a reduction in hours raised three pounds, seven shillings and tuppence.' The pipe he'd stuck back in his mouth rattling, he turned to address the others. 'What sort of measly collection's that, eh?'

'Three pounds, seven and tuppence better than bugger all,' cashbox man said without looking up.

'The eight-hour day would do us just dandy. And we might get it if these bloody agitators'd keep their noses out.' He puffed and wheezed over a flaring match. 'Have we had anything in from the Trades Council about our brother masons?'

After exchanging sidelong glances, the men at the desk looked up at Iza as though they'd discovered a pressing engagement.

'And how can we help you, hen?' said ledger man. The way his bushy eyebrows arched as he peered over his specs was discouraging, but the wee tilt of his head was friendly enough. Cashbox man leant back, stretched, scratched his bald head. His lower eyelids hung loose, so that Iza worried those watery eyeballs might slip out, slither down his cheek, catch on his black moustache. He was about to speak, but slobber-mouth got in first.

'Looking to start in the caseroom are ye? Well, ah can

tell you for nothing girruls don't bother themselves with tedious matters like union organisation. They go straight into the masters' pockets.'

Iza narrowed her eyes at him as she laid her father's union contributions card on the desk and said, 'Mah dad's sickness benefit.' She added a curt 'Please,' when ledger man picked up the card.

That very week a man from Ballantyne's Pauls works had come to her class to talk to school leavers. He'd given out a handwritten sheet and a printed sheet that had the same story on and told them to find errors and mark them with squiggles from a list. He gave them some sums too. And not just boys. Girls got to do it. The man from Nelsons' Parkside works, where Iza's dad and brothers Rab and Jack worked, only talked to the boys. Iza spotted eleven mistakes and found the right squiggle to mark most of them. She loved it. And though she didn't love them, she got the sums right. After the class handed in their work she saw the Ballantyne's man and schoolmistress look her way, so she wasn't surprised when her name was called. She was surprised to be the only one called, though. Girl or boy. She knew she was good at spelling and grammar, but she'd never come top of the class. That evening she'd asked her dad could she start in Ballantyne's caseroom. And her dad had nodded, slowly, and said, 'We'll see.'

Iza watched ledger man write 'James Ross' and a number in one column and '9/6d' in the next. She waited while he scratched his head over a running total she'd worked out in her head, upside down. She watched him write and initial '9/6d' and '23/9/91' on her dad's card. When cashbox man had counted out the coins, she carefully lifted them into her pocket and, saying her thanks, made to leave.

'You'll be wanting this, hen.' Ledger man was holding

out the subs card. As Iza took it, he said, 'Tell your dad we asked after him.'

She almost said, 'No you didn't. You never asked,' but she held her tongue. He'd spoken kindly enough. It was raspberry nose got her dander up. As she left Typo Hall she minded how, after saying, 'We'll see,' her father had said it might go hard on her. There were some would say she was taking a man's job. Still a lot of ill-will over lassies entering the caseroom in the wake of the '72–'73 strike. He hadn't said any more and she hadn't asked. Her dad was warning her what she'd be up against, not refusing her, and that, in the coming weeks, had helped steady her resolve.

Her eldest brother Jamie, too, had helped. Jamie had fair confounded their father by refusing to follow him into Nelsons' machine room. Daft, James Ross had said, when ah can easy get you a start in a steady trade. There'll always be a call for printed matter. Choosing his own path, Jamie had gone into the ironworks. And this remove from Edinburgh's print trade, along with his couthie nature, had led Jamie to side with Iza in her wish to work in the caseroom. Well, at least he'd kept out of family disputes over the matter, offering her sympathetic looks and a change of subject.

Iza's sister Violet, turned sixteen, and her wee brother William, nearly nine, had kept out of it too. When words were raised on the matter Violet would be out with her chums, eyeing up lads, or, if she'd left off and come home, helping with housework. Her only intervention had been to tell Iza, out of earshot of the others, that she couldn't for the life of her see why anyone would want to go into a filthy dirty print works.

'And who'd want to be at the beck and call of toffee-nosed madams,' was Iza's answer to that.

Violet had started in a wee drapers shop, but hadn't taken to the bossy wifey who ran it, nor to handling men's drawers, and had gone up in the world, to fancy lingerie in Thompson and Allison's department store.

Matters with William were more complicated. Until summer just gone, though Iza had to help with chores, still, come grown-up talk she'd escape with William ben the bedroom or out to the woods by the park. She'd have been a bairn with him, doing what bairns do. Now that Iza had joined the grown-ups, she knew William felt the loss because she felt it too.

Jack, second eldest, would take the opposite tack to Jamie. Not that Jack had any burning interest in how Iza was to earn a living. It was simply not in his nature to keep out of any dispute. After following their father into Nelsons' machine room, Jack had now served his time. With no females in Nelson's caseroom the issue was not pressing there, but this seemed to give Jack all the more leeway to be contrary, one evening arguing black was white, the next that it might be red, and, later the same evening, that it was indeed white.

Along with Rab, their mother, Vi Ross, formed the opposition. The two had different reasons, though. Vi Ross was not bothered about Iza taking a man's job. Her objection was born of hard-nosed calculation.

'What the hell's the use of bringing in a pittance for your keep while you spend years learning skilled work,' she'd say, hands on hips, eyebrows hitched up, 'when you'll no sooner be on decent money than you'll be wed and having bairns and never use your precious trade again?'

Folding envelopes had been quite good enough for her, she insisted, red hands going like the clappers to demonstrate the folding.

'Ah was giving mah mother good money for mah keep soon as ah left school,' she'd say, scrubbing carrots like they were fighting back.

Gritting her teeth, Iza chopped at the carrots, whacking the knife down and slicing a finger in the process and so giving her mother the satisfaction of saying, 'You see, just like ah said, you're too clumsy for that type of highfallutin work.' There'd been no point in telling her mother she'd said no such thing, but Iza had told her anyway.

And Rab? A newly time-served comp in Nelsons' caseroom, he'd fumed at talk of Iza entering the caseroom.

'So you'll allow yourself to be used to undercut agreed rates, to be used as cheap labour? Ah'll tell you for nothing ah'm not about to stand by and let a sister of mine...' at which point he'd be pulled up short by a warning look from their father. He'd not give up, though. Adopting a tone he must have picked up in lecture halls he frequented, a tone that drove Iza mad, he'd launch into: 'Do you know that working men have had to fight long and hard to win decent rates. Back in...' Iza would hear no more. Like the rest of the family she'd give full attention to fiddling with the lamp wick or clearing used matches from the box. Then, tutting and muttering, Rab would turn to sharpening his pencil to underline and write notes in a tiny, neat hand in the margins of his Scottish Typographical Association journal.

On the eve her father agreed to Iza accepting a start at Ballantynes, Rab had quoted chapter and verse from a journal article by an eminent French physician – he'd stressed every syllable of that – on the detrimental effects of print works on women's fertility. 'Unnatural,' he'd said. And as if saying it once wasn't enough he'd underscored it. 'Unnatural.' He'd blushed when he said 'women's fertility' though. And he mispronounced 'puerperal'. And even though Iza was only thirteen she knew it and her dad knew it too and a wee smile he'd given her had emboldened her to say, 'Who cares. Who wants bairns anyhow?'

# 1894: Time-served

§§§§§§§§§§

She's made the measure allowing for squeeze and, elbows hinged soft but firm, set herself to face e in its compartment just left of centre of her Old Style lower case. Though she'd never let on, she's even said 'mornin' to the letter that curls in on itself as though it doesn't need the others. When it comes to it, though, she silently informs it, you're nothing on your own, just like the rest. Eyes fixed on the first line of the first folio of 'The Dwarf with the Long Beard', she sharpens them on the particular tilt and curl of the hand – a fairly good one this – to pluck into her mind the day's first string of words. 'In a far distant land.'

Arms raised to the upper case, slight swivel of shoulders and fleet lever of wrists, and she nips up her first sort, a cap *I*, slips it into place in her setting stick and snares it with a black-and-yellow-furrowed thumbnail. And so her hands set off on today's nine-and-a-half hour journey round the case, right plucking, left gathering in.

IN a far distant land there reigned a

Narrowing her eyes to see the line as a pattern of black and white, she chinks out a thick between *t* and *l*, nearest thing to two uprights, and slips in two thins to increase spacing a fraction. Same between, let's see, *d* and *t*. Still a bit of give. It'll have to be that *N* and *a* and, there now, her first line's justified snug.

> an only daughter who was so very beautiful that no one in the whole kingdom could be compared to her. She was known as Princess Pietnotka, and the fame of her beauty spread far and wide. There were many princes among her suitors, but her choice fell upon Prince Dobrotek.

Arms too tightly strung. You'll not last like that she tells herself. Replanting her boots straight and square – sawdust and metal filings already settling on the sheen from her father's spit and polish – she lowers her chin a fraction and hikes her slight shoulders back and down to slacken the tension a notch. There now.

> She obtained her father's consent to their marriage, and then, attended by a numerous suite, set off with her lover

for the church, having first, as was the
custom, received her royal parent's
blessing.

As though she's drawn a thick veil about her, all that is
not manuscript and case of tiny metal slivers fades clean
away. Ranks of frames the length of the caseroom, each
with its crowning head, women's on this side, men's on the
other, gone. Squat slabs that dot the central aisle, each with
its brown-aproned stoneman bent over it, gone. The print
works' din, too, fades: machine room's distant rumbling
thuds; clatter of next door's casters; near-at-hand, tap-tap
of mallet on metal. Wheesht. Listen. Just the clink of sort
meeting sort, of tiny wee pieces of tin and antinomy and
lead lining up, and that's a sound for fingertips to feel, not
ears to hear. And now, concentration set, fingers flying,
lines building sure and even, she can pay some heed to her
mind's wanderings.

As she thinks of giving her wee brother a proof copy
of this job, last of the *Slav Peasants and Herdsmen's Tales*
she's typeset these past weeks, pictures his eager eyes, his
voice intoning 'The dwarf with the long beard,' her mouth
softens into a smile. But will she manage to rifle a proof?
Linger by the proofing press to admire the pressman's
work, find the right words to butter him up without giving
him the wrong idea. Depends who's on the press. Some of
them have minds, hands even, liable to wander where they
oughtn't. Her nose wrinkles like it's got a sniff of the gas
works and, catching this thought-trail threatening to stall
her hands, she cuts it short.

Most of the princes who had been

unsuccessful in their wooing of
Pietnotka returned disappointed to
their own kingdoms: but one of them,
a dwarf only seven inches high, with
an enormous hump on his back and
a beard seven feet long, who was a
powerful prince and magician, was so
enraged that he determined to have
his revenge.

That lad at the works' gates this morning. Now what's
he doing slinking into her mind? Her lower lip pouts as
she tries to add features to a sun-browned face and thick
brown hair that needs a cut. Tall, bare-headed, standing like
a boulder in a burn so that the surge of printers had to flow
round him. No. Not a boulder. More a branch, buffeted as
he held out his handbills and folk swept by, some grabbing
one, someone near her muttering 'bugger off'.

So he changed himself into a whirlwind
and lay in wait to receive the princess.
When the wedding procession was
about to enter the church the air was
suddenly filled with a blinding cloud of
dust, and Pietnotka was borne up high
as the highest clouds, and then right
down to an underground palace.

A rattling wheeze plucks at her nerves. Bent over his
stone not two yards from her, heel of a hand pressed to

the edge, John Adams has set down his mallet to cough and gurgle. She doesn't want to see the alarm in his face, that same safety lamp flickering down a black tunnel she's seen in her father's eyes. Holding her setting stick aside while her fingers scamper through *ts* to nip out *ns* strayed from an overfull box – time saved in the long run she tells herself – she silently hums a tune that's been playing in her head since a slurred strain of it wove its way up the tenement wall last night.

Pause. Listen. John Adams rakes up phlegm. She casts an eye over her learner's practice piece, set three year ago now in ruby, minion and all the font sizes up to 14, both justified and in quad left ragged right, in upper and lower case roman, in italic, in small caps and all caps, read, proofed, corrected —

### Habits to be Acquired

First and foremost, maintain a quiet and thoughtful manner. The compositor must not sing, whistle or talk or allow the mind to wander from the work to be set.

— and, quietly at first, sings *Daddy wouldn't buy me a a bow-wow*. When her voice rises, Netta Strachan at the next frame picks up and echoes *bow wow*, then a handful of voices take up *Daddy wouldn't buy me* and women's voices, men's voices, a good two score of them, this whole end of the caseroom, chorus *bow-wow*.

Voices drop. She lifts her head. John Adams is darting a warning nod up at the gallery. The singing stops. Fifty pairs of eyes take a quick keek up while heads stay down. Wight the overseer is out of his lair, leaning over the iron rail to survey. She swallows a lump in her throat, taking down with it a musty mothball tang of nepthaline laced with black oil and ink.

> There the dwarf, for it was he who had
> worked this spell, disappeared, leaving
> her in a lifeless condition.

And so the day slips along, sorts plucked, words composed, lines justified, folios turned until, light sunk to dirt-speckled oatmeal, eyes stretched to bursting, legs stuffed with yeasty dough, it must be about half five. Half an hour to go. She unfurls and stretches the fingers of her left claw and releases them to coil back round her setting stick.

One of three casting machines next door judders to a halt. Then another. Then another. Tap-tap of stonemen's mallets stops. It's so quiet she can hear her ears throb. Nearly there, and like a fiddle coming in to lift a tune, a few lines of verse give a wee lift to her arms.

> The prince made the sign of the cross
> and resumed his journey. When he had
> gone some way along the moorland
> he stopped, and without looking back
> tried the effect of the magic words,
> saying:

> "Dappled Horse with Mane of Gold,
> Horse of Wonder! Come to me.

Walk not the earth, for I am told

You fly like birds o'er land and sea."

Then amid flash of lightning and roll of

thunder appeared the horse.

# -4-

Great chorus of works' hooters fading and clatter of boots swelling, Iza tramped down iron steps. Out into late summer's silver-grey light she blinked and rubbed her eyes with the back of a hand as she and her work chum Margaret Scott joined warehousemen, typecasters, bookbinders and bindery lassies, machinemen and machine-feeder lassies to shuffle through the yard gates into Causewayside. Nearing the gates, Iza found herself craning for sight of the tall, bare-headed lad who'd been blocking the way that morning. And there he was, head above the crowd. When folk in front brushed past him his outstretched arm swung back like a briar into Iza and Margaret's path. Margaret took a handbill. Lowering her eyes from his keen look, Iza followed suit. The lad shook a pail. Coins jingled.

'Support the miners' fight for a living wage.'

He was broad-shouldered. A bit hollow-chested, and that crumpled linen jacket was made for someone with shorter arms, but she saw why he had caught her fancy this morning. That thick brown hair and strong, clean-shaven jaw. Big, squint mouth. Like his skin, his eyes were unusually dark for these parts. It was his voice, though, that had her step out of the flow and stop. Like treacle toffee. Quite well-spoken. Edinburgh, aye, but with a trace of somewhere else altogether. Ireland?

'Will you not spare a halfpenny?'

No, not Irish.

By Iza's side, Margaret dug in her pocket and dropped a coin into his pail.

'Thank you. Much appreciated.' Margaret got treated to a broad smile.

Highlander? No. As Iza stuffed the handbill in her pocket the lad eyed her expectantly.

'Ah haven't got any money,' Iza said, wishing she had.

'Pity. Never mind. Will you not read the handbill?'

When he looked down at her she held his gaze for a moment before muttering 'Later.' As she hurried to catch up with Margaret she felt his eyes soak into her back, through her jacket and blouse and onto her skin, like sun or like frost. She glanced over her shoulder. A few loping strides and he was by her side, close enough for her to get a whiff of spicy tobacco and Coco Castile soap.

'Two Fife miners are in town. They'll be in Jim Connolly's cobbler shop in Buccleuch Street this evening. That's where I'm taking this.' He jingled his pail.

'How much did you get?' Iza took a keek.

'A fair bit. Come and help count it.'

The cheek of him. 'No thanks,' she smiled.

'Come and hear about the miners' dispute. Months on strike for a living wage.'

Margaret had walked ahead but stayed within earshot.

Now she stopped. 'I'll tell me dad about it,' she said over her shoulder. 'He'll want to know.' She clasped Iza's arm.

'I hear there's a dispute brewing in your works?' the lad called after them.

Iza stayed her step. Though female comps couldn't help but get wind of a dispute in the offing, and earlier in the week Iza had got just that, she knew little or nothing of the matter. That didn't mean, though, that it didn't concern her. It did. And it concerned her all the more now this lad wanted to talk of it. But disputes were men's affair. With a wee glance over her shoulder and a hint of a smile she let Margaret lead her off.

It was a dry evening. Nights starting to draw in and a wee nip in the air. Deep pink streaks of cloud slid over tenement roofs. The morning's fresh wind had dropped, but the tail end of it still hung about in side streets to slap cheeks and swirl skirts. Causewayside was thick with folk leaving off work. The haberdasher had shut up shop and the greengrocer was lugging boxes inside, but the tobacconist and chemist had lit their lamps. As usual, a fair few men peeled off from the homeward tramp to disappear into the brown fug of pubs.

Iza dragged her feet, in no hurry to be home, but Margaret tugged her along. She'd be set, Iza knew, on seeing to her dad's tea. Just the two of them in their house, Margaret's mother having died giving birth to her, the firstborn. 'Me mam's buried down south.' Margaret had gazed into a distant south when she'd told Iza that. Her dad had brought her up to Edinburgh from England, from Preston, when she was eight and that's why she said 'me mam' and 'me dad', a strange sound that to Iza's ears carried a deep affection. Turned eighteen, Margaret was nearly two years older than Iza, but whereas Iza had started straight from school at thirteen, Margaret had worked in the ticket office at the Caledonian Railway Station before getting a start in the caseroom two years back. The pair of them had chummed up soon after Margaret started and these past two year had sat together on a crate in the yard at dinnertime on fine days and chummed each other home of an evening.

After Margaret waved her cheerio, Iza dithered. Just a single red streak in a sky turned deep smoky grey and streets were emptying now, the stream of folk pouring into stair doors thinning to a trickle. An oily tang from fishwives' baskets of herring and mackerel had a pair of scavenging gulls squabbling in a gutter already pecked clean. Staring along a gully between tenements at the blackening outline of Salisbury Crags, Iza pictured herself back home, in a room bulging with big brothers wanting their tea and her sister Violet and mother busy seeing to it while their dad coughed his lungs up or, worse, took to his bed sick and silent. Iza would get told to make herself useful then get bustled out of the way by a Violet going on all the while about the latest hairdos and fashions, which was fine if you'd got lovely copper waves and a shapely figure like Violet's, but not so fine when you'd been landed with fair wisps stuck atop a fencepost with a couple of dabs of poorly risen dough. That'd leave Iza to help William with his homework, which would have suited her fine had William not stopped accepting her help, had given up on homework altogether if truth be told.

Poor William. He hated school. Iza hadn't much liked it herself, but she'd been better equipped to withstand sarcasm and tedium than William seemed to be. He was losing interest, too, in stories she'd tell him when she was working on something good, like these Slav fairy tales. He'd been all ears at the lion who knew every hidden and secret thing in the tale of the twelve huntsmen, though when she resorted to making it up because she'd been too busy setting type to take in the sense he'd lost interest. Sometimes, though, he himself would make it up and, for the most part, she was glad he was a better storyteller than she was. These days William occupied himself drawing comic book stories. 'Och,' she muttered. She'd forgotten to bring the scrap paper he'd been asking for. A cab clipping by had her jump to the pavement. A gust of wind whipped at her skirt. She shivered. She wanted … she wanted something.

On the main road, a motor car's roar drowned out for a moment the clip of hooves and rattle of cabs and carts. Still dawdling, going the long way round, Iza took a cursory interest in enamel jugs and stacked cans of corned beef, anything on show in shop windows. A shutter banged. Two dogs snarled over scraps. She paused at a newsagent's billboards to read headlines: Mine owners stand firm; Canonmills cooper crushed; Battle of Yalu River. Yalu River? Where's that when it's at home? Further along a display of hats caught her eye. Quite fetching, that brown one with the yellow ribbon. Could she afford it? Probably not. What were fetching hats to her anyhow? As quick as she questioned herself, the answer came to her. Though you'd not want to be making a song and dance about it like Violet, there was nothing wrong with looking nice. And the morn was Saturday. Pay day. More than pay day. Much more. The morn's morn she'd get her first time-served pay packet.

Her eyes glazed as her mind drifted back to knock-off time last Saturday when the women comps had performed a mock version of the men's time-served ritual for her, parading the caseroom chanting the Cuz's Anthem – but skipping straight from *caca ceecee ca cee ci co cu* to *zaza zeezee za zee zi zo zu* rather than going through the whole rigmarole – and taking a not-so-formal vote to put Iza's one-and-sixpence donation towards an evening at the Gaiety music hall rather than the men's Saturday afternoon downing of buckets of beer and whisky. Back home that day she'd announced to her mother she was time-served, a journeyman. 'How much more will you be getting?' her mother had asked, wiping floury hands on her pinnie before stretching out a spread palm for the pay packet.

'That's not the point,' Iza had said.

'Would you hark at her ladyship. What's the bloody point then, pray tell?'

Iza had held her tongue.

Holding her hands up to inspect stained nicks and dents made by three years of clasping a setting stick and plucking type, Iza frowned. Not that she minded work-worn hands. Quite the reverse. She wanted to show them off, to tell someone she was time-served, someone who'd say, 'Well, fancy that. A compositor! Good for you, hen.' And if that someone wasn't in the print trade, they'd ask, 'What is that about? What do you have to do?' And she'd tell them, though she'd mind not to go on about descenders and pica breviers and overrunning matter. She bit her lip at the thought of a childhood chum's nose wrinkling like she'd stood in dog dirt when, in the street the other Sunday, Iza had launched into an account of her work. The lassie had soon interrupted to talk about a lad who'd walked her home from the dancing, then she'd gone waltzing off across the road trilling, 'Yes, I'm just about the cut for Bel-gra-via'.

'Daft place to stand gawping.'

Someone bumping into Iza jolted her back to the here-and-now.

'Sorry. Ah was miles away,' she said as she turned, to find herself face-to-face with Rab.

'Best place for you.'

'Aye. Miles away from you,' she batted back. But then, finding herself wanting company, even Rab's company, she changed her tune. 'Where're you off to?' she asked as though she cared.

Since her early days in the caseroom the pair of them had settled into a hostile silence, skirting round or avoiding each other, though when Rab read out letters on the scourge of female labour from his union journal, addressing another family member or the wall, he spoke for her ears.

'The library.'

'Have you been home?'

'Aye. Had to get mah own tea. No-one in. Only wee William.' Rab, too, seemed to want company. Even her company.

'Can ah come?' she said. When Rab glowered at her she kicked herself for giving him the opening.

While she'd been dithering, the street's clatter had dropped and black dye had soaked into the sky. Rab looked ghostly pale as he peered at her over his specs. 'It's not for lassies,' he said, his scrawny ginger moustache twitching. 'Lassies don't go.'

'Ah thought it was for tradesmen?'

'Aye.'

'Well ah'm one. Me and mah work chums. That's what we are.'

'So you're a man now, are you?'

'No, but ah'm just as good as.' She said it, but it came out squeaky.

Rab stiffened. Iza could see him stepping onto his high horse, but he bit his lip, humphed, gave her a scunnered look. 'Och, come on then,' he said. 'They'll not like it though. There's no girruls in there.'

'There will be in a minute,' she muttered. She knew what he was up to. He was going to show her, teach her a lesson, let her see for herself just how out-of-place she was. Thought of her wee brother William at home alone, a strange state of affairs, had her look back for a moment, but she hurried after Rab. She'd eyed the Mechanics Library and wanted to get a look in there but had never got up the nerve. Now she was time-served, why on earth shouldn't she? This she told herself, but it didn't wash right through. If she were honest, she'd been feart to go in there on her own.

'How's things at Parkside?' she said when she caught up, putting on an airy tone, like she was passing the time of day with a normal human being.

When Rab didn't deign to answer, she persisted. Softening her tone, she asked what job he was working on. This, a question likely to hook a response from any comp, he ignored, but when she asked if he thought she should join the Warehousemen and Cutters trade union he slowed his pace and, scratching his chin, said it'd be worth finding out what they paid in benefits, what they gave out for dowries, totting up your contributions for say, three or four year, see if you'd be quids in when you left to wed.

'Their representative came round our frames asking us to join. There's a meeting in the warehouse the morn.' Thinking aloud, Iza found herself asking for more of Rab's opinion.

'Go then.'

'But their union's for unskilled workers like the machine feeder and bindery girruls.'

'Don't go then. Don't join. What are you asking me

for anyhow? You well know what ah think and you never bloody listen.' Rab sheered off up a short flight of broad stone steps.

'Thanks a lot,' Iza called after him, watching how he pinned his eyes on the library's double doors to avoid acknowledging two men with handbills and pails who stood either side of it. Whether it was annoyance at Rab's want of manners or simple curiosity that made her stop she couldn't have said, but stop she did. She took a bill, had a look and, since it was the same as the one she'd got from the tall, bare-headed lad, she made to give it back. When the older of the two men, a wiry Irishman with a quizzical smile, asked politely would she not keep it and leave it on a desk inside she said aye, she would.

Stopped just inside the lobby, Rab was holding the door open for her.

'What the hell are you doing encouraging them?' he hissed. 'They're not miners you know. They're agitators. Layabouts and Irish and that.'

'Ah'll do what ah like,' she said, stuffing the handbill in her pocket.

Snatching off his bunnet and muttering under his breath, Rab left her. As he disappeared into a room at the end of the lobby she could see that lamps were lit in there, but when he shut the door behind him the lobby was dark and for a moment she looked from one closed door to the other, not knowing which to choose before, bracing herself, she walked determinedly into the reading room.

Inside she stopped short. In a mustard-brown room doused in smoke hushed rows of folk stood at long lecterns to pore over newspapers, books, journals. Rab was right. No sign of a woman. Sidling by, she made for a wall of shelving and row of desks at the far end of the room and there ran a finger along leather, cloth, thick, thin, tall, short spines. Head tilted to read titles and publishers, she stopped by a set of tall, brick-red volumes that took up the whole of a shelf: The *Encyclopaedia Britannica*, ninth edition. The Ency Brit she said to herself, as though in a crowd she'd happened upon Walter Laburnum or some such famous person. The Ency Brit was known throughout Edinburgh printerdom as a source of plentiful work.

Needing to look like she knew exactly what she was doing here, Iza picked out a volume, Volume XIX Phylactery – Provins, and carried it to a vacant spot. Elbow planted on the lectern, chin resting on a fist, she turned a wad of pages and read at random. 'At the very time when Lithuania was thus becoming a compact, united, powerful state, Poland seemed to literally be dropping to pieces.' The other readers were paying her no mind, but still she couldn't settle. Her eyes drifted down the page. 'Casimir's few wars were waged entirely for profit, not glory.' Whispering had her look up. The man opposite's head had slumped onto his chest. He snortled, shook his head and looked at her baffled-eyed and open mouthed. Now, try as she might to glue her eyes, they skidded from capital to capital – Louis of Hungary, Wladislaus Lokietek, Mendovg. She heaved the volume shut and closed her eyes to rest them. When she replaced the book on the shelf she thought of fetching the final volume to look up Yalu River that she'd read on the billboard, but instead she composed herself to have a slow yawn and stretch before walking unhurriedly to the door, averting her eyes from where she knew her brother stood.

Outside, street lamps up the town end of the road were spluttering into life as, way out along the countryside end, distant stars did the same. As she came down the library steps she saw that the lad from outside her works had joined the other two agitators. They were packing up, carrying off their bills and pails. Hearing her footfall, the lad turned, cocked his head and smiled.

'Evening,' he said. 'Is this you coming to Buccleuch Street after all?'

'Ah have to get home.' She was chuffed he knew her though. Only later did it occur to her that he might have said the same to any number of folk he'd shaken his pail at.

'You ought to hear the miners' talk of their strike. They're remarkable men.'

'Ah have to see to mah wee brother,' she said. Funny way to talk about miners was what she was thinking. But she didn't mind at all when he lagged behind the others to walk by her.

'So, d'you work in the bindery?'

'No. In the caseroom. Ah'm a comp.'

He quizzed her with a tilt of his head.

'A compositor. Typesetter.'

'Well, fancy that. A compositor,' he said.

She smiled up at him. Her wee laugh had him asking what was funny.

'Nothin,' she said.

'So you're one of Edinburgh's famous female compositors? You do men's work?'

'It's women's work too.' She spoke in no uncertain terms, but now thought twice. 'But lads serve a seven-year apprenticeship; we spend just three years learning.'

'So lassies are smarter and quicker to learn, eh?'

Iza studied his face. He wasn't having her on, so she felt a need to put him right. 'We don't make up at the stone. And we generally set straightforward matter, slinging plain dig as we say in the trade.'

'Ah'm sure you do a fine job. But do you get properly paid for it?'

'Mind your own business,' she said. And she meant it, but her tone was light.

'And will Ballantynes be striking work over the fifty-hour week dispute?'

This shift in his interest from her and her job didn't please her, but since she couldn't for the moment think how to get the talk back to herself she answered as best she could. 'Ah've heard mutterings. Ah suppose we'll find out soon enough. But we're not allowed in the Typographical Society Chapel. It's just men.'

'Is that so? So what will the women do in the event of a strike?'

'Ah haven't a clue.'

Her honest reply surprised her. She wasn't normally so quick to admit ignorance. But, then, unless she was deceived, this lad was asking for her honest opinion. His 'Is that so?' didn't mean 'little you know' as out of others' mouths it well might. He wanted to know more and he believed she could inform him. And, then, there was that voice of his. And that smell. Not so much spicy tobacco, she thought now, more parsley and pepper.

A silence fallen between them made her glad when he followed the others across the road to where they were disappearing down a narrow side street. But when she looked over her shoulder and caught him looking too, she wasn't glad. And as she turned into her street, tapping her fingertips on a rough stone wall, a flaking windowsill, a stair door, she eyed the crags that fringed the sky above the roofs and wanted to be not under but beyond them. Wanted to be with the agitator lad and his striking miners. 'Don't be daft,' she told herself. A bell chimed the hour. She counted.

Seven, eight, nine. Up the stair, she found herself tramping to the slow time of a ditty dredged up from childhood: 'Strike, strike, strike for dee-dee dee-dee, We demand the nine-hour day.'

# -5-

Not a soul in. Colour had rinsed from the living room, leaving a wash of tarnished silver and inky blue-black over sink and stove, table littered with bowls and crumbs, empty fireplace and mantelpiece with its framed photograph of her grandfather, her dad's pipe rack, her mother's china posy and a mantel clock that, in the empty room, tick-tocked as though it were head of the family. Iza reached up to pat its head. A muffled 'Aye' came from the bedroom when she called William. He was on his spot, lying on the floor by the window to read by streetlamp light. Aye, he'd had his tea he muttered. No, he didn't know where the others were.

Evening chill had chased away autumn's warmth. Seeing as her mum wasn't there to moan, Iza went back through to the living room and lit the stove as well as the lamp. She stood for a bit staring at hissing blue and gold flames, then thought better of it and turned off the stove. The broth pot was nigh-on empty. Just a heel of a loaf in the bread bin. She soaked up what broth there was with the bread and ate it cold. Milk? Just a spot in the jug. She made to drink it but thought better of it. Her mother liked milk in her tea, claimed it eased her innards. Iza put the jug down and cleared the table.

Gone half nine. Rab, she knew, was at the library; Jamie would be off courting Jessie; Jack at the new gymnasium down Canonmills; Violet must be out winching, or working late, tidying lacy drawers. Their dad? Must be feeling better and off to the pub for a wee half. Mum? She should be here.

'Have you done your homework?'

William snaked himself and his *Halfpenny Surprise* out of the bedroom and across the floor towards the lamp. Skinny, all legs, William would never be tall, but he was getting too long to be taking up space sprawled on the floor.

'Ah'm doing it,' he said without looking up. 'It's reading.'

'What about writing?'

'Ah've did it.'

'Done it.'

Through in the bedroom she picked up overalls and a jacket and hung them on door hooks. She gave bedding a quick tug and stroke. The chanty wasn't emptied and clumps of her father's dirty green gob dotted the surface like frog's heads. She'd take it down to the ashpit in a minute. Funny, though, mum leaving the house in this state. William's school jotter was under a work shirt on a chair. She held it up to the window. Those angry red scrawls. Even though she'd left school more than three year ago now, those marks made her shiver.

'*H, e*, capital *R, t*,' she read out. 'Why can't you even spell "heart"?'

No answer.

'William!'

He scrambled to where Iza stood by the bedroom door

with his jotter, snatched it from her hand, flung himself back on the floor.

'Mind your own business.'

Iza winced. It was as though she'd slapped him.

'Anyhow, see if ah care. Ah'm never going back.'

'But you need your Standard 5,' Iza said softly.

'You do not. Not to go to sea you don't.' William had a spark in his eyes.

'If you get your Standard 5 Dad'll get you into Nelsons. Jack never even got Standard 5 and he got him in. Rab got it when he was eight or something, naturally.'

'Ah'm not going into the print works.' William rolled over, sat up and hugged his knees.

'You might get into our works. Ah can ask for you. We do some good stories.'

Looking up from under hair that needed combing, William pulled up a leg of his breeks to pick at a scab on his knee.

'Want to know what's happening to the dwarf with the long beard?' Iza said. 'He's changed himself into a whirlwind and got a magic horse. He just has to say the magic words: "Dappled horse with mane of gold, horse of wonder come to me, walk not the earth, for I am told you fly like birds o'er land and sea."'

Just a year back William would have rolled his tongue round that. The pair of them would have have chorused it out the window or down the stairwell. But though his face lit up for a moment, William didn't take it up.

'You don't do *The Prairie Chief* or *Ungava* like Nelsons, so they're better than you. Anyhow, ah'm going to sea. Ah'm going on an expedition,' he said.

'But you like books.'

If looks could kill. 'Just because you like something

doesn't mean you want to spend aw day making it. Anyhow, you don't get to write them. You just have to put what others say.'

William's words stung. Rab was always saying things that hurt, but Rab made her angry and anger was an ointment for hurt. William being crabby with her was such a rare thing that it silenced the both of them. And William was right. But he was being stupid. How could she write her own books? That was just daft.

When, gone ten o'clock, their father and mother and sister Violet arrived home together, James Ross went straight through to bed. A slight man to start with, he seemed to have shrunk. Vi Ross, too, looked smaller than she had this morning, and though she did start on about hour-upon-bloody-hour waiting in the infirmary just to be told to get him home to his bed, she quickly ran out of steam. She sank into her armchair and shut her eyes, so that Iza found herself wanting the usual sharp looks that took in the state of the house, sharp hands that snatched up a tea-towel, sharp voice saying, 'You'd let the house fall down round yer ears and not lift a finger.' What with her mother's rare silence putting the wind up her, Iza could even have taken a dose of her 'Ah should have gone off to America with mah sisters when ah had the chance' refrain. Then someone, Jack usually, would get their mother laughing about how she'd be so busy getting a sailor's breeks off him to mend a tear – and making the poor bugger blush by drawing attention to his equipment – or telling the ship's cook where he's going wrong with his stew, that she'd fail to disembark and get herself carted all the way back across the Atlantic.

Vi Ross sat hugging herself, staring at an empty fireplace. Iza fetched a woollen shawl to drape over her

44

lap and knees. When her mother looked up with a half-smile, Iza saw foreign matter in her eyes. What was it? Sadness. That's what it was. Now how had that got into her? True, hunched over a steaming bowl or in bed much of the previous winter, the man of the house, James Ross, had had too much time to dwell on this being the start of his family's downhill slide, the beginning of the end of a few brief summers on the summit with six pay packets coming in: Jamie's time-served metalworker's, his own plus Jack and Rab's journeymen printers' and a quarter of that for Iza, half from now on, plus Violet's shop assistant's. What with him laid up again and another winter not yet set in, Jamie off to start his own family any day now and Jack about take a place at Morrison & Gibbs' Tanfield works and go off to lodgings in Canonmills, James Ross could see the end of the family having a bit to put aside and talk of keeping William on at school. The chances of the last were slim, Iza knew, but William's reluctance would not stop his parents from dreaming. Already, they'd had to dip into savings for the half-year's rent. All this Iza could not fail to know. But she knew, too, that while her father worried himself sicker, her mother was not one to make things worse by worrying. Though full of good grace she was not, Vi Ross set herself to making the family's ends meet, greasing her days with moans and the odd tot of whisky and dose of laughter. Iza's mother had never had time for sadness.

Violet brushed Iza aside to put the kettle on and tidy up round the sink. Iza shooed William off to bed then made herself scarce, curling up by the wall in the set-in bed, shutting her ears to Violet's soothing tuts and crisp ordering of affairs by fixing them on the silence of the coal depot. Though the clatter of wagons always sank as night fell, clanks and hoots of the odd train shunting on into the night had accompanied her falling asleep since the day she was born. Now that the miners' strike had stopped the coal trains, she found herself listening out for them, missing them.

When her mother hauled herself up into bed and elbowed Iza over, Iza elbowed back just hard enough to show she wasn't about to budge far. When the springs in Violet's bed creaked, she wondered for a moment if she would miss those creaks, miss her mum's backside pressed to her hip, the snortles and snores, if, like the coal trains, they absented themselves. Hard to imagine them gone, but Violet was sure to get wed and take her squeaks off to another bed in another house and then Iza would get the small bed and be rid of her mother's backside. And once Jamie and Jack were gone and William off to sea – the thought made her heart lurch – her mother and father would take the bedroom and she'd get the living room to herself. Then she might invite that agitator lad in for tea and a game of whist. Now where did he come from, sailing into her mind with that voice of his? The fact that she'd erased Rab from her reckonings didn't occur to her.

She heard but paid no heed to her brothers coming in and going through to bed. If ah can put a bit by when we're done with the Slav Tales and on to a better-paying job, maybe take a day trip across the river to the seaside before the summer's out? Train or ferry? Train. With Margaret? With the agitator lad? There he was again, insinuating himself. Fat chance anyhow, since soon she was to have a learner lassie perched by her side to read copy and be instructed – a prospect that excited her more than she'd let on. Bound to slow you down. And if she joined the Warehousemen and Cutters union there'd be dues to pay. How much? She'd find out. She'd see if Margaret would come to the meeting in the warehouse at knock-off time the morn. On that thought she sank into sleep to the sound of Jack bashing his shin on a chair, cursing.

§ § § § § § § § §

While the prince was awaiting the
answer to his challenge he heard a
great noise in the clouds, and looking
up saw the dwarf preparing to aim at
him from a great height. But he missed
his aim and fell to the ground so
heavily that his body was half buried
in the earth. The prince seized him by
the beard, which he at once cut off
with the sharp smiting sword.

Must tell William about that, she thinks as she goes to grab
the next string of words from her manuscript, but before
her eyes get hold of them they sheer off, snatched up by the
antics of two figures. At the far end of the caseroom Fred

Henderson, Father of Ballantyne's Edinburgh Typographical Society Chapel, has left his frame to make his way up the central aisle. A bristle to his walk, teeth champing at stray tufts of tobacco-stained moustache, he holds up a foolscap sheet as though he fancies he's a bairn straining at the pavement edge with a golden jubilee flag, or a signalman at the rail depot, red face matching his red flag. The other figure is out of his lair up in the gallery. Belly pressed hard to the iron rail, hand raised to block a shaft of light that's pierced the glass roof's layer of filth, Wight the overseer looks likely to call out 'Land ho', though no sound from his open mouth reaches the ears of those working below him. Despite the good span between the two men, they lodge in far corners of her eyes as she pins her senses back onto her manuscript.

> Then he fastened the dwarf to the
> saddle, put the beard in his helmet, and
> entered the palace. When the servants
> saw that he had really got possession
> of the

Her fingers stutter. Thumb and forefinger fail to pick clean and she's scuffling metal slivers round their wee box until a voice in her head instructs: select your sort before you reach for it; seize it the moment your hand's at the box; if you miss, never fumble; go back to your stick and start again.

> terrible beard, they opened all the
> doors to give him entrance. Without
> losing a moment he began his search

for Princess Pietnotka. For a long time he was unsuccessful, and was almost in despair when he came across her accidentally, and, without knowing it, knocked off the invisible cap.

As her fingers dart, she keeps a corner of an eye on Fred Henderson's progress round the men's frames. She knows full well that his foolscap sheet is a strike notice. She knows he's collecting signatures of men willing to strike work and she knows, too, that most, if not all, will sign. That's what's got knotted veins in overseer Wight's temples pulsing. As part of the fifty-hour-week movement rumbling through the entire trade and beyond, the Edinburgh Typographical Society wants a reduction in hours. Everyone knows this. She's heard her dad and brothers talk of it. She's seen headlines on billboards and read reports in newspapers. But she knows, too, that though a reduction in hours will affect women comps as much as men, Fred Henderson will not be bringing his sheet to her frame to ask her to sign, nor to any frame on the women's side of the caseroom.

This whole business agitates her no end, but seeing as it's too big a matter to dwell on when there's work to be done, she shuts it from her mind and revisits sums she's as thoroughly drilled in as classroom times tables. Every Saturday she's known the sum will come out much as the previous week's, yet still every Saturday she tots for the sheer pleasure of it. And now she's times-served the sums are new. Her learner's piece rate is doubled. The thought thrills her. So, let's see: 2464 ens a page equals tuppence farthing a page. 10 pages Monday to Friday and an extra half on Thursday is 50-and-a-half, plus 5 today is 55-and-a-half.

> He saw his lovely bride sound asleep,
> and being unable to wake her he put
> the cap in his pocket, took her in his
> arms, and, mounting his steed, set off
> to return to the Monster with the
> Basilisk Eyes. The giant swallowed
> the dwarf at one mouthful, and the
> prince cut the monster's head up into
> a thousand pieces, which he scattered
> all over the plain.

Ears prick at the distant ironworks' short blast followed by a long, piping dweeeee. In anticipation of Saturday dinnertime's chorus announcing the end of the working week, the caseroom's splash of blether and curses sinks to a low burble. She fills her last line with em quads, sets down her stick, clasps leading front and back, wriggles, clips the ends of her block of lines with hinged middle fingers, swings the type to the galley, loosens her grip to let the sorts settle then grips again to slide her lines into place.

With an eye on Fred Henderson tramping up the iron stair to the gallery, strike notice clasped to his chest, she finishes her sums. Two 55-and-a-halves is 111 divided by 12 is nine shilling and thruppence plus 55-and-a-half divided by 4 is 13 and three farthings equals one and a penny farthing, equals ten shillings and fivepence farthing. Her fingers tingle at the prospect of taking hold of a wee brown envelope thick with coins.

As she locks up her galley she watches Fred Henderson tramp back down the stair. Though his face gives nothing away, it's clear from the way he holds himself that he knows hungry eyes are on him. And now overseer Wight too descends, chin up and gaze straight ahead, holding himself as though he's unaware of the man a few steps below him. She gives her last quoin a tightening twist and runs fingertips over the solid web of metal she's fashioned. Good work.

Head like it's stuffed with a wad of damp wool, sinews fit to seize, arms and hands that need cajoling into putting tools in their proper place, wiping crusts of metal filings from between her fingers, lifting a tumbler of cloudy water to her lips, stretching to lift her jacket and hat from a hook. Hanging loose, her hands are dead weights.

Down the far end of the caseroom Wight sniffs the air. Maybe he'll bother to notice the fumes and sweltering heat in here, she thinks. Fat chance. He's at Margaret's frame. He's stopping to have a word. What the devil is he wanting with Margaret? Fred Henderson will be wanting to know exactly that, but he doesn't let on as he makes his way past Wight and, there's a thing, he keeps his eyes down and his papers by his side. Not feeling so sure, then.

John Adams starts to whistle a gay tune. Netta joins in with a dum-de-dum. Iza gives it a dee-de-dee. Even though the corridor it rattles along is the other side of a brick wall, their ears have picked up the rattle of the wage clerk's trolley.

'Ouch, ye bugger ye.'

John Adams sets down the mallet he's just brought down on flesh and bone. Eyes raised to the roof, he clasps a hand to his armpit.

'Sounds like knock-off time,' Iza calls.

'Aye, right enough, while ah've still got a few fingers left.' John Adams sucks in through clenched teeth.

The wage trolley is in sight now. It comes stuttering up the aisle. Hands stretch out for envelopes. When Iza gets hold of hers she weighs it in her palm and shakes it to hear coins clink before stuffing it in her pocket.

# – 6 –

Though they all knew it was coming, still Pauls works' hooter had comps' heads jerk as though in surprise. Iza let out a sigh as she put on her hat, all the while keeping an eye down the length of the caseroom. Folk were hanging up aprons, putting on hats and bunnets, trickling from between frames and down the central aisle, women to hurry off alone or pause for a moment by a work chum before heading off in pairs, men to cluster round Fred Henderson's frame.

Iza paused in the aisle to watch Netta Strachan's hands going like a fairground card shark's, eyes darting as she grabbed phrases from her manuscript.

'You staying all day?'

Hardly breaking beat, Netta swiped at a drip on her squint nose with the back of a hand, leaving a sparkling trail across her cheek. 'A few more lines,' she said.

Knowing Netta's mind was taken up with totting up farthings, pennies, shillings, racing against a clock ticking towards her wedding day, Iza left her to it. She dragged her feet down the aisle, waiting for Wight to make himself scarce. After skirting the men gathered round Fred Henderson across the aisle from Margaret's frame, Wight moved on to saunter round the proofing presses, running fingers along surfaces to inspect them for dirt, picking up a proof page to frown at it, before leaving the caseroom. Iza stood by Margaret, watching her chum riddle through boxes of metal slivers, every so often raising a stray sort to bloodshot eyes before dropping it into its proper box. This place'll have her stoop-shouldered, Iza thought. Margaret was a good head taller than the other women comps, the only one of them who didn't need a wooden platform to stand on. She was solid built, mind, so maybe she wouldn't bend.

'You still coming to the meeting in the warehouse?'

Margret nodded. 'Give me five minutes.'

'D'you want a hand?' Iza said.

Margaret shook her head.

'You're best doing that as you go along.'

Margaret flinched. Sometimes she'd take Iza's say-so; sometimes she wouldn't. Margaret had another year to go as a learner and though she loved the work her fingers were not always as keen as her mind. More than once Iza had stopped late to help her lock up a galley.

'What did buggerlugs have to say for himself?'

'Asked how ah was finding it. Said he thought ah've the makings of a damned good comp.'

'Sooking up.'

Margaret bristled. 'I was not.'

'Not you. Him, ah mean.'

'It's still nice to hear it. You have to listen to enough snide remarks in here.'

'Aye. Right enough. "We'll aw be oot on our backside and hoards o' girruls at our frames. A caseroom full o' skirrrts."'

Iza whined through her nose in a fair impression of George Seggie. Margaret's raised eyebrows warned Iza she was talking too loud and, sure enough, when she glanced over her shoulder she saw Seggie's scraggy neck craning.

'Did Wight say anything about the Chapel's doings?' Iza whispered. 'That's what he stopped here for. To eavesdrop.'

'I know what he was up to.'

Iza kept quiet now, letting Margaret finish in peace. What with Fred Henderson and his crew close by this was indeed a good place to eavesdrop and, though women were not party to union discussions, she well knew that if you'd eyes to see and ears to hear you'd soon find out what was what.

'Aye. Ah raised it. Just as ah did last week and every other week.'

'So we have to breathe our last afore they'll address it?'

'And have more lassies step into our boots when we drop down deed.' Seggie, of course.

'Last ah heard the female of the species needed good air to breath just like us.' John Adams. The voice of reason.

Ah. They were on about ventilation. And with good cause. Three years in the caseroom and already Iza could feel her lungs tightening. Her eyes were blunting too, though the intricate job of making up meant that the stonemen suffered most from want of light.

'Today, as you know, ah asked for your signatures.'

Iza and Margaret's eyes met and flicked towards the pool of men. As Margaret carried on with her sorting and Iza tinkered with leads, lining them up, they kept their ears sharpened, barely acknowledging Netta's 'Cheerio. Behave yersells,' as she hurried by.

'Aye. We know that. Get on with it. Some of us have got wives and bairns to get home to. So, what's the outcome?'

Over her shoulder, Iza watched Fred Henderson tug at a lopsided ear.

'In a minute. Hawd on. Ah just need to go over where we've got to in this matter of working hours.'

Seems happier studying the wee chess board under his frame, muttering to himself, than telling folks what's what, Iza thought.

'We know where we are. It's where the hell we're going's at issue.' Dour Dougie Gossman, lanky comp with rickety legs who was cliquer, or leader, of her chumship, the small group of comps typesetting *Fairy Tales of Slav Peasants and Herdsmen*.

'At twelve-thirty today ah submitted the notice every last one of you signed.' Henderson's voice plodded like it was tramping up the iron stair to the gallery. He looked up in that direction. All eyes followed his. No sign of Wight. Like dark ripples on loch waters when a cloud covers the sun, anxiety ran through the men. Better a Wight up in the gallery spying on them than a Wight gone upstairs to report to the masters.

'What about the girruls? If we strike work we'll be oot on our backsides and...'

When someone burst in with, 'Och, God, give me strength. Will you cease your girning?' Iza knew that she and Margaret weren't the only ones rolling their eyes at Seggie's whining.

Fred Henderson pointed with his chin. Heads turned towards Iza and Margaret. An apprentice's broom bashing a frame and the rattle of another's bucket of fresh sawdust echoed in the hush that fell on the men.

'Ah'll wait for you down the stair,' Iza said.

'Be with you in a minute,' Margaret called after her. 'I'm starving.'

Margaret was always starving, though you'd never know it from the way she nibbled wee bites from her piece and chewed like she'd got all day, and that only after dusting down her clothes, taking a comb from her pocket to tidy her sleek brown hair, cut uncommonly short, and treating her face to a wipe with a wetted handkerchief and a dab of cold cream. Margaret's attention to her toilet would cause Iza to tuck up loose strands of her hair, conscious of her own slapdash approach.

Swaying gently to the machine room's rumble-roar-thud, Iza scrubbed her hands. Though the works were still in summer's slack time, a couple of presses were running on for a rush job. Though she'd been warned of the need to rid her hands of noxious muck, the habit hadn't stuck and, like many of her work chums, her scrub-up was usually cursory. Today, though, she took time to soap and knead between her fingers and scour her nails with a worn brush, inspecting them in a block of dull light from a wee high window. The rattle of a barrow and heavy clomp of footfall echoed in the yard outside.

'Watch out. Watch out. Girruls about.' She'd had the cludgie to herself until two apprentices burst in. She gave the lads a purse-lipped nod over her shoulder. This pair had started the same year as her, three year ago now, which meant they were not halfway through their apprenticeship, still fetching fonts from the foundry, mixing ink, sweeping up, so they had no cause to look down their noses at her, a time-served comp at her own frame. She knew, though, that these lads picked up their snash from the likes of Seggie along with tricks of the trade, so she couldn't blame them. At least she didn't think she could. When, soon after Margaret started in the caseroom, Iza had told her to just ignore them, they knew no better, Margaret had said well they should know better, they ought to have minds of their own. Margaret's assurance had taken Iza aback. It had her wondering if she herself had such a thing. She'd thought she had a mind of her own, but just then Margaret had her doubting it. Now, listening to the apprentice lads splash and snigger, Iza decided her chum was right. After all, some of the women comps were old enough to be their mothers. They ought to mind their manners. She shut her ears to them till the door banged shut behind them.

It struck her now that the Warehousemen and Cutters union might get the women comps their own cludgie. When he'd come round the women's frames to invite them to the union meeting, the representative had been on about how they'd be protected if the dispute over hours came to strike action. Never mind that, it'd be worth joining just to get a cludgie, she thought. After all, the bindery lassies got one to themselves.

Where had that Margaret got to? Out in the yard, leaning against a wall, Iza fingered the pay packet in her pocket, counting coins by shape and size until the paper was worn, thinned almost to bursting, and the thought of her mother's raised eyebrows made her leave it be. Vi Ross and no one else was opener of pay packets in their house. Clasping her hands tight and blinking in hazy sunlight, she watched Pauls works empty. Millions of metal slivers set, thousands of sheets of paper carted, fed into presses, printed, cut and folded and bound and the print workers spilled through the yard and out into the street as though each and every one were letting go of breath they'd been holding back all week.

Iza didn't know she was looking out for the tall, bare-headed lad by the gates until her heart skipped when she thought she spotted him. She stretched on tiptoe. No. Not him. She scolded herself for feeling disappointed, but it didn't stop the feeling. A burst of noise from the back of the yard had her turn to see women stream out of the bindery. By a cart piled high with packages the flow split, one part following the men out the gates, the other skirting barrows to make for the warehouse's hefty double doors. Off to the union meeting. Would they discuss strike action? Iza winced. Strike was a word that bore a heavy load. This she had known for a long, long time, ever since she was wee.

A summer's day, and Iza and her big sister Violet stood in the soft grey light of a narrow sash window. The two wee lassies noticed a rumble of rolled barrels, a ragman's yelps, only because the baby's papery eyelids batted, for they had lived their few years – Iza's five, Violet's eight – in the guts of the city, close to a main road that clattered with carts and carriages heading south past the rail depot with its great heaps of wet coal, past sprawling print works and belching foundries, through the sweet malt reek of breweries, before stretching itself past squat houses framed in gardens, past pig pens and potato patches, coal bings and turnip fields, and on through hills and wet woods where wild raspberries grew under a thin blue sky.

Iza crouched to grip the side of a drawer that lay at their feet. She shoogled it. It wouldn't rock. A tug with both hands had it judder an inch or two across the floor. Violet prodded her aside to lift a grizzling baby.

'There, there, mah wee man.'

The bundle drooping from her scrawny, freckled arms hiccupped.

Baby William was the first since Iza to hold on for nine months, to come out alive and, three months later, still be living. And the rupturing of their mother's innards, already ripped ragged from the birth of Harriet who died of scarlet fever, Jamie, Jack, Robert, Violet, a wee boy stillborn and, worst of the lot, their mother was wont to say, Iza, meant this baby would have to be the last.

'It won't rock,' Iza girned. 'Why can't we get a proper crib?'

When they'd slept with the neighbour's lassies next door while, through the wall, William burst into the world, Violet had got a shot of rocking a bairn in a fine wooden crib. Iza had watched, happy just to stroke the crib's sleek brown sides.

'Ours had to go in the '72 strike. They couldn't carry it aw the way to Glasgow could they? It's miles,' Violet said.

'Where's Glasgow?'

'Ah just told you. It's miles.' Violet nestled the baby's fuzzy head before straightening his cap and treating him to a dose of her scratchy, earnest 'Oh dear me' song.

'Why did they go to Glasgow in the '72 strike?' Iza persisted.

Violet laid baby William down.

'When? When did they go?'

'Ah told you. It went to the pawn in the '72 strike. Ages ago. When Jamie was wee.'

'What's the pawn?'

'They give you money.'

'What's the '72 strike?'

Violet had had no answer to that except a fingertip pressed hard to clasped lips.

The yard was nigh-on empty and Iza was heading back to the caseroom to find Margaret when the men came tramping down, mouths clamped in heavy silence. The first of them bumped into her at the foot of the stair.

'What's this. Are we locked in?' said one.

'Ah'm waiting for mah chum. Is she still up there?'

'Aye, there's a girrul up there.'

'No doubt assuring Wight you lot will rat.' Not Seggie, but one of his kind.

'It's not our fault,' Iza muttered, earning herself a withering look.

Fred Henderson was last down. Iza blocked his path.

'What'll happen to us if you strike work?'

He pushed his bunnet back, lowered his head to rub at raw-looking eyes with bony fists. 'It won't come to it, hen.'

'How come?'

'The masters will see sense is how come. We try it on, the masters try it on. They give a bit, we give a bit. If we stand firm, we win a bit.'

'Or lose like in '72?'

Eyeing her like she'd voiced unholy thoughts too close to a church, Fred Henderson excused himself and she stood aside.

'Should we join the Warehousemen and Cutters' union?' Iza called after him.

He stopped, turned, lifted his bunnet to scratch his head and took in breath as though for a full answer, but 'Up to you, hen' was all he said.

# - 7 -

Guided by a buzz of voices, they made their way between a long narrow table and floor-to-ceiling shelves, Margaret striding, head high, Iza trailing a finger over stacks of folded sheets and bound books. At the far end of the warehouse the bindery lassies had gathered with a small group of machine-feeder girls, still in oily overalls, and a bigger cluster of warehousemen. A few sidelong glances and whispers greeted Iza and Margaret when they reached the back of the crowd, but, then, they were the only caseroom lassies here and, besides, Margaret did look striking. Trust her, Iza thought. She'd taken time to comb her hair and freshen her face and she was wearing her green hat with its jaunty red-brown feather.

Voices fell and heads turned as the union representative climbed up on iron shelving and, gripping a strut, leant out as though about to perform acrobatics, all the while stroking a bushy dark moustache between thumb and hooked index finger.

First off, he extended a warm welcome to newcomers. He scanned heads and, here and there, nodded. New members by the finish, he hoped. But on to the day's important business. The trades – machinemen, compositors, bookbinders – were to serve notices to strike work over the issue of working hours. A fifty-hour week was the demand.

'A fine demand,' he intoned as though bowling the words to someone perched up in the rafters. 'But I say to you that what's good enough for skilled workers in caseroom and machine room is good enough for unskilled toilers in bindery and warehouse.'

'And machine room.' A woman's voice.

'Aye. Not forgetting our gallant machine feeders.' He gestured to the machine-feeder lassies with an outstretched palm and a bow of his head. 'In fact, our heavy work means we are the more, not less, in need of a shorter working day. And ah ask of you now that you vote to strike work along with the trades.' He added a pinching and wiggling of his upper lip to his moustache stroking.

His words were met with mutters that cracked the crowd's attention and, try as he might, he now failed to mend the crack. Bindery lassies began to call out for all to hear so that he had to busy himself parrying what was tossed at him, free arm swinging like he was on a tennis court.

'It's all very well for yooz on stab wages. What about us on piecework?'

'Aye. Less hours. Less money. Did you think of that?'

'No-one's going to lose out,' the union man pleaded. 'We're demanding fifty hours with no loss of pay.'

'So how does that work? They increase all the piece rates? Fat chance.'

'Get them doubled while you're at it, will you?'

'Aye. And a bonus for the strain of carrying all that money hame.'

The union man patted the air above their heads. 'Girruls.

Girruls. We know it's not straightforward for piece workers. We're not forgetting you.'

'Don't you worry, son. You'll not forget us in a hurry,' a bindery lassie called out. To laughter, she bared her teeth to snarl, 'We'll get Bessie to gi' ye the evil eye.'

Iza felt Margaret stiffen and take a step back. She knew why. She, too, felt that this was no way to conduct yourself. She was torn, though. It could have been lassies in the street or her mum talking.

'Let's hear him out,' she whispered to Margaret, eyes on the union man as he asked for attention.

He didn't get it. Warehousemen, who, other than telling the women to wheesht, had been holding their tongues, now let loose.

'We don't have a hope in hell of getting a reduction to fifty without loss of pay when they're working fifty-four in London.'

'Fifty-six in Beccles.'

'Who gives a shite what they're doing in Beccles, wherever the hell that is. The trouble is the trades can hold out. Aye, they can dredge up the odd time-served machineman or compositor to rat, but there's no stock of them ready in a cupboard. Us though? They'll have rats out of their sewers and in our places soon as we're out the door. We've seen it all afore.'

'And what will these rats be doing? Cutting and folding blank sheets?'

'That's mah point. If the trades come out we're laid off anyhow, so why risk serving our notices?'

'For chris'sake hear him out or we'll be here all bloody day,' one of the machine-feeder lassies at the front bawled.

The union man got nowhere till he thumped on a shelf and went on thumping. He called for a show of hands in an indicative ballot. 'Like ah said, the trade societies are submitting a memorial asking for a reduction to a fifty-hour week. Are you in favour of our society submitting a like memorial? All those in favour. Members only.' Though some arms stayed down, most went up. Necks craned, heads swivelled. There was no need for a count.

Iza had been ignoring Margaret's elbow nudging her. She wasn't ready to leave. Those alert faces and arms rising in chorus stirred her. Still, Margaret's insistent elbowing had her turning to go when the union man, waving and calling for them to hang on, made his way towards them. He held out an open ledger, asked would they print their names and sign to join.

'You'll be joining a national society with thousands of members throughout Scotland and England.'

It was Margaret who piped up to ask the question that was bothering Iza.

'But why should we join a society for unskilled labour?' Her voice carried and earned her a muttered, 'Pfuh. Who do they think they are?' from a passing bindery lassie. When the union man said the Warehousemen and Cutters union represented all manner of tradesfolk, that they'd be more than glad to represent female compositors, Iza burst in with, 'But your members aren't in trades are they? Like mah chum said, it's for unskilled.'

'We all need a cut in hours. We all need improved rates of pay.' The union man's spread palms bobbed, weighing hours and rates. 'You need better ventilation in the caseroom,' – his head bobbed from one side to the other – 'they need ventilation in the bindery. We all breathe the same air, eh?' He sniffed and smiled.

'True, but you have nothing to do with our rates, do you?' Margaret was telling rather than asking.

Tugging at his moustache, the man looked away, held up a hand to bid them wait and, saying 'back in a minute,' made off against the current of folk heading for the door. Iza and Margaret didn't wait for him.

Out in the yard, sun seeped through a smoky haze. Iza paused to smooth the blank paper she'd managed to snatch and stuff under her jacket. When an old brown cuddie left harnessed to an emptied cart raised its slumped head, turned weeping eyes on her and snickered, she stopped to rub its grizzled star. Eyes narrowed in concentration, head and shoulders tilted back as though pulled by invisible strings, Margaret kept her distance, eyeing the cuddie as though she might catch some deadly disease from it.

'I think we should be demanding a women's section of the Typographical Society,' Margaret said after a bit. 'And I'm not the only one saying it.' She'd taken a wee step closer, but she was talking to herself as much as to Iza.

'You're probably right,' Iza said, 'but...' She paused. She was sure there was a but, but before she could think what it might be the nag turned a big bony head, bared clagged teeth, took a lazy lunge at an itch under its traces and, shifting its weight, clomped a splayed hoof down on her toe. Crying out, Iza shouldered the beast aside and heaved her foot free. Leaning on Margaret to hop across the yard, she found her but, 'But d'you know what?' she said, 'Ah'm sick to death of the lot of them. "Are you in favour of our society submitting a like memorial?"' she mimicked, tweaking an imaginary moustache.

'Girruls. Girruls,' Margaret twittered.

'And not forgetting our gallant machine feeders.' Iza stopped hopping to test her foot on the cobbles. 'Heh,' she said. 'It's Saturday. We're free. Can you get out the night?'

'Aye. The dancing? There might be a do on at Nelsons' Institute.'

'Can you see me dancing?' Iza hobbled a circle. 'Anyhow, Nelsons'll be full of printers. Full of Rabs. What about the Gaiety for a sing-along? It's on me.' She took out and shook her pay packet. 'Feel the weight of that.' Her face fell as the paper burst and coins spilled. Picking them up and stuffing envelope and coins in her pocket, she added, 'If mah mother'll let me keep any, that is'.

Coming out onto the street they were agreeing they'd not wait for the evening but go straight home to change and be out again within the hour when Iza spotted the tall lad. He wore an earth-coloured Tam o' Shanter. No pail this time, but, squinting a smile at them, he held out a handbill. As she did last time, Margaret took one and walked on a few paces. Iza stopped.

'The miners?' she asked.

'No. It's about the fifty-hour week dispute. The miners are back at work.'

That voice of his. She wanted to hear more of it. 'Did they get their rise?'

'No they did not. Not this time.' His eyes clouded. 'They went back on the masters' terms.'

He nodded towards the works and asked if they'd all knocked off now. Still a handful at the warehouse union meeting, a few on overtime in the machine room she told him. Is that where she'd been, at the union meeting, he asked. From down south was he? No. Not down south. Aye, she and her chum had been at the meeting, but they weren't members. A raised eyebrow. 'Why ever not?' he asked. Face as dark as a tinker's and yet manners you'd call posh. Iza shrugged.

'She's sick to death of unions,' said Margaret, stepping forwards. 'She's had enough of them.'

The lad's quizzical half-smile made Iza wince and throw Margaret a pleading glance. 'No ah've not,' she blustered. 'Well, ah have for now, it being Saturday and all.'

When she and Margaret turned to go, Iza saw his eyes dart from them to the yard and back before he shoved his handbills into his haversack.

'Would you let me walk you home?' His mock bow made Iza smile.

'If you like,' she said, 'but me and mah chum are going out.'

Until Margaret and she parted at the corner he kept behind them, but once she was on her own he walked by her side, shortening his stride to match hers. When his arm pressed her shoulder as they skirted passersby she found she liked it.

'You should have heard the Fife miner that night. A fine man. He told us about a frog.'

She stopped short and studied his face to see if he was having her on. And there was mischief in his eyes, but an uncommon delight was what struck her as he related the tale of how, on a morning's stroll to Methil docks where a ship was in from Riga, Russia, the striking miner had watched a sailor come down the gangplank with hands cupped in front of him; that in those big hands sat a wee frog the sailor had lifted from among the ship's load of railway sleepers; how the miner had watched that big, lumbering man carry a Russian frog to a patch of grass and set it down in a Scottish puddle. A great ring of metal on granite from a stoneyard they were passing drowned out the rest of the tale, but she stashed what she'd heard of it in a cubbyhole in her mind so she could give it to her wee brother William.

As the lad leant in to say something more to her, his breath on her cheek had the feel of lemon sherbet fizzing in her mouth. She drew away to keep safe inches between them as they made their way through backstreets and alleyways. Stopped on the corner of her street, she got a word in to ask where he was from.

'I was brought up in Calcutta,' he said.

'What, in India?' Iza was wide-eyed.

'Aye. That's where it was, last I heard.'

Fancy him making her feel stupid like that. Thinks he's clever. She'd have none of it.

'Ah have to go,' she said.

When he took hold of her arm to stop her from walking off, she tugged. He didn't let go. But the feel of these fingers, long fingers that went right round her arm, was nothing like Rab's bruising grip. It felt grand. It felt stirring and comforting and perplexing. She looked steadily up into his eyes and smiled.

'Leave go,' she said. 'You'll make me late for mah chum.'

# – 8 –

They never got to the music hall for a sing-along. A bright afternoon slipping into a mild evening kept them out of doors till well after dark. Arm-in-arm in their good clothes, Margaret in powder-blue dress with a ruched bodice, Iza in faded charcoal skirt, cream blouse and her sister's cast-off slate grey jacket, they headed for Princes Street Gardens.

'Your dad didn't mind then?' Iza knew that Margaret's father's infirmity often kept her at home. In fact, Margaret's mindfulness of her father made Iza aware of, and a bit troubled by, her own lack of it. But, then, Margaret had no mother and big sister seeing to things.

'No. He never minds. He's always on at me to get out and enjoy meself.'

'Maybe he's wanting rid of you. Maybe he's got a fancy woman.'

'If only.' After smiling to herself for a moment Margaret tilted her head to ask, 'Did that lad at the gates pester you?'

'No.' Feeling a need to keep the lad by the gates to herself, Iza skipped over her chum's enquiry. She was in high spirits. Money jingled in her skirt pocket. In a fit of generosity her mother had given her two shillings of the coins she'd poured from Iza's pay packet, counted and stashed in her old wooden tea caddy.

When, at the top of the Mound, the strains of a pipe band skirled up on a stiff breeze, Iza and Margaret marched in time down the hill, their disorderly march turning into a skip then a jolting run. At first they ignored glowers from folk they buffeted, but after they lost hold of each other and barged into a black-clad woman with a walking stick, her sharp, 'I say!' pulled them up. Apologising, they collected themselves.

Iza was glad to see all the benches in the gardens taken so that they had to sit on cropped grass. Since stains would show on Margaret's pale skirt, Iza took off and spread her jacket. Shame, she thought, you can't pull up your skirt and pull down your stockings as you would round the back greens or up by the crags. In no time, heat drove them to the shade of a rowan tree, which was fine except when smoke from passing trains belched their way.

'So you had a good week?'

'Aye. Twelve-and-ten. Ah've got two bob to spend. And you?'

'Low this week, but a nice job. It's got a dedication in half-diamond indent, you know, in, in, in till there's just the one word on the last line?'

Iza nodded as if she knew.

'It took some working out. Then the whole of the first chapter – eleven pages – in italic.'

'What's it on?'

'This woman's garden. In the Arcady Library series? Says she didn't even bother looking inside when they got a new house, seeing as the garden was so beautiful. According to her you need a border of scented things round the house for when you lean out the window – China roses, eucalyptus, jasmine. Good for your spirit she says.'

'Aye, we could give it a go, 'cept the neighbours wouldn't be well pleased with us digging up the pavements or shovelling horses' doovers on the roses round the side, which in our case would be in Ma-Findlay-next-door's living room. Not that she'd notice, mind, her being a boarded-out loon, poor soul. She thinks her daughter's trying to poison her. And she likely is.'

'Anyhow, there's no shortage of spirits in St Leonards. Just wait till tonight. The place will be reeking of them,' Margaret added.

When a baggy white cloud slipped across the sun the leaves above them darkened. A cool gust tugged at their skirts. It was time to move on. Iza wanted to look at hats. There was one in Jenners she'd seen in an advertisement in the papers. Not that she'd have enough for it, but if it took her fancy she might be able to put a bit by. As they climbed the steps into Princes Street, a pair of grey-uniformed soldiers made as if to let them pass then mock-stumbled into their path. The tall one cleared his throat and said, 'Ladies. Excuse us. We was blinded by your charms.' The other grinned then looked at his feet. He was frail-looking, like he could be knocked over by a bairn's rubber ball never mind a bullet. Iza glowered at them as she swung past, but, still, the look in the frail one's eyes, like a sunbeam striking smudged glass, bothered her.

They crossed the broad expanse of Princes Street, dodging a tramcar and honking cabs, to join thick columns of folk, one headed west, one east past sparkling shop windows. Well-to-do-looking folk for the most part and, seeing herself through their eyes, Iza was checking buttons and stray hair when she spotted, among a gaggle of unkempt young lads clotting the column like smudged ink, a figure she took for her wee brother William. She stopped and called out, but the pretty-faced lad with his cap set back on wild hair didn't look round and she knew she'd been mistaken. Daft to think it. William would not be in this gaggle. William would be alone, in the bedroom or, if it was peaceful enough, on his belly on the grass round the back green, buried in a book or drawing stories in the jotter he'd make out of scrap paper. Thought of him made her sad. Why? She didn't want William to be alone, not when she wasn't. The morn. The morn she'd spend time with him, if he'd let her. Stretched on tiptoe, she picked out Margaret's green hat and feather bobbing ahead and hurried to catch up.

She couldn't make up her mind about the hat. Did it not make her head look awful wee? Too square? How about this one? No. Looked like an upturned bucket with a swan's backside stuck to it. Where Margaret could get away with pert green or navy, Iza fancied something bigger, with a splash of colour, to cover her wispy hair. Oh, now, how about this wavy grey and yellow affair? What began as a fairly serious attempt to choose a hat turned into a grabbing of the funniest concoctions and a striking of poses, until, when Iza strutted off along the aisle in a huge purple bush, a walker showed them the door. Margaret tutted, mouth pursed in annoyance and outside, stopped by the kerbside in late afternoon sun, they were awkward with each other for the first time that day, tucked back into themselves.

'Just a bit of foolishness,' Iza said.

'Yes, you're right.' Margaret smiled. 'We're young yet, eh? At least you are. I'll be nineteen soon.'

'An old maid, eh? Tell you what, let's get a train across the Forth bridge before we're any older.' Iza took Margaret's arm and gave it a wee tug. 'Come on. Have you been on a train? You must have.'

'Never. Saw and heard quite enough of them when I worked at the ticket office.'

'Before you burned the Caledonian station down?'

'Only in my dreams.' Margaret looked up at the huge clock on a towering wall by Waverley station. 'It's getting on. We'll have to check times for the last train back.'

Iza had to squint to get the outline of the clock's hands to settle, but as she was peering the clock struck five and she and Margaret set off at a run, weaving through a thinning parade of window shoppers.

It turned out Margaret, of all people, was feart of trains. She clenched the side of the carriage with one hand and Iza's arm with the other as the train chugged along below high dark walls and out past a green bank fringed with the crags which, from here, looked like a pleated red band hacked along the top with blunt scissors. Iza was thrilled to be rollicking along, watching the curved band narrow to nothing. They were off to Musselburgh, a small grey stone town a few miles along the shore. They'd have missed the last train back across the bridge from Fife. This was Iza's first ride on a train, too.

'Ah nearly got on one when ah was wee,' she said. 'With mah dad and Jamie and Jack. We were going to stay at Uncle Lawrence's, who settled in Glasgow during the '72 strike, but we got to the station to find the railwaymen had struck work. Could have waited till we'd had our holidays, says Jack. Could have waited till doomsday and got bugger all, mah dad said.'

A dull orange ball of a sun slid down the back of the town as they made their way along Musselburgh High Street, sniffing at shellfish and vinegar and fried white puddings and hot sugar and beer in sea air. Clumps of men had spilt out onto pavements by pub doors, and when Iza and Margaret stretched their ears they caught the far end of a bundle of roars and yells, but otherwise the street was quiet. But before they'd decided what they'd fill their rumbling bellies with, horses' hooves clattered and a wave of noise rolled towards them. Riders and carriages, just a few at first then more and more, trotted and skittered by. Of course. The horse races were on. Jack had said that's where today's Tanfield's work's outing might end up, to catch the last race once they'd beaten Nelsons in the swimming round of the printers' five-sports tournament.

Now folks queueing for fish suppers appeared like stars in a darkening sky, first one, then twos and threes, then hundreds before you knew it. Iza and Margaret were too hungry to give up waiting and, anyhow, they were soon tangled up in the crowd's boisterous warmth. They sat on a step to eat hot, salty, battered haddock and bread rolls, Iza gobbling and licking her fingers, Margaret plucking with pinched fingertips before wiping them on her handkerchief. Then they joined the tail end of a trail of people making for the station, but before they reached it the folk in front were turning about, saying too late, last train's full up, looks like we're on Shanks's pony. It turned out the only concern both Iza and Margaret had was that the other might be anxious to be home, but neither of them was. They both fancied a walk, might even have a paddle, and they set off along the estuary shore, dawdling so that others soon passed them by and figures and voices ahead of them thinned and dissolved in dusky light. At first they held to the road, but on an open stretch of shore they skirted off to slip and slither on pebbles sucked by wavelets. Iza took off the boot that was pinching her trodden-on toe and they sat on a fat boulder to blether under a great expanse of sky that had turned ink-blue-black dotted with white stars and a silver disk of moon.

Iza was surprised by Margaret's confession that the taller of the two soldiers they'd bumped into in Princes Street had taken her fancy. She didn't offer her low opinion of him, though. If she knew anything, she knew there was no accounting for taste in these matters. Anyhow, talk of soldiers had brought her wee brother to mind.

'Mah wee brother wants to be an explorer, but it scares me the army's the nearest he'll get.'

'You're lucky though.'

'Eh?'

'To have a wee brother to care about.'

'Aye, but you've got a bedroom to yourself. Ah'd give a hundred brothers and sisters for that.'

'What about swapping them for a man? Getting wed?'

'Not if ah can help it,' Iza dismissed the idea. 'Do you want to?' She had an inkling Margaret would say no, and she was right. Margaret said she'd certainly never marry any of those she'd met, that she was well used to cooking and cleaning for her dad and, when he passed, God rest him, she might want the company, but, no, she wouldn't marry because she didn't want bairns. 'I know it's daft,' she said, 'but I couldn't wish being the cause of my death on any child. I know me dad doesn't blame me. And he says me mum wouldn't. She'd be too busy being proud of me.'

'Must be hard never knowing your mum.'

'I've got a good dad, though. Plenty don't get that. When I had doubts about starting in the caseroom he told me I was as clever and strong as anyone and I'd be as good at the trade as any man, and better than most.'

'Ah'd quite like to have bairns.' Gazing out on dark

waters, Iza tried to picture a wee bairn in her lap, a crackling red fire, and at her back, leaning in but out of view, a man who was dear to her. The picture was dim at best but she knew who the man was and it felt nice. 'Who wants bairns anyhow,' she heard her young self say. Well, ah can change mah mind, can't ah? She picked a pebble and stood to toss it. As it plashed and sank, she shivered. A chill sea breeze had got up. As she pulled on her boots she told Margaret about Rab's lecture on fertility. 'So it seems we're scuppered in any case.' 'Unnatural, unnatural,' she intoned as she hauled her chum up and took her arm. 'Ah'm not so sure ah want the man anyhow and seeing as you can't get one without the other, supposing you haven't gone and wrecked your fertility of course, ah'll likely do without.'

'Well, I mean to stay a comp.' Margaret stopped to toss a pebble far out into the water. 'So that settles it for me.' Plash.

Iza tried but failed to throw one as far. 'Aye, who wants bairns and men anyhow,' she said. Must be nice to be so certain, she thought but didn't say.

'I thought that agitator lad at the gates had caught your fancy.' Margaret eyed her, nose wrinkling.

'What agitator lad?' Giving Margaret a wee smile, Iza stepped up the pace, heading to where town lights daubed the dark.

'What if we lost our jobs?' They'd been wrapped up in their own thoughts. Margaret broke the silence. She was deadly serious. 'All those mutterings about clearing us out the caseroom.'

'Just let them try it, eh?'

They clasped each other tight to walk briskly past the silent bulk of fat square houses strung out back from the road. In the throng around Portobello High Street's pubs, though, they slowed to an amble, dodging swayers and staggerers, past a man slumped in a cloud of boozy vapours. Wrapped round palings like bindweed, he bawled 'What have ah done wrong? Tell me what ah done wrong,' up into the sky.

'Mind out the way. Let the ladies by.'

They'd crossed the road to join a pile of men clamouring to get on board a tram already full to bursting when someone barged through the crowd, jostling to part it.

'That's no lady, that's mah wee sister. She can walk.' Barging his way towards them, Jack spread his arms to force a gangway. 'Just joking, hen. You and your pal get on.' He took their elbows to guide them to the stairway then clambered up behind, calling back that he'd like the walk himself but he needed to see the ladies home safe, didn't he, what sort of brother would he be.

The driver wouldn't start till passengers settled. 'No standing,' he barked. 'Off you get if there's no seats.' Jack tugged at Iza to get up and sit on his knee, then, failing to shift her, perched himself on hers instead. The tram juddered as the horse leant into the traces.

'Rab's here. Rab. Where are you?' Jack bawled as they heaved off. 'He's got the sulks because they got beat,' he said before drumming the air with his fists to 'We, we the Tanfield men beat the Parkside girruls again', a chant taken up by his chums. From behind them, Rab's voice called out 'It's the likes of you Tanfield crew let girruls into the caseroom. We wouldn't put up with it at Nelsons.' His stern tone earned him a belch of laughter.

'You don't need to. You're aw wee girlies at Nelsons.' Jack turned to grin at Margaret. 'No offence, hen.'

'You are being offensive. You want to mind your manners when there's ladies about.' A reedy voice had heads turn.

Iza felt Jack bristle. She blushed. Though it'd been a good three year since she'd heard it, she recognised that voice.

She'd not long started in the caseroom when one autumn morning, as she turned into Oxford Street to tack her way through backstreets to Pauls works, a south-easterly had her skirt up round her thighs so that she'd had to snatch and hold it down. It was a bit early for folk to be setting off to Nelson's Parkside works just round the corner, so Oxford Street was nigh-on empty. As she passed the first of a row of low tenements a ginger-haired lad with a chiselled nose marched out of a stair door, new haversack over his shoulder, head high to sniff the air, looking off along the street and not at what was in front of him. The Oxford Street tenements were set back a yard or so from the pavement and this had Iza looking to see what folk had made of their wee patches – most were just dirt or scrag bushes but one had crazy paving and flowers and a wee stone bench – and she'd stopped to get her skirt in order and look at a pot of pink flowers when the lad stepped straight into her. He started, stumbled, muttered, flung his haversack onto his other shoulder and, fists clenched to his sides, marched off across the road. After that he kept appearing of a morning and even took to hanging about by his stair door of an evening. They barely spoke, but he'd nod to her, mumble a few words in a voice that ran away with him, rising to a squeak before he yanked it down. He'd walk along her side of the road at her shoulder before sheering off with a curt cheerio.

Then, home from work one Saturday afternoon after seeing him at the street corner with Jack and his work chums, Iza had asked was he at Nelsons. Aye. Apprentice machineman. So he was leaving for work earlier than needs be. Jack had chaffed her about her interest, said it was mutual, John Orr had asked about her, she was on, he'd fix it up, the lad had the makings of a good machineman, though he was a might touchy, needed to learn to take a joke. Look who's talking, Iza had said, and got a clout for it, playful but hard enough to sting. After that, she'd taken to using other streets and alleyways to get to work.

John Orr, the ginger-haired boy whose jittery ambushes had caused Iza to avoid Oxford Street, sat wedged beside Rab a few seats behind them. At least his voice seemed to have settled its pitch, she thought, though it had settled a touch higher than you'd want. He certainly showed some guts talking to Jack like that, unlike Rab, who was blinking nervously, head bobbing as though he'd got a spring in his neck and a weight on his nose.

'Oh, ah do beg your pardon, son. At least the lassies can take a joke. Can't you girruls?' Jack was subdued for a bit, but soon perked up. 'Anyhow, you're all girruls at Parkside. Ah ken. Ah was there before ah got started at a decent firm.'

'Just you wait till next year,' John Orr called out in an attempt at levity.

Iza nearly pitied him, but Jack was busy calling out to his chums how they should have boxing in the tournament next year, wouldn't that be grand, and ah bet our girruls could beat the Nelson mob at that too. Iza pushed to get him off her lap. Her legs were numb, but she couldn't switch places with him because that would leave Margaret crushed up against him and she'd felt how Margaret was trying to draw herself apart. Jack tumbled to the floor, arms swaddling his head, crying, 'Get off. Leave me alone. See what ah mean. They girruls are devils.' His chums had to yank him down the stairs when they got off to walk to Canonmills. And as they tugged him across the road he was still calling out that next year their team would head straight down the pub and leave it to their lassies to beat the Parksiders.

When the tram reached the terminus Iza and Margaret set off quickly, in and out of North Bridge's cold puddles of white light from the new electric lamps that smudged the sky and blotted out stars above them. It was spitting rain and from Market Street below came a peevish howl of, 'Wait for me, will ye?' and snarls and yelps from dogs after scraps. Iza wanted to get clear of Rab. She'd rather put up with Jack's belligerent clowning than Rab's pious sermonising. And though John Orr, coming along behind them with Rab, had sounded tonight like a decent enough sort, he was not the easiest of company.

'See what ah mean about brothers,' she apologised as she and Margaret parted. Margaret had been quiet since they got on the tram and she said little now. 'The other two are better, mind. Jamie and William. You'd like them,' Iza said by way of apology.

# – 9 –

All night it rained, but come morning the world shimmered. A slow, soft Sunday of powder-blue air. Side-by-side with her mother peeling potatoes and carrots, Iza looked through a window opened wide on the finest bone china of a day, a soft breath of north wind through the tiniest haircrack. Just she and her mum and dad at home. William had gone out to play. When she leant over the sink to look down at the street she caught sight of him. He was on his own, sitting on the kerb, head turned to watch a gang of lads charging off down the road.

Just a week to go till he was wed and away to stay with lovely Jessie, a girl who seemed to bring sunshine into a room, Jamie had wetted down his wiry brown hair, tossed a towel over Iza's head, birled her round, and, leaving a trail of sweet whistling in the stairwell, was off. Jamie's presence could go ignored. He went about his business without ruffling feathers. But when he was gone from the house it felt to Iza as though nothing fitted quite so well, as though a door hinge was off-kilter or the table needed a wedge of folded paper under a leg. And she knew from the way other family members looked about them when he'd gone that they all felt this.

Rab was off to the kirk. Violet too. They'd all been taken to the back door of the kirk for Sunday school, Jamie by their father, then each sibling by the one above. But there was no compulsion to go a second time, their father having fallen out with the minister over him and his sidekicks, women who'd never done a day's work in their lives, coming poking their noses into working folks' affairs, drumming up business by threatening God's displeasure. Rab and Violet were the ones it had stuck on. Iza hadn't much liked the screechy voice of the woman who'd lead them in singing and she'd liked even less the sour smell of her fingers when the woman had nipped her chin to jerk it up. After the service Rab would stay on for a talk by some missionary fresh from Africa. For Violet, too, there was an appeal other than the service. Smoothing her skirt, she'd be leaning in to whisper to her chum, pretending she wasn't watching out for her fancy man, Angus, an office clerk whose father was an elder at the kirk.

'Are you on a go-slow?'

Iza felt her mum's bony elbow dig her side. Her hands had slowed to a stop.

'Leave it, Vi. Come away out for a walk in the park.'

Well there was a surprise. Her dad not just up and about but heading outdoors.

And with a 'Finish getting the dinner on, will ye? And see your wee brother doesn't tear his breeks again,' her mum dropped a half-peeled potato in the sink, wiped her hands and picked up her cardy.

'Let the lassie alone. She's big and ugly enough to see to it herself.' Iza's dad winked at her.

Another surprise. Her dad not just off out but telling their mum her business. His sickness making a stranger of him. And what Iza heard behind his words was that everyone could be left to their own devices, that everything could be left to see to itself. Standing in the doorway between the two rooms of their emptied house, she was no sooner pleased to be left to her own devices than she was wanting her family back, filling the place, making a din, settling round the table for dinner then a game of whist. When she caught sound of William out on the landing she felt joy.

Sitting on a stone step, she watched William drill his army. Three years earlier, soon as she'd saved enough of her first year's pay packet, she'd bought him four soldiers and a cavalryman on a black horse. She'd thought it a shame that by the time she was able to buy them, William was too old for them, but she'd needed to make up for telling him, 'Because you can't, that's why,' as she'd yanked him away from a shop window years earlier. Though William had been pleased, and he'd kept his soldiers safe in a tin can, he'd never shown much interest in playing with them. Now, chewing at a ragged nail, Iza wished she'd had enough to buy him the model ship his eyes had fixed on.

'Who're they fighting?' she said like she cared.

'The seaboys. That massacred us in Lucknow.'

One of the soldiers marched towards her firing, baahm, baahm, baahm. Iza clutched at her breast, lurched forwards, swayed, toppled.

'You're not hit. His rifle's jammed.'

'Why did it go baahm baahm then?'

'Sometimes they do that. It blew him up. Look.'

A soldier went flying over the bannister and down the stairwell. The others followed. Snatching up his cavalryman, William galloped down the stairs and, his baahm baahm baahming echoing, disappeared into the street. Iza felt sad. The agitator lad's tale of the Riga frog had just awoken in her mind, taking shape in words ready to tell her wee brother.

She got scrag-end stew and dumplings simmering on the stove then, feet up to hug her shins, sat in her mum's armchair to chew on morsels of yesterday's outing: train ride, sea shore and big sky, Margaret by her side. But as her mind conjured scenes of yesterday it played tricks on her, introducing into them the agitator lad, who was so persistent a presence that soon she let her imaginings settle on him alone, sucking her fingers at the thought of that smell of him, liquid voice, dark speckled eyes you wanted to dive in.

Violet bustling in startled her. She watched her sister give the stew a sniff and stir before angling a pocket mirror to study parts of her pretty face, dab her paste of lampblack and elderberries on her eyelashes, pinch her cheeks, nibble her lips. Face fixed as close to satisfaction as she ever got – though her face fixing was done with great assurance it never seemed to satisfy – Violet pulled the ends of a lacy black shawl under her arms and, tying them at the back to make a bolero, paraded the room, hiking up the skirt to show off the cream cotton stockings she'd embroidered trails of green vines up. She pointed her toes, glided, stopped, twirled and curtsied before making a show of studying Iza.

'Your legs are a bit thick, eh? Shame. Your chin's fine with that wee dimple and you've got mum's nice nose, only yours is fatter.' She leant in close. 'Your eyes are odd. One's more green than blue and the other's more blue than green.' She peered closer. 'That one's got a dark streak in it.' Straightening up, finger on her chin, Violet pondered. 'Unusual. They're quite big which is good. Ah'll put some of this on for you to make them look even bigger.' Violet spat in her paste. 'You want to put lemon juice on your face at night. And bite your lips like this, look.' Violet nibbled at her lips with her buck teeth. Next she was plucking at Iza's faded, striped grey skirt. 'What a mess. Here, try this on.' She fetched her dark green Thompsons and Allison frock from a hook by her bed.

'That's your work one,' Iza said.

'Ah know, but you have to be smart in shops not like in factories. You might get into our shop.' Violet sounded doubtful. 'Try it on.'

When Iza gave the dress a cursory glance and tossed it back, Violet held it against her front and smoothed it. 'You have to go, "May I be of assistance, mawdum?" It's a mortal sin, all those gorgeous clothes on some of the ugliest old puddocks in Scotland. These bicycle suits with breeks up here, like this, and stockings under. And this lang jacket, in at the waist then out, right down to here and big puffy sleeves at the top. You want to see them.'

'Who wants to see ugly puddocks in stupid clothes.'

'Anyway, you'd be useless behind the counter. You'd stand there gawking then ask them the wrong questions. They'd go, "That cream satin blouse, so elegant, do you have it in my size?" – Violet larded it – 'and you'd go, "How would ah know what size you are?" or they'd go, "I'm looking for an outfit for my daughter's wedding. Flattering, elegant, not too showy," and you'd go "Why's she getting married?"'

'Has she got a bun in the oven?' they chorused.

'Ah saw you with yon lad yesterday.'

Iza scowled. Though to her mind her sister was none too clever, Violet was too good by half at wrong-footing her. And how had she managed to be out and about when she worked the full day Saturday? Best not ask, Iza was thinking, when Violet carried on plucking at the thread she'd got hold of.

'He's not from round here, is he? You better watch yourself. He's got the look of a student. Is he a student? From a good family, is he? But fallen on hard times? Or he's fallen out with them? Has he fallen out with them? What's he called?'

'Don't know.'

Their mum and dad coming in, towing William and wanting their dinner, put a stop to Violet's prodding.

Iza had told the truth. She didn't know if he was a student or if he'd fallen out with his well-to-do folks. She did know his name though. His name was Roddy Mac.

§§§§§§§§§

After a ruckus by Fred Henderson's frame that has necks craning, a spate of growls and mutters as men settle at their frames and stones, an uneasy hush descends on the caseroom. Above their heads a blustery wind tugs at a loose roof strut. But the voices of the caseroom fall silent. George Seggie and John Adams are the last to shut up.

'Should have held out,' Seggie snivels. 'Marching us up the hill to march us down again.'

'You'd have done no better in negotiations yourself.' John Adams shakes his head, leans to his work. 'You'd have had us marching straight into a bog,' he says to the beat of his mallet.

Tempers are frayed. The caseroom is sweltering and word is out the working hours dispute is settled. There'll be no strike. Just as Fred Henderson said, the Chapel tried it on, the masters tried it on. The Chapel asked for a two-hour reduction: the masters conceded quarter-of-an-hour shaved off Saturdays. After a bit of umming and ahhing, the Chapel committee agreed and accepted; Chapel members will be officially informed at a dinnertime meeting. The men's faces display a heady brew of irritation, relief, anger, resignation.

Through a heavy silence that's making her edgy Iza calls to Netta, 'What're yours up to now?' Netta's working on a job called Rosemary Lane. Without her busy hands breaking beat, Netta reads out from her manuscript. She's good at doing the voices.

'Come here, dear, and sit close to me, and I will tell you a story about Christmas. But, mother, I am so hungry,' Netta whimpers. 'The kind lassie from down the stair gave the wee boy a herring and dry bread but she's in trouble for it and she'll probably catch the scarlet fever from him.'

'Why's she in trouble?'

'Ah don't know. Ah didn't set that chapter. Ah do know the father's a boozer but it seems it's the mother at fault. "I tell you Sarah Pierce, if you don't make your home more comfortable you'll have to answer for making your husband a drunkard and a brute and your little Alistair will grow up to be just such another." So, what's happening to yer wee dwarf?'

'Gone. He got eaten by a monster with basilisk eyes.'

'He'll have been in Paddy's bar down the Grassmarket,' John Adams calls.

'Aye, and asked for a clean glass,' Iza calls back. 'But now the prince has chopped the monster up into a thousand pieces,' she tells them.

'Well that'll learn him,' John Adams concludes.

A sixth sense has the three of them glance up. Overseer Wight's looking down from the gallery. He's got wind in his sails now the strike's called off. You can see it, the way he's drumming the rail like he's playing piano. Word is out he's doling out fines: sixpence apiece to two apprentices for fooling around and spoiling type; a shilling to Dougie Gossman for getting caught smoking. Iza gives Netta a warning hiss and, swiping sweat from her brown with a flick of her sleeve, buckles down to the last few paras of her Slav tale.

> Meanwhile, poor Prince Dobrotek, seriously wounded, was slowly recovering consciousness, but he felt so weak that he could hardly utter these words:
>
> "Come, Magic Horse with Mane of Gold,
> Come, Dappled Horse, O come to me.
> Fly like the birds as you did of old,
> As flashes of lightning o'er land and sea."
>
> Instantly a bright cloud appeared, and from the midst thereof stepped the magic horse. As he already knew all that had happened, he dashed off immediately to the Mountain of Eternal Life. Thence he drew the three kinds of water: the Water that gives

Life, the Water that Cures, and the
Water that Strengthens.

She smiles. Nearing knock-off time and she's picturing Roddy Mac at the yard gates. She tuts. You were having none of him and his Calcutta, she chides herself. Not sure about Roddy for a name, she ponders, though Roddy Mac sounded fine.

Clink, clack. Shower of metal slivers. Though the sound is just a wee rushing tinkle in the printwork's regular cacophony, every pair of ears in the caseroom hears it. She braces, but it's not her lines buckling and spraying as she lifts them to the galley.

'Och, ye-fucker-ye.' A man's voice. George bloody-frocks-at-the-frame Seggie's.

She takes a keek. Seggie glowers as he kicks at sawdust and scattered type.

'Who pied, he pied, he, she or it pied,' a male comp sings out. The other men join in chorus.

As Seggie bawls for a useless sod of an apprentice to get himself here toute suite with a broom, she looks over her shoulder to share a snigger with Netta. You wouldn't wish pieing type on anyone, but if you had to wish it on someone...

Returning to the prince, he sprinkled
him first with the Life-giving Water,
and instantly the body, which had
become cold, was warm again and the
blood began to circulate. The Water
that Cures healed the wound, and the

Strength-giving Water had such an effect upon him that he opened his eyes and cried out, "Oh, how well I have slept."

As though Seggie's pieing is catching, she feels a wee stutter in her fingers as she lifts her lines, but before the hooter sounds she has them down safe, slipped into place in the galley and secured with leading and quoins.

# −10−

In a poky back storeroom, the flame of a single candle flickering over spilt bags of tacks, odd split boots and rusty tools, she sat pressed close to Roddy Mac's side on a lumpy sack of leather scraps. Breathing in glue and rubber and sweet pipe tobacco, she gripped her knees to keep them clear of those of James Connolly's, while, head tilted, mouth slightly ajar, she studied his face. A fine-looking young man: thick dark eyebrows arched over steady black eyes; matching thick curtain of dark moustache covering all but the middle of a full lower lip. Another Irishman, Eamonn, completed the circle. Iza held back in the shadows as the men leant in, feet splayed as far as was possible in the cramped space, elbows on knees, three pairs of hands dangling: Roddy Mac's white and lean; Jim's blunt, palms dyed bark brown and fingers scored with nicks and scratches; Eamonn's small as a bairn's, and one smaller than the other, on account of a wasted arm.

The previous evening Roddy Mac had been absent from his post by the work's gates and, viewing the blank spot where she'd been picturing him standing, Iza had wondered for a moment if she'd imagined his very existence. Don't be daft, she'd told herself. Margaret met him. Violet saw him, for goodness sake. He grew up in Calcutta. Ah couldn't have made that up. And sure enough, this evening he'd appeared in the flesh. He had no handbills and no pail and he was paying scant heed to the workers streaming by. He was scanning faces, on the lookout, she could tell, until his eyes lighted on her. Walking her home, he'd persuaded her, with no difficulty, to walk out with him this evening. A dander in King's Park? Might call in at Jim's cobblers shop for a brew and a blether afterwards? When he spoke of James Connolly, Roddy Mac changed from the confident young man she fancied to a wee laddie captivated by a seafaring uncle. Did this reduce him in her eyes? She thought not, but she wasn't sure. She was curious. Besides, James Connolly's name had sprung up everywhere this week, chalked on walls and pavements all over St Leonards. So curiosity had her agreeing to go. Well, that and wanting to be with Roddy Mac, wherever that happened to take her.

She barely knew what the three men were on about, much of their talk being as foreign to her as the Latin and Greek she sometimes had to set. But just as with John Adams sharing with her his pleasure in getting familiar with foreign words – a pleasure that went way beyond extra farthings and halfpennies on the rate for setting them – so their talk did not set her aside but stirred her in. Over a steady drone and occasional bursts of raised voices from the pub next door, the three men relived the previous night's local elections public meeting: how their calls of 'Off-side' and 'Half-time' had caused McLaren, the Liberal with the look of a sick badger, to leave the platform saying he'd 'take a better opportunity of speaking when I do not have such a motley lot to contend against'; how jeers and laughter from the socialists had rippled well beyond their own ranks at the Tory candidate's 'dust is being thrown in the eyes of the public. Mr Connolly is trying to raise a great cry of politics'; how cheers had been likely to bring down the roof when the chairman announced that James Connolly had won the nomination. Caught up as they were in relishing their recollections, still they drew her in as their audience, Jim Connolly speaking straight to her, Eamonn a bit shy, squinting at her from under his bunnet. And when it came to the final exhilarating announcement, 'Mr James Connolly has the majority and is hereby selected as the candidate for St Gile's Ward,' they choroused it for her.

A rap on the shop door interrupted their revelry. She thought to ignore it as they seemed to be doing, but instead asked, 'Shall ah go and see?' First time she'd opened her mouth since saying hello and her heart thudded at the sound of her own voice, but Jim's 'It'll be Alex. Aye, hen, if you will,' had her up and opening the door like she was at home. In the near-dark she couldn't quite make the man out, but she thought she recognised him from Ballantyne's machine room. The sight of her jolted the visitor. He made to keek round her, but when she stepped aside to let him by he shook his head and thrust a small thick package at her, saying simply 'Handbills.' After this interruption, she settled back easier on the lumpy sack. When the candle guttered and she asked where she'd find another, Jim said 'Roddy'll see to it. You stay where you are, hen. You'll have been on your feet long enough today, eh?'

Handbills on the floor at their feet, they leant in to lift wads to their knees to fold them. She wanted to ask if Alex who'd brought them had printed them at the works. He couldn't have, could he? But the men were now speaking with a sober urgency that demoted her from audience to listener-on. Next day's mass meeting – they always seemed to be having meetings – at the Corporation Cleansing Department. Aye, Roddy would be at the gates at five-thirty sharp. Aye, Eamonn would be at the yard with the lorry at twelve noon. No, nobody had seen so-and-so about taking handbills inside, but Jim would try to catch him first thing. Having taken in this much, Iza let their words dissolve into sound without sense. She wanted to indulge in the sensation caused by Roddy Mac's side pressed against her, a warm softening and stirring, like marg and sugar creamed for a pudding, but all too soon she knew her sensation was not shared. The body against hers felt brittle. She pulled apart, bending to smooth and tuck her skirt round her legs. The men's words resumed shape and form. They were on about matters afoot in Dublin. Somebody's rousing speech from the Custom House steps. A plan to advertise Jim's services as an organiser for the Dublin Socialist Society. Had Roddy noticed her pull apart? She turned to look at him and knew he had not. Taken up with Jim Connolly's every word and gesture, he had quite forgotten her company. The question, 'What on earth am ah doing in here?' rang in her like an alarm bell. Straightening up, arms clasped tight round her breast, she took a steady look at this strange room and these strange men, then stood up and announced, 'Ah'm off.'

It was James Connolly, not Roddy, who protested, asking could she not stay a while. He'd like to hear about her job. They'd have a wee drink. What would she like? As she hesitated, Roddy Mac stood, bent to lift her chin and give her a squint smile, so that when, with a nod at the pub next door, Jim sent Roddy to fetch drinks, she sat down.

Tugging at frayed stitching on a burst boot he'd picked up,

James Connolly asked about her work and listened intently as she told, first off, how she'd got her start. Smiling at the remembrance, she said how she'd taken her dad's 'We'll see' for an 'Aye' and Jim said 'Good on you, hen.'

On the intricacies of typesetting, Jim wanted to know how fonts were chosen, how corrections got done, how lines were made up into pages, and her animated account had him saying how grand it was she had a trade she loved. The honest-to-goodness way he said it warmed her heart. He even tolerated her going on about phat and lean, chumships and cliquers. More than tolerated. He took delight in her delight. When he asked what jobs were in Ballantyne's pipeline, his ears pricked at mention of a new edition of *The Wealth of Nations*. What about wage rates? How many were on set pay – 'We call that stab,' she told him – and how many on piece rates? He pondered the numbers she offered before adopting a solemn tone to say how he'd heard the Edinburgh Typographical Society didn't admit women. What did she think to that? This was no demand for a correct answer, so she took a sip of shandy – she'd barely noticed Roddy's return with drinks – while she gave the matter due thought.

'It's wrong,' she replied after a bit. 'They ought to let us in. But there's ill-will from us getting paid less, nearly half the union rate. The Typographical's against cheap labour. Mah brother Rab won't let me forget it and though ah'd never admit it to him, he may be right. A family could never make do on mah wage packet.'

'Aye. Your brother has a fair point. The masters certainly capitalised on the hammering the Typographical took in the '72–'73 strike. But you do the same job?'

'Aye. Mostly the same. We don't lift formes though. They're too heavy.'

Jim Connolly silently weighed this up and, with narrowed eyes, invited more.

'The Warehousemen and Cutters Union wants us in,' Iza said. 'There's lassies in it. Machine feeders and bindery lassies. But they're unskilled labour. We're skilled.' She waited for Jim's response to what she'd voiced as a puzzle to be solved, like the knotted thread and flapping sole of the boot he'd worried at before tossing it aside.

'Ah see your difficulty. But skilled and unskilled – whatever that may mean – have interests in common and a common enemy. No?'

Iza chewed on this. 'Enemy?' she said.

'The masters who pay you too little.'

'Mah dad's always on about them fleecing us, but that's just the way of the world, isn't it?'

Roddy Mac had been silently drinking in their talk with his beer. Now he burst in with 'So long as we let them.'

Iza saw how James Connolly quieted him with a glance. 'You need to be in a union do you not?' he said softly.

'There's talk of forming a women's section of the Typographical. That's what mah chum Margaret thinks we should do and she may be right, but ah can't see the men having anything to do with it, especially the national union, the Scottish Typographical Association, not when Edinburgh's the only place with women comps. It's all wrong.'

'There's much wrong in this world, the thing is to make it right, and to make it right working folk must be organised.' Though there was grit in it, Jim's tone was so generous Iza nodded agreement. And by the time he'd told her how lassies at Bryant and Mays in London, unskilled matchmakers, Irish, many of them, had got monies stolen from them restored and their union recognised, she agreed wholeheartedly.

'Though they'll always try to make you act otherwise, all workers – men and women, skilled and unskilled, Scots and Irish – must make common cause. Simple as that.' Jim's wry smile gave his final words a question mark rather than a full stop. He eyed Roddy Mac, who'd been drinking in their talk with his beer, and said, 'You'd best see the lassie home, eh?' Then, as she neared the door, he called after her, 'When trimmers and compromisers disavow you, I, a poor slum-bred politician, raise my hat that I lived to see the resurgence of women.'

In a dark, sleeping house Iza slipped into bed to tuck close to her mother's warmth. Her mother stirred.

'Where the hell have you been till this time of night?' she muttered.

'At Netta's, helping her finish her wedding dress,' Iza said. A daft story from someone known to be useless at sewing, but her mother wasn't awake to hear it.

Drowsy as she was, her mind teemed. The world she'd got a glimpse of in that tiny storeroom was vast. What, in there, had seemed to make sense now confounded her. She tried to recall what Jim Connolly had said, but his words slipped from her, washed away by a yearning in her flesh.

Walking her home, Roddy Mac had gone some way to soothing her hurt at his neglect of her. Winter had not yet come, but already the night air held a touch of frost. He'd draped his jacket round her shoulders and pulled her close to him. His liquid voice had lapped her ear as he told her how she'd caught his eye. Not that she was a great beauty. (She clipped his ear for that.) She had something better. The way she walked, head up and with a bounce to her step, he'd said, like she knew just where she was headed.

'Aye. Getting clear of ruffians shaking pails at me,' she'd said.

'And that curious look you give me with those odd eyes. Inviting and warning at the same time. Shows gumption. Spirit.'

She'd been enjoying this, but he'd no sooner pleased her than he was on about the fifty-hour-week movement, how nigh on a century ago it had been the forty-hour-week movement – eight hours' labour, eight hours' recreation, eight hours' rest – and Australian workers had won that back in the '50s. Hands waving and thumping the air, he'd left her to clutch the jacket to her chin and wrap her own arms round herself. She'd kept listening, even though she'd have been a lot happier if he'd spoken more of how come he'd picked her out among hundreds. When a century ago and Australia stretched it too far, she'd begun to tell him about the '72 printers' strike, what little she knew of it, and how they'd had to sell their crib so baby William got laid in an old drawer. But he wasn't listening. Mention of '72 had him cutting her short to head off to Paris, people's assemblies, barricades. As they neared her house he was off down south, to English agricultural labourers, 10,000 of them locked out and their families evicted and she'd heard enough and made to turn into her stair with a curt good night. That had pulled him up short. He'd apologised and pulled her close and kissed her forehead, her nose, her mouth.

And the kissing was delicious. And all those English families evicted and Australia and Paris made her head reel. It swelled the world from a wee burn to a wide river and, maybe, beyond, to a great sea. As a bairn, she'd paddled in the burn. Just the other week she'd sat by the shore of a river whose passage to the sea she'd once tried to trace, from up Arthur's Seat, the big humpy hill behind her house. But smoke belching from a thousand chimneys had smudged her eyes and blotted out the river, and she'd never seen, let alone sailed, the sea. She'd never learnt to swim. Would Roddy Mac be there to keep her afloat? A chill ran through her. There'd been times this evening when Roddy Mac had been willing and able to reduce her presence at his side to a blank page you skip over. She'd felt that. Her flesh had felt it. She clutched the blanket to her chin and hugged herself to ward off a gnawing fear in her guts, trying hard to savour the sensation of his kisses. And it worked. Warmth soaked through her. She was bathed in it. He's taken with me, she thought. Ah can tell he is. You can't fool yourself about such matters. Or can you? As sleep took her down, her sister Violet's warning, 'You'd better watch yourself,' bobbed into view.

§§§§§§§§§

At the week's end Jude was again
walking out to his aunt's at Marygreen
from his lodging in Alfredston, a walk
which now had large attractions for
him quite other than his desire to see
his aged and morose relative.

The new job she's on is a jigsaw of printed pages from
a serial edition with all manner of deletions, amends and
insertions. Fanny Begg, cliquer on the job – the first and
so far, the only Ballantyne's woman to rise to cliquer – had
tried but failed to get extra for the difficult hand. In fact,
Iza's not found it so hard once her eyes got the hang of its
loops and twirls.

Doling out chapters to the four of them in the Jude
the Obscure chumship, Fanny had said, only half joking,
they should be getting extra for damage to their morals.

Word had soon got round about the scandalous nature of this book and two apprentices had come in for a good skelp for rifling through the manuscript looking for saucy bits instead of getting on with filling cases. Though she'd not admit it, she'd kept an eye out for sauce herself when she skimmed through her chapters to get the measure of them.

> He diverged to the right before ascending the hill with the single purpose of gaining, on his way, a glimpse of Arabella that should not come into the reckoning of regular appointments.

'What's happening?' Next week Netta's hands will be gripping a broom, not a setting stick, or pounding laundry, not pinching up sorts. And before winter's out she'll be dangling a bairn. Some mornings she's had to set down her setting stick to throw up porridge. She'll be wed and gone from her frame. And because she'll be gone, she's not been assigned to a chumship but given a short, one-comp job that's boring her to death.

'He's off to see his old bat of an aunt, but it's just an excuse to go coorting.' Clasping the last en space firm with a thumb that, now she notices, has taken on the comps' blackened claw look, Iza rounds her lips to mouth the strange oooo.

'What's coooorting when it's at home?'

'It's winchin. What you and your man have been up to this past year.'

'Christ, they've not gone and put that in a book, have they?'

'Ah've read stuff like that. You can get these penny...'

Iza had clean forgotten the learner lassie by her side. With raised eyebrows and pursed lips she informs the lassie that her part in the blether is not wanted. A bit too quick with that tongue Iza judged when, on her first day, the lassie announced 'You're Iza? Same as me. Ah'm Bella. So, the pair of us make a whole, eh?' Too smart by half. And that way she has of watching out of slanted eyes. A bit sneaky Iza had thought, until, that is, the look had put her in mind of her own first few days of suffering groans as she stuttered her way through copy, watching hands with the look of bared tree roots pluck and place type till she was skelly-eyed. Scuttling fingers, horny thumbnail click, click, clicking along, line upon line justified in a flash. But getting her own fingers on type had been a different matter. Like a bairn with its first spoon she'd felt. The comp had gripped her wrist with one hand, flattened her left palm with the other, bedded her setting stick in it, pressed her fingers under and thumb over, given her wrist a sharp tweak. 'Right. There's your case. Learn it. Get the feel. Right hand leads, left follows. Like a man and his Mrs,' he'd said. 'You want a full ridge of nicks at the top or you'll wind up with a bish when you're wanting a pish.'

'Type wants to fall,' she tells Bella, the learner lassie, the memory of her own early days softening her manner. 'Always make sure it falls the way you want it to.' She tilts back and slows the motion of her fingers for a moment so the lassie can see how it's done. 'Right, on you go.'

Before quite reaching the homestead,

his alert eyes perceived the top of her head moving hither and thither over the garden hedge. Entering the gate, he found that three young unfattened pigs had escaped from their sty by leaping clean over the top, and that she was endeavouring unassisted to drive them through the door which she's set open.

Just yesterday Iza had felt justified in her doubts about having a learner. Slowed you down like she knew it would. The lassie mumbled, read out too many words or too few, stumbled over easy words, breathed through her mouth. Maybe that sharp wee nose can't take the fumes. And her own eyes had kept flicking back and forth to pluck the next string of words from the manuscript when there was no need. Today, though, her ears are beginning to take over partnering her fingers, and it's certainly a balm to her eyes to let them glaze. Besides, the lassie's learning fast. Ah'll likely relent and give her a high stool this afternoon, she thinks. She's chosen to have Bella stand because learning to set type is useless if you don't learn to stand all day. Poor wee thing, she thinks in a kinder moment, having no chum to sit in a corner with at dinnertime and moan about the bossy old bissums always on at them. Bella is the only learner lassie started this year.

# -11-

At dinnertime Iza told Margaret she had an errand to run. Margaret wanted to know more. Iza didn't enlighten her. She was quite certain of her purpose. Jim Connolly's words had had their effect and walking out with Roddy Mac these past weeks had sealed it. She'd join the Warehousemen and Cutters Union. But, firm as her purpose was, she had a sense that it needed shielding from searching eyes. Since she would not entertain thoughts of *why* this was so, her mind conjured an illustration. A mustard yellow scarf. She could picture it clear as day. Her first attempt at knitting. A squint apology for a garment full of holes where she's dropped stitches. Her mother is holding it up alongside the even, shapely stocking on her own needles. 'Would you take a look at that?' her mother's saying. She's laughing. 'Looks like a fishnet and that one wouldn't stop a whale.' Iza's upset, but only for a moment. As her scarf is unravelled to reclaim the wool they're both laughing. You're right, Mum, she thinks. Ah'm not the most nimble-fingered. But only round the house, not when it comes to handling tiny metal slivers. With them ah'm in mah element. So, Rab, stick that in your pipe and smoke it.

'What's funny?' Margaret sounded miffed.

Iza said it was nothing, she'd just minded something, see you later.

Seeing as it was a fine day out, she stopped a wee while in the yard, not to drag her feet, but because that block of bright blue sky above roofs and chimneys was a braw thing to look on and that air, sooty though it may be, was a precious balm to lungs, and she took in her fill of sky and air, hoping upon hope that the coming Sunday, just two days off now, would be just such as fine day when she walked out again with Roddy Mac. With that thought in mind she set herself to march straight by the timekeeper in his cubbyhole at the warehouse door without explaining herself. She didn't need to bother, though. He'd nodded off, bunnet peak down over his eyes, chin on his chest, upper lip drooping.

'D'you know where the union man is?' she asked the first man she came across in the gloom of ranked shelving.

'Ah'm a union man, hen. Will ah dae?'

'Ah was wanting the Warehousemen and Cutters representative.'

'He'll be doon the far end, hen. Ah'm no sure if he's there the noo, mind. Sit yersel doon.' He nodded at a low stack of packaged paper. 'Ah'll hae a look-see.' From the Highlands. Broad smile.

At first Iza perched on the edge, but as minutes ticked by she shifted herself to sit atop the packages, legs stretched, back against the wall, glazed eyes on roof rafters. She dozed, and as she dozed her mind drifted back to that scarf. Why had it come to mind? Because it wouldn't hold water, that was why. And that's why she'd not been honest with her chum. Because though she was sure of what she was about to do, she was not so sure her reasoning would hold up to Margaret's objections. So, you've taken the coward's way out, she tells herself.

'What's this about cowards? What is it you're wanting, hen?'

Iza opened her eyes. The Warehouse and Cutters Union man was leaning to wave a hand close to her face.

'Nothin. Sorry. Ah was dozing. Talking to myself,' she muttered.

Five minutes later she'd written her name, job, work number and address in his ledger and signed to say she'd abide by the rules of the Warehousemen and Cutters Union. She hadn't read the rules, but in her pocket she had a printed copy folded into her dues card. She'd paid this week's dues. And she'd told the man who took her tuppence and pointed to where she should sign that she'd come to the warehouse each week to pay.

Iza gobbled her piece as she walked back to the caseroom. Just five minutes of dinnertime left and, though she knew she owed her chum an explanation, she was relieved Margaret wasn't waiting on their perch in the yard.

§§§§§§§§§

> The lines of her countenance softened
> from the rigidity of business to the
> softness of love when she saw Jude,
> and she bent her eyes languishingly

When Bella has a job getting her mouth round languishingly, Iza sounds out each syllable for her. A puzzled look on Bella's sharp wee face has Iza say 'Languish means droop. Or something like that.'

'The fancy woman's bending droopy eyes on him.' A glance over at Netta as she calls this out has Iza imagining looking over at an empty frame. The thought scares her. Next week Netta won't be there. She won't be back. And what with the Typographical Society flexing its muscles against cheap labour, fewer and fewer lassies are being taken on. There's mutterings that Bella will be the last of them. Iza casts an eye round the caseroom. While there's a head at every frame on the men's side, the women's side is dotted with gaps left by women who've left to get wed. Like bairns' milk teeth, you can't miss the first gap but then you stop noticing. And if, like milk teeth, the gaps get replaced, Iza realises with a jolt, they'll get replaced by those apprentice lads who seem to be everywhere. Three of them near-on time-served will be needing their own frames any day now.

How could Netta go and be expecting, get married, leave? Iza tuts. Not that we've ever been that close, she thinks, not outside of work anyhow, but in here we've been within sight of each other, greasing the days with blether and laughs, for fifty-two hours – fifty-one-and-three-quarters from this week on – for a good three year, nearly four.

'On you go,' she tells Bella in a softer voice than she's tended to use on her.

upon him. The animals took advantage
of the pause by doubling and bolting
out of the way.

They were only put in this morning
she

'Was that reported speech?'
'Aye.'
'Well you have to say so. Read out "inverted comma cap T". And, look here, you take your comma, so, and invert it, so. Right. On you go.'

'They were only put in this morning'
she cried, stimulated to pursue in spite

of her lover's presence.

Iza wonders for a moment if it's right to be exposing this thirteen-year-old lassie to languishing lovers, but she suspects young Bella knows as much about these matters as she herself does. More, probably. The thought that since walking out with Roddy Mac she's catching up fast has her blush.

Come Saturday the caseroom always subsides into a calmer, dogged rhythm. Limbs are wearied. Backs and eyes ache. Lungs are fume-laden. Saturday afternoon and Sunday's freedom are close enough to allow a breath of the outside world to seep in and give faces a faraway look. This morning's calm, though, is disturbed by two ructions, men marching up the stair to see overseer Wight. By pricking her ears Iza gleans that the first is pleading for extras on Canon Law on account of the tiny, very bad hand. This deputation stomps down grumbling that a farthing a thousand ens is too little. The second delegation complains that some comps on The Monks are getting text to set while others are getting the notes. They tread down the stair quietly, lower lips jutting, heads nodding, clearly vindicated.

When the hooter sounds at quarter past twelve, Iza and Bella have already tidied up. Netta too. John Adams, though, is startled. Iza sees him look about him, shake his head, take out his pocket watch and blink at it.

'Early! Well that's a new one.'

'We finish at quarter past now,' Iza says.

John Adam's brow wrinkles.

'Your strike notice that got us the quarter hour reduction.'

'Och, right enough. How could ah forget our great victory?' He starts to clear up. 'You get so used to the hooter being late and them thinking we're too daft to tell the time.'

# -12-

His fingertips stroked the back of her neck, along her shoulders and back up. She didn't flinch. The sensation was a million miles from that feeling of cobwebs pulled across your skin you got when lads tried touching you up. She let her head loll. He gripped her upper arms for a moment then slid his hands round onto her breasts. His breath on the back of her neck, tongue slicking stray hairs. Thighs clasping her sides, he hooked his chin onto her shoulder, nibbled her ear. She lifted his hands from her breasts to wrap his arms around her. He fingered the calloused tips of her fingers.

'Horny hands of labour.'

Pulling her hands away to stuff them in her pockets, she turned to kiss his cheek, missed, felt the scrape of bristles on her lips, laughed, suddenly awkward. He disentangled himself and crept round on all fours to stroke the feathery seed head of the blade of grass he was sucking up the inside of her thigh. She pulled his Tam o' Shanter off and tossed it, leant back and clenched her knees to his ears. The sun had slipped down, the earth gone cold under her backside and when she felt it the grass was damp.

'Kinda weety wye.'

'Kinda what?' He raised his head to kneel facing her.

'Weety wye. Wet. Mah dad's teuchter talk. The other night he said "Ah'm fair doon apon it, hen. Ah'm awa back to Fetlar." But he's never lived in Shetland. That was his granny that came down to mind them when his mum died. He was born in Edinburgh, mah dad, so he isn't a teuchter, even though he talks like one sometimes.'

'There's nothing wrong with country folk. Except of course for those that stole all the land. Poor folk like your father, they're just workers, or tomorrow's workers if they're still up there in the Highlands.'

'Mah father isn't poor,' Iza challenged. 'We're not poor.'

'I don't mean it like that. Anyway, there's nothing wrong with being poor.'

'Aye there is.'

'Well, yes. No one need be poor in the richest country in the world, but...'

'If you work hard you won't be poor.' Said as though she was telling him night follows day rather than asking if it might not be the other way round, and she got the reply she suspected she deserved.

'Simple as that is it?' Roddy Mac got up, strolled to the edge of the brown waters that burbled through the Braid Burn valley and squatted there to gaze up at a patchwork of shadow and light shifting across flanks of mounded purple hills.

Wind whistled through dry grass and set red and gold leaves spinning. Late October. Every day the sun gone paler and further away and nights coming in fast. Since the evening in Jim's shop a few weeks back Iza had spent her scant spare time as close to Roddy Mac as she could get. She hadn't been back to the shop, but she had waited on street corners till he and Eamonn were done with giving out handbills, noting how they got precious few thanks from folk bundling themselves to work or home from it. On one such occasion she'd had to nip into a doorway when she spotted her brother Jack in the crowded street. On hearing Jack berate Eamonn, she'd seethed but kept herself scarce. She and Roddy Mac had walked streets and parks. Like bairns, they'd climbed and sat up a tree one day and like sweethearts they'd lain in a secluded hollow at the foot of the crags and she'd opened herself to him. Now, just a few blissful Sundays outdoors all day long and this might be the last of them. Where would they go then, she wondered. Talk was of a harsh winter coming.

A gang of bairns who'd spent the afternoon piling stones to dam the burn and leap and splash were running off home dangling jam jars full of tiddlers. Other couples who'd dotted the grass slopes of the glen had pulled themselves up, fixed their clothes and sauntered off towards town, voices trailing behind them. Iza got up, sat down again, plucked at grass stems while in her mind she told the man swishing a stick across bubbling water, a few yards from her, about Jamie's wedding do. How her dad had dug out his fiddle, first time in ages, and set it reeling, scratchy at first, but back to his old self, almost, once a neighbour took up the lilt with a squeeze-box and Jack set spoons clacking; how she'd never in her born days seen a face glow as Jamie's bride Jessie's had that day; how she had searched for him, Roddy Mac, among folk piling into the house, hoping against hope he'd have a mind to ignore her 'Best not come. They're a bit funny'; how, as drink and dancing built up steam and floorboards groaned she'd tugged William into a dance and, for a brief spell, spinning and clowning with her wee brother, had forgotten to miss Roddy Mac; how when the round of music ended she'd gone to the back room to gaze out at the dark crags, alone and wanting him, willing him at that very moment to chance past their door and be swept up the stair with the flow of neighbours still being drawn by the music.

But she said none of this. And seeing as he seemed to have forgotten she was there, she pulled herself up and walked away without looking back. On a rutted track leading down to where the town was bursting its banks to form trickles, puddles, pools of new houses among fields, she sensed rather than heard him behind her. When he came alongside her they walked in silence until, as they skirted the hulking Royal Asylum, a man's white face peering through the bars of a high iron fence made her jump and Roddy Mac wrapped an arm around her and she steadied herself by taking up where she'd left off talk of her father, saying how her dad believed some of the old wifey's tales he'd got from his Shetland granny, how he swore that if the house wasn't cleaned before they went to bed of a night it'd be witched for a year and a day.

'And do you clean the house?'

'Aye.'

'Then he's not so daft, is he?'

On a patch of scrubland, they stopped to pick brambles. At least, Iza picked while Roddy Mac opened his mouth for her to poke fat berries in.

'When we were wee mah brother Jack picked a fight with lads bigger than him when they laughed at mah dad's teuchter talk. Mind you, Jack would pick a fight with Jesus Christ himself. Now he's learning to box so he can punch people officially.'

'Grand idea. Working folk need to learn how to fight. Not that daft waving your arms around they do outside the pubs. Proper fighting. Disciplined. Warlike.'

'Mah dad says the army's for fools.'

'I'm not talking about the army.' He didn't add 'stupid' like Rab had a habit of doing, but he might as well have. 'Mind you, Jim's talking of signing up. To learn how to use a rifle for the cause, though, not to fight bloody imperial wars.'

'What, Jim the cobbler?'

'Jim can turn his hand to anything.' Roddy Mac's sharp tone stung.

'He can walk on water, can he?' she hit back.

It worked. 'He wouldn't win any prizes at cobbling, mind,' Roddy Mac conceded before picking up a twig to whack at nettles and add, 'He only took it up because he's blacklisted.'

The awestruck wee laddie again, Iza thought. Though she smiled to herself, she wasn't so sure she wanted the company of this Roddy Mac, the one bragging about how tough his big brother was. But what with those eyes of his, those long sinewy arms, that smell of him, she wasn't about to dwell on what she didn't want. Out of sight out of mind. She'd change the subject. First, though, she wanted to know something.

'What's blacklisted?'

'Barred from employment for the terrible crime of standing up for his fellow workers, encouraging them to combine to challenge the masters' right to treat them as they please.'

Eyes down, Iza chewed on this. First she'd heard of it. She'd heard how strike-breakers were hounded from the works. Not just heard it. She'd seen it. Just the other week the appearance of a new comp, set on a frame by the overseer, had raised hackles. 'Notorious rat,' Iza had heard. 'Send him to severe Coventry.' As she left the caseroom late one evening that same week she'd glanced at him. She knew he was waiting for the caseroom to empty so he could leave unharried. He'd glanced round at the same moment. His face was twisted. He wasn't at his frame next morning and was never seen again.

'So, are you blacklisted?'

'No.'

'So where do you work? You must start late.'

'I'm studying.' His clipped answer suggested she'd given offence by prying. But now he grinned, stood to attention and, clenched fist raised, called out to a darkening sky, 'Like Jim says: educate, agitate, organise.'

She'd like to have asked how he lived without working but sensed it would set them at odds. Instead, she responded to the grin by giving him a hefty shove. He mock toppled but righted himself to pin her along the sights of a pretend rifle.

'Take that, Irish rebel-rouser,' she called out, raising her arms and firing.

Roddy Mac clutched his chest, staggered, then turned heel and sauntered off, kicking at loose stones, calling back, 'So the Irish don't meet with your approval? More poor folk trying to put food on the table.'

'Some of mah best chums are Irish,' she protested. 'At least they were.'

'So what are they now? Red Indian?'

'Mah chums ah played in the street with when ah was wee, ah mean. Ah never see them now ah'm in the caseroom.'

He stopped and turned to face her, arms folded. 'Can you

not see how it suits the masters for you to be down on other working folk just because they talk different?' Walking on again, he tossed 'And, by the way, though I was born in India I'm as Scots as you are, but if I were Irish I'd be proud of it,' over his shoulder.

'And ah'm not down on anyone except you when you talk to me like a schoolmaster, like ah'm stupid.'

They were nearing town now. She crossed to the other side of the road and they walked a while on opposite sides of an empty street of brand new stone houses set way back, some still being built. Backstreets had garages for motorcars at the end of long gardens. Lamps were being lit and curtains drawn across big bay windows. A candle flitted past a wee window in a round tower.

Roddy Mac turned into what would be the garden of a big half-built house. Calling 'Let's have a shufty,' he disappeared over rubble into the black hole of a doorway. She didn't follow him. She didn't like the look of it. But standing alone in this raw street, the bang of a gate blowing to and the bark of a guard dog coming at her as solitary sounds thudding in thick silence, she felt more alone than she'd ever felt. Though he was within shouting distance, Roddy Mac could have been across the high seas in a far-off land. And it struck her, not for the first time, that even as their flesh touched he could be at a great distance from her. One minute their beings were as close as you could get, the next ... Gripped by a need to escape, she set off. Though she called out 'Ah'm off,' she didn't wait or look round.

As he'd done earlier, he soon rejoined her, and when he did her fear left her and she took the hand he stretched out. With stars coming out high above them but no streetlamps to go by much of the way, they stumbled through a field, smell of crushed turnip tops and soot in the air, walked past middens and pig pens, along railway sidings, while up ahead an amber glow blurred the outline of tenement roofs and wisps of pale smoke from the first of autumn's fires trailed from chimneys into a rust-red sky.

By Nelson's Parkside works he led her through a gap in a hawthorn hedge into the work's allotments. She knew this place. Her dad had kept an allotment here before shredded lungs had him gasping for breath. Roddy sat her down on a low plank bench by a hut, disappeared in the dark, came back with a handful of over-ripe raspberries and fed her, sucking juice from her mouth. And though she felt something of her dad's presence in the still, dark bushes and black earth, she was settling to their lovemaking when an owl swooping close by startled her and had her jump to her feet.

Other than a drunk slumped by a lamp post, tankard dangling from a hooked finger, the street was asleep when they reached her corner. They'd walked in silence, both lost in thought, Roddy she knew not where, herself picturing him in her house, exchanging a few words with her mum and Violet, letting William win at draughts, having a beer and a game of whist with her dad and Jamie. No. Jamie was gone with his Jessie. With Jack then? No. Jack would pick a fight. Rab? Impossible to imagine. Violet and her Angus? No. That stuffed-shirt would stick his nose up at Roddy and Violet would likely go along with him. Just her and William and her mum and dad then, Rab and Violet having conveniently vanished. Aye, she'd invite him in next Saturday afternoon or Sunday. That's what was needed to seal that split that kept opening up between their two worlds.

They'd reached her door when Roddy Mac took hold of her shoulders and turned her to face him. 'I'm away to

Dublin on Monday,' he said. Though his eyes were on her she could see he was looking through and beyond her.

'Dublin in Ireland?' She didn't need that scathing look to know she'd said a stupid thing. 'For how long?'

'As long as needs be. They're setting up a Trade Union Congress. Jim's hoping to be paid organiser for the Socialist Society. I'm to go on ahead for a look-see, make soundings while he fixes his affairs.'

He talked over her head and his solemn tone did not mask an eagerness to be off and away. So when he now looked into her eyes and said, 'Come. Come with me,' it knocked her off balance. She held her breath. Ah can't. Can ah? Her head spun. Aye, ah can. Why not? Not sure what would come out of it, she'd opened her mouth, but he got in first.

'Mind you, Jim says you're best staying here to work in the union.'

Eyes turned inwards and nods of his head told her loud and clear that he'd agreed to this. So it's not me he cares for, she thought. It's his bloody handbills. Miserable beyond measure, the thought that his handbills and pails *were* matters of importance was of no comfort.

When Roddy Mac pecked her forehead with his lips she almost said 'You'll write to me, won't you?' But lips that just a half-hour past had melted on hers now rasped. She said nothing.

'Don't you go keeping yourself out of trouble now,' he joked, and he was off across the road, and when, turning in at her stair door, she looked over her shoulder, he didn't.

As Iza gripped the bannister to pull herself slowly up the dark stairs, someone came rushing down towards her. When the figure reached her, it stopped. Even in the dark she could see her sister Violet was beside herself.

'Where've you been? Ah'm going for Ma Coutts.'

Ma Coutts meant a birth or a death. Though there were always new bairns coming into the world, none of the neighbours that Iza knew of were due now. Violet held still a moment. 'Dad's dead,' she said before hurrying on.

§§§§§§§§

'He's off to the big town.'

'What, with his fancy woman?'

'No. On his own. She's left him. Gone away to Australia.'

'What, on her own?'

'Ah don't know.' With this, Iza snapped off the conversation.

> that city, had seemed to be visible. A
> milestone, now, as always, stood at the
> roadside hard by. Jude drew near it,
> and felt rather than read the mileage
> to the city.

She's been going along with this 'what's happening now?' as though it's Netta standing at the next frame. But it's not. It's young Bella at Netta's empty frame, set there to learn the lay of the case.

Snap. Her fingers fail her. Lines buckle. Sorts scatter over case, over frame, to tinkle to the floor. 'Who pied? He pied. He, she or it pied,' she mutters. If anyone chants it, she doesn't hear them.

Hunkered down on haunches, she riffles through mucky sawdust for stray type, a good penny's worth by the time she gets the lines reset. She finds a halfpenny and she gets a metal shard jammed under her thumbnail. One or two sorts have chinked between floorboards. She gives up trying to dislodge them but stays down on her haunches to suck a thumb that's already starting to throb.

'Say one for me while you're down there,' John Adams calls. Then he ceases his tapping. 'You aw right, hen? You look like you're saying your prayers.'

'Mah dad's died,' she says.

John Adams sets down his shooting stick and mallet and, with a 'Bide there a minute. Ah'll fetch your chum,' he walks off.

# -13-

It was dry out but a wild wind was up, sending low clouds scudding across the sky. Iza followed Margaret to a sheltered corner of the yard where, behind a stack of crates, they found a perch.

'Poor you.' Margaret looped an arm over Iza's shoulders. 'Should you not go home?'

Iza shook her head. Last night Violet had said she'd stay home to help see to things. 'Aye. You get away to your bed,' Vi Ross had said. 'We'll be needing every penny of your pay packet from now on.'

She'd set off early, eager to be away from a dreadful hush in the house. It was raining. Aiming for the bakers for a roll, she'd found herself stopping to peer in through a watery window at Jim Connolly. Pipe gripped in his teeth, he was turning the page of a book propped on a rickety music stand. A candle set on his wax-covered last still flickered. He looked like he'd been there all night. Though his eyes were set firm on his book, she ducked away before he looked up.

'You're shivering.' Margaret hugged her.

'Ah got drenched this morning. But ah've joined the Warehousemen and Cutters union so just five months to hold out and ah'll be in benefit and can take to mah bed with pneumonia and get sick pay.'

'You did what?'

'A few weeks back,' Iza said, making light of it because heaven knows why she'd said it. It just came out. Because she needed to mend a rift she'd created? Aye. She hadn't shared it with her chum and that was wrong. But, then, she hadn't shared much of anything with Margaret these past weeks. Taken up with Roddy Mac, she'd given little time and less thought to her chum.

'But we agreed. What changed your mind?' A good dose of irritation had entered Margaret's concern. 'We've nothing in common with them,' she tutted, as much to herself as to Iza.

'We need to be organised. Simple as that,' Iza said. Out of Jim Connolly's mouth that had rolled round and strong but out of hers it came thin and shrill, even though she thought she believed the truth of it. 'Besides,' she rushed on, 'with mah dad dead and Jamie wed and Jack gone to lodgings we'll need the benefits.' This was true, but she well knew that her family had been far from her mind when she joined the Warehousemen's union. Roddy Mac had not, though. Her mind had been full of him. And when, just then, she'd listed the men gone from her life, the unspoken words that rang in her head were 'and Roddy Mac's gone and left me.'

'Anyhow, it can't be right us getting half what the men get.' They'd been talking quietly till now but a rush of anger had raised Iza's voice.

Margaret blanched. 'Joining that union's not going to help matters. And you know perfectly well they'll never pay us the same as the men,' she snapped, taking her arm from Iza's shoulder and shifting along to put inches between them.

Now, that the lassies earned half the men's rate was as obvious as night follows day. That the scales might be altered in the women's favour would enter your mind as a fancy. But to speak of it was to step onto thin ice and Ballantyne's women comps never did. Apart from two labourers heaving bales of paper the yard was empty, but, still, voicing these thoughts set the both of them on edge.

'We'll be getting ourselves no pay at all at this rate,' Iza said flatly. 'Best get back to our frames.'

Margaret was screwing a lock of hair round her finger.

'Sorry to snap, Maggie. Ah'm not feeling mahself.'

'Aye. I can see that,' Margaret said.

By mid-afternoon, light a grey broth, comps having to lean in close to peer at manuscripts, Iza had had enough, and, since it was going to be a lean day's pickings in any case, what with a throbbing thumb slowing her down, she went down to the cludgie to sit a while in a dingy cubicle. To a rumbling of presses that seemed to come up from the depths and a slow, steady plonk of dripping water that might be in her head, she hugged herself and rocked. She felt raw. A voice called in the corridor outside, the door creaked and thumped, footsteps clomped, a cubicle door clunked. Then, after a low growl, a tinkle, a splat, it was back to drips echoing in silence.

She stopped at the chemist for a drawing paste for her thumb and a poke of powder for colds. On the way out with them she thought to turn back to ask for something for her mother's nerves, and while the chemist rooted in drawers, slid jars from shelves and spooned powders onto scales, she sat quiet on a stool.

'Ah said, how's her tongue?' The chemist rattled his pestle in the mortar to get her attention. 'Your mother. Is her tongue still furred?'

'Ah don't know. Aye.'

'Tell her to put a spoonful on her tongue with a wee bit of water or sweet tea. The same if she wakes in the night and another spoonful first thing. And you want to wrap yourself up warm.'

As Iza turned to go, the chemist asked how her dad was doing.

'Mah dad's passed away,' she said, matter-of-fact, like she was saying 'it's windy out'.

Folk were stuttering along St Leonard's Street, buffeted by gusts. Clouds swirled round the russet crags. Round a corner, out of the wind, Iza stopped, leant against a stone wall to catch some sun, not ready to face home. But her bones soon juddered as cold seeped in from the wall. In her street, a passing neighbour lowered his head to say 'Sorry to hear about your faither, hen.'

# -14-

The breezy jig of an accordion came to Iza in scraps as she neared her stair door. In the stair, a familiar tune settled and swelled so that she opened her house door prepared for it to fill her ears. But the music was elsewhere. Her house was hushed. The room smelt of coal tar soap masking a whiff of blocked drain pipe. A sickly sweet tang, too. Burnt sugar? Sparse hair combed and greased flat except for a lick of curl by his ear, James Ross lay in a deal coffin stretched between two wooden seats. His jacket, dyed sheer black for the occasion, had been tucked under to take up slack and a Paisley pattern cravat Iza had never seen before, bunched under a startlingly white collar, caused his chin to poke. Book-ended by two neighbours, Vi Ross sat in the middle of a short row of borrowed seats set along the coffin's sides. She grimaced when Iza proffered the poke of powder but said a doleful aye to a splash of whisky in her tea.

Violet stood at the draining board lighting candles she'd put in jars and tumblers. Her copper hair gleamed. She'd coiled it in a neat knot held by a black and silver comb. Face pale against a blouse that had gone in the vat of black dye with their dad's and brothers' jackets, she looked older and grander. Violet had taken another day off work to borrow seats and crockery, boil a ham, buy rolls and biscuits, greet and serve callers.

'There's been a steady trickle,' Violet said when Iza joined her at the draining board. 'There'll be a lot coming soon. Make up some rolls and see to the fire. And tear up some paper for the cludgie, will ye.'

Iza did her sister's bidding with good enough grace, but when she came out of the cludgie after sitting there a while willing Roddy Mac to make an appearance, just as she'd done at Jamie's wedding do, only shifting herself when someone kept rattling at the door, she said 'You seem to be managing fine,' when her sister told her to make herself useful.

Ben the bedroom William lay across the bed on his belly, legs hinged back, ankles crossed, reading his book. He looked up, rubbing at his eyes with slight, grubby hands. When Iza went to fetch a ham roll and a candle for him, Violet and she exchanged strained smiles and were about to find words to share when the front door opened to belch Jack and Rab and a good score of men from Nelsons' print works into the room. Close behind came Jamie and Jessie with more folk, neighbours, in their wake. Iza slipped back into the bedroom, shut the door behind her and lay on her belly pressed to William's side. Letting a rising babble of voices from next door fade into the background, she watched William's thick lashes quiver and his pouty lips move as he read. Teasing knots from his hair till he slapped her to stop, she told the tale of the Russian frog's journey. At first he tutted at her interruption, but by adding a bit of colour to the outline she'd heard she drew first a little and then all of his attention. Face lit up, he asked what happened next. When Iza said she didn't know, he stared up at the ceiling for a bit, thoughtful, before turning back to his book.

'What's happening?' she said. 'Read me it.' And he did. Or, at least, they did. 'Ah'll be François the half-breed. You be Massan and the other one.' William held the candle close. 'There,' he said, pointing. And Iza read, 'I've seen more than enough o' these rascally Huskies (Esquimaux). Tis well for me that I'm here this blessed day, an' not made into a dan to bob about in Hudson's Straits at the tail of a white whale, like that poor boy Peter who was shot by them varmints.' By the end of her lines she had her voice tugged down to gruff. She was about to nudge William, but didn't need to. '"What's a dan?" asked a young half-breed who had lately arrived at Moose, and knew little of Esquimau implements.' William read poorly, stumbling over some easy words, but still his wide-eyed intensity brought him close to being the young half-breed Iza now addressed. '"What a green-horn you must be, François, not to know what a dan is!" replied another, who was inclined to be quizzical,' – Iza made a great flourish of quizzical – '"Why, it's a sort of sea-carriage that the Esquimaux tie to the tail of a walrus or sea-horse when they feel inclined for a drive. When they can't get a sea-horse they catch a white whale asleep, and wake him up after fastening the dan to his tail. I suppose they have conjurers or wizards among them, since Massan told us just now that poor Peter was–"' William's mouth was open ready. '"Bah! Gammon," interrupted François with a smile,' – William tugged the book to him – 'as he turned to the first speaker. "But tell me, Massan, what is a dan?"' Here, the deep blue eyes that looked to Iza for an answer were no longer William's but François', and they were looking not at her but at Massan. "'It's a sort o' float or buoy, lad, used by the Huskies, and is made out o' the skin o' the seal. They tie it with a long line to their whale spears to show which way the fish bolts when struck.'" William's fists came up to clasp his cheeks. "'And did they use Peter's skin for such a purpose?" inquired François earnestly.' "'They did", replied Massan.' "'And did you see them do it?'" William whispered. "'Yes, I did,'" Iza hissed.

When William lost the struggle to hitch up his eyelids, Iza lay on her back listening to a fine bass voice rise through next door's burble. *My grandfather's clock was too big for the shelf.* She got up and stood in the doorway. Other voices took up the song, as Iza did under her breath. *So it stood twenty years on the floor.* Now the whole room sang or stayed their tongues to listen. As they neared the end of the song, voices dropped off until the lead singer was left to finish alone. *But it stopped, short, never to go again, when the old man died.* A hush fell on the room.

By the coffin, in the middle of a huddle of bodies wreathed in tobacco smoke, Jack had propped himself up on Violet, trying to detach herself, on one side and their mother, looking up at Jack, on the other. Violet caught sight of Iza and, miming the filling of a glass, nodded over to an old boy sitting in a corner on his own. A machineman, Iza knew by the lean, angular cut of him. She fetched his empty glass and held it out for Jack to fill from the bottle of whisky he now waved about as he talked, not bothering to let him know it wasn't for her when Jack started on about girruls not being able to hold their drink. She pulled a stool over to sit by the old boy, asked was he at Nelsons.

'Aye, hen. Used to be.'

They sat silent for a bit. He had a soft, far-away look about him that soothed her.

'So you worked with mah dad?'

'Aye.'

Thin, blue-grey lips like her dad's. Same rattle in his chest as he breathed, like he had pebbles loose in his lungs. Same clouded eyes with a tiny spark deep in them.

'Ah've got the cancer,' he said to the empty space in front of him before turning to her to say, 'Ah was wi your faither in '72. Ah mind him playing his fiddle at Drummond Street hall.'

Iza held silent for a moment before asking, 'The '72 strike? What was it like?' She wanted to know, but she also sensed the old boy might like a trip back to a time before cancer sneaked into him. And, right enough, his eyes cleared and he sat taller.

'We were out for the fifty-one hour week. Part of the national movement. They'd just made strikes legal. Trade was good. Start of November, close to 800 of us served our notices. Mid November we were out. A bitter winter that.'

Aware of Rab glowering over at her, Iza clasped her hands between her knees and pinned her eyes on the old boy. She'd sit for a blether with this man if she pleased.

'By the new year the town was teamin wi rats. Tenth of January 1873 ah lifted mah card, took mah thirty bob – down from the four quid ah'd've got in November – and me and the missis packed up what wisnae in the paund and spent two-and-six on the train to Glasgow.'

'Mah Uncle Lawrence went to Glasgow during the strike. So there was work there?'

'Aye. For some.'

Rocking gently as though he were riding on a swaying cart, the old boy peered straight through the cluster of bodies and out the window into darkness. Watching him, Iza saw the embers of a burning intelligence in the spare lines of his grey face and that brought her the closest to spilling tears that she'd come these past few days.

'A fair few headed off to America.' He nodded slowly as though he were bidding farewell to them. After a bit, he blinked and turned to her. 'Some of us wound up back here. Some tramped down to London but couldn't get a start on account of the masters telling their pals down there to black us.'

He sounded so dejected Iza almost changed the subject, but curiosity got the better of her.

'Could the London Society not get them in?'

'Aye the big shops did, right enough. They had the organisation.'

Two printers standing nearby had cocked their ears and a natty wee man smoking a pipe too big for him joined in with, 'And we have to mind it was the London boys' levy kept us going as long as we did.'

'Them and donations from the Kirkcaldy floorcloth workers and the Newcastle corkcutters and others we'd never even heard of,' his chum said.

At first Iza ignored empty glasses, but the old boy's puzzled look when he raised his to his mouth made her think better of it and she got up and, giving Rab a wide berth, wove her way through thick-packed bodies towards Jack. This time, rather than pour, her brother hung himself on her shoulder by a limp arm and dribbled slurred talk in her hair, 'Whityewantinhen? Ah'mnogivinyenomore.' And he and his bottle were still draped on her when she excusemeed her way back to the old boy and his chums. There she dislodged Jack, leaving him to sway until he found a prop in Rab, who'd come to listen in with that pinched look of his.

'Mind thon first day in the big hall in Drummond Street?

Alex Smart drummin' us up into battalions – draughts battalion, dominoes battalion, the mighty chess battalion. That's when ah learnt to play chess, and beat the wee bugger that showed me the moves,' the natty wee man was saying.

'Ah mind the fitba on the Meadows,' his chum said.

'Gettin slaughtered by Blackwells. Blackwells for christsake.'

The old boy perked up. 'Mind that hike over the Pentlands? The hills ringin wi the call of printers coughing their guts up.'

'Aye. And Ernie Poulson going, "There's bugger aw oot here except sheep and when ye've seen one sheep ye've seen the bloody lot."'

'And sitting doon on his bumbaleerie in the middle of a field saying he wisnae shifting till the bugger whose bright idea this was got a cab to get us to the nearest pub.'

Now Jack righted himself to barge to the middle of the group. 'Get us to the nearest pub,' he sing-songed. 'First sensible thing ah've heard you lot say. All this bloody stuck-in-the-bloody-past '72 strike nonsense. It's dead and gone. Life's for the living.' A pause to poke his chin towards the coffin and beg his dad's pardon and he finished with a stamped out, 'Mah faither's no wantin to hear all this shite. Respect for the dead for christsake.'

'Right enough.' The old boy sank back into himself. 'May we never see the like again. That's what Jim Ray wrote at the end of the strike minute book. Ah seen it. "May we never see the like again. March 1873."' His eyes shuttered.

'A-bloody-men,' Jack slurred.

When the singing ended and the blether sank and most of the mourners had bowed a head to James Ross's body and left, Vi Ross, who'd sit out the night by her man, repeated to Iza what was become a nightly refrain. 'You get yourself some sleep. You'll need to be at your work first thing.' Iza tried lying down by a sound-asleep William, but couldn't settle. She'd only have to shift herself when Rab came to bed, so she got her hat and scarf and coat and slipped out, down the stair, round the back and into the park. Cold had set in good and proper. A crust of frost crisped the path. Spiked grass glistened under a full white moon.

Following the path she'd walked with him, she told Roddy Mac that William loved the tale of the Russian frog, told him what the old boys had had to say about the strike, and that her dad's face had more colour now he was dead. Though she spoke in her head only, still she was going on as though he were there by her side till a big tuft by the path moved and she gasped and stopped dead, hand to her heart. A small head emerged, two black eyes pinned on her, and a shaggy ewe bleated and ambled off. Turning, Iza shooed Roddy Mac from her mind and walked quickly home.

§§§§§§§§§

How long they bode so they didn't
know, but when they came to
themselves a terrible thunderstorm
a-raging and they seemed to see in the
gloom a dark figure with very thin legs
and a curious voot

Eh? What's this? 'Ever heard of a voot?' Iza calls.

'A what?' John Adams lends an ear without looking up.

'A voot.'

'What's it say?'

'Very thin legs and a curious voot.'

'It'll be boot.' He coughs in time to the tap-tap of his
mallet then gulps air. 'Could be foot, mind.'

'Right enough, he had volk for folk earlier. But it'd be
voots, surely. Boots come in pairs. So do feet, mind you, so
maybe it should be veet.'

"You still on the Jude job?'

'Aye. Part Fifth. Just the one part to go.'

Page upon page assembled, her last chapter of Jude, and with no one asking what's happening the story's passed her by. It strikes her that if John Adams were to ask what they were getting up to she wouldn't have a clue. It was blethering with Netta had her picking out matters of note in all those tens of thousands of words, like William pointing out tiny creatures in a jam jar of murky water scooped from the burn. Netta's frame's empty, and no man would ever ask. Curious facts they'll share. So, she'll hear them call out 'Here's a good word for an imposter: a lampresado,' or 'Did you know St Alban of Mainz carried his chopped-off head to the place he wanted to be buried?' And sometimes she'll prick her ears and learn something. The men must be right scunnered that Neills, not Ballantynes, prints the Encyclopaedia Brittanica she's thought. They'd be in heaven with all those facts in the Ency Brit, calling out this and that all day long. Mind you, she'd quite fancy it herself, finding out about the world and its doings, having things to tell to... Roddy Mac. God damn his soul. Giving a wee glimpse of faraway places then it's up and away without a backward glance. Gone. But what if he's changed his mind? What if he's at the gates this evening? Don't be daft, she chides herself. If he waited for me every day from now till eternity ah'd have no truck with him.

She goes to shelves at the end of the caseroom to look up the dictionary. Vomitory voodoo voracious. No voot. Back at her frame she has another look. Och. It's in inverted commas. 'He's doing this English accent, ah think,' she calls.

'Maybe they only have one voot down south.'

voot, a-standing on the ladder, and
finishing their work.

Just in case, she goes to circle 'voot' on the manuscript
for the author, but her pencil is not in its place and she
doesn't bother.

Dull. Dreary. Deadly. All of a sudden, she's sick of the
lot of it: windowless walls with their fat, ugly pipes; filthy
soot-smeared roof panes that make the sky grey every day
of the year; infernal din bashing her lugs; aching back, sore
fingers and stinging eyes. She feels sick in the stomach. She
wants to be out of here. She wants to drop her stick, tip
up that galley of type, walk out of the caseroom, out of
the yard, and never look back. And go where? Home? Up
north? Down south? But no. She'd never drop her stick.
She'd set her lines and dump them to the galley and go on
doing so until the hooter goes, as she now does.

# -15-

That winter was bitter. Worst in living memory. Five months of blistering, sleet-laden winds, gutters hung with icicles long as your arm, snow that stayed white because no sooner had soot dirtied it than low grey skies dumped fresh loads. Snow upon snow, frozen pipes, chilblains, cracked lips, hacking coughs.

'As well your father left us when he did,' Vi Ross said. 'He'd never have survived this. And ah'm likely to be joining him.'

Of an evening, Vi Ross stayed hunched over the fire until it died. Her spirits had taken a beating. Within a few months her family had been halved. What remained of the Rosses, she, Iza, Violet and Rab, had flitted a few doors along to a top floor house: two rooms, same as their old one but smaller, so cheaper. In this house the three women shared a back room that looked out over woods and crags, while Rab, gone from younger son to man of the house, had the front room and set-in bed to himself. The family writing bureau and mantel clock never made it up the stairs. Along with those of James Ross's tools that Jack had no use for, they'd raised part of the half year's rent. A machine room bereavement subscription had been generous, but that and the union benefit and funeral club didn't make up for pay lost through James Ross's long sickness.

Not just her husband's death, but Jack going off to Canonmills had taken the stuffing out of Vi Ross. Jack could rub people up the wrong way, but his way of rubbing suited his mother just fine. It wasn't Jack that Iza missed though. It was her wee brother. No one had noticed William skipping school, not until the truant inspectors knocked, or at least not until a neighbour came to say she was sure that's who'd been asking for Mr and Mrs Ross. The neighbour, one of those too keen to know everyone's business, had assured Iza she'd acted dumb, which was no more than you'd expect of any neighbour, but, taking exception to her poking her nose in, Iza had seen her off, saying their mother needed to be left in peace to grieve. If anyone should have noticed, Iza knew full well she should have. But she'd paid William scant heed until it was too late and he'd lied about his age and got a live-in job in the kitchens of a serviceman's club in the New Town.

Without the clomp of feet, scrape of chairs and bouts of yelling from upstairs, this was a quiet house. These days Iza's shrunken family made little noise. Each of them, Iza noticed, seemed to stick to their own separate spot – at the sink, by the window, at the table – as though they'd forgotten how to move through the space between them. Even Violet's arm round their mother's shoulder looked stiff, like it was jammed in a sleeve shrunk in the wash.

For her part, Iza was more than willing to keep herself to herself that winter. She spent those bitter months doing what she knew best. She worked long hours in the caseroom, taking advantage of what overtime was going.

Coming out of the works into dark nights she hurried home against icy winds, got messages if she caught the grocer still open, fetched coal, stoked the fire and helped Violet get hot food into bellies. Evenings, Violet would be out winchin if she wasn't working late openings to save for her wedding. Nigh-on engaged and full to bursting with it she was. If Rab stayed in you'd get only mutters out of him. Often, though, he was off to the library. After tidying up Iza would join her mother poking and staring at flames or she'd go straight to bed to grip blankets to her chin and fall asleep quick as she could. Weariness made that easy enough, though a dread preying on her made her whimper and moan in her sleep.

Young as she was, she knew the signs. Still, it was a good three months of the curse missed and a patch of throwing up porridge of a morning before she paid any mind to her condition. Her mother, she knew, knew it. Questioning eyes showed that. But Vi Ross said nothing until one evening in November when, after Iza had turned in early, she came through to the bedroom. She came without a candle and Iza was glad of that. Streetlamp light barely reached this top floor and unless there was a bright moon the back room was pitch dark.

Vi Ross sat on the edge of the bed. 'You're in the family way, aren't you?'

'Seems so.' Iza kept her eyes tight shut.

'So what are you planning to do?' Though there was a trace of accusation in it, her mother's tone was woebegone. One more trial to add to a heap of them.

Iza gave no answer.

'Will he have you?'

'Will who have me?'

Her mother tutted. 'You know perfectly well. Him. The father.'

'And you know perfectly well there is no father.'

'So you're the Virgin Mary now are you? Chosen by an angel, were you?' Vi Ross had perked up. She was almost enjoying this. More of her old self.

'He's gone.' Iza turned her back and pulled covers over her head. Then, as her mum sighed and heaved herself up, she turned to say, softer, 'Don't worry. Ah'm seeing to it.'

Though eyes said a great deal in the coming weeks, Iza's 'Ah'm seeing to it' were their last words on the matter. One evening soon after, though, Iza's big sister did voice her opinion. After dishes were washed and Rab went out and Vi Ross dozed by the fire, Violet silently invited Iza through to the bedroom. At first Iza refused her by busying herself scouring the sink, but when Violet, lit candle in hand, stayed by the open bedroom door grimacing and nodding, she wrung and hung the cloth and followed her.

In flickering light, Iza made out Violet patting the bed for her to sit by her side. She held back. Though she could not deny her condition, keeping it to herself was the next best thing. At work in the caseroom she could forget it for long stretches, whole days sometimes. When Violet persisted, though, a yen to be close to warmth carried Iza to her side.

'How're you feeling?'

Though her sister's voice sounded warm enough, her flesh felt ungiving.

Violet held silent for a bit then spoke in a rush. 'Mum says you're seeing to it. Do you know what to do? Where to go? Can ah help?'

Forearms propped on splayed knees, Iza stared at where the candle flame was drawing shfting patterns on the wall.

'Are you...?' Violet paused. Not words, but a grimace and nod towards Iza's belly said 'getting rid of it.'

For a moment, Iza wanted to confide. She turned to look her sister in the face. She opened her mouth. But nothing came out. Seeing, or imagining, Violet's intended, Angus, standing in the shadows, she clammed up. It's shame that's bothering her, she thought, and though she knew she wasn't being fair to her sister, that though not unalloyed Violet's concern was real enough, she replied not to Violet but to a phantom Angus.

'It's mah business. You don't need to concern yourself.'

Violet put an arm round her. 'Silly girl. No wonder he flew the coop. He'd got what he wanted.' It was said tenderly, but Iza was having none of such tenderness. She pulled free, got up, moved out of the light to undress for bed.

'Ah'm only trying to help,' Violet said. 'We'll find out for you if you haven't already. Mum and me. Ah'll come with you.'

'Come where?'

'You know. To the...' A weighted silence said the rest.

Iza's head hurt. She slumped on the opposite side of the bed, back to her sister. Maybe ah should, she thought, leave it to them, let them see to it, do what they say. But no. That wouldn't do. They'd never understand, never know how she'd loved Roddy Mac. Still loved Roddy Mac? How he'd loved her. Had he loved her? How this was not a thing to be flushed away, though it had to be flushed away, hadn't it? It had to be gone, as he was gone. But for it to be gone she'd have to go back to summer and never let Roddy Mac walk her home, never go with him.

She stood up and went to the window. Pitch dark out there but you could make out snow crusted on trees. Not the crags. She couldn't see the crags beyond the trees. Feeling her silent sister's eyes on her back the thought came to her. Mum and Violet don't deserve this. I do. Ah've set mah own path and ah'll stick to it even though I amn't sure where it goes. She knew she was leaving it late. She'd felt the quickening. But then she wasn't leaving it. Her brother Rab had had more influence than he would ever know. His eminent French physician had been vindicated by reports in the papers about Sheffield, about women's periods being brought on by lead poisoning. You had to feel sorry for these poor women but there must be girls like me, it had struck her, for whom it's a blessing. Iza was trusting to the caseroom to do its work. Day after day she'd been sucking dust from her fingers. A good doze of lead, antimony and tin. In her heart of hearts she knew this was leaving it to chance, but her hearts of hearts was buried under swelling flesh and layers of clothing.

'It's all right,' she told Violet as she turned from the window and climbed into bed. 'There's a girl at mah work knows a woman.' This was a lie. She'd told no-one at work, not even Margaret, and she didn't intend to.

'What does it feel like? Is it nice?' Violet's tone was curious. She's not asking about my condition, Iza thought. Or at least not just that. She wants to know about the begetting. And with that, she slammed the door on her sister.

'Why don't you try it for yourself and find out.' Not what she'd have said in a kinder moment, but she wasn't feeling kind and she didn't care.

Violet was on her feet and making for the door. 'Ah will,' she said. 'When a respectable man's put a ring on mah finger.'

§§§§§§§§§

Have you any ground for supposing
that if the eight hours' day were now
conceded, the men would do as much
work in eight hours as they now do
in nine?

Last of the questions dumped to the galley, she heaves up
her 10 point case, scolding her arms for having so little life
in them. After sliding the case into place in her frame, she
tugs out her 11 point case and, grunting with the strain,
sets it down. She then rearranges a bunched shawl she's
using to cushion where her front presses on the edge of
a case.

At least seven months gone, she wears a loose smock
of her mother's draped over her dress. She's sewn panels
into the sides. Her sewing is abysmal but it serves. Skinny
to begin with, she's a slight thing even with the swelling.

Her smock is something you'd expect to see on a wifey howking potatoes in a field by the hills, but, then, this winter folk are wrapped up in all manner of odd clothing to keep body and soul from freezing, and if anyone in the caseroom has noticed they've kept it to themselves.

Rab. Damn him to hell. He knows nothing about anything. The thought gave Iza a rush of bitter glee. He's useless. Him and his French physician. The pair of them.

> In view of the results obtained by Mr. Allan at Sunderland, and by Mr. Mather at Manchester, probably the most important matter covered by these questions is that of the experience of the engineering firms generally as to the result of the introduction of the nine hours' day some twenty-three years ago.

A short job. A horrid job. But being sole comp is a blessing. No need to listen, take instructions, consult. No need to talk. She's sealed off from the day's comings and goings. And this job has tied up her mind in sums. Her first proper go at casting-off: 11 point, 2 point leaded, page 32 picas deep, so 32 times 11 is 352 divided by 13 is ? She has to write it down.

> "Not one jot more per hour than when ten hours were worked."

> "The nine hours, when it came into

operation, had with us a ruinous
effect."

Slow going. All thumbs. Though the caseroom is chilly, sweat gathers on her chin and drips to her chest. Easing the weight off first one foot then the other, she rocks just a fraction to the caseroom's tap taps and rumbling thuds from the machine room that find a softer echo in her belly.

Dimly aware of rain lashing the glass roof, she sets lines, dumps to galley, sets lines.

'It's raining!' John Adams calls out in jubilation.

'It's pouring.'

'The old man's snoring.'

Rain. Who'd have thought you'd welcome it.

'Ye can come out of thon tent hen,' John Adams mouths to her. 'Winter's passing.'

A lamp pops and swells into life for those who'll be working on late.

# -16-

Spring thaw was a long time coming and its coming meant days of slush to wade through so that Iza and her work chums stood at their frames in sodden boots, sodden skirts sticking to stockings, steam rising from clobber draped on heating pipes. Come one Thursday in late May, though, all but the stubborn remains of shovelled heaps of snow had vanished in the night.

Arrangements had been made. Her mother had seen to it. Two months back on a Saturday afternoon, the two of them alone, she'd sat Iza down and told her how it would be. Jamie and Jessie would raise the bairn as theirs. Jessie was due around the same time. The pair would make twins, no-one the wiser. 'Aye, right enough Jessie's dark-haired, but then Jamie's quite dark and there's no doubting he's your full brother. Ah should know.' And because there was nothing else for it and because it brought relief beyond measure, Iza had nodded her agreement. She'd wanted to cry but had chewed hard on her lip to hold it back. When it came on, she was to go straight to Jessie's. Jessie's mum was among the best granny midwifes in St Leonards. Their talk had been cut short by Rab coming in. As he'd done for these past months, Rab managed to occupy the same room without setting eyes on Iza, but still his presence added a weight that was hard to bear.

The following day, Sunday, she'd let her mum lead her to Jessie's house. Hand on her back, her mum had pressed her in the door then left. Jamie was out. Told to make himself scarce, Iza realised, and she was glad of it. She'd spent a good hour with Jessie and her mum, the three of them sorting laundry ready for the morn. Then, while her mother listened on, knitting needles clacking like there was no tomorrow, Jessie had shared intimacies about carrying a baby. Green eyes sparkling – my, how her thick hair shines, thought Iza – Jessie had been full of warmth. She'd even taken Iza's hand and laid it on her belly, asking, 'Can ah?' with a smile and tilt of her head. Aye, Iza had nodded, and Jessie had placed a spread hand on her. To Iza it felt the best thing in a long while.

'Two love babies,' Jessie had whispered in her ear.

And though her eyes didn't, Iza's mouth smiled, a strange sensation after months of it being downcast. But when Jessie then started to take out her bottom drawer, to show two fine frocks, two bonnets, four cardies, Iza's face fell. Jessie saw it and hurriedly put the clothes away. Her mother, a crisply efficient woman with Jessie's fine dark eyes and full mouth and a little of her warmth, told Iza what to expect and what she was to do when the time came. As Iza left, Jessie had taken her by the hands to say firmly, 'We won't be telling the wee one. You'll be auntie Iza.'

Pains coming on in the night barely woke her. Wakening from a turbulent dream, a dream in which a loaded trolley spraying loose sorts careered down a sloping caseroom aisle straight towards her, she was up and pulling her dress over her head when an almighty pain poleaxed her. Though she kept her lips clamped, a slaughter yard squeal escaped them. While Violet didn't wake, or pretended not to, Vi Ross was up out of bed to take Iza by the shoulders and, without words, tell her to go to Jessie's.

Jessie came to the door with babe in arms. Her boy had come into the world less than a week before.

'Is it...?'

Well used by now to hearing words not spoken, Iza nodded. Her drawers were drenched. Turning into the stair door she'd had to stop, hands clasped to her crutch. Her waters had broken. Shuffling her way up the stair, legs splayed, she thanked her lucky star Jamie and Jessie were only one floor up. Thought of her lucky star tickled her but the laugh that came out was hollow.

'Ah'll go get mah mum. In you go.' Jessie went to hand her bundle to Iza but thought better of it. In the front room she went to hand it to Jamie who was sitting for his breakfast, but again thought better.

'Yer brother's just off to his work.'

Iza caught a look that had Jamie on his feet, into his jacket and out the door with a shy nod in her direction and a smile that was more of a grimace. Jessie went through to the bedroom and reappeared without her baby.

'He shouldn't wake. Ah'll not be a minute,' she said as she filled a big pot with water and lit the stove under it.

'Can you send someone to tell mah work ah'm off sick,' Iza called out as Jessie hurried off.

Left alone, Iza was drawn to the bedroom. By the side of their bed, Jamie and Jessie's baby slept. Looking down at the crib, fine if a bit rough-hewn, Iza was back for a moment looking down at her wee baby brother William asleep in an old drawer. She let loose a keening mewl that turned into a yowl as the monstrous pain that had stalked her through the streets snatched hold again.

Next thing, a figure loomed into view, blurred, loomed again. Iza gawped, confounded, as Jessie's mother set a steaming basin and cloths down, pulled two bottles, one blue, one misty, from a bag and placed them by the basin, tidied stray hairs under a big white cap. Out of the corner of an eye she saw Jessie lift her baby and disappear with him. Then she felt cool, nimble hands pulling off her clothes, getting her into a stiff, scratchy nightgown, pressing her onto all fours by the bed, rubbing her back. Like a lump of dough, she let this all happen until, when this woman who was working her turned to leave, she caught hold of a wrist, dug her nails in, pulled the hand to her mouth and tried to stuff it in. The hand was wrenched free.

'Bite on this.'

Though the cloth Iza clamped her teeth on smelled of bleach, she found herself puzzling over something bitter. And a trace of cinnamon was it? But now bleach, bitter, cinnamon, were swept away as her teeth unclenched themselves to let out a great bellow.

'There now. There now. You'll not be long. Yer bairn's coming quick.'

Panting like a broken-winded cuddy, Iza felt a hand clap her as though she were indeed the animal – horse or cow – she felt she'd turned into. Though she'd been a thin wall or ceiling away from the raw sounds and smells of childbirth all her days, becoming one with them was another matter.

She woke knowing she was not at home. She did not open her eyes but let her ears sift the peace and quiet of this strange place for familiar sounds. Rattle of coal wagons close by, louder than she was used to. Whoops and calls of bairns playing in the back green. After a wee lull, a chorus of girls' voices, clear as anything. *On the mountain stands a lady*. A wave of longing had her shut her ears and tune her senses on her body. A dull ache it was, the whole of it. She shifted her bottom a bit. Twinge of pain. Nothing to speak of though. Nothing to stop this comfy bed calling her back to sleep.

When she woke again she'd have known where she was even without Jessie's soft voice in her ear. She opened her eyes and looked about. Jamie and Jessie's bedroom, all spic and span. Just the two of them here, her and Jessie.

'Here. Let me help you sit up. Drink this.'

Jessie puffed pillows. She offered her arm as a hook but Iza shuffled herself to sitting without it, took the cup and drank warm beef tea.

'What's the time?'

'It's gone five.' Jessie fussed with bedclothes, smoothing and tucking.

Not herself, Iza thought. Jessie never fussed. And now there she was wringing her hands. Jessie wasn't one for hand-wringing.

'Ah best be getting home,' Iza said.

'Are you sure you're able?'

Jessie spoke far too quick and keen and it came to Iza as a sickening blow that she had an ear pinned on faint grizzles seeping through from the front room.

'Ah'm fine.'

'Jamie's back early. He'll walk you home. Or maybe get a cab?'

As Iza gathered wits and energy to show more than willing, the grizzling swelled to a piercing squall.

Help, Mummy, help, sounding inside her, Iza was on her feet and into her clothes and at the open front door where Jamie stood waiting, with barely a glance at Jessie's mother

154

cradling a baby and Jessie, back turned, shoulders rounded, nursing another.

Out in the street the world was going about its business. The low sun dazzled. A work's hooter sounded. Folk rounded the corner headed for home. Against the flow, buffeted, faces forming and dissolving, Jamie gripping her to his side strong and firm, she was fine, just a bit light-headed, a bit unsure of her legs and where her feet would land. Round the corner, flowing with the stream, it was easier going. Fit to float she was, but her brother kept her pinned to the pavement.

At the foot of her stairs she needed to stop to gather strength. Jamie waited patiently. At her door he stood to face her, hands clasped tight in front of him. At first he lowered his head and turned shuttered eyes on the floor to the side of their feet, but he jerked his head up to address her in a deep, grave whisper that sounded nothing like her brother.

'You understand she'll grow as ours. She's our daughter.'

So it's a girl, Iza thought. A wee girl. Lips pouting, she nodded.

'What will you call her?'

'We'll see. You get in and get some rest.'

She clasped the doorknob. 'What's the date today?'

Jamie searched the ceiling for an answer. 'Not sure. Thirtieth ah think.' With that and a clap of her shoulder he was gone.

Thirtieth of May. A day till her own birthday. Her seventeenth. Eyes clamped shut, she waited a moment before going in. She's Rodella she thought. Della for short. She'd no idea where the name came from. Strange name. Welsh? Must have heard it somewhere. In a song? But she didn't say it out loud. She'd never say it aloud. It was for her alone.

# 1896: Custom and practice

# -17-

Another year, another thirtieth of May and a bit come and gone and St Leonards slowly scratched and stretched itself awake to thrushes' song and a lone steamer's horn sounding far off over the sea. No hooters, no clatters, no thuds that morning. Start of the city's July summer trades fair and, Monday forenoon, yells and whoops of bairns at play ringing round the street, Iza, alone in the house, leant over the sink to open the window and take in a good lungful of air. With few of the city's chimneys belching smoke it went down deep. The street below looked broader, brighter. Men with shirt sleeves rolled were gathered by a lamppost for a smoke and a laugh. Women called from open windows or, hands on hips, stood in doorways squinting up at the sky. Three young women in short-sleeved blouses sat on the sunnyside pavement, backs to the wall, chins up, legs outstretched, hands loose in their laps.

Stretching her arms out and up, Iza felt sinew and muscle and bone creak and give. She went through to the back room and, forehead on the window pane, watched a crow sweep across the sky ahead of a block of shadow that turned the crags' rusty hue from fresh to blackened. Above the crags clouds scuttled to gather into a great white billow; below them whin in bloom tinted the air yellow and when Iza raised the window she got a whiff of the scent she fancied you'd get if you picked up a coconut from hot sand and pierced its eye to pour its milk. She heaved the window wide open. A fat bee bumbled past her ear, round her head and straight out again. Ruffled squawks and clucks from the back green below had her leaning out over the sill. Uttering clucking noises herself, Ma Coutts tossed handfuls of grain to bring brown hens loping on long pins from all corners, heads high, bodies waggling. When the big cloud overhead sailed off, sunshafts turned their feathers brilliant chestnut.

She turned back to putting the house in order, taking care to smooth Violet's yellow frock across a chair back, easing the skirt off a split strut. After sweeping the floor and shaking her mum's red rag rug out the window, she cast an eye round the room. How bare it looked. Clean and tidy, but bare.

From the rifle range beyond the crags came a sharp crack-woosh, crack-woosh, a sound that had peppered her days but which now entered her ears in a way it never had. It was the quiet of this house heightened it. Until today, until the holiday opened the world up like a bursting bud, that quiet had suited her. Not now though. Not with rifles cracking and folk out in the sun and her in here on her own. She had to get out. Had to go somewhere. She had a good wash at the sink, changed into her white blouse and good grey skirt, brushed her hair and looped it in a coil pinned with her good-as-real-tortoiseshell clasp before hurrying down the stair and along the road, past the lassies on the pavement, past the men at the lamppost, as though she knew where she was headed. At the street corner, though, she stopped still. Where was she headed? Her mind scurried about for an answer. William's lodgings at his work? No. He'd not be getting the holiday. Not at the club. Not waiters. They worked all hours. She never got much chance to see William, though when she did it always made her forget herself. Jamie's house? No. No. That was no place for her. She hadn't been back since. The odd Sunday when Jamie brought his family round she made herself scarce. Walk down to Canonmills to see Jack? Aye. That might do. No telling what sort of company he'd be, mind. Join the lassies sitting on the pavement back there? She wished she could, feel sunlight soak in, share a joke, free and easy, but these days she only knew them to say mornin and evenin to. Most worked together in the biscuit factory or in Menzies folding envelopes.

She was on the point of turning for home when it came to her. She'd go to Margaret's. Last time, ages ago, they'd had scones and jam and tea from a fine china pot. Mr Scott, Margaret's dad, had poured. An interesting man. Different. But that was before the union business chilled her friendship with Margaret, before winter and Iza's troubles that she'd kept to herself, kept it frozen right through summer and another winter and spring. Recently, though, they'd shared smiles, exchanged a few words. Saturday knock-off she'd asked Margaret did she have any plans for the holiday. Nothing to speak of, Margaret had said. And now, minding the pair of them walking home from Musselburgh, sitting by the shore for a blether, she decided Margaret's house was at least a place to head for. She winced as she walked on, though, hearing herself tell Margaret that evening that she'd like bairns but not the man. My, how she'd taken herself at her own word.

# -18-

The Scotts stayed on the ground floor. Mr Scott was outside tending a display of yellow and purple blooms in his window box. Iza slowed her pace as she neared. Margaret and her dad, she knew, discussed union matters and Mr Scott knew a lot about them. Margaret would have told him about her and Iza's differences. He might not be so friendly.

'It looks lovely,' she ventured.

Mr Scott stepped back to survey. A wiry man with keen eyes that seemed to take everything in, to sift and reckon but not judge, he gave her a quizzical smile. Getting ready for the flower show, he said. Preferred to keep it plain and simple, not like some. What did she think? She meant to say it was grand, but it came out as 'Ah'd love one like that,' which had Mr Scott offering to make her a window box, her saying she didn't mean that, him saying I know, but. Margaret must have got her height from her mother because her dad was no taller than Iza. There was a shrewd, agile cut to him, stringy neck stretching as he cocked an ear towards her when she spoke. He winced when he turned, though. He had rheumatism and, Margaret had told Iza, a wonky heart.

'The door's open,' he said. 'Go right in. She'll be pleased to see you. I was just saying she wants to be off out with her chums and not hanging around old codgers like me.'

And sure enough, Margaret did look pleased, if a bit surprised.

'Well, well. I was just thinking about you.' Margaret swept her hair with the back of a floury hand and wiped her hands on her pinnie.

'You've got a clump of dough in your hair. Come here.' Iza reached up to pick it out. 'What were you thinking?'

'Just wondering what you were up to.'

The Scott's house smelt of wax polish, lavender and a buttery sweetness that had Iza eyeing a griddle on the stove. Margaret whisked a white tea towel from a plate to reveal a heap of drop scones. She told Iza to sit herself down at the round table by the window, made a pot of coffee and poured it into china cups with rosebuds round the rim, then made tea for her dad who, she said, couldn't abide coffee.

'Ah had a mind to go down Canonmills to see mah brother Jack. Mind him? On the tram that night?'

Margaret squinted, thinking back. 'He's at Tanfield, Morrison & Gibbs, eh? I heard there was a lot of bother in that Chapel. A to-do about favouritism and lassies getting too much overtime.'

'A to-do would be no surprise with Jack around. He might have decided to defend the lassies, mind. Or to punch one of them. Unpredictable's Jack's middle name. Never know what he'll do next.'

Margaret smoothed her lace-edged tablecloth. 'It runs in the family then?' A wee playful smile creased her lips.

What was behind that? Iza sipped her coffee to consider.

Is it me she's talking about? But there was no sting in Margaret's voice. Margaret had a way of making Iza feel both settled and unsettled in herself. Safe to question herself, it now came to her. That was it. Just the look of Margaret did that. Something about her was so definite you'd think she'd sprung into the world just as she was.

'No. You could set your clock by mah brother Rab,' Iza said. 'And mah mother's medicinal toddy is getting worryingly predictable.'

Margaret's skewed smile invited more, but her dad came to join them just then. After washing his hands he brought a beautiful miniature rosewood cabinet to the table, opened a wee drawer and handed Iza a postcard, pointing with delight at an emu on a stamp from Australia. Iza admired it. Mr Scott was a joiner who knew the French polishing trade. Now that his joints and heart stopped him from working at his trade, he made and restored miniature cabinets when his health allowed; he knew how to select and propagate seeds to get the best blooms; and he could knock up an excellent pot of pea soup. A right mongrel, Margaret said. Her dad looked pleased with that.

Iza and Margaret debated the merits of his window-box display, acting out the parts of flower show judges Mr Scott sketched for them, first in words then in fine pencil drawings of a woman with no chin and a stacked cauliflower and twig hat, a man in a bowler with a tiny wee mouth and a fat slug of a moustache and a working man lifting his bunnet to scratch his head while he scowled at a bent carrot. When Iza, doing the working man, announced Mr Scott the winner by a mile, Margaret puffed out her bosom and tucked in her chin to object that while she commended the quality of the contestant's blossoms, she found his display too paltry an affair to warrant a prize.

Iza went to wash up but Mr Scott told her to sit herself down and have a blether. She was the guest. He'd see to it. Now there was a thing. A man at the sink. Iza had never seen the like. When he'd dried and stacked dishes and wiped the draining board, he went through to the bedroom and came back unwrapping from tissue and holding out an ivory satin garment with fine embroidery work on its wee bodice.

'Now what do you think to this for a piece of work?' It was a christening dress his wife, Eleanor – he lingered over the lovely name – had made for Margaret but never got the chance to put on her. 'For her brood now,' he said, nodding towards Margaret.

Though sight of the dress pained her, Iza fingered and admired it.

Margaret turned her head away. 'You know I won't give up my job, Dad,' she said after a bit.

'Yes, I know that. Nor should you. I've told you. Marry and stay at your trade. Have babas and stay at your job.' Mr Scott made to hand the dress to Margaret, but she shook her head.

'Nobody does that, Dad.'

'Be the first then.' Mr Scott tenderly folded and rewrapped the dress.

'It's not done. It's not allowed,' Margaret said firmly.

'Says who? What law says you can't?'

Margaret was stumped. Iza too. She'd been pulled up short like a yank on reins that had her mouth gaping. She gulped. If only they knew. You can have a bairn but you can't keep it. Do they know? No. They wouldn't be saying this. But maybe they would. She hunched, arms crossed over her belly to hug it, pressing into the table edge so's not to show it.

'There's no law says you can't. No rule. It's mere custom and practice.'

Mr Scott's calm, measured tone had Iza straighten up to listen.

'Now, laws and rules can be changed, though it's not us as often gets to change them. Custom? Change it. Get wed. Have a bairn. Stick at your trade. If they knock you down, get back on your feet.'

Iza was all ears now. When Margaret gave her a knowing look that said 'Me dad likes to be fanciful, eh? We're agreed on that?', she wasn't about to share the intimacy. Eyes wide, mouth ajar, she was set to thinking. Like a fish in a still pool that you don't see till a gill twitches and you pick out its dark brown length against dark brown stones, an idea took shape in her. And she could see not just the outline of it, but mottled patterns and gills and wee black eyes. She could do it. She could get herself a husband, a common-or-garden man who wouldn't go swanning off to Dublin or some such godforsaken place. She could have a bairn, a new bairn that would be hers, and stay at the case. Why not? That she could get with child, carry it and stick at her trade she well knew. And all around her were mothers who went out to work. Not in the caseroom, right enough, but out to long days of hard toil nonetheless. They did it. They saw to their man and their house and their bairns, which was, it now struck her, a marvel. And what of neighbours who, within days of their confinement, were lugging heaps of washing to the laundry, hanging it out, fetching messages, sweeping landings. Like Mr Scott said, like Jim Connolly would have said now she thought on it, there was no law against it. None. There'd be folk dead set against, mind. This thought had the chief of them, her brother Rab, spring to mind, but rather than daunt her

164

the prospect brought a rush of glee because this Rab stood helpless. He had steam coming out of his ears because, try as he might, he couldn't grab hold of her, couldn't stop her. As she wallowed in her victory, right pleased with herself, the fish darted off. It had left its mark, though, and she had an inkling of a lesson learnt. Indulge in pettiness and her plan, if it was a plan, would come to nought. Treat it honestly and it might, just.

'I've told Margaret you're wrong to dismiss the claim for equal pay. That's conceding the ground before you start. Demand equal pay.' Mr Scott's addressed this to Iza. His hands beat out the final three words.

Iza blinked. Realising her mouth was open, she shut it. She had a scone raised half way to it. What was he saying? Before she could get a hold of Mr Scott's striking idea Margaret brushed it aside.

'Och, Dad. What world do you live in?' She turned to Iza. 'Not hungry? Leave it if you don't like them.'

'Sorry. Ah was thinking. Aye. They're lovely. Ah'm starving.'

'Taking a leaf out of my book,' Margaret said.

Many hours later, after rounds of whist and a lesson in bridge and a bowl of mutton stew and tales of Mr Scott's days as a young journeyman tramping Lancashire, Iza left for home. Outside, powdery dusklight rinsing colour from the flowers in the windowbox, she watched a flicker of light behind the Scott's pulled curtains swell to a fuzzy ivory glow. Though she felt shut out from it, something of that glow was inside her.

# – 19 –

'Will you do me the honour?'
She'd recognised him from those awkward
encounters in Oxford Street years back, noticed him
eyeing her, but still she was taken unawares when the
ginger-haired lad, John Orr, took hold of her elbow before
she could think and Margaret, laughing, nudged her on.
Looping his arm over her shoulder, he clasped her right
hand and stretched in front for her left as they edged into
the ring of couples looping the dancefloor. Two pairs of
work-worn hands, same size, loosely clasped. A long,
sweeping chord from fiddles had them drop hands and turn
to face each other – they stood near eye to eye – bow and
curtsey. Turning side-on, they fumbled the re-clasping of
hands so that the couple in front were off and away and
the one behind barging into them before they got hold of
each other and surged forwards. Once he loosened, John
Orr was a good dancer, even if there was a bit of a flimsy
feel to him. When he tried to keep her for the next dance,
Iza nodded towards Margaret and made her excuses, and
though for the rest of the evening she was aware of him

standing by a wall sipping a small beer, on his own for the most part, though one time she looked over her brother Rab had his ear, pouring poison most likely, she stuck close to her chum, the pair of them skipping and birling themselves silly.

When they spilled out into the street she spotted him among folk lingering for a blether under a midsummer night's pewter sky. He was on tiptoe, craning. He saw her and waved. She caught hold of Margaret and the three of them set off, the women arm-in-arm, John Orr stepping on and off the kerb to loop round passersby, shifting to the inside as they skirted belches of noise and heat from pubs. A good do, they agreed. Aye, but wait till they see Nelsons' Christmas dance, he said. A very grand affair, evening dress, dinner suits, bow ties. Though she balked at his bragging, his enthusiasm had her warm to him despite herself. Would they be going on Nelsons' outing to Wemyss Bay next week? A day at the seaside. Had her brother said about it? She was Rab Ross's sister, wasn't she? Iza humphed in reply.

He talked in fits and starts, pausing after each burst almost long enough for Iza or Margaret to get a word in, but never quite. When they reached Margaret's stair door Iza's 'help me' grimace had Margaret say, to Iza but for his hearing, 'You're staying at mine tonight, eh?' It wasn't the case, but it served. John Orr went to shake hands, pulled back, nodded goodnight and strode off.

Though bells had chimed midnight the air was still mild and they stopped out a while before parting. Just a few days into the holiday the city's canopy of smoke had lifted and a few stars showed above roofs. When it came to John Orr, Margaret thought he had nice enough manners. Aye, but a touch jittery said Iza. The way he scratched his moustache as though he'd got nits in it. Good enough looking if you like the type, Margaret mused. What about those eyes? Iza questioned. That raw look, like they're hungering after something in you. Well, Margaret could hardly offer an opinion seeing as he hadn't noticed her existence, his eyes being stuck on Iza.

'Only because he barely reaches your chin. He'd have to stand on tiptoe, on a crate. Or you'd have to get down on your knees.'

Margaret humphed. 'Fat chance of that.' She cocked her head. 'You'll not shake him off so easy, you know.'

'Ah will if ah want to.'

'If?'

'When. When ah want to,' Iza said.


Back home, Rab was still up, poring over his union journal by a guttering lamp. As was their wont, Iza ignored him and he ignored her. Practice had made this arrangement tolerable, almost comfortable. As she poured a tumbler of water and drank, though, she felt his eyes on her.

'You might want to read this.' Rab's tone was hesitant, nigh-on inviting. He spoke like he meant it. 'There's talk of a motion to clear frocks from the frame.'

This caught her unawares. She rinsed and dried the tumbler, taking time to compose herself.

'No thanks. Ah'm off to mah bed.' She almost succeeded in answering in like manner, but her voice had a crack in it.

'Look. This is not about you. It's not personal. You've always taken it too personal. It's about...'

'Ah know all too well what it's about, Rab.'

In the bedroom, snuffly bleats came from her mum's side of the big bed the three of them shared, as if in her dream she'd become a stray lamb. Violet half-opened her eyes, muttered 'Where've you been?' and lapsed back into sleep. Keeping herself clear of her sister's hunched backside, Iza lay on her back with palms spread on her belly to ease the churning pain of the curse coming on. A single voice from the street below fell away. Silence pressed in. With no house above, no weight of folk coughing, twanging bedsprings, bairns crying out their night terrors, she felt as though she might float up through the ceiling, through the roof, weightless, up into the night sky.

The room was stifling. She got up, tugged the window wide open and knelt on the floor, arms and chin on the windowsill. A hobgoblin's hollow eyes leered down at her from the dark crags. When she blinked to be rid of it, it turned into a different face. A smudged impression, aye, but a face she knew to be Roddy Mac's. Like a bairn, she stuck her tongue out at him. 'Ah'll show you,' she muttered. Alarm bells rang. Don't be so daft they said. She blinked again and willed another face to replace it. John Orr's face? It would not. Why should it? Fine. Then she'd stare Roddy Mac out. She'd let him into her mind one last time, invite him in by the front door, not let him sneak in at the back, then give him the shunt for good and all.

Low sun on clear rippling water. Sweet smell of grass. His thighs gripped to her sides by her elbows hinged to his knees. His chin sliding down the back of her lowered head. Lips on the nape of her neck. The flush of it. And now she turns her head and he looks up. Their eyes meet. She tries to hold his gaze.

Downstairs a door banged to. In the other room feet shuffled. A groan, a mutter, then the creak of Rab's bed and, in no time, full-throated snores.

Was that it then? A kiss and tumble by the burn? No. That was no small matter, but it was not the whole of it.

169

She'd only pared away the outer skin; there was the corn itself to root out, the stringy chord that pressed on nerve ends. And that was – her mind shied but she yanked it back – it was being happy in strange company. It was feeling herself and more than herself, as though she and he had been walking off together, hand-in-hand, off the beaten track, off to foreign lands she'd caught a whiff of and, for a brief spell, almost pictured. And not just the two of them walking hand-in-hand. Between them, clasped to them, wee hands. She closed her eyes to conjure Roddy Mac, to tell him, 'There now. See. Did you know? Do you know we have a bairn? A wee girl?' But the result of her conjuring was little more than a musky scent that made the back of her neck and privates prickle. There was no face. No wee hands. She held the smell, the sensation, a moment, then attended to its fading. There. Gone. She'd sent him packing. But the bairn? What of the bairn? Now Jessie and Jamie rose in her mind. The bairn is ours, they said. She's well cared for. And it was true. She couldn't deny it even if she'd wanted to.

The bed shoogled and creaked as Iza's mother heaved herself up and dragged the chanty from under it. She crouched a long time and groaned as she rose. Vi Ross's bent form in the room's murky light was that of an old woman. Was she all right? Iza asked.

'Och, mah insides are killing me. Mah waterworks are aw to pot.'

'Can ah get you anything?'

'Not unless you can get me a new body, one with the bits working.'

Iza watched her mother heave herself back into bed and fall asleep. Curled up on her left side with her palms pressed together under her cheek, she took the same position as

Violet, and Iza realised she thought of them as a pair, her mother and her big sister. But that was daft. There was her mother, an old woman having to heave herself up on to her pins. And Violet? Just three years older than she herself, Violet would soon be wed, in her own house, then lots of bairns round her feet. Get old young and spend her days groaning? No. Not Violet. Her Angus was a clerk. He'd get made up. They'd have a nice house. Violet would make a good job of seeing to her family. She'd be a lovely mum.

Nowhere near sleep, Iza went ben the front room where, curled into her mum's armchair, she studied the lump that was Rab. Dead-to-the-world he was, but grinding his teeth. A horrible noise, but instead of bristling with irritation she felt something almost akin to affection soften her flesh and bones. Poor Rab, she muttered. Almost said it aloud. You don't sit easy in this life, she thought. Then another thought came tacked onto that one. Me neither come to think of it. We're a right pair. Now where did that idea come from? What a thought. Still, maybe ah ought to be nicer to him. After all, he's going to lose this battle. Isn't he? She turned her eyes from her brother to stare at dark window panes.

A great yawn coursed through her. No work the morn, nor the next or the next. A year ago, six months ago, she would have dreaded empty days ahead. Not now. Now it felt grand to wonder what she would do with herself. She let her mind go for a wander into the caseroom. After taking time to show her the intricacies of making up formes the other evening, John Adams had agreed to ask Fred Henderson if Iza could get a start on making up. The thought of working at the stone, assembling pages of text and illustration blocks into an intricate web of metal, excited her. Her hands itched to get at a mallet and shooting stick. Still, she intended to go to see her brother

Jack and ask him about Morrison & Gibbs. Did the lassies at Tanfield get to make up? And then there was Neills' Bellevue works next door to Tanfield. Word was they had a new edition of the *Encyclopaedia Britannica* in the offing. Years of steady work, never mind what Rab and his moves and motions had to say for themselves. Interesting work at that. Aye. Monday she'd take a walk down Canonmills and ask around. There'd be plenty printers out and about for the holiday. She might get a word with some Neills' lassies, ask if there was a place going there. Imagine that. A new caseroom in a new part of town. A safe distance from Jamie and Jessie's. Now there was a thought.

And Tuesday? Tuesday she'd buy a piece of scented soap, take her mum to the baths for a hot soak and scrub, do her hair that these days had a straggly look, come home and make coconut tablet and, if the greengrocer had strawberries, a pot of jam.

And the morn? Sunday? The morn she'd go and find her wee brother William. She'd barely caught sight of him this past year. Leave it much longer and they'd be passing in the street and not knowing each other.

# Part II   A memorial to the masters: 1910

# -1-

'Where is he?' William scanned the room and eyed the bedroom door. After knocking, he'd waited until she called out for him to come in as if they were no more than acquaintances.

'Overtime. Saturday afternoons and Sundays these past few weeks.'

'Leaving you all on your ownsome?'

'Long may it last.' Catching her wee brother's questioning look Iza quickly added 'It's good money.'

She helped him off with his dripping wet jacket and bunnet, sat him down, gripped his shoulders, rubbed his hair. First off she went to use an old pink towel from a hook by the sink, but instead fetched a newish wedding gift blue one from her chest of drawers.

Rain streamed down sparkling window panes. April, and after a week when winter had seemed to be settling back in, spring had arrived bright, crisp, wet. Wondering how come fair silk turns into brown wire, she combed and smoothed her wee brother's forelock back over his head. And why, when he's just – let's see, ah'm thirty-two so he's twenty-seven – why has his hairline's scooped back so far at the temples. Not fair when you're born into this cold country and need all the covering you can get. She faced him and lifted his chin to take a good look. Too much bone showing, cheeks the colour of winter, but he was bright-eyed enough and the grin was the same as ever.

'It's needing a good cut. It's down to your shoulders.'

'Don't be daft.'

'Well, it's too long, 'specially for a waiter. Folk'll think it's been trailing in their soup. Sit still till ah get the scissors.'

'Did ah not tell you, ah'm behind the bar now. Your hair could be down to your knees and they'll not notice so long as you keep pouring.'

'What, those officers at the serviceman's club?'

'No. Ah left there ages ago. Ah'm at the Caledonian Bar now.'

'Where's that?'

'Down Leith Walk.'

Dark coils stuck to the towel and dropped to the floor. When the rain stopped as suddenly as it had started, pale gold light bursting through the window set off red sparks in William's hair. From their mum's side. When William pulled his head away to take a good look round the room, Iza followed his gaze, smiling at her mahogany-veneer gate-leg table, her good-as-new his-and-her armchairs, her longcase clock.

'No books?' William said.

'A few in the closet. There's a *People's Friend* or last night's paper if you want a read, but you could just talk to me while you're here.' She clasped a hand either side of his head to right it. When she raised the window to shake the towel a squall of young sparrows burst out of a patch of scrub bushes across the road. Folk out and about in the street peered up at scurrying rain clouds. Some of the older folk, and even a couple of youngsters, wore black armbands for the king's funeral.

'Where are you staying?'

'Where d'you think? Lodgings.'

'What, down Leith?'

'Aye.'

'Is it not a bit rough?'

'The warl's a tap-room owre and owre, whaur ilk ane tak's his caper, some taste the sweet, some drink the sour, as waiter Fate sees proper.' William rolled the words round his mouth like treacle drops. 'Rab Tannahill, in case you didn't know.' He squinted up and she saw that he saw she didn't.

'You could be on the stage,' she said, her smile failing to mask a touch of sadness at not being in step with him, at being left behind by him and, too, at the thought of William stuck behind a bar.

'Ah've got a parrot,' he said, as if this were an answer. 'An African grey.' Then, proving her right, he proceeded to be a seaman talking to a caged bird he'd brought into the pub and set down on the bar. 'Come closing time, ah'm busy wiping and he's up on his pins and headed for the door with a "Look after him till ah get back will you, son?"'

'So when's he back?'

'Who knows? He'll be getting a look at New York's skyscrapers by now.' William raised his eyes to the ceiling. 'Or having a bevy in Riga.' He raised a glass. She clasped his head still as he turned to say, 'That's in Russia'.

'Ah know where Riga is. Remember the tale of the frog's journey from Riga to Methil ah told you?' She expected William to have forgotten but he knew straight off what she was talking about.

'Was it you told me? Ah thought ah must have got it from one of the seamen in the bar.'

It hurt that her part in it was gone from his minding. She gave his hair a final clip and comb and tugged him out of his seat. 'Come on. You sail yourself down the stair to see Mum. Ah've got to get messages.'

'Why's Mum gone to stay at Rab's?'

Good question. What with Rab's wife Jeannie's two bairns from her first marriage, plus one of their own and another on the way, not to mention Jeannie's mother, Rab's house down the stair had been full to bursting before Vi Ross decided to move out of Iza's house and into his. And here was Iza and her man left with two rooms to themselves. Mind you, she told her brother, just the other day their mother was on about Jeannie's bairns driving her mad, never mind that mother of hers, so she'd likely be back here any day now; would have been already except that when they were carting her belongings down the stair Iza had said she'd have them carting them back up again within the week and now her mother, she knew, would go to lengths to prove her wrong.

Iza handed William his jacket and picked up her purse and message bag.

'Ah suppose you could do with her here?' He grimaced at the bulge in Iza's middle that till now he'd ignored. 'Ah never saw you as a wee wifey,' he said, 'and here you are, quite the part with your nice wee house.' Iza swiped at him with her bag, William ducked and grabbed, she charged, and the pair of them careened round the room, into the bedroom, out again, squealing like bairns until Iza crashed into a seat and bashed her shin.

'Anyhow, you're a fine one to talk. Leith's about half a mile nearer the sea than St Leonards, right enough, but it's hardly an expedition.'

Panting more than he should at his age, William sank down in her armchair as though stuffing had got ripped out of him. Now she saw how pasty his skin looked. And, for just a second, she caught a glimpse of distress in his eyes. She scuttled to bury what she'd said, shovelling encouraging words on top. Leith was the best place to learn where to head for, find out about likely ships, hear tales of how to make your way in foreign lands. But she succeeded only in making William put on a carefree mask.

'All that girlie stuff.' He squirmed, nodding at her bulge. 'Yeuch.'

Iza turned from him to set her house in order, frantically wondering if William knew about her daughter, Della-Mary. She'd never told him and she was pretty sure, though not certain, no-one else had. Waiting for the right moment, it was one secret she'd never brought herself to share with him. She stood in the bedroom doorway looking at her wee brother. No. This wasn't the right time.

'According to Rab, Mum moved so she didn't get stuck looking after it.' Iza patted her lump. Sucking in her cheeks, waggling a finger, she did a fair impression of Rab saying, 'Our poor mother's had quite enough of bringing up bairns.' In telling William this, Iza was trusting her wee brother not to say what anybody else would have. And, sure enough, William didn't say 'How come? You'll be giving up your job to see to the bairn, won't you?' He just smiled. Iza knew in her bones that William's sense of what was right and proper was not the same as that of other folk. It wouldn't occur to him that she'd have to leave the caseroom, that no-one could possibly be a comp and a mother.

Being in the house all day on her own was the reason their mother had given for going to stay with Rab and Jeannie. Gave her the creeps, she said. Iza had brushed this aside with, 'It's no different to St Leonards when we were all out at work.' But she'd had more trouble brushing aside the next part of her mother's complaint, the bit tagged on in a low mutter, 'And it's not much better when he's in.' That her mum was not at ease with her husband had been plain enough to see. It was embarrassing, the way her mother's upper lip curled as she gave him sidelong glances. Iza thought it would get better. It hadn't. But this she couldn't tell her wee brother because if she told him she'd see that look on his face. Though he'd try to hide it, she'd see it and read it. That look conveyed the question William never voiced: 'Why on earth did you marry him?' A question that would leave Iza silently rehearsing answers. Because he's hardworking and sober and steady. Hearing this with William's ears, she knew she might as well shorten it to 'Because he's dull as dishwater.' Besides, she wasn't so sure about steady. Dogged in his affections for her, aye. From their first encounter in Oxford Street when she was thirteen till the day four year ago when, turned twenty-eight, she'd agreed to marry him, there'd been not the slightest sign of John Orr's attentions wavering. Not that they'd kept company through those years. There'd been long spells when they'd seen nothing of each other, especially after Iza got the job at Neills' Bellevue works and moved to Canonmills. Whenever they did resume relations, though, John Orr behaved as though they'd spent the intervening time together, as though their companionship was as natural and unavoidable as the seasons. That steadfastness, she knew, had counted for a great deal in her reckonings. There was something in John, though, that hinted at the very opposite of steady. He was liable to be excitable one day and withdrawn the next. He could be difficult in company. So had these intimations of *lack* of steadiness been a source of attraction? Hidden depths to be discovered? She suspected so. So, why had she married John Orr? More than once, when that look of William's had raised doubts in her, she'd retraced the progress of their relations.

Nelson's Wemyss Bay outing. Since Margaret was stuck at home looking after her sick father, Iza sat on the train with Jeannie, the widow who was to become Rab's wife. This put her too close to her brother for comfort, but Jeannie was light-hearted company, the very opposite of Rab. At the seaside, they paddled, tossed a beach ball, ate sand-coated egg and cress sandwiches, collected tiny pink shells. John Orr peeled off from men clustered round the golf links to sit close by and swipe at sandflies plaguing them. Then they clambered over rocks and John hunkered down by a pool and, signalling to be still, gazed into the water and pointed out a tiny crab she didn't see till it scuttled under a rock.

An invitation to the Empire Palace with him, accepted since it meant an evening's relief from hearing about her mother's kidneys. Did she fancy the unveiling of the statue of the late queen in Leith Walk? This was rejected in favour of a climb to the observatory on Calton Hill because Iza's dealings with Roddy Mac had tarnished any affection she might have felt for the queen and, besides, as she reminded John, he didn't like crowds. Within the year he was turning down overtime to call for her regularly on Saturday afternoons. He wasn't the easiest of company. Just the two of them and he'd talk ten to the dozen; meet up with others, men especially, and he'd have hardly a word to say for himself. He could never be still, was all the while checking his pockets, fingering, shifting, wiping, tucking. But. But?

But he was a good worker, he spent his free time on his works' allotment or playing bowls, an old man's game according to some, but a sight better than the horses and dogs and every night in the pub. He'd had a go at Nelsons' rifle club, and though he wasn't one for union meetings he'd collected machine room signatures on the Trades Council petition to get the botanic gardens opened to the public after kirk on Sundays; wasn't a churchgoing man, but, then, this they shared. And they were the same age and the same height, whatever that was worth. And she was getting no younger. Now or never.

She'd gone through this totting up umpteen times, lying awake, nudging her mother over to quieten the snortles from her gaping mouth, an evening out with her, her what? her husband-to-be? having tugged at a knot in her. Trouble was, the knot was nowhere near her mind where the totting went on. Once or twice, trying to get at the knot to slacken it she'd felt that flush of her flesh that was Roddy Mac's presence: neither heat nor cold, neither wet nor dry, but an unholy mixture of the two. And in bed one Sunday night after John Orr proposed for the second time, there was Roddy Mac's breath on her neck, the scrape of his chin on her cheek, his hands turning her face to his. But not his face because he'd never looked at her quite like that. Pitying? Sneering? No. Indifference was what she'd seen in his face. She'd wanted to wail, but she'd kneaded the bedsheet to her mouth to stopper it.

She'd marry John and become Iza Orr. She'd known as much that Sunday afternoon she agreed to go to the botanic gardens with him, though the outing had tested her resolve. When he'd taken her hand as they stood in the sweltering palm house, she'd left it there, acutely aware that were it not for her glove between their two skins she'd have taken it back. Strolling up the path through pink-daubed rhododendrons, a brittle gloss to John Orr's pale blue eyes and a wee patch of stubble missed on his chin, like a tiny paint brush, had her pull away and walk on ahead. At the top of a rise, though, seated side-by-side on a bench, both of them looking off to where ragged clouds were catching on the city's spires, her mind was made up, depending.

'Ah'll want to stay on at mah work,' she said.

'Is that allowed?'

'It's not the custom, but that doesn't mean it's not allowed. There's no rule or law to stop me.'

He hadn't turned his gaze from the clouds to look at her, but he had squeezed her hand. He hadn't answered straight off, but he'd said, 'Whatever you think's best,' quickly and honestly enough.

Iza steered William out the door and onto the landing. Her wee brother could usually see more than she wanted to show, including, she suspected, things she herself couldn't see. Once, just before the wedding, she had answered William's unvoiced question. She'd told him she was marrying John because John had agreed to her staying on at her job and that was a rare thing in a man. Now, face-to-face with William, she doubted herself.

'Why didn't Mum go to Jack's? That's what she'd like.' William stopped halfway down the stair.

'Jack's wife Maggie won't have it. At least that's what Jack says. Rab says it's Jack, not Maggie, who's not having it.'

'What about Violet's?'

In the clipped voice their mother used when she was digging her heels in on slippery ground, Iza said she was not about to stay in that part of town, that she didn't know anyone there and didn't want to, seeing as they were all Hearts supporters.

'Mum, bothered about football?' William scratched his head, messing his hair.

What bothered Vi Ross was not football or any such thing, and both William and Iza knew it. What bothered her was the scattering of her family. With Iza and, later, Rab following Jack down to Canonmills, Iza to work at Neills, Rab at Morrison & Gibbs, and Violet off to one of the new houses in Dalry with her husband Angus and her wee boy, Victor, only Jamie and his family had stayed on in St Leonards. Vi Ross had been torn. St Leonards was home. She'd been born there. But being near Jack had decided her. She hadn't settled, though, and there was no consoling her with reminders that the family were all still in the same town, just a tram ride away. It was definitely a mistake to say that, unlike some families, they were hardly at far ends of the earth; this, on top of Jack's loose talk of opportunities in Australia, had their mother convinced they were all about to emigrate in secret. First thing she'd know would be when she got word the ship had gone down.

Iza flicked a hair clipping from William's shoulder as she prodded him down the stair ahead of her. When, at the bottom, he made for the stair door, she swivelled him about and nudged him towards Rab and Jeannie's door. He resisted.

'Heh. It's stopped raining. Let's go down the Puddockie and see the frogs first, eh?' he said.

Iza scowled. 'Water rats big as cats, more like.' But William poked his chin at her, patted his cheeks, said, 'Ah need some sun.'

Stretched on his belly by the water's edge, jostled by a gang of bairns, William dredged green slime with splayed hands to scoop tadpoles into their jam jars, lunging at streaks that slithered through his fingers. When he raised a speckled blob of frogspawn high and flung it at skinny outstretched hands, the bairns shrieked. A splash. Yells. One of the bairns was flailing in mud and reeds. When William grabbed his wrist to haul him out, the bairn hauled back and his chums joined in, tugging and pushing. William staggered as if to fall then dodged the bairns to run off along the bank ahead of a shrieking, galloping charge.

Stretched out in a patch of long grass and buttercups, face lifted to a pale sun in a lilac sky, Iza listened to their shrieks fade. She stroked the mound that had taken root in her. Her bairn. Her own. Her first, but not her first. So what of the other? Ah know no more of her than ah know of the young lass who lives next door, Iza mused. But no. That wasn't so. When Jamie and Jessie, seven bairns in tow, had dropped in at Hogmanay, hadn't she felt a kinship, a deep knowing that was of the blood, if not of the mind, when she looked at Della, or Mary as she was known? And hadn't she felt the lass eye her in a manner that said, ah know you better than you think ah do? But, then, though she didn't have much to say for herself, the girl had doubting eyes that scratched at the surface. Just a slip of a thing, though a good head taller than her brother the same age, but that look of hers had put Iza in mind of the way Fanny Begg had eyed her on her first day in Pauls' caseroom: puzzling, weighing, judging.

'Ah'm going to call him William.'

Low sun had cast a band of shadow along the tenements of her street. They'd stopped outside Iza's stair door. She needed to hurry for the messages now, get the tea on before John got in from work. William still resisted going in to see their mother. He couldn't go looking like this, clothes all wet and clarty. She'd think he'd gone to the dogs. What if she's looked out the window and seen you? Iza argued. She'll be that upset. That had William eyeing the ground-floor window, grimacing, but then Iza squandered her advantage by suggesting he take the opportunity to ask Rab what books Morrison & Gibbs were doing. Useless, it seemed. Nelsons did all the best ones: Buchan, H G Wells, Joseph Conrad. Or, better still, *The Heritage of the Desert*. He said this with all of his youthful relish. Had she not heard of it? About the wild west. Zane Grey. American?

'How come you know all this?'

'It's not just talk of football and horse racing in the bar. There's folk in there have seen the world. Better read than all you printers put together, some of them. They've got stories to tell.'

Knowing he'd stung her, William made amends. 'It might be a lassie. What will you call mah wee niece?' he grinned.

Iza started.

'You all right? Have ah said something?'

'No. Just thinking. Williamina she'll have to be...'

William turned to go. He'd come back the morn, smartened up, he said. 'Don't tell them about the pub, will you?'

'No,' she said, 'but ah think you should come and stay with us.'

'What, and get in the way of your marital bliss?'

She gave him a shove. Sauntering off with his jacket slung over his shoulder, he raised a hand in farewell.

§§§§§§§§§

> aneurysm which is false — loose
> tissues of the armpit — crimson, blue,
> purple

Like odd beads strung together by someone colour-blind, these lumps of words make no sense to her. Pipes gurgle and clank, but it's still freezing in here. Just yesterday, sun glistened on window panes making folk blink their way along the road to work; this morning, a north-easterly drove hail in their eyes and now it moans in Bellevue's pitched roof. Still. Rather this cold than the sweltering heat of the caseroom in summer.

> queen of Bohemia — remains of a
> magnificent castle — the poem is very
> obscure — Ancient Books of Wales

To the surface of a deep pool of noise – caseroom's regular taps and occasional thuds, click-clack of monotype machines, churning thump of the presses – bobs a rich, round voice. A male comp working at a frame on the lassies' side of the aisle sings out In the bleak mid winter. He's joined by another and another as a flotilla of lassies take up the song. Frosty wind made moan. From the men's side, a fine baritone, a steamship, say, lends ballast. Earth was hard as iron.

'It's like a bloody morgue in here. Can we not have something cheerful. It's spring for god'sake.' The optimist has a go at Come Josephine in my flying machine, but his effort is not taken up and his voice tails off.

Iza leans to peer over her spectacles down the length of the aisle. Overseer Purves is out of his seat, stroking his thinning black hair, coming out of his box. His office is at the far end of this caseroom so he has more trouble spying than Wight did from up in his gallery in Pauls works.

> second Bishop of Rome — Mal'akh
> Ylweh seems to — guardian angels —
> mortified negative asceticism

Her mind refuses another clump of words. She retches, gagging over her case. It's not the first time, though it's been a good while since the last bout of sickness and she'd thought she'd seen the last of it. Though she's not quick enough to turn her head, but she does manage to stopper her mouth with a cupped right hand and clasp tight till she's snagged the nick of the last sort with her left thumb and laid her setting stick down before fumbling for a muslin cloth she keeps tucked under her frame.

'Here. Let me.' Grace comes hurrying from the next frame to hand Iza the cloth and hold her hair back till she's done throwing up. It puts Iza in mind of doing the very same for Netta, all those years back. Why on earth's Netta gone and got herself in the family way she'd thought then. And now look at me.

Sick has dribbled down her blouse. With a nod towards the cludgie as she catches the eye of Charlie Dewar, Bellevue's Father of the Chapel, she goes off to clean up.

# -2-

The lassies had their own cludgie in Bellevue, and not just because these works were new and Pauls was old. They were a different lot down here, the women comps. They outnumbered men and they made their voices heard. Some of them even flung their weight around. Agnes Galloway certainly did. Lizzie Amos too, though Lizzie threw it in a less bruising fashion. Not Grace, though. Grace kept her head down. And me? What about me? Iza asked herself as she dabbed her blouse with water so cold it stung her fingers. She didn't much like the answer that came to her: neither nor, a bit of both.

Holding her hair back, she drank from the tap, rinsed her mouth and spat, then sipped and swallowed. As she dried her face and hands on her skirt and headed back to her frame, she rubbed the bulge in her middle and comforted herself with the thought that being wed and expecting was a daring bit of affrontery that was bound to limit her involvement in organisational matters. Besides, being a longstanding member of the Warehousemen and Cutters Union gave her a bit of a say. Where she'd been the only women comp at

Pauls to join, here a fair few of the lassies were members. They'd even got a caseroom representative in Agnes, who'd bend their ears when she came round collecting dues. Iza had puzzled over the difference between Bellevue and Pauls. Hard to imagine being at her frame in Pauls with a ring on her finger and bulge in her middle, yet here, despite choppy waters in the form of raised eyebrows and the odd mutter, she'd sailed through, so far. Being younger, many of them second generation comps, the women in Bellevue acted like they had the right to stand at the frame. And, too, she'd felt for herself how typesetting the prestigious eleventh edition of the *Encyclopaedia Britannica* gave you a sense of your own worth. Still, she was the only one with a man and a bairn on the way. And, she well knew, she and her work chums were going to need every bit of their sense of worth. Like a delayed long-distance train to an unknown destination, anxious folk craning on the platform for sight of it, rumblings about getting women out of the caseroom had taken shape and, belching smoke and steam, burst into view. Six months ago the Edinburgh Typographical Society had submitted a memorial to the Master Printers Association demanding there be no further introduction of females into the trade. The Masters had been taking their time to chew on this. Now the Typographical meant to push, and pushing meant threatening to use industrial muscle. There was to be a meeting in the storeroom this dinnertime.

Back at her frame, a raised voice had Iza look up. Since it was Agnes's voice she'd no trouble hearing it, but she had to stretch on tiptoe to catch sight of her. Five foot nothing, Agnes Galloway barely reached the top of the frames. She was broad and solid, though, and there she stood in the aisle, hands on hips, fat brown bun bobbing from side to side, berating George-bloody-frocks-at-the-frame-Struthers, the George Seggie of Bellevue works. And there was Lizzie, with her marigold mop of hair, joining in. Iza couldn't catch every word, but it was clear that Struthers was standing his ground. It was a right scunner, the likes of him, close cousin to her brother Rab, being full of themselves these days. Mind you, Agnes was a match for him, and the way he snarled under his breath as he walked off showed that she'd punctured his bluster. Iza caught the glower he tossed at her from under bristly eyebrows as he marched by. She knew exactly what he was thinking. He was thinking: not just a frock-at-the-frame but a bloody wife-and-mother-to-be-at-the-frame.

Ring of mallets on metal ceased. Clanking chorus of monotypes dribbled to silence. Out of his office, hands on hips, overseer Purves watched men leave their frames and stones to stream down an iron stairway to the cellar storeroom. Despite their stiff-shouldered strut, the male comps talked under their breath. Women followed, a bunch of monotype keyboard operators at the top of the stairs replenished by a queue of comps pressing their way up the central aisle. Apprentices looked on while making a show of going about their business. The dwindling crew of learner lassies – not one new starter for years now – watched out of the corners of their eyes, biting their lips.

It was near dark in the storeroom. Thin strips of filthy window high up on a long wall that ran along a back alleyway let in only a scrap of murky light. It was stifling too. Someone opened a door to let in light and air, but seeing as it was the door to the lavatories by the works entrance that just let in a fetid reek.

'Jesus wept. Who's been at the cabbage and molasses?'

'Beef olives, ah'd say. Must've been one of them.' A nod at the ceiling.

'Can we not go outside?' a voice called.

'What, and get ourselves locked out?' called another.

'Shift along. Make way for the girruls.' From his perch on an open stairway in a far corner, Charlie Dewar narrowed his eyes on a mass of heads and levered an outstretched hand through the air as though to push bodies along. Having stopped to persuade Grace to set down her stick and come to the meeting, that this was for all comps, not just union members, Iza was one of the last down the stair. She pulled a wary Grace through to stand by Lizzie. Easy to spot with that heap of hair, Lizzie was the one they all went to if they thought their pay packet might be short but weren't sure enough to test Agnes's patience with it. Lizzie would take time to listen and, if they'd got their totting up wrong and the pay was right enough, she'd say 'It's easy done.' Agnes, stood by Lizzie's side, was a different kettle of fish. You might as well bump into a loaded trolley as clash with her. Even with no bruise to show you'd feel it. These past few weeks Agnes had been collecting strike levy contributions along with union dues and, even if they'd wanted to, no-one felt inclined to question her or make excuses. But, then, as Agnes was quick to remind them, she could always leave it to you to trudge over to the warehouse with your thruppence every week and put up with comments that'd make a whoor blush, or you could give it to her and save your modesty.

Iza found some relief in being propped upright by the work chums pinned to her sides. Her breasts throbbed and her insides churned as if the curse was coming on, though it couldn't be. Lizzie linked her arm and gripped tight.

'Your attention please.' Charlie Dewar coughed and

198

kept coughing until voices dropped away. 'For the benefit of anyone who's been away to the South Pole these past months, let me remind you of our position. You are all party to the memorial the Society submitted to the masters to the effect that, from the start of this year, there will be no further introduction of females into our trade and that in future, machine composition will be solely undertaken by male union labour. These past months we have been reasonable.' His chin rose and dropped. 'We have been patient.' He held out spread palms.

'And look where it's got us,' a male comp called out. 'Up the pole.'

'Aye. We'll all be history before they budge,' another called.

'And the lot of us replaced by lassies.' That was Struthers.

'You *want* replacing,' Agnes flung in his direction before addressing the whole room. 'You know what you lot can do about it. Support our case for improved rates and we'll support you.' Only those right next to Agnes could see her, but the whole storeroom heard her. Like a jagged crack appearing on a frozen pond, men shuffled to put an inch between them and the women. Eyes stayed fixed on Charlie Dewar.

Iza wanted to ask what Agnes was on about. What did she mean by 'case for improved rates.' First she'd heard of it. But now wasn't the time nor the place. Charlie Dewar was calling for attention, and, besides, just taking in breath was proving hard. She felt stifled. Her head swam like she'd gone under water.

'Girruls. Ladies. Please.' Charlie Dewar's wounded tone would have been enough, but coupled with raised hands and the solemn look of a minister in his pulpit it had tension dissolved in calls of 'Hallelujah' and laughter. He took it well, waited for silence, and got it. 'We'll come to the question of the girruls' grievances, and you will see that your Society has not been idle on that matter.'

'But it's not our Society,' Lizzie cut in.

Heads jerked round.

Iza gathered her wits. 'She's right,' she called out. 'You won't have us in *your* society.'

'Ladies. Please. You'll get your chance to have your say.'

'Right you are. But don't go calling it our Society when your Society's not prepared to have us,' Iza shouted.

Charlie Dewar conceded the point with nervy nods of his head. His reminder that disunity in their ranks could only put a smile on the masters' faces won him the few minutes' peace he needed to retrace the dispute's stuttering progress: the masters had indicated a willingness to reduce the ratio of females employed on hand-setting; they'd offered a five-year ban on new learner girls; the Society had balloted all members on the committee's resolution to reject these proposals and adhere to their memorial calling for no further introduction of females into the trade and for all future machine composition to be undertaken by male union labour. Here, he paused, fingers drumming on a jutting lower lip. A few men called out their approval. Most kept quiet. The women held their tongues. The Society had balloted and that ballot had returned an overwhelming vote in favour of tendering notices to strike work in the event of the masters failing to sign.

Like a fire bell in a nearby street, this brought an alert hush, and in the hush Iza heard a roar in her ears. As folk around her blurred and bobbed, she felt her knees buckle. The crook of Lizzie's arm stiffened against her.

'Hold on there. Out the way!' Lizzie called out, making to tug Iza through the crowd. Iza tried to resist. She didn't need that glower from Agnes to tell her that a display of female frailty was the last thing needed.

'She's taken a turn,' Lizzie shouted. 'Let us through. Get water, will ye?'

Elbowing her way through thick-packed bodies, Lizzie guided Iza to the front, turned her about, sat her down on the bottom step and shoved her head down between spread knees before nodding up to Charlie Dewar to say, 'Sorry. On you go.'

Trying to get to her feet by snatching at clumps of words floating above her head, Iza failed. Her body was too heavy. If you don't stand up now, she told herself, that's it, you're beat. Rab will be vindicated. She brought to mind tugging free of Rab that first morning, walking into the caseroom, stepping to her frame. That nearly did the trick, but it wasn't enough. Then Mr Scott's voice came to her. If they knock you down, get back on your feet. Right you are. She'd have one last go at it, and if she couldn't heave herself up she'd nod off till it was all over then she'd go home and never come back. Next thing, she was on her feet, pushing her way through to Lizzie, taking her place.

Charlie Dewar took his watch from his overall pocket. 'Any questions? We've only five minutes and ah need four of them with the girruls.'

'What about the machinemen?'

'They're with us.'

'The labourers?'

'Labourers, lithographers, warehousemen stone polishers, bindery. The lot.'

'Is it all the shops together?'

'Aye. Except Nelsons where they've never used female labour.'

'What if the masters send work there?'

'It'll be blacked.'

'Ah heard the Tanfield masters have signed?'

'No, they have not, but they soon will.'

'A report in the *Evening Dispatch* said they'll send work overseas.'

'And our international brothers say they'll send it straight back.'

Charlie Dewar checked his watch again, said they'd run out of time but if the lassies would come back down at knock-off time he'd hear them out and be sure to relay every particular of their grievances to the national joint union committee meeting that evening. Calls of, 'And who's going to get mah dad his tea?' and 'Who'll get the messages in?' had his fingertips back drumming his chin.

'Can we not have someone speak for us?' Iza called. 'Agnes or Lizzie.'

'Aye, if that's the consensus,' said Charlie Dewar, drawing the meeting to a close.

Iza told Lizzie to go on ahead, she was fine, she'd wait for the room to clear a bit. When the crowd thinned, she saw Grace was waiting by the back wall, on her own and looking anxiously about her.

'What's going to happen?' Grace was close to tears. Her family's sole earner, she provided for an infirm mother and a brother who hadn't been right in the head since a lump of masonry fell on him when he was working on a building site.

'It's going to be all right, that's what. Did you not hear him? They're talking about stopping new lassies for a bit, not us losing our jobs.' Iza clenched Grace's hand.

'Can we trust them though? One minute they're saying one thing, the next something else. And are they going on strike? What'll happen to us then?'

Relieved by what she'd just heard about their jobs, Iza brushed this aside. 'Did you not hear Agnes talking about us getting improved conditions? Wouldn't that be grand.'

'Aye, but ah don't know what she's on about.'

'Neither do ah, but we'll soon find out.'

# -3-

The sun had gone down and street lamps were lit, but a wee patch of sky above roofs and chimneys was dim rather than dark at knock-off time. Summer in sight. Start of long days that stretched on into evening. Down the alleyway, out into the main road, turning down side streets, Bellevue print workers walked home at an easier pace. Not having to bundle themselves up to battle against hail or sleet, folk greeted chums or neighbours coming from nearby Tanfield works, stopped for a blether at corners or stair doors. To join the queue in the corner grocers Iza had to skirt round a cluster of printers – machinemen by the look of them – who were leaning in, heads bowed, to talk in hushed voices. What she could see of their grave faces had her prick her ears. Discussing the dispute, for sure, but she couldn't catch their words.

There was quite a queue in the grocers and the woman being served was buying the shop.

'Ah'm only wanting shrimp paste for mah man's pieces,' a wee woman in front of Iza moaned.

Mention of shrimp paste had her gagging, but she

swallowed and managed to join in with 'Ah'm just wanting a tin of corned beef,' before turning away to get her mind off food. Her back ached. Her head too. But she got her corned beef and a tin of mustard and was on her way home with a weight off her mind and a wee bit of life in her legs. For as long as she could remember she'd heard moans about frocks-at-the-frame and mutters about clearing them out. And now the men were going to let them stay? Hard to credit. She needed another opinion. If anyone knew the ins and outs of it, Rab would. But would he deign to tell her? And could she stomach being told by him? Climbing the stair to her house she felt juice drain out of her like a squeezed lemon.

Once John had rolled his smoke and opened his *Evening Dispatch* and she'd tidied up, she went down to Rab's. Sitting at the table with Jeannie's eldest, who was chewing his nails over homework sums, her brother acknowledged her with a curt nod. Rab had finally managed to grow a full moustache, but he'd lost most of the hair from his head and eye strain had furrowed his brow. He was taking it for granted, she knew, that she'd dropped in to see Jeannie or their mother about women's business. She saw him glance at her lump then over to Jeannie, coming through from the bedroom, and to his mother and mother-in-law sitting either side of an empty grate, Vi Ross knitting, Jeannie's mum darning. He kept his eyes on the lad's sums when Iza said could she have a word with him.

'What about?'

'What do you think? About the Typographical Society's intentions, the dispute over female comps.'

Still Rab didn't look up. 'None of your business,' he humphed.

'Don't be ridiculous,' Iza burst out. 'Of course it's mah business.'

Jeannie and the two mothers eyed each other, grimacing. Rab's shoulder's stiffened. He opened his mouth to protest, but when he turned to look at Iza he'd adopted a look of strained patience.

'Sorry, hen. You're right. Sit yourself down.' He told the lad to get himself through to the bedroom with the other bairns and asked Jeannie if there was any tea left in the pot.

Bad news, Iza thought. He's feeling cock-a-hoop. He looked weary, though.

'Ah need to know what's going to happen about our jobs,' she said. 'Ah've not been able to follow it.'

Rab pinned his eyes on hands he'd clasped and laid on the table. 'We're demanding no more lassies get taken on,' he said. 'You know as well as ah do they're training up lassies to operate the new monotype machines and paying them half the agreed rate. No more learner lassies and no women on the monotypes. That's the demand.'

Iza nodded, 'Aye.'

There was a hush in the room. Jeannie and the mothers were all ears.

'We can't let it go on,' Rab went on. 'We're hardly living the life of Reilly on *full* rates.' When he swept a hand round the room, inviting her to look and agree, the two mums nodded their approval.

Iza kept quiet while Jeannie set the teapot down and poured.

'But what about us?' She'd composed herself, but not enough to keep her voice calm.

'Who's *us*?'

The way Rab clenched his hands told her he was mounting his high horse. She knew that to get anywhere she was best off soft-talking him down but she couldn't do it.

'Who d'you think? Time-served women handsetters like me. What'll happen to us?' she snapped.

Rab didn't rise to it though. Eyes pinned on the door behind Iza's head, hands now spread flat, he spoke evenly. 'We need to stop the flow of cheap labour. Stop it and within a few years we'll be back to a caseroom full of men on agreed rates. Families able to make ends meet.' The tiniest tilt of his chin told Iza he was stopping himself from looking round for applause.

'What about lassies like mah work chum Grace? Her wage packet feeds her family.'

'She'll be there till she gets wed and has a man's full-rate wage packet coming in.'

'What if she doesn't get wed?'

'Well, it's looking like she might be at her frame a while longer, more's the pity. But one way or another females will go and in the meantime we'll have turned off the tap of cheap labour. It's been too long coming.'

'Turned it off for a bit, surely? Five years they're saying.'

Iza watched Rab's hands clench again. The eyes he turned on her were awash with rancour. Knowing he was about to jump down her throat, still she persisted.

'So we get to keep our jobs?'

'*You* get to keep *your* jobs!' Sucking in a lungful of breath and thumping the table with a fist, Rab was on his feet. 'You know perfectly well what ah think to it. Ah think you need clearing out now, the lot of you, once and for all, and ah'm not alone in thinking it. It's a man's job and you belong at home seeing to your man. A fine example of a wife you are! Why he puts up with it is beyond me. And now this.' He glowered at Iza's lump then turned from her muttering, 'What sort of a man is he anyhow?' just loud enough for her to hear.

Doing the same, turning away and talking just loud enough, Iza said 'What would you know about that?'

She felt four pairs of eyes on her back as she went out the door, but as she walked slowly back up the stair to her house she didn't give a jot. They could look all they liked. Ah'll keep mah job, she was thinking, and so will Grace and Agnes and Lizzie, and Margaret at Pauls too, and that's just grand. She slapped the matter out on the bannister. The men tell the masters they'll strike work unless the masters stop taking on lassies. Slap. The masters hum and haw then say, right you are, we'll stop taking on learner lassies for a few years. Slap. The men say not good enough, ten years, and all machine work goes to men; and since cheap labour's the issue, you'll up the rate for time-served lassies while you're at it. Slap. The masters give a bit; the men give a bit; it's settled.

Settled? She stopped short, gripping the bannister. Margaret. What would Margaret be making of the dispute? She and her chum had stayed in touch over the years, by postcard and letter for the most part, since Iza's move and marriage. Margaret had written about a campaign for a women's section of the Typographical Society. She'd sent accounts of meetings, including the inaugural meeting of a 'We Women' movement formed to oppose the men. She needed to talk to Margaret. She'd write a postcard. Go to see her if she got a chance.

John looked up expectantly as she came in. She didn't know what he was expecting but right then she needed to be giving him something. Perched on the arm of his chair she asked if he'd found anything interesting in the paper. John liked to read advertisements. Some evenings he'd read to himself, with just the odd humph, fancy that; sometimes he'd read aloud.

'Listen to this,' he said. 'Throw away your old burning,

ill-smelling electric belt. Ajax dry-cell is the newest and most successful cure for nervous and sickly people.'

'What's Ajax dry-cell?' she said to keep him talking. She nearly asked if he thought it might help his mother, but she wasn't sure if 'nervous and sickly' properly described John's mother's condition, and she sensed John wouldn't take kindly to her bringing it up. The frayed state of John's mother's nerves was not something they spoke of.

Anyhow, John was on to canaries, reading aloud again. Tuppenny stamp for a guide; 250 illustrations of birds, aviaries, cages. He'd like to see that. Might send off for it. Hair destroyer. Last thing he wanted. Stammering. Effective cure by correspondence. How the hell can your correspondent tell if it's worked? He looked up at her. She was smiling obligingly when an image of a round gent reading a composition sent by the stammerer formed in her mind – an image straight from the pencil of Margaret's dad, Mr Scott, she realised. She laughed and John smiled. But her laugh was cut short. She frowned. Thought of Mr Scott brought Margaret back to mind and, with Margaret, nagging doubt. She shoved it away again, this time with the thought that she'd ask Margaret to be godmother.

'Ah'll ask Margaret to be godmother,' she said, fingering John's wiry ginger hair. 'It's needing a trim,' she said. 'Shall ah do it?'

'Not now. Let's get to bed,' he said.

'Ah'll just write Margaret a card.'

When she staggered and clutched her lump as she got off her perch, John caught and steadied her.

Next morning, sunlight already starting to filter through smoky haze, Iza watched out for Grace among the stream of folk headed for work. But there was no sign of Grace and all day her frame was empty. Where on earth could she be? Grace was always at her frame. Iza decided to drop in at her house on the way home. First time she knocked there was no answer, but when she knocked louder Grace called to come in. Busy trying to spoon food into her brother, who was slumped with his chin nearly touching the table, Grace's face fell when she looked up.

'Och, ah thought that was the doctor turned up at last,' she said. 'Ah've been waiting all day.'

Grace's brother had had a seizure. First thing this morning she'd been getting him up for breakfast when his eyes rolled and he'd collapsed and lain on the floor twitching. He'd come round quick enough, but hadn't been himself all day. Iza asked could she do anything. Nodding to a pan on the stove and over to the bedroom door, Grace asked would she mind taking her mum some pudding. Grace's mum was a bent wee woman, head lolling on piled-up pillows. She looked ancient, Iza thought, though when she got close she saw she wasn't that old. Iza lifted an empty plate from her knees and handed her the bowl of rice pudding. Could she manage, Iza asked, thinking she didn't look up to feeding herself. She was wrong. She spooned away with relish, cleaning the bowl in no time and wanting more, with a spoonful of jam this time, eh?

Grace was wiping food dribbled down her brother's front.

'It's going to be all right,' Iza said. 'Our jobs are safe.'

'How do you know? Are you sure?'

'Aye. Ah'm sure. We'll get to keep our jobs. And after a few years there'll be new learner lassies coming in, and if more stay on like me, there'll be no getting shot of us. The only pity is ah'd like to have seen them try to shove Agnes out the door.'

There was no time to say more because the doctor turned up and Grace said she'd be back at her frame next day.

§§§§§§§§§

What with the fit so tight it's down to counting every single word. She's tried averaging, like normal, and learned better. So, 327 words times 6 is 1,800; 1,920 plus 42, that's 1,962 ens in a 21 pica column; so 12 times 21 is 240; 252 points divided by 8.

'Keep it to yourself will you. Ah'm trying to work here.'

Most printers are cloth-eared from the din. Not Alistair McWhirter. He can hear a six point sort hit the deck. Famous for it.

'Sorry. Never realised ah was talking out loud,' she calls. 'Miserable old sod,' she mutters.

'Ah heard that.'

Sanitary Condition—Dr John Tatham constructed a Manchester life-table based on the vital statistics of the decennium 1881–1890, from which it appeared that, while in England and

Wales of 1000 men aged 25 nearly 800
survived to be 45 and of 1000 aged 45,
569 survived to be 65, in Manchester
the survivors were only 732 and 414
respectively.

She dumps her lines, pauses to wipe sweat from her brow with a forearm then lays her right palm on her front and gently rubs. On occasion, she's thought the bairn will be coming out dented from being pressed to the edge of the 10 point case. More than once she's urged him to shift himself. And now, as though he's heard and decided to do her bidding, he's dropped to lodge himself on the edge of the 12 point. Then there's swollen breasts getting in the way of raised arms. She's bound them tight to keep them out the way and now, what with the caseroom's pipes needing shut down, they're stewing like dumplings.

The expectation of life, at 25, was, for
England and Wales 36.12 years, and
for Manchester 30.69 years. But the
death-rate has since rapidly decreased;
in 1891 it was 26.0 per thousand living;

Down to 9 point and leading reduced to nought. Such ugliness pains her eyes, text crammed in like a ragman's full load, but the rush towards publication is on and there's no time for niceties.

Though no-one looks up, everyone sees. At the far end of the caseroom Charlie Dewar's in the aisle waving a sheet of paper like a wee flag, putting her in mind of Fred

Henderson at Pauls. Must learn it when they get elected Father of the Chapel. Except Fred Henderson would not have a woman by his side and there's Agnes set to accompany Charlie Dewar on his strike notice round. Hard to imagine a Ballantyne's man with a female lieutenant.

Though she keeps her mind on the job, still she takes heed of the pair's progress. A few steps to a frame, a few words exchanged, sometimes more than a few, a smile and a nod as the comp bends to sign, or a scowl and about turn if she refuses, and they're on to the next. Male comps on the opposite side watch from the corners of their eyes. This goes on for a good half-hour before the pair are by Iza's side and Agnes is saying 'We can count on you, eh?'

'What is it we're signing?'

'We're signing to say we'll back the men.'

'Back them how?'

'Strike work alongside them.' Agnes thumps the side of Iza's frame.

'If it comes to it.' Charlie Dewar nods sagely.

'And will it come to it?' Iza wants to know.

Agnes shrugs. 'Who knows? But it's a lot less likely if we all sign. That ah do know.'

'They'll cave in,' Charlie Drawer says assuredly. He looks at his feet. 'More than likely,' he adds, with a trace of doubt a sharp nose can sniff.

'But we get to stay put?' Iza looks him in the eye.

'Aye. You get to stay.'

'And what's this about improved rates?'

'Part of the negotiations. On the table.'

'Where they stay till they're agreed.' Agnes gives the frame another thump.

When Charlie Dewar lays down his paper and Agnes

points with a stubby finger, Iza signs next to her name. Her hand shakes, and her name looks scrawny, unlike her true signature, but it's done and Charlie Dewar and Agnes are at Grace's frame and Grace glances round like a startled bird before leaning in to sign her name.

Taking in a deep breath of hot air, Iza turns the best part of her attention to her work.

> The "singing beach" is a stretch of white sand, which, when trodden upon, emits a curious musical sound. Manchester, originally a part of Salem, was settled about 1630 and was at first known as Jeffrey's Creek.

Her inner ear pricks at this mention of a singing beach. She repeats the phrase, quizzing herself. Her memory finding no match for the sound, it offers the swish of sandflies being swatted at Wemyss Bay. Her inner eye does, though, find an image for the stretch of white sand; not something she's ever seen, but her father's talk of the Fetlar Foy on Tresta beach in Shetland, where he'd never ever been.

She glances at Grace, who like everyone else has fallen silent. To break the spell, she calls 'What are you on?' She has to repeat it.

'Maps. A big entry on Africa. How about you?'

'Still Manchester, but a different one.'

'How many are there?'

'How many do we need?' calls McWhirter. 'One's one too many to mah way of thinking.'

'Miserable old sod.'

'Ah heard that.'

'Aye. Just checking.'

> On the east side of the city are two connected lakes known as Lake Massabesic (30 m. in circumference). Manchester is known for the attractive appearance of the residence districts in which the factory operatives live, detached homes and 'corporation boarding-houses', instead of tenement houses, being the rule.

'This one's got attractive detached homes for the factory operatives.'

'It'll not be our one then.'

She calls for an apprentice to fill her case and while she waits she chews on a question that's stuck in her gullet. How long will she need to take off for the birth? As she's done many times these past months, she tries telling herself that she's done it before so can do it again. But it's hard to imagine the she who walked to Jessie's that morning, walked home the same evening and was back at her frame within the week. Was that really and truly her? Though she knows it was, she can't credit it.

This time round though, as if she's timed it when she's done no such thing, the bairn should come just before the city's trades fair holiday. With an overtime ban in the offing, the works will shut down for the full fortnight. Better still, it might be a biddable bairn that, to please its mother, decides to enter the world during the holiday. But that happy thought is chased away by buts. But this time the bairn will be staying put. But you couldn't have picked a worse time or worse reason for taking time off, handing ammunition to male comps who say women are not fitted to the work.

# -4-

A tingle in the blood and bristle of hairs on the nape of her neck had Iza's eyes snap open. The midwife was leaning over, arms outstretched to take hold of her newborn. Iza clasped him tight.

'Now, now. Ah'll just put him down afore you crush him.'

Iza clung on, shouldering the woman's arms away. 'Ah'll keep him by me a wee while.'

The midwife straightened. She didn't need to say 'So you think you know best do you?' Folded arms, raised eyebrows and a pulled in puffy chin said it loud and clear.

'Just to get the feel.' Iza felt limp but she clung on.

The midwife went bustling about her business, stuffing the tools of her trade into her carpet bag.

They'd got off to a bad start from the outset.

'Yer first you say?' Rising from where she'd been poking and peering between Iza's legs, the midwife had let out a wee humph that said pull the other one. 'Late to be starting a family,' she'd said, inviting Iza to confide.

'Aye.' Eyes on to the ceiling, Iza had kicked herself.

Better to have come clean. But the woman's high-handed manner had got her back up and now it was too late.

She was certified and came well recommended. Best in the district, if a bit on the expensive side. And she certainly knew her business, and that you could admire. Hard to warm to, though. When she'd first surveyed the room Iza had read her mind, or thought she had. What with two good pay packets coming in they'd got some nice bits of furniture and that fine crib, right enough, but what kind of a mother would she make, this woman who did a man's job and meant to be back doing it. Money and being clever never made a good mother.

But now, to Iza's relief, she was out of her smeared pinnie and cap, had primped her hair and was at the door, bag in hand.

'If he wakes afore ah'm back do like ah said. Head firm in one hand, teat in the other and stroke his lips with it.' She shoogled an ample breast. 'Keep stroking till he latches on. If he won't nurse, don't fret. Ah'll be back to see to it.'

She made to leave but stopped in the doorway for a look round.

What's on her mind now? Was that worry on her face? Hard to judge what lay behind those sharp eyes of hers. Iza glanced over to her mother, perched on a stool by the window. Did she look worried? Far from it. She was dead to the world. She'd nodded off hours ago, slumped sideways, a hand gripping the side of Iza's new crib. Iza smiled. Trust her mother to sleep through all this bellowing. She'd opened the window when she first sat down there. The midwife had objected. That her mother had stood her ground had pleased Iza no end. The way her mother had wrinkled her nose behind the midwife's back had told Iza she had an ally and right then she'd needed one.

'Wait. Wait a minute.' Seeing where the midwife's eyes had lighted, Iza grappled her legs out of bed. 'Your money's in the dresser.'

'You stay there. Ah'll get it. Which drawer?'

But Iza was up, gripping the bairn to her baggy middle to shuffle across the room and rifle in a drawer, back turned. Money pocketed, the midwife leant over Vi Ross to close the window.

'Tell yer ma she's been a grand help, keeping herself out the road. Ah cannot abide folk getting under mah feet.'

'Leave it open eh? It's turning warm.'

That had the eyebrows up again. 'It's not recommended.' She shut the window.

Left in peace, Iza sat on the edge of the bed studying the baby's wee puckered face. Those pulsing blue veins alarmed her more than last night's contractions rolling through her had. Where the pain had been hers and hers alone to deal with, the baby was no part of her yet latched on to stay. She put her nose to the bundle and sniffed. Cloudy sour-sweet. Hay and curd cheese.

When she laid the wee one down in the crib, the echo of a stabbing pain had her fumble, tapping his head on the hard edge. She froze. Beads of slaver on his lips bubbled, but he stayed quiet. The callouses on her fingers grated on embroidered white leaves as she tucked and smoothed the cover. She crouched, ran a palm along sleek wood, began to rock herself, which rocked the crib. Back and forth. Smooth as anything. *Bye baby bunting, daddy's gone a hunting, to fetch a little rabbit skin, to wrap his baby bunting in,* she sang under her breath, her heart singing at the thought of a wee miracle. Her baby bunting had come into the world just in time for the start of the trades holiday. The morn's morn the works would close for two whole weeks. She could let caserooms, Ency Brits, Agneses and Charlie Dewars, memorials and masters go to hell in a handcart, the lot of them.

While her mother slept on, mouth agape, Iza lay listening to the sounds of daybreak in Canonmills: far off, squall of gulls swooping on a catch coming in off the North Sea; nearby, hoot of a locomotive and clatter of wagons heading out of Scotland Street station; somewhere close, the low of a lone cow; up the road, scrape of the muck carter's spade on stone; down below, clomp of hooves and clank of tin as a milk cart came to a halt at the dairy.

'Open the window will you, Mum?' Iza called out. She wanted her company.

Vi Ross woke with a start. 'What's going on?' She looked about her. 'Where's she gone?'

'Take a look, Mum. You've got another grandson.' Iza nodded to the crib at her mum's feet.

'By Christ, but you don't hang about. Ah just close mah eyes for a minute...'

'Aye, Mum.'

'Ah had a nice crib just like that. Mine went to the pawn in the big strike,' she said as she heaved the window open. She'd said the same more than once since John carried the new crib in.

The first of the street's voices were cutting up through still morning air – 'Can you not fit a stopper in her erse?' – and Iza put a face to the voice. The skinny lad with big ears and a gallus grin who did most of the shovelling and hauling for the muck carter. It was an Irish erse he had, not a Scottish one, and that word, uttered with that cadence, brought to mind folk she'd barely given a thought to in years. She heard Eamonn's 'We'll kick their feckin erses for them,' burbled out the side of his mouth, saw James

Connolly's eyes crease in amusement even as he raised his eyebrows and flicked an apologetic look her way, as well he might. Even though a belch of rotten egg from the gas works had wafted in through the opened window, Iza got up to lean out.

'And put your tribe out of work?' the dairyman called out. 'No, son. This mare's got a hert, a hert so big she'll keep dropping her shite so's even an Irish tinker can eat.' Chummy but hard as nails.

Now a mewl from the crib had the dairyman look up, churn balanced on the edge of his cart ready to howk onto his back. 'Another brat to feed,' he said.

'Miserable old fekker,' said the muck carter's lad, who stood scratching the carthorse's withers. 'God bless them, mother and child.'

When Vi Ross lifted the baby and handed him to Iza, her smile had a touch of sadness in it. Though no words were ever spoken about Iza's first, her girl, Jessie and Jamie's daughter, words were not everything.

As the baby nursed, moth-wing eyelids flickering, petal mouth puttering, shuffles and mutters rose from next door. John getting himself up.

'That's your man up,' her mum said. 'Ah'll get him his breakfast.'

Given the way she felt about John, this was gracious on her mother's part, so even though Iza wanted her by her side she said 'Aye. Right you are.' She heard John and her mum exchange a few words, but it was as if their voices reached her from another house, another town, another country.

Lying in bed with babe asleep in her arms Iza dozed, the sound of barrows and carts rattling by, hooters blasting, clomp of feet and coughs and calls of folk off to Bellevue and Tanfield, to the gas works, the paper mill, to Lindsays the coopers, rose as though a giant broom swept all before it along the road then dropped away as the last few strokes of the broom cleared up straggled odds and ends. While the streets where Iza had opened her eyes on the world were always awake with carts, carriages, bicycles, her son's new eyes would look on factories and workshops clustered by a river on the north edge of the city. As hers had, his ears would tune on clatter, but for him it would be a clatter that ebbed and flowed, interrupting whistling wind, chirrup of birds and croak of frogs. And while most of the piggeries and cow byres had been shunted beyond the river, still he'd hear the odd grunt and low. Just like his mother, though, he would fall asleep and wake to trains' hoots, wagons' clanks and the rush of tipped coal.

Coming out of deep sleep, Iza felt warmth stroke her eyelids. She conjured a soft breeze, scent of grass, yellow flare of buttercups, misty blue sky, tried to draw them back even as they faded. Her eyes opened onto sun slanting through the window, dividing the room into two triangles, one bright, one in deep shadow. Must be mid afternoon. Sensing a presence, she turned to see her mother standing in her green and pink floral short-sleeved dress, looking down at the crib, the ghost of a sweet smile on her face. Were it not for skin hanging loose on her neck and upper arms and grey in her red hair, she could have been a young mum.

'You stay there. Ah'll get you a drink. Ah've put stovies on for your man's tea.'

While Iza sipped lemon barley water, her mother busied herself about the room, fussing at the hang of blue cotton curtains, easing in a jutting end of a dresser drawer. Rearranging framed family photographs atop the dresser, she studied them: Jamie and Jessie with their big batch of bairns, Rab and Jack with theirs. Though when they appeared in the flesh she paid her grandchildren scant heed, Vi Ross took great pleasure in totting them up. Their very existence, their survival, supposing they survived, was a personal triumph. So her face clouded as she lifted and studied the photograph of Violet and her man standing by a parlour palm, hands resting on the shoulders of their young Victor, togged up in tweed breeks and jacket. Just the one. Two or three lost and no signs of any more.

'And she makes such a lovely mum.' Vi Ross tutted, then, turning to Iza, said 'You'll be having more, eh?' like it was an instruction rather than a question.

Iza just smiled at her. She was thinking about how her wee brother William was missing from her photograph gallery, how she must ask him for a photograph, a nice portrait, William on his own.

Vi Ross had gone back down to Rab's and Iza was in the living room buttoning herself up from nursing the baby when John got in from work. He stopped short just inside the door to test the air like an alerted bird before going about his business, hanging his jacket and bunnet on the door hook, washing his hands and splashing his face and neck at the sink, placing his tobacco pouch on the mantelpiece, sitting down and lifting his spoon ready. All just as usual, except for a slight wait for his tea to be dished while Iza got the baby settled. But even though he must have missed sleep, what with refusing to go and stay the night at his folk's, and spending a good hour at shift-end banking up tatties at his work's allotment before making the mile's trek home, the way John went about the usual had the crispness of a fresh-picked apple to it. He didn't have much to say, any talk being kept for after he'd finished eating, the dishes were cleared and he'd rolled and lit his smoke. But that, too, was just as usual. Like his movements, though, his few words – 'A boy is it? Aye now. That's braw,' – had a brightness to them. There was just one rank note: a scunnered humphing at his first taste of the stovies Vi Ross had made, a banging down of his spoon, a 'What's in this? It tastes funny.'

Settled in their facing chairs in evening's tarnished silver light, Iza tried to tease words out of her husband. Though she'd told herself the looming dispute could go to hell in a handcart, part of her hadn't been listening. The chances of getting information out of John were slim. With no females in their caseroom Nelsons weren't directly involved and hadn't taken part in the strike ballot, but there was more to John's attitude than that. Iza had long ago decided to take his lack of interest in union matters to be just that: a lack of interest. And this suited her well enough. It was a lot better than it being a bone of contention. But one Sunday when her brother Jack called round she'd been unable to dismiss it so readily when the topic of the dispute, which Jack had plenty to say about, had John fidgeting in his pockets and looking about him like a bairn who's lost his favourite marble. Even as she'd winced at this display of jitters, she'd felt alarm. The looming dispute scared her enough without signs of her husband's lack of steadiness.

Still, she needed to know what was afoot. Maybe if she came at it at an angle?

'Did you get a clean run today?'

'Aye.'

'No more snarl-ups with the new machine?'

'No.'

'So, a good day?'

John looked up from his paper. 'Aye. A clean run. Went like a Derby winner once ah'd readjusted the settings.'

Said chatty enough, but now his brow knotted and his gaze turned inwards. 'Ah'd got it right, but someone must have tampered with it when mah back was turned.'

'That's not likely, is it?' She wished she hadn't said it. Better to have skipped over it. John's claim made her doubt not just his word but his judgement. Both seemed to her to be off kilter.

John just gave her a look that said 'a lot you know', shut his eyes and seemed to nod off.

A knock at the door broke a long silence.

'Ah've kept the cab waiting so ah won't be stopping. Just popped in to greet the new arrival. Mum got word to me.'

Dressed in a fine ivory shirt, cream fitted jacket and nut brown skirt, Iza's sister Violet looked elegant but pale and far, far too thin, as if she'd been hollowed out.

'Ah thought you might want to make use of this. Good as new.' Violet unwrapped a cream satin christening dress. Its intricate lacework bodice was beautifully laundered.

As Iza took the package from Violet's hands her mind conjured up a day many, many years ago when Violet had decided it was time to pass on to her wee sister a rag dolly she'd carried around under her arm for all of her seven or eight years. Though Iza's coveting of the dolly's yellow wool hair and blue gingham dress had been intermittent, and she hadn't much wanted it at that moment, she'd taken it nonetheless, dimly aware that she was less grateful for her big sister's sacrifice than was due.

Violet was looking round the room.

'He's in the crib, ben the bedroom.'

Iza stayed where she was while her sister went through to see the baby. Violet was back and heading for the door in minutes, her face set in a strained smile.

'He's lovely. Ah'll be back to see you both soon.'

'Sit yerself down for a minute.'

Violet didn't sit, but she did stop at the door.

'Mum tells me you're going back to your work.'

'Aye.'

'What on earth for? What about the bairn? Who'll see to him? Mum won't you know.'

'Ah know that.'

'So who'll see to him?'

'Are you offering?'

'No I am not.' Violet's decided tone was belied by a wistful look.

'Ah'm getting a minder.'

Violet laughed. 'You're what? Who do you think you are? You can't.'

'Why can't ah?'

'Leaving your bairn with a stranger. Ah'd never do that.'

'Nobody's asking you to. Anyhow, she's not a stranger, she's a neighbour.'

'You'd think you'd have learnt a lesson or two about motherhood after…'

When Violet stopped short, Iza narrowed eyes at her, daring her to finish. She knew perfectly well what was on her sister's mind. Just because she hadn't dwelt on it all these years didn't mean to say her wee girl was deleted like a piece of text that didn't fit and didn't belong.

'Since you bring up motherhood, ah think you spoil your bairn rotten. To mah way of thinking he'd benefit from being left out of your sight for a minute.'

Violet winced. She was dumbfounded. And, fully aware that her sister treasured her bairn, what with him being her only child and likely to stay that way, Iza felt bad and was about to apologise when Violet said out loud what Iza knew she was thinking.

'You should be there for your bairn and your man who's earning good money. You ought to be ashamed of yourself.'

Iza was well used to Rab saying such things, but her sister?

A rap-a-tap had Violet open the door and take a letter from a postboy's outstretched hand. Without saying another word, she handed it to Iza and was gone, leaving behind a trace of sweet floral scent.

Iza took a quick keek at the envelope, recognised Margaret's hand and stuffed it in her pinnie pocket. The baby was rousing.

Sitting by the bedroom window watching the wee face crease and smooth as the baby sank into sleep, Iza wondered for a second if Violet was right, but she let the idea flit off. Beyond tired now, she sat on in gathering dark. Two whole weeks to doze and wake and doze again, to gather strength for the work's reopening. Someone up there was looking out for her. Shifting her wee bundle to get a handkerchief from her pocket, she felt Margaret's letter. Wincing, she tried to put it from her mind, but it wouldn't go.

With hardly a greeting and no mention of Iza's condition, Margaret launched straight into an account of a meeting she'd just attended. What was odd, and a little alarming, was that the letter read as if Iza knew about the meeting and had asked for an account of it, as though she and Margaret had discussed these matters just the other day, when in fact Iza's recent postcard had been their first contact for a good few months. The meeting at the Women's Social and Political Union offices last night was very lively, Margaret wrote. The invited speaker, Women's Freedom League organiser, Madge Turner, said we are being filled with promises of better wages and conditions, but what use will they be to us if we are shut out? Amelia McLean, a comp at Skinners, reported that 300 women had joined the We Women movement, set up with the aim of keeping the trade open to women and that they planned to set up a union of Edinburgh women compositors, readers and monotype operators. Miss McLean spoke most persuasively. Buckner from the Scottish Typographical Association was roundly challenged about shutting us out and encouraging us to join the Warehousemen and Cutters Union. He was sent packing with a flea in his ear. At the finish I signed the We Women statement. Have you seen it? You must. The letter finished with a plain 'Yours.' That was it. Like it was intended for someone else and Margaret had put it in the wrong envelope. Except that it started off with 'Dear Iza.'

# -5-

They sat to a plate of the year's first tatties from John's allotment. He'd brought a bunch of mint and, for a treat, Iza had bought a pat of butter to melt into burst brown skins. Head dipped over his plate, John hummed to himself between mouthfuls. A glance round the room assured Iza everything was neat and tidy. Another few days of the holiday still to go, the baby was fed and settled so she just had to keep the corner of an ear out for him, and she was hungry and enjoying her food, but still her mind scuttled to those stains she'd noticed on a muslin over the baby-minding neighbour's shoulder. And her house? Not filthy, but not clean enough. Sticky smears on her table, a burned pot in the sink, a dirty cloth on the floor. And her bairns' noses were always running. The trial run was not proving reassuring. And another worry. Was baby William getting all the milk she gave the minder? She thought not, but there was no way to be sure. And, then, the whens and hows of expressing her milk and keeping it good and clean were a worry. Should she ask the minder to bring the baby round to the works at dinner time, once she started back?

Or find a wet nurse and let her own milk dry up? An image of one of the neighbour's snotty-nosed bairns sooking on William's bottle formed in her mind. Aye. Tomorrow she'd ask around for a wet nurse. Should be easy enough. Some poor woman was always losing one round here. As though he'd been listening in on her thoughts, the baby grizzled.

Cooking pot scoured, rinsed, filled with water and set on the stove, she leant over the sink to catch a whisper of a breeze from the open window. The street rang with life. Boys skeltered by, throwing a ball fashioned out of a stuffed and tied bit of trouser leg. Lassies huddled by the kerbside to share secrets or lined up to skip into a length of rope stretched across the road and hauled up and over by a scrawny arm each end. When their skipping chant rose, Iza joined in under her breath: *On the mountain stands a lady, who she is I do not know*. Across the road a couple smooched in the scrub patch, while a wifey leant out of a ground floor window, resting her breasts on the windowsill, listening in to three women having a blether by the stair door. A bank of shadow slid up the tenement wall. Pink dye seeped into a silver-blue sky. Iza pulled rubber teats and valves from two glass feeders, poked them into a bowl of scalding water scooped from the pot and lowered the bottles into the pot.

'No vinegar. No trouble. Away with prejudice, away with old methods.' As usual, John had started with the advertisements in his *Evening Dispatch*. Many a time he'd doze off before he got past them and onto the news. When Iza sat opposite him to do her mending she caught a glimpse of the front page. Trouble in the Welsh coalfields. Threading the needle, her eyes swam and the cotton was no sooner in the eye than it was out again, snagged on horny fingers. She peered to re-thread it, kept missing, dumped the mending down. How on earth had anyone the patience for this? Maybe Rab's wife Jeannie would do laundry and mending for her for a bob or so? Rab wouldn't like it though. Violet? She knew just what Violet would say. Violet would say you should be at home doing your own laundry.

She studied John studying his paper. He'd stopped reading aloud but his lips still moved and his forehead creased as he puzzled then smoothed as he humphed in a 'Well, fancy that.' When a voice called out in the street below, he lifted his head and, mouth slightly ajar, looked over at the window. A man off to the pub was calling up to his chum and John looked like he was waiting for the answer. Iza felt a rush of affection tinged with sadness. She wanted that voice to be calling to John, wanted him to be going to the window to call down to his chum 'Hang on. Ah'm just coming.' But John didn't appear to have a chum to call to him and he rarely went out for a drink. Then, at the same time, she didn't want that at all. She wanted John here in his chair, reading his paper, so she could feel his presence even as she ignored it, so she could ask him where her scissors had got to and get irritated when he fussed about looking for them, so she could see him kept safe from the scorn of men like Rab and Jack. And, then, who was she to talk about having no chums? Where were all hers? Grace and Lizzie? Just work chums.

Not a cheep from the bedroom. She went through to check, heard a crackling in the baby's chest, and, in dusky light, saw a flush to his cheeks. His forehead was clammy to the back of her hand. She opened the window then carried the baby to it, took off his cap, loosened his arms from the swaddling, and watched the quick pumping of his wee chest under his bodice.

232

'There, there, wee lamb. Is that better now?'

Red soon faded from his cheeks, his chest eased and his limbs slackened, but even as she saw and felt the effects of cool air she doubted herself. Always keep them well wrapped, away from draughts. She'd heard it so often it must be right. She wrapped him up and set him down on the bed, lay on her side by him, nuzzled his stiff dark hair.

'Ah'm away out for a drink.'

Framed in the doorway, John looked sparse, like a single tree left where a clump had been felled. Iza was pleased by his surprising announcement. 'A game of crib maybe?' she said encouragingly.

'Aye. We'll see.'

If her dad could see her now. A bedroom to herself – excepting the sleeping tot of course – and a set-in bed, like the one her mother and she used to share, for John alone. Who'd credit it? She strolled round their two rooms, smoothing bedclothes, angling her good-as-new white wicker chair in its corner, tucking seats under the table, wiping an already clean draining board. After dusting the mantelpiece, she stood with her back to an empty, swept fireplace, trying to conjure her father to her side.

'Well, Dad. We'll not be witched the night.'

And she almost succeeded, almost saw his face and smelt his tobacco and oil and turpentine, but he was too exposed in this empty house and would not settle. He'd find much the same were he to visit Violet, she realised. What if her dad were to visit William and find him not set up in a good job after staying on at school, but in some crummy lodging house in Leith? Didn't bear thinking about. Rab's then? Enough folk in that house for their dad's ghost to slip in unnoticed. But if he did go in there for a look-see, the sight of his wife biding in the house of a stranger – for Jeannie and her mother and her two bairns would be strangers to him – would have him confounded. Better to cease her conjuring, leave her dad in peace.

The street had fallen quiet, light dimmed to dark mercury. Resting in her armchair, head back, she told her sister about the hot baby, about unwrapping him. Alone, eyes unfocused in near-dark, she could talk to a phantom, attentive Violet. Well, at least Iza could talk. Soon as her mind wandered to the neighbour's filthy muslin and likely wet nurses, her sister had things to say and no mistake. And when, despite herself, her thoughts drifted to the union business, the strike notice she's signed, she was most definitely talking to herself alone.

She pictured Violet setting down a piece of embroidery to draw her curtains, the same lined maroon curtains with a gold border Violet made for her first house, the house where Iza and John had had their wedding tea, the tea that was supposed to be at Nelson's Social Institute, 'cept there was a muddle with the booking, then was to be at John's parents' house, 'cept his mother's nerves hadn't been up to it.

Deep red glow of a banked fire, yellow flames licking up back bricks. Cake stand piled with shop-bought meringues in fluted white nests, set in the centre of a starched white tablecloth. Iza's mother in Violet's kitchenette, slicing and buttering bread, elbows clacking, pinnie ties loose down her lumpy rear-end. Iza trying to help but being urged by her mother and Violet to go and stand by the door to greet her guests. John leaving her side to tinker with glasses and tumblers, sorting them into sets, into pairs, shifting odd ones to the back, straightening the lines, starting again, as if everything depended on it, so that he was not by her side with a tray of poured drinks when guests came in pinched white by frost, stamping their feet. A March day, still in the thick of winter. Violet's husband Angus taking coats and hats through to the bedroom. Violet weaving her way to the table with a baked ham on a platter. Rab and Jeannie, not long wed, sat on a bench eating bread and ham as though they'd been side-by-side for a hundred years. Jack was away to Glasgow for a boxing championship. William was working, but he'd try to get there. Jamie was at the centre of things.

The guests filled the small room to bursting, yet still the clusters of Rosses and Orrs – one of John's three sisters and three of his four brothers, two with wives in tow – managed to keep bare floorspace between them. By marrying, Iza and John had drawn two families into the same room for a couple of hours, but neither quite had it in them to tack the seam, and it was left to Jamie, and John's father, both metalworkers, to forge a link of sorts. They shared tots from bottles of whisky they'd brought, offered them round, drank much of it themselves. Jamie toasted the bride and groom, again. Rab chipped in with a surprisingly gracious toast to the couple doing their bit for the historic amalgamation of Edinburgh's machinemen and compositors' unions, then spoilt it by launching into a lecture on female labour. Iza was giving Rab daggers when John's big brother Alex, twice the bulk of John, bashed into a tray of drinks and sent them crashing to the floor. As folk shuffled clear of shattered glass and Violet's broom, John's father set about Alex. Cursing something rotten, he strode up to him and gave him a skelp round the lugs. Alex was a good foot taller, so his father had to stretch up to do it, but he didn't miss and Alex cowered and let out a yelp. Iza wasn't the only one shocked. Alex was a grown man, for goodness sake. When John rushed to the scene, Iza saw the look of black rage and white hatred he aimed at his father's back before skirting round him to pat a bumbling Alex on the back and whisper to him.

Through all this the bairns had been mingling well enough around and under the table, but now scuffling arms and legs caught at the tablecloth and rocked the cake stand, getting them sent out to play, all except Violet's Victor who had to be wrapped up warm and got left behind, and Jamie and Jessie's eldest two, the twins, who, in their last year of school, louched by the window, the lad with an eye on the street, the girl with an eye on proceedings in the room, and particularly on Iza.

Tall for her age, sallow complexioned and dark eyed, Della-Mary would have stood out among the Rosses had she not had a way of making herself scarce in company, of setting herself apart without drawing attention. Hard to tell what she was thinking, but she had the look of someone full of thinking. Though Iza had plenty to occupy her, still she'd been feeling the girl's watchful eyes on her, and she was steeling herself to go over and have a word, to ask how she was doing at school, when she saw the girl catch her dad's eye, saw them both look in her direction. Next thing, Jamie was by Iza's side, leaning to whisper 'Can ah have a word?' He nodded to a quietish corner of the room and she followed him there.

'She's asking about getting into the caseroom when she finishes school in the summer. Can you get her in?' Jamie didn't need to say who 'she' was.

Iza's heart pounded. For a thrilling moment, she saw herself leading the girl, her daughter, through the bindery, through the casting room and into the caseroom; heard herself name stone, frame, case; saw the girl's face glow. Quick as they came, though, the thrill and glow were gone.

'No, ah can't,' she said. 'They're not taking on any new learner girls.'

'Right you are. Ah'll tell her. Unless you want to?' There was a rare challenge and tinge of bitterness in Jamie's voice.

'No. Best if you do.'

Excusing herself and avoiding the girl's gaze, Iza went to attend to John's mother, who'd been sitting by the door looking a bit too like a lavatory attendant for her liking. Hat still on, Mrs Orr was gawping at a meringue on a plate on her lap as though it might talk to her. Iza had noticed that she had a way of twisting her head and cocking an ear as though attending to a sound just beyond hearing.

'He's a sick man you know,' Mrs Orr muttered.

'Who? Your husband?'

She took a good look at Iza before saying 'Aye. Him.'

When Iza followed Mrs Orr's eyes they landed on John. He was scanning the room as though trying in bright sunlight to spot a familiar face among strangers in a park. He straightened his narrow black tie and plucked at invisible specks on his sleeve. Iza went to him and touched his arm. He patted her hand then went to join Alex, who was sitting hunched in a corner.

After the last of the guests had left William turned up in a bottle green velveteen jacket, book sticking out of a frayed pocket. He asked had he missed the music, which made Iza sad, then, riffling in his pocket as though he'd just remembered, he handed her a flat, square ivory box with a lattice carving of vines and birds. He showed her how the lid slid off and tipped into her palm two wafer-thin squares that broke into a pile of wee geometric pieces.

While Iza tried, and failed, to fit the pieces back, William took a mouth organ from his pocket and played a sailors' hornpipe.

The longcase clock struck the hour. As she counted chimes, roaring fire, meringues, wedding guests, William and his jaunty tune, faded, dissolved. The girl, Della-Mary, was last to go. At the stroke of eleven, two pieces lingered: ivory box and shattered glass. First, she attended to the glass. That incident, she realised, had taught her that another's life, their family relations, were as foreign a world as you could imagine. John's face! Pure hatred for his father one second, tenderest love for his brother the next. Did she have such feelings? Pure hatred for Rab? Tenderest love for her wee brother William? Something like it, maybe, but nothing as raw and pure as she'd seen in John. Brothers and sisters tussled as part of their growing and Rab and she had always rubbed each other up the wrong way, even before her becoming a frock-at-the-frame set a match to it. Her heart went out to her husband for being so torn.

And there was William's ivory puzzle box with pride of place on her mantelpiece, by the wooden letter-holder she'd prop her pay packet in soon as she got in of a Saturday, where it would stay till John got in and they'd sit together and she'd empty two pay packets on the table and John would watch as she counted and wrote the family accounts in an exercise book. As she got up, fingered the ivory box and blew specks of dust from its crevices, her blessings counted themselves: lovely box in a spic-and-span two apartment house, a husband who'll serve, a healthy baby boy and her place in the Ency Brit chumship at Bellevue safe and sound.

Still wide awake though the clock had chimed twelve, she

lay in bed listening to the front door open, to John shuffling towards the bedroom, to a tiny clink as he took hold of the doorknob, at which point she called out 'Goodnight John,' turned over and listened to him pad across to the set-in bed.

In the still of night she woke with a start. Margaret! All those folk swilling around at her wedding do and she'd erased Margaret from the scene. Margaret who'd been her witness and whose smiles through the crowded room had steadied her. She reached to the bedpost for her pinnie, took Margaret's letter from the pocket and put it under her pillow. She must meet up with Margaret. The morn's morn she'd see about a wet nurse. Then she'd take a tram up to the Bridges and walk up to St Leonards.

# – 6 –

She knew Mrs Cossar only in passing. They'd shared the odd word in the grocers of a Saturday afternoon and greetings as they passed in the street of a Sunday, though one time a few weeks before their confinement they'd found time for a blether. Iza thought she had two or three weeks to go, Mrs Cossar about the same. If he carried on like this, Iza's would kick his way out any minute, feel this. Mrs Cossar's quiet wee thing was content to stay curled up asleep. A lassie she was sure, making the most of peace and quiet while she could get it. With a sad smile, she'd patted her lump. It was her fourth, her sixth counting the stillbirths. And she'd started her family late, though not as late as Iza. Mrs Cossar had been reassuring. Aye, it hurt like the devil but there was a good end to it, if they were for this world. Iza didn't say she well knew about the pains. They'd had a moan about heaving great lumps up and down stairs, parted, and hadn't bumped into each other since. Iza couldn't remember who'd told her about Mrs Cossar's wee lassie. You always heard.

Mucky boots, a broken chair, a burned pot, scuffed

newspapers for a doormat littered the other door two floors up, but Mrs Cossar's side of the landing was scrubbed, they had a nice doormat and a door fresh painted. Baby William slung in one arm, a bag of plums in the other, Iza nearly used her full hands as an excuse to leave the poor woman be, but she took a deep breath and knocked. Mrs Cossar stood ironing a stack of laundry with one of those new kerosine irons. Her bairns were at the table crayoning, the eldest lassie, in a fresh green gingham dress, playing schoolmistress.

'Have you come to see our wee sister?' a wee boy said, climbing down off his seat.

The baby lay in a white-painted coffin set on a wooden chair near the fireplace. A white satin dress had been carefully tucked down her sides and over her feet. She wore a white lace-edged bonnet. A wispy fair curl stuck to her forehead looked almost alive.

'She looks lovely,' Iza said.

'Aye. Bless her. We've had a fair few in to see her today,' Mrs Cossar said.

'Was she ailing from the start?'

Mrs Cossar said she'd been fine until she'd taken a good keek at the world and hadn't thought much to it. Iza said that it must have been something she'd caught sight of outside, not in this house, that the house was kept lovely. Mrs Cossar admired Iza's baby then busied herself putting the plums in a glass bowl. She offered a cup of tea or coffee.

'Ah won't keep you,' Iza said, fishing out a wad of scrap paper she'd brought for the bairns. 'Ah just wanted to ask. Just say no if...'

'Go on. Take the weight off.'

'Ah wondered if you'd nurse him for me while ah'm at mah work. Ah don't want to impose. Just say no.'

Hugging herself, rocking slightly and looking through

Iza to the far wall, Mrs Cossar didn't answer. She'd just pulled heavy eyes back into the room and leant forward to talk when her husband came in – the bow-legged man with a limp who whistled down the road of a morning and who you'd catch still whistling, though quieter now, if you passed him coming back at nightfall. Iza got up saying she'd come back another time, but the Cossars both said no, no. After kissing his wife on the cheek, Mr Cossar stood for a bit over the coffin, hands clasped to his chest, lips moving but making no sound, before going to the table to study his bairns' drawings from different angles, telling them how clever they were, lifting a wee boy to the ceiling and swinging him round upside down before letting him slither to the floor.

'Mrs Orr was asking if ah'd nurse the wee one while she's at her work.'

Mr Cossar blinked and cocked an ear to hear what more his wife had to say.

'What do you think?' she asked him.

'It's up to you. Whatever's best for you.'

'A neighbour's minded him these past few days. Ah was expressing mah milk for her. But it's not working out and we're back to work Monday,' Iza explained.

When the wee boy made to give his dead baby sister a bite of his plum, Mr Cossar gently stayed his hand.

'You'll want to think about it. Ah'll call back the morn if that's all right.' Iza stood up and edged towards the door.

'No. No,' Mrs Cossar said. 'It'll help him, the wee lamb. It'll help you. And it might help me. If it's not too late, that is.' She was up and pacing now, her eyes brighter. 'We can always find out. Will he be hungry?'

'Aye. He's always hungry.'

Crossing to the sink, Mrs Cossar bared first one breast

then the other to clean crusted nipples under a running tap. After drying her breasts with a clean towel, she sat and held out her arms for the baby. Watching the wee mouth putter and latch on set Iza's nipples on edge. The baby wriggled, arched his back. Iza watched Mrs Cossar cup his head, rock him gently, shift him to the other breast where he settled. Just what a mother should be like, Iza thought. She looked about her. Just what a family should be like. Like in a story. The thought had her smiling. Were they ever at odds? Hard to imagine. They must be though. Surely. If you were working on this story and read it out, someone, Netta, would say 'Oh aye, and when do the bairns start fighting; the woman bawling ah'm sick to death of the lot of you; her man out the door to the pub quick as his legs'll carry him?' Iza found herself thinking back to when she was wee, comparing. Her family hadn't been so bad, not as families go. Vi Ross always kept them clean and fed. But she'd never taken much interest beyond that. Iza's dad had though, sometimes, when he was well enough.

When Iza took the sleeping baby back from Mrs Cossar's arms he smelt different. Mr Cossar saw her down the stair. At the front door he followed her eyes over tenement roofs to where Bellevue's chimneys scored the sky.

'You work at Bellevue, eh? A compositor?' With a slight tilt of head and lowering of voice, Mr Cossar apologised for being nosey, for voicing the common knowledge of the street about everyone's business, while conveying something like high regard.

'So you might be at home yourself soon, eh? From what they're saying in the papers about the elimination of female labour?' His voice was tender.

'No. We're getting to stay. At least that's what they're telling us.'

'It'll be hard on you, eh, what with the bairn and all?'

'Knowing he'll be in good hands will help.' Iza nodded up the stair.

'They say the women are divided on it, some with the men, some against?'

'Aye. Mah chum's been going to meetings with suffrage women and that.'

'They certainly have a strong case. But then, so do the other side, what with the undercutting of wages.' Mr Cossar pondered before saying 'So what do you make of it?'

Iza studied his face. Though it was coarser and fleshier, she saw something of Mr Scott, Margaret's dad, in it. Same keen eyes alight with interest and concern and understanding. A good soul, she thought. She opened her mouth to reply. He wanted to know her opinion and she'd like to give him it, but she could hardly inform him on a matter that, hard as it was to miss talk and newspaper accounts of the We Women movement, she'd managed to keep at arms length. That she could not satisfy Mr Cossar's curiosity was, she knew, a pity, because he was, she sensed, a person who would take a reasoned, balanced view, and these days that was a rare thing.

# – 7 –

On the last Saturday of the holiday Iza boarded a tram for town. Margaret had replied to her postcard straight away to say yes, she'd love to meet up, which was grand, except she'd gone on to mention a Women's Freedom League tea that day. Iza would be more than welcome. It should be fine to bring the wee one. They'd be among modern women. 'I confess their ideas have on occasion shocked me,' she wrote.

Iza tutted. 'I confess?' 'On occasion?' Doesn't sound like Margaret. And why on earth would ah want to go to a Women's Freedom League tea? Couldn't Margaret give it a miss? But then she chided herself. Of course, her old chum hadn't been sitting at home for years waiting for her to grace her with a visit. She'd been at outdoor women's suffrage rallies and fundraising bring and buys. Her postcards had been full of it. Except for the big suffrage procession the previous year, Iza had never seen it close at hand. And that day Princes Street had been so thick with folk she'd only got keeks at floats of women in costumes and marching bands and ranks of banners and a wee lassie playing the pipes, red in the face and getting out of puff trying to keep up. Along with thousands of other folk, she and John had gone to gawp, but seeing as John didn't like being in a crowd they hadn't stayed.

She'd go to this tea affair with Margaret, she decided. It'd make a change. Get her out of herself. Besides, she could take advantage of having found the best wet nurse money could buy. Mrs Cossar would mind the baby. Get him settled into it before the holiday was out.

Margaret was waiting at the tram stop by the Bridges. She wore a crisp white blouse and a lovely duck-egg blue skirt. Her hair was longer, tied back in a small loop under a pert hat. She was thinner and her features looked sharper, but the smile that made Iza feel special was the same as ever. She said Iza didn't look like she'd been with child. Skinny as ever. Iza looked down at her baggy chest and gave Margaret a quizzical look. They walked arm-in-arm up the Bridges as though they'd done it regularly since that evening after their trip to Musselburgh, all these years ago. The streets had been dark and quiet that night. Now they were bright and bustling with street hawkers and working folk at their ease.

When Margaret asked after the baby it sounded like politeness rather than interest. Iza said he was fine and left it at that. But she'd misjudged. Margaret now spoke with passion as she said how proud she was of her, a married woman and a mother to boot, staying at her frame, refusing to give up her job.

'You're a fine example of womanhood,' she announced, clenching Iza's hand and raising it high. 'A pioneer.'

Iza gave a derisory laugh and, when Margaret's raised eyebrows asked for an explanation, said, 'You want to tell that to mah brother Rab and listen to what he has to say about me and examples of womanhood.'

Margaret looked at her with concern. 'I've been worrying about you,' she said, her face turned serious. 'We hear the Neills' lassies are backing the men. Terrible, eh? It must be putting you in an awful position.'

Iza gulped. How stupid. She could have seen this coming. But in days of sleeping on of a morning after interrupted nights, of boiling and hanging out nappies and bathing and applying salve to sore nipples, of sitting on a grassy bank by the river, baby asleep in her lap, hearing bees buzz and birds sing, the Edinburgh Typographical Society and their blessed dispute had barged in the door once or twice only to be shooed away. And now here she was, setting out for a merry get-together with her old chum on their old stamping ground, wanting to talk about it, needing to, and yet without having put her mind to it. Viewed from her frame in Neills' caseroom, siding with the men, after a bit of umming and ahhing, had seemed the most sensible thing in the world. Viewed from here, from the place where she used to belong, it might very well look otherwise.

She took time to collect herself before saying simply 'Aye. Not easy,' as she pulled away from Margaret to stop by a drapers' window.

'This used to be McReadie's greengrocers. Ah mind one day some bairns from our street grabbing apples and running off with them and me and a chum got nabbed by old McReadie when we hadn't even got a sniff of an apple.'

'What happened?'

'He shut us in his storeroom. Said he was going to get the polis. Ah mind the reek of onions. There was a crate of pears and mah chum was stuffing one up her jumper when he opened the door and frightened the life out of us.'

Though what happened next was hardly worth relating,

she was about to do just that when bells struck three and Margaret was off, saying they'd be late, she didn't want to miss the speaker. Iza hurried after, puzzled, anxious. A speaker at a tea? What was that about?

Half way down a street of big detached houses they turned in through a scrolled ironwork gate and up a paved path that led to what might have been the very house Roddy Mac had disappeared into all those years ago. Half built then, its stonework was now draped in deep green foliage. After following Margaret through a porch and glossy red door, propped open by a brass dog, Iza found herself softening her tread along a wood-panelled lobby, aware of the clomp of her boots, loathe to draw attention, feeling as though she were sneaking in unbidden. A murmur of voices guided them to a large bay-windowed room where a good twenty or thirty women sat. As they entered, voices were hushing as heads turned to a stocky woman who'd taken up a stance in front of a banner draped from a huge black mantelpiece. Emblazoned with a thistle, the banner was in the same green, white and gold as the sash the woman wore across her high-collared white shirt.

A tall, angular woman in an ill-fitting beige linen suit came to greet Margaret, shook her hand, smiled at Iza and introduced herself in a deep whisper as Mrs Sinclair. Pressing a finger to her lips, she ushered them to seats in the bay window. Iza kept her head down, but from under her brows she recognised a few faces from Ballantyne's caseroom. That surprised her. She wouldn't have imagined her old work chums, apart from Margaret of course, coming to such a tea. And where was the tea? No sign of it.

'We're just about to start,' Mrs Sinclair whispered. Before she left them she bent to pin green, white and gold ribbons on their blouses.

The woman by the fireplace cleared her throat.

'Ladies, sisters, women of Edinburgh.' She swept a hand round the room then paused to hold it up and, smiling and dipping her head toward two men, called out, 'Ah, and gentlemen. Welcome all to our wee gathering.' Her voice was flutey and nasal.

Iza missed what she said next. She had an awful feeling she'd leaked on her blouse. Since working at the frame with milk-full breasts didn't bear thinking about, they'd agreed that as well as nursing during the day Mrs Cossar would express milk into bottles for night and early morning feeds. They'd begun the routine to get ready for holiday's end, but Iza's milk hadn't yet dried and Mrs Cossar's advice to apply cabbage leafs and avoid breast binding meant a constant green-tinged seepage. Arms crossed over her chest, she lowered her head and fingered her hair as if to tidy it, then drew her palms down to feel for damp. Aye. Wet. It would be showing. She bent her arms to clasp her shoulders, trying, by holding her head high, to make it look as though she always sat that way.

'... the peculiar helplessness of women...'

These, the first of the speaker's words to reach Iza's ears, made her wince. Could have been aimed at me, she thought. But then she felt a burst of irritation. 'Speak for yourself,' she muttered under her breath, then bit her lip when Margaret gave her a warning look.

'... the men printers exclude them, the master printers exploit them and the women printers have no right of appeal.' The speaker's hand beat the three parts into the air: men printers, swipe; master printers, thump; women printers, whack. After a slight tremor in her voice on 'no right,' she clipped 'appeal' off clean, tilted her head and held silence for a second.

Iza felt blood drain from her face. 'What's she on about? Why's she talking about us?' she whispered to Margaret.

'Ssshh,' Margaret hissed.

'The men of the medical profession tried to prevent women from engaging in their work. Now it and other professions once closed to them are open to women. Everywhere the clock moves forward, except in the printing trade, where men mean to set it back.' The speaker drew a circle in the air, forwards then backwards. 'But you have not come here today to listen to me,' she continued. 'You already know what I think.'

'Aye. You think we're daft.' Iza muttered, hearing Agnes's voice in her ear.

'... a marvellous woman, a woman who plies the trade of compositor and who will not be cajoled or gulled by empty promises, who will not stand by and see women deprived of the opportunity to embark on, or remain in, a trade for which they are eminently suited and in which they have been employed for the past thirty and more years, who will not stand by and allow the total elimination of the employment of women in typesetting.'

As the speaker paused to let the weight of this sink in, Iza felt blood flood her cheeks.

'You didn't say. Why didn't you say?' she hissed in Margaret's ear.

Margaret laid a hand on her arm. 'Wait till you hear her,' she whispered before clamping a finger to her lips.

Iza took a quick keek round the room: lovely burgundy wallpaper; ornate white cornice; big gilt-framed portrait of a gentleman above the fireplace; crystal vase of lilies on a fine-grained occasional table. 'Who do they think they are?' she thought to herself.

'Ladies, gentlemen...' Again, the speaker paused to poke

her chin at the two men and wait while one of them half-stood and took a mock bow. As light laughter rippled, she held out a hand to announce, 'I give you Amelia McLean of the We Women's movement and...' She lifted a card and, putting on pince-nez, read 'the newly inaugurated Women's Compositors, Readers and Monotype Operators Union.'

'The Skinners' woman? You should have told me,' Iza muttered. When two women in front looked over their shoulders, eyebrows raised, she scowled at them.

'Ssshhh,' Margaret hissed, as a striking, dark-haired woman with a single string of jet beads tight round her long neck stood, took her place in front of the banner, peered at a notebook then took off her spectacles.

Amelia McLean set out too fast and not quite loud enough, but she took a deep breath, stood taller and cleared her throat. 'Sisters,' she said, 'I won't bore you with the intricacies of a matter you are all thoroughly familiar with by now. What I want to say to you, loud and clear, is that it is inconceivable that nowadays men should be allowed to dictate in the high-handed fashion of the male operatives what women shall do and shall not do. The men complain that we women are not organised. But the Edinburgh Typographical Society, and their national body, the Scottish Typographical Association, have excluded us from their organisation.'

The audience was rapt and Iza could see why. There was passion in her every word, but no trace of hectoring. She spoke well, in a clear, low, unaffected voice. There was no fuss about her manner either. The fact that she was addressing these women, gathered in a grand house, about caseroom matters angered Iza, but, try as she might, she couldn't dispute the truth of what this woman was saying.

'Now that we are organised, now that over 400 women

have signed the We Women statement in opposition to our exclusion, they say our society is a bogus union.' A pause, a tilt of her head and, lowering her voice further where others might raise it, she said, 'Well, I say, if that is so they have nothing to fear from it.'

As Amelia McLean paused to sip from a tumbler of water while the room rang with 'hear hear' and applause, Margaret whispered, 'She's amazing, eh?'

Iza said nothing.

'But I must report to you that the saddest part in this affair is that women in one or two of the larger firms are supporting the men. They have been filled with the promise of better wages, better conditions. The fact is that if women are shut out of the print industry, better wages will be of no use to them. They will certainly be of no use to generations of women to come. This ugly fact the men have taken care to gloss over.'

Without willing it, Iza's hand rose to clamp her open mouth. This was awful. It was as though she'd been standing well back from the estuary shore watching far-off waves and now water was lapping her feet, her ankles, her knees. She looked for a boulder to stand on. She found one. But they're not shutting us out, she thought. Not taking on new learner lassies for a few years is *not* shutting us out.

'The men say they are not seeking our elimination. A mere pause in taking on young women is what they claim to be seeking. But mark my words, they mean to see us gone from the caseroom.'

Slithering off that boulder, Iza found another to clamber on. But you're not addressing the heart of the matter. Cheap labour. The men are right. They can't stand by and see wages driven down. How would folk live?

'The men say it is about cheap labour,' Amelia McLean

said, 'but by refusing us representation they have done nothing to remedy that.'

Iza's hand slipped to clasp her throat as she stared at Amelia McLean. Like she's reading my mind, she thought. But that's daft. Impressive she may be, but she's not a mind-reader. Truth is she's thought about both sides of the matter while I have not. This realisation was a big wave hitting.

'The men have recently shown a curious and novel diligence in coaxing, bribing and even frightening lassies and women into joining a trade union. But not *their* trade union. Not *our* trade union. Their answer is to bring in a male organiser from the south to cajole women into an inferior English union, the Warehousemen and Cutters Union, a union of unskilled workers.'

'That's not right,' Iza muttered. But she couldn't have said whether she meant that Amelia McLean's claims were false or that her claims were true and that that truth was an injustice. Both at once? No. It couldn't be. It had to be one or the other.

'Fortunately, the majority of women compositors cannot see their way to joining that union, for we are skilled worker just as male compositors are.'

True enough, Iza thought.

'And having been refused admittance to the union for skilled workers, we have no alternative but to form a union of our own.'

Aye, ah see your point.

'Our movement is resolved to keep the trade open to women and to better the conditions of women presently employed. And with your support we shall do so.'

You might at that, Iza thought. You've certainly got the gumption.

Amelia McLean finished with a call for everyone present to attend a coming mass meeting at the Assembly Rooms. 'A meeting called by the men's union, so we will not be given a platform to put our case. But we will speak from the floor. We will make our voices heard. And they will listen.'

A rattle of crockery announced two maids wheeling trolleys of tea and sandwiches and folk were up out of their seats, gathered in groups to sip and eat and talk. Iza stayed in her seat. It was easy enough to make excuses to Margaret – aches and pains from the birth, you know – and after bringing her tea in a fluted white cup and a plate with a sandwich on a doily Margaret left her to join a wee group of women Iza recognised. When Margaret leant in to say something, the women looked over, smiling smiles that seemed to Iza forced. One of them beckoned her, but she stayed put, nibbling a sandwich she'd no appetite for. She couldn't have begun to talk to these women, her old work chums from Pauls. She felt foolish. Confounded. Dead tired. She had to get out of here. First, though, she needed the cludgie. She'd go and find it then slip away.

As she was frantically eyeing dark wood doors in the hallway, Mrs Sinclair startled her.

'The powder room?' she hailed. 'Just here.'

The cludgie was an Aladdin's cave. It had a sink with hot water, sweet-smelling soap and a clean, fluffy towel. Iza took off her blouse and bodice to rinse out stains and bathe her breasts. She took time to relieve herself before redressing. She checked her front. The damp didn't show too much and out in the sun it would soon dry.

She'd got safely to the front door when Margaret called after her.

'Ah have to be getting home,' Iza mouthed to her.

'Don't go yet. Stay a bit, eh?' Margaret called, beckoning with an outstretched hand.

She'd got a hand to the gate when Margaret clutched her shoulder. When she turned, Margaret took hold of both of her hands as though for a dance. Her expression was not inviting, though.

'You won't sign to strike with the men, will you?' Margaret said, half pleading, half instructing. Then, before Iza could think of an answer, she said 'You'll tell your work chums at Bellevue not to sign, won't you?'

This was pure instruction and Margaret was gripping her hands so tight it hurt. She wrenched them away.

'They're not getting rid of us, Margaret. It's just no new lassies for a few years.' She meant to fling the words, but they were too lightweight to carry far.

'You believe that?' Margaret didn't need to add, 'More fool you.' Her face said it. 'Every week women leave to get wed. More and more are getting too old for it. We're not replaced and before we know it there'll be just a handful of spinsters like me. If they get this through, it'll be the finish.'

Iza took a step back, stuck out her chin. 'Ah didn't leave when ah got wed.'

'But we're not talking about you,' Margaret snapped. 'We're talking about our trade being closed to the daughter you might have had.'

Eyes on the ground, Iza scrabbled about in her mind. Margaret didn't know about the girl, did she? As far as she knows mah bairn's a boy, not a girl. She chewed her lip. Even so, it was too feeble a point to be voiced. Unworthy. She scrabbled some more. Give it a few short years and learner girls will be stepping to the frame, fumbling with setting sticks, sniffing in fumes. Though she didn't say it and Margaret said nothing, she heard her response. You truly believe that? She winced. Ah, but you lot in Pauls haven't reckoned with the likes of Agnes and Lizzie. The men are as likely to fly through the air to singing white sands on a coral island as they are to budge Agnes Galloway. She raised and turned her head to look towards Canonmills, towards Agnes and Lizzie. But her view was blocked by a bush's thick glossy leaves and pink flowers and, when she stretched to look over it, by solid stone walls of a huge house whose roof hid the red crags. From where she now stood, Agnes and her like were nowhere to be seen. She had no more answers. She opened the gate. When she turned and looked Margaret in the eye, all she could find to say was, 'Ah need to think about it.'

Margaret held out a journal. 'Amelia McLean's got an article in here. Read it,' she said.

And Iza took it and, holding it in pinched fingers as if it might burn, left.

# – 8 –

Her head swirled. To the fore, rows of pale rapt faces brayed 'hear-hear'. Elbowing through them, Agnes's round, freckled face yelled, 'She said what? And you just sat there listening?' And while Rab snarled from the sidelines, a ghostly, silent Della-Mary stood at the work's gate watching and waiting. Hurrying, close to running to escape her own thoughts, Iza wove along teaming pavement and across busy streets. How she did so without bashing into folk or being mown down by a cart or cab or one of the motor cars that roared along she couldn't have said. First thing she knew she was in Buccleuch Street staring in the window of Jim Connolly's cobblers shop.

'All workers must make common cause.' The words chimed in her ears. Grand words. But where's the common cause in this matter, eh? You tell me that. James Connolly might just have had the answer, but James Connolly was not sitting at his last. Instead of boots and shoeblack and laces and a fine-looking man with a book on a music stand, her eyes were on second-hand washtubs, wooden tongs and irons stacked round a rusty mangle. James Connolly was in

Dublin. She'd read about it. After catching a headline, she'd waited till John put the paper down. Edinburgh agitator returns to Dublin. He'd been in America, it seemed, but other than that she hadn't taken much of it in. As she'd laid John's paper down, a sinking heart had made her aware she'd been after seeing Roddy Mac's name.

She needed to talk to somebody about this business. Somebody on the outside of it. But who? Mr Scott came to mind, but she couldn't go to Margaret's dad, not behind her chum's back, supposing she was still her chum. And, anyhow, she couldn't admit to Mr Scott she'd signed the strike notice when she hadn't had the guts to tell Margaret.

'Ah don't know what to do.'

'What are you saying, hen?'

Iza hadn't noticed the old woman by her side.

'Och, talking to yerself were ye?' the woman said.

Iza gave her a wan smile. 'Ah was talking to that mangle.'

'Aye, well, you'll get more sense out of it than some folks ah could mention. Ah'm needing an iron. Wonder how much that one is?'

'Ah was just telling the mangle ah don't know what to do.'

'And did it give you an answer?' The woman gave her a gap-toothed grin.

'Aye it did. It said to go and see mah wee brother,' Iza said before she knew it.

'And have you got a wee brother to go and see?'

'Aye.'

'See. Like ah said. More sense than some.'

She would. She'd go down to Leith, to the pub. She'd go and find William. Though he might not have much to say on the matter that confounded her, he'd set her to rights. Even when he said things she'd never thought of, things that opened up a gulf that made her sad, William never made her feel stupid. The baby would be fine. She'd told Mrs Cossar she might be a bit late and Mrs Cossar had said fine, don't you worry yourself.

Crossing Princes Street to head for Leith Walk she wavered for a moment. What was the name of the pub William worked in again? Did he say? A tram's horn blasted and she leapt back as it rollocked by within an inch of her. Safe on the other side of the street she looked up at the big clock. Six o'clock. The pubs should be fairly quiet. She still couldn't mind the name, but William had said the top of Leith Walk. There couldn't be that many pubs there, could there?

There were though. Every second door led into a pub. The first one she came to wasn't at all quiet. A rabble of men who'd already had a skinful lounged round its door. She walked on, unable to bring herself to squeeze past them to take a look inside. Last drinking day of the holiday. All the pubs would likely be full even at this early hour. She had hold of the door handle of the next one, which was quieter, before she lost her nerve. But just along a bit the Alan Breck looked inviting and she walked straight into its dim interior and up to the bar, noting but ignoring glances from men lounging there. One of them smiled and raised a glass to her. She gave him a nod and went to the other end. No barman in sight.

'Can ah get you a drink, hen?'

The one who'd raised his glass had edged along the bar. She told him no thanks, she was looking for her wee brother. He came to her side and leant on the bar. Ah'm sure to know him if he's a regular, he slurred. What does he call himself? Something was telling Iza she should get out of here but she wasn't listening. She moved aside to

259

put a few inches between her arm and his. He works behind the bar, she explained. Not sure this is the right pub, mind. The man kept his distance. Though he'd had a good skinful, he seemed harmless enough. What's his handle? he asked. William Ross. Short, clean-shaven, hair that needs a cut, she told him. Wee Willie? Aye. Course ah know him. Shouting, 'Willie. Customer,' he lifted and shook a brass bell.

Emerging from a back room with bottles in hand William saw her straight off. He showed no sign of surprise. He smiled and said, 'Evenin. What can ah get you?' then 'mind out' to warn her to keep her sleeve clear of spillage. Like ah'm any old boozer she thought. But no. Not a bit of it. The way he smiled as he wiped the bar told her he was pleased as punch to see her. Though he asked for no explanation for her visit, Iza felt the need to give one. It was as though some mysterious force had brought her she told him. One minute she was in St Leonards having a blether with a wise man she once met, only he'd disguised himself as a mangle and got an old crone in league with him, next thing she was in here. What did William think to that?

'Ah think you've had a few already,' William said as he poured drinks, lifted the hatch and led her to a bench and table near the door which, apart from an old boy lodged in the corner, was free.

'Try that,' he said, setting down a half of beer and a shot of whisky.

'Ah can't drink that,' she said.

'Course you can. Get it down you. Ah'll be with you in minute.' He refused the money she offered.

In between sips and watching William pour drinks and clear tables, catching his eye and a smile every so often, she flicked through Margaret's journal, more out of a need to appear occupied than out of real interest. 'Pageant! The word conjures up a vision of pomp and splendour ... as learned women and saintly women, artists, heroines, rulers, and warriors pass before you, as you hear of the work they have accomplished, give rein to your enthusiasm.' She turned the page. 'Who Votes? At a Suffrage meeting at Portsmouth, Mr. Hugh T. Barrie, M.P. for North Derry, said he had always been in favour of giving the Parliamentary vote to women who were the owners of property.' She closed the journal.

However busy he was, she noticed, William took time to listen, exchange a few words, share a joke with a customer. But though he seemed happy enough, he looked sickly pale and as he bent to clear glasses he fell into a bout of coughing. She saw him try and fail to control it before disappearing out the front door for a spell. When, after seeing to a build-up of customers, he joined her again, his skin had the look of creased paper. She asked had he had his cough long, had he taken medicine? The tobacco smoke in here didn't suit him, he said. William had never liked tobacco. An evil substance, he claimed. His brothers had scoffed at that, but he'd stuck by it.

'What's this? *The Vote*?'

'Ah've been to see mah friend,' Iza said apologetically.

William tweaked the ribbon she'd clean forgotten was pinned to her chest. 'And joined the suffrage movement?' She went to take it off but he stayed her hand. 'Leave it,' he said. 'Votes for women. Quite right. Good for you.' Iza was on the point of telling him about Amelia McLean and her We Women movement and Agnes and her strike notice and how she'd got herself somewhere between the two with no solid ground to stand on, but William had to be up and away and the moment passed.

All evening her brother was back and forth for a few

words, but he could never stop for long. When she emptied her glasses he brought full ones. She couldn't possibly, she said after the second round. Of course she could, William said. Get me a shandy, she pleaded.

That had the old boy in the corner roused from his reverie. 'What? And waste good beer.'

'Tam will relieve you of the onerous task of drinking good liquor, eh Tam?' William sat by her side to pick coins from a stack old Tam had set down by his deck of cards. My, but it felt good to have William close.

'She's a compositor, you know. Mah sister,' he told old Tam. There was pride in his voice.

'Well fancy that,' old Tam said.

'Mind you, ah bet she doesn't know who Alan Breck is?' Seeing Iza's puzzlement, William added, 'The name of this pub you're sat boozing in. The Alan Breck'.

'See,' he said to old Tam. 'Told you. Printers.' He shook his head. 'Ignorant.'

Iza nudged him hard and he pretended to topple.

'Who is he then?'

'Not telling. Since you mean to stay a printer, you best stay ignorant.' And he was off again.

Iza sipped shandy. She watched men come in and drink alone or join in bands to blether and laugh, their voices swelling and dropping away as they came and went. She tried to make out a framed picture on the opposite wall, a book jacket by the look of it, but her eyes didn't stretch that far. The man who'd offered her a drink when she first came in smiled over and waved 'Night, hen' as he and his chums left. She laid her head back against the wooden-panelled wall to keep it steady. It seemed to have come loose. But she felt safe and sound on her bench in this bar watching old Tam shuffle cards, catching William's eye whenever he passed. Close to dozing, she shook her head and yanked herself awake.

'Deal me in,' she said to old Tam.

'What's your game, hen?'

'Your choice.'

Old Tam dealt two hands with bony, stained fingers that put her in mind of her dad's. His deep, moist eyes had something of her dad's in them too.

'Ah'd put mah money in mah pocket if ah was you. She'll clean you out,' William said as he swept by with a tower of empties.

They'd played rounds of whist and pontoon and old Tam was teaching her crib – pity he'd left his board at home, he'd be sure to bring it next time – when his 'at home' had her gasp and stand up. The baby. Mrs Cossar. For goodness sake. What was she thinking? She burst past drinkers and, without stopping to say goodbye, hoping William would see her frantic wave, was out in the street and breaking into a trot, the cool night air clearing her head.

A blustery wind announced a coming storm and as she neared the corner of her street the heavens opened to splat rain that had her soaked through in seconds. Head down, she tried to skirt round a group of men blocking her way, but one of them clasped hold of her arm.

'Heh, look who it is out galavanting.' Her brother Jack.

She shook free, but he blocked her way.

'What's this,' Jack said, tweaking the soggy ribbon on her chest. 'Votes for women. Where've you been? Up the West End to mah lady's tea party?'

'Out the way, Jack.'

Jack stood aside, patted her on the backside, said cheerio hen, but now she was faced with Rab and one of his Tanfield chums, a square, flat-faced man.

'So, just when we're getting the masters cornered, you're giving them something to clutch at,' Rab said.

'What are you on about? Ah'm not giving them anything.'

'Then what are you doing at their meetings?' Rab said. 'Lending credence, that's what.'

'Don't you go parroting your union journal at me. Lending credence! Anyhow, if ah am it serves you right. They're setting up a women comps' union, and good luck to them, seeing as your lot never let us in.'

'That West End suffrage brigade? Stuff and nonsense. No more a union than ah'm King Leopold.'

Unnerved not so much by Rab's words as by her own, Iza wanted no more of this. Trust Rab to rile her into defending something she wasn't sure she wanted to defend. But now Rab's flat-faced chum piped up in a thick voice, 'This is no picnic, you know. We're talking about families having food on the table.'

'Oh sorry. Ah never realised,' Iza said, hands on hips. 'But then ah'm just a woman. What would ah know about putting food on the bloody table.'

'Go on, hen. You tell them.' Laughing, Jack told Rab to leave her be, that it was hardly the lassie's fault that he and his compositor chums had been too stuck in their old-fashioned ways to see that machines were the future; that in no other town in the country had comps been so daft. 'First you stand by and let lassies take your frames and then you stand there snivelling when they take the new monotype machines. You lot want your heads seeing to.'

'Well now we're putting it to rights.' Rab was still blocking Iza's way.

Chest taut as a drum, she stretched to her full height so they were nose-to-nose. 'Excuse me,' she said. 'Ah need to see to mah family.'

'*Your* family. Ah thought you were quite content to let mah wife see to *your* family.'

'Your wife is not seeing to mah family.' Iza fumed.

'Aye she is. She's minding your bairn right now.'

'No she is not.'

'Aye she is. That wifey came looking for you. Your man brought the bairn down to us.'

Iza felt sick. Barging past Rab she rushed to her stair door, paused a second at Rab and Jeannie's door before belting up to her house and flinging the door open.

'Where's the bairn? Is he at Rab's?'

John was sitting at the table in near-dark, shoulders hunched and hands pressed between his knees. He looked round, startled, like a bairn caught out in the wrong. 'Aye. He wouldn't settle. Ah couldn't manage. Sorry.'

When she'd fetched the sleeping baby from Jeannie – thanking the heavens for keeping Rab out in the street a while – she handed him to John till she got out of her sodden clothes. Watching his body ease as he swayed and hummed, she wondered for a moment could she tell him about what she'd heard today and how it had knocked her off-kilter. But she knew straight off she could not. How could she tell her husband she was slewing about in the wind when she'd led him to believe she knew her own mind, that he could rely on her to know it.

§§§§§§§§§

The responsibility to notify falls on both the head of the family (or nearest relative, or person in charge of or in attendance on the patient, or the occupier of the building) and the "medical officer attending on or called in to visit the patient".

She pants for breath. Air hangs hot and heavy. But poor ventilation is the least of it. Throbbing breasts don't help matters, but she can live with them. What irks is that she's been put on to short, urgent Merchant Company and government jobs. Aye, there's something in Charlie Dewar's claim that he's doing her a favour, that it's lighter work and so more fitting, but his more fitting doesn't allow for the extent to which her hands and mind are alloyed with the stack upon stack of tied-up letter boards of type that are the makings of the eleventh edition of the Encyclopaedia Britannica; letter boards that must be heaved out, carted, set down, loosened, unpicked and amended in line with alterations in the world: the acreage of cultivation of Lucerne in Kansas; improvements to the Japanese Hotchkiss since the war with Russia; the mapping of the French Africa Colonies. Though there's undoubted satisfaction to be had in calculating and making up tabular work on government jobs, and Greek and algebra examination papers pay double rates, still, it doesn't compensate. The Ency Brit, all 28 volumes of it, will take its place on library shelves all over Scotland and England. They'll be shipped across the Atlantic to America. Rumour has it it's already owned by an American firm and that this, the eleventh edition, will be the last to be printed in its home town. It will be taken down and consulted by all manner of people for decades to come. Its progress is reported in newspapers. And, then, the government job she's on today isn't even tabular and it's not Greek or algebra, though some of it might as well be.

Infectious Diseases (Notification) Act 1889 defines "infectious disease" as: any of the following diseases, namely, small-pox, cholera, diphtheria, membranous croup, erysipelas, the disease known as scarlatina or scarlet fever, and the fevers known by any of the following names, typhus, typhoid,

enteric, relapsing, continued, or
puerperal, and includes as respects
any particular district any infectious
disease to which this Act has been
applied by the Secretary of State in the
manner provided by this Act.

Half way through a sluggish forenoon, a flash of lightening
sears the caseroom and an almighty peel of thunder has
Iza's thoughts fly along the alleyway, down the road, up a
stair to where right now her baby William is hearing his
first ever burst of thunder. What will he make of it? Is he
bawling his wee lungs out? She quells a pang of longing with
the thought that he's in safe hands. Mrs Cossar had been
worried rather than annoyed at being left holding him the
other night; she'd brought him round to Iza's not to be
rid of him but to make sure his mum hadn't met with an
accident, a fear which John had not been able to allay.

Lodging her locked-up galley in a groove between breasts
and belly, she carries it to the proofing press, lowering her
head to hurry past Grace's frame. All morning she's avoided
meeting Grace's eyes. So far she's avoided Agnes and Lizzie
too, though they visited her while she slept and have been
stalking her mind since she woke. In fifteen minutes or so,
she'll have to face the music.

# -9-

Washed clean by a downpour, air sparkled as Bellevue's comps joined machinemen and laying-on lassies, stereotypers and stone polishers, bookbinders and warehousemen, engineers and labourers to fill the yard. Charlie Dewar climbed onto a cart to stand side-by-side with Alex Stewart, an agile wee bloke who was Father of the machine room Chapel, and big, lantern-jawed Jack Goodall, Warehousemen and Cutters' union representative. The cart wobbled. Blokes at the front hurried to prop its shafts and, while they were at it, give it a wee jiggle to send its occupants teetering.

Having made excuses to stay a few minutes at her frame, Iza stood on her own at the back of the crowd, relieved that Grace was using dinnertime to snatch fifteen minutes at home. Lizzie's hair shouted her presence a few yards in front, while the gap beside her announced Agnes. Looking towards that gap, Iza's insides clenched.

Eyes pinned, folks paused from snatching bites of dinnertime pieces to jeer at an announcement of the masters' claim that the unions had broken trust by going round the city inducing every employee to sign strike notices and encouraging lassies to join the Warehousemen and Cutters union. Whoops mixed with a few grumbles greeted a report that the overtime ban was solid and beginning to bite. Then, after a pause that lasted longer than gaining full attention warranted, Alex Stewart announced slowly, deliberately, what they were gathered to hear.

'Soon the whole of Edinburgh printerdom will begin tendering notices to strike work.' His words echoing like a gong struck, he went on to tell a tense crowd that though some of the masters had signed the memorial, many still refused to do so, including – he wagged a finger at the upstairs offices – those biting their nails up there right now, the very ones who make the most use of females in the caseroom. 'We are now approaching the buffers,' Alex Stewart called, leaning forward to scan the crowd.

'Would that be the buffers that keep shifting down the tracks?'

A ripple of laughter was cut short by chants of 'When? When?' drummed out with a stamping of boots. Seeing Agnes's clenched fist rise above the heads, Iza leant back against the wall and shut her eyes.

Now Charlie Dewar was bellowing. 'Most of our female comps have already signed notices to strike alongside the men. The others will be persuaded.' Iza opened her eyes to see Agnes, on tiptoe, turn and, catching her eye, beam and punch the air with a clenched fist.

'Tell them they'll be fined three quid same as us if they don't sign. That'll soon persuade them,' a man called.

'Only one machineman has refused,' Alex Stewart cut in. Above a chorus of jeers he called, 'No, no. At seventy-two-year old, a staunch Chapel member for nigh-on sixty of them, through the '72–'73 dispute that got us here in the first place, he's earned the right to draw pay to stand by a silent machine.'

'You never earn the right to be a rat.'

'Och, leave the old sod alone. We'll get a barrow and wheel him in through the picket.'

'Aye and gie him a good kicking on his way oot.'

Faces eased into smiles, bodies slackened, but only for a moment.

'What about strike pay? What will we be on?'

Though the different trades formed discrete clumps in the crowd, they tensed as one, sniffed the air as one.

'As is customary, strike pay will be what the Society can afford. In the region of eight shillings.'

'Ah heard the lassies will get full pay.'

'Aye. The Society has agreed after a bit of gentle persuasion from the lassies,' – Charlie Dewar nodded over heads towards Agnes – 'to pay them full wages for the duration of a strike.'

'So you're handing our dues and strike levy to unorganised lassies?' The spluttering voice came from nearby and Iza recognized it. George Struthers, which brought George Seggie to mind, and, close behind him, Margaret. She drove them from her mind.

'Aye. Organised and unorganised alike, if they agree to support us.'

Over a mixture of jeers and cheers from the men, Jack Goodall waved papers at the clusters of women in the crowd. 'There's Warehousemen and Cutters union application forms here. If you've not done so already, sign up before you leave,' he shouted.

Most of the men stayed pensive-looking, but there were odd calls of 'What a liberty' and 'Why don't we just turf our strike fund in the river while we're at it.'

'Och, go turf yourself in the river.' Agnes's voice rang round the yard. 'What about our grievances?' she bawled.

'Not forgotten. Improved rates for female comps is on the negotiating table,' Charlie Dewar called back as, sensing the hooter a good few minutes before it sounded, the crowd started to break up.

'Well, get it off the table and into our pay packets.' Agnes was earning herself attention, but dinnertime was over.

As the hooter sounded and folk made for the doors, Iza, from her stance by the wall, watched Agnes and Lizzie go to have a word with Charlie Dewar. The yard had emptied and still they talked on and still Iza waited. When at last Agnes and Lizzie, deep in conversation, made for the door, she stood in their path.

'Ah need a word,' she said. She meant to come at it slow and sidewise, but time was pressing and 'Ah've heard the men *do* mean to get rid of us all,' burst out of her.

'What? Who's telling you that?' Agnes poo-pooed.

'Mah old work chums from Ballantynes.' Best not mention Amelia McLean and her We Women movement, Iza had decided. 'They're saying this'll mean the total elimination of women from the caseroom.'

'Stuff and nonsense.' Agnes tossed her head.

'Well that's what they're saying.' Iza squared up to her.

'And ah'm saying that's rubbish and you shouldn't be listening to them.' Agnes added an exclamation mark by stomping a foot. Her face flared like a fire catching.

Squinting at Agnes's face then feet in a plea for calm, Lizzie lifted a hand and went to speak, but, riled by Agnes's 'shouldn't', Iza got in first. She wasn't sure what to think, but she was quite certain she didn't want to be told what she should and shouldn't be doing.

'Hold your horses. Think about it. If they're right, we're throwing away the chance for women to get into

272

the caseroom. We're helping the men deny generations of women to come.' She'd managed to look Agnes steadily in the eye as she spoke. Now she turned to Lizzie to say, 'Ah'm not saying they're right. Ah'm saying we've never heard their side of it.'

Again Lizzie went to speak but, wagging a finger, Agnes butted in with 'Ah've got better things to do than listen to that suffrage brigade's havering.'

'It's not them saying it.' That wagging finger had Iza snap back, voice raised. 'There's comps saying it. Amelia McLean's a comp at Skinners.'

'Ah, so now we have it. Amelia-We-Women-McLean. Her! She does not speak for me.' Agnes's head bobbed from side to side.

'Keep your hair on. If you're so sure of yourself, what harm can it do to listen?'

'A whole lot by the sound of it,' Agnes sniffed. 'Anyhow,' she said, quieter now, 'you've signed the strike notice.' With that, she marched off and in the door.

At last Lizzie got a word in, though not the word Iza hoped for. Mention of Amelia McLean had swept away what sympathy Iza had sensed in Lizzie's bearing. As she followed Agnes, Lizzie turned to say, 'A bit late to be swopping sides is it not?'

§§§§§§§§§

She stops by Charlie Dewar's frame. School dinner tickets? Her face falls. And it works. He says 'Tell you what, ah'll knock that job out mahself. The morn's morn you're back on the Ency Brit.' Then he backtracks, narrowing his eyes to study her. 'Are you sure you're up to it, hen? You're no looking so good.'

'Aye,' she says, pulling her face into the closest she can get to a smile.

'See the cliquer and get your copy. Get your case filled ready. Plenty of dollar signs, mind, though you'll need to wait for them. We've run short and the lads need to go to the foundry.'

The thought of empty time, of not enough to occupy hands and head, is dreadful. 'Can ah spend the time by a stoneman? Watching him make up?'

'Aye. Why not.'

Tall, thin Dougie Black bends over the stone like an f.

He wears the male comp's uniform of brown linen jacket hanging open over an apron that brushes his shins. Though the apron is stain-splotched, still it is bleached bright white. His hair's like a well-worn scrubbing brush and long, wiry tufts sprout from his ears. His manner puts her in mind of John Adams at Pauls, and thought of John Adams comes with a longing to be back there. Not now, not with all this strife, but back, just turned sixteen and newly time-served and full of it. Dougie Black halts hinged elbows and turns strained-looking eyes on her just the once, then goes on as if she's not there, as though he's talking himself through his work.

'Wooden furniture, never metal, against the chase. Sixteen-page scheme, four pages per quarter. Lock-up to the outer edges of each quarter with pressure towards the cross bars. There now. Point-cut furniture head and foot. Side-stick overlaps to secure the corner, but not, no, never, past the foot-stick.' She watches lithe, stringy hands make a compact mesh of metal.

Engrossed, she manages to keep Agnes and Amelia McLean from her mind. Only once does her attention stray from Dougie Black's hands. As he taps a sliver of metal into place the thought comes to her: if ah have to rat, so be it, ah'll have to rat. But she shudders as that thought takes her back to a time long, long ago when her father and his work chums came into the house one workday morning, talking in gruff voices of rats swarming up from London and Liverpool, rats that she pictured black and fat with muckle yellow teeth jutting from pointed snouts. She remembered how their talk of rats had her keeking over the banister before skeltering down the stairs and out the door as quick as she could in case greasy beasts jumped out of the cludgie or the coal bunker and landed on her. She'd like to have believed her dad and his chums would keep the rats out of their street, let alone their stair, but from the way they snapped and snarled she didn't believe they could.

When the knock-off hooter blasts the air, Dougie Black immediately downs tools. All the men do, every last one of them. Overtime ban.

# -10-

'Your mother's needing you.'

On her way out to empty the chanty, Iza recognised Rab's voice before she saw him coming up the stair towards her. His tone had her hackles up.

'Be there in a minute,' she said.

Rab blocked her way. 'She's sick.'

'She's your mother an' all.'

'Aye, lucky for her seeing as her daughter does bugger all for her.'

'Would you like to empty this for me?' Thrusting the chanty at him, Iza flicked off the old towel that covered it.

Rab's grimace was part disgust, part shock.

And Iza was shocked at herself. When you passed folk on the stair carrying a bairn or bag of messages or pail of coal you met eyes, said your 'mornin' or 'evenin'. With a full chanty, covered and tucked well into your side, you might as well not be there. No meeting of eyes. No greeting. Manners dictated you went about this business in private.

The back green was full of thickening shadows. When she tipped the muck on the midden a rat scurried. On her way back she paused by Rab and Jeannie's door. Leave the baby on his own another five minutes? With Nelsons' Parkside works unaffected by the dispute and so not on overtime ban, John was working late. No. She ran up to fetch the wee one. All these years of hankering after room to breathe she'd never given a thought to this side of it, never imagined that anyone, let alone a baby, could be left alone in a house.

Jeannie stood by the sink strapping a bread and milk poultice to an angry boil on her wee boy's neck while her mother comforted a newborn in one arm and brushed a wee lassie's hair with her spare hand. Iza's mother sat hunched forwards, her maroon shawl bunched up and clutched to her middle. The shawl needed a good wash and so, by the look of her, did her mother. And she smelt of whisky. Iza eyed Rab. What on earth was he thinking of? Pernickety Rab putting up with this.

'Your stomach?' Iza asked her mum.

'Aye. It's giving me hell. Ah canny move.'

'What have you taken?'

'Magnesia.'

'And?'

'Ah canny keep anything down.'

'Have you had the doctor?' Iza asked Rab.

'No. We've no time to go for doctors. And if we did he'd be lucky to get in the bloody door we're that packed in in here.' Rab looked round him then leant in to say quietly to Iza, despondent rather than angry, 'Ah've no money to pay for doctors. Ah've got a full house to feed. Or hadn't you noticed?'

'Ah'll go for the doctor now,' Iza said. 'Ah'll pay.'

Seeing her look round for somewhere to put her baby down, Jeannie called to her eldest boy to take him. Out of her mother's hearing, or so she thought, Iza asked Rab if their mother was drinking a lot.

'Just a wee toddy to settle mah innards,' their mother whinged.

'Nothing wrong with her ears, eh?'

The doctor's was in a quiet terrace of houses over the river. By the bridge, lights from Tanfield's offices glanced off iron railings to splinter on dark waters. Iza pulled the brass bell three times before a housekeeper answered. The doctor was out. No, she couldn't say when he'd be back. No, there was no point waiting. No, she couldn't ask him to call, not tonight. Try the infirmary. Before going back in to Rab's, Iza ran upstairs to see if John was home. He was sitting alone with the pieces of her ivory puzzle box spilled out on the table in front of him. She was shamed to feel an urge to snatch it from him and tell him to leave it alone. Back in Rab's house, Jeannie's newborn was quiet at the breast, Jeannie's mother was busy at the sink and the other bairns had taken baby William to bed with them. Iza told Rab she'd stay off work the morn's morn to get the doctor in or, if needs be, take their mother to the infirmary.

Still buckled over in the armchair, her mother tugged at her arm as she made to leave. 'Ah need to come back up to yours,' she whispered. 'Ah canny abide it here.' She clamped a finger to her lips and grimaced towards Jeannie's mother. 'See her, ah canny have any ailment but she's had it first. If ah said they'd had to take mah head off at the infirmary, she'd have had her's off years ago.'

They were off to the infirmary, heaving up the brow of the hill to trundle down to Princes Street where they'd change trams. Saturday, but Iza was glad to have a good reason to stay clear of the caseroom despite the loss of a half day's pay. She'd gone back to the doctor's first thing and got sent to try another doctor along the road, where she'd been told to try some new doctor, a good half hour's walk away. Walking arm-in-arm with her mother up the alleyway to the tram stop, past Bellevue's muffled roars, had brought to mind trailing after her mother to stand by Nelsons Parksides' yard gates. And, like fitting an awkward piece of her puzzle box, it struck her that it must have been Saturday knock-off times when they went and that her mother and the other women standing by the gates, heads up to sniff the air, would have been waiting for pay packets to flow out of the works. And she remembered the pleasure of looking up to see her mother tear open a brown packet and tip coins into a cupped hand.

This morning the sun had come up white and low, the moon had stayed on late and the air had a nip of autumn in it, but when they stepped off the tram in Princes Street the day was set bright and fair. Watching folk saunter by shops and cafes in Princes Street, Vi Ross forgot all about the state of her stomach.

'What's she got on her head? Looks like a cockerel that's lost a fight.'

'Wheesht, mother. She'll hear you.'

'Look at that. What a sight. Ah wouldn't be seen dead in that.'

Now her mother wanted to have a look at the floral clock. Iza objected but gave in. Red, white and blue petunias and begonias were patched with brown, past their best. Iza said they'd better get going. Her mother wanted to stop and watch a gardener who'd turned up with a wheelbarrow of pansies.

'You've got a good job there.'

'Aye. On a fine day like this. Mind you, ah'd rather be out in wind and rain than stuck indoors.' His bunnet, breeks and waistcoat were the colour of earth. Vi Ross leant over a low iron railing to confide. She was just like him, couldn't abide being cooped up, didn't know how she – a nod towards Iza – could abide it.

They leant on a wall for the first hour's wait at the infirmary. No seats free. Then they sat a good hour wedged between a mother whose shaved-headed bairn had a bloody cloth wrapped round his leg and a youth whose thin shirt clung to his bones as he drooped forwards, shuddering with ratcheting coughs. The air was thick with sweat and antiseptic and urine. Iza made to hand her mother a butter roll from her message bag, but Vi Ross shook her head. The reek in here had turned her stomach. She pulled a bottle of milk of magnesia from her pocket and took a swig.

Faced with a woman when they were shown into the doctor's room, Vi Ross muttered that if she'd thought a nurse could see to her she'd have called in to Ma Souness for a poultice and bottle of mixture.

The doctor gave her a toothy smile. 'Doctor Elizabeth Gordon,' she said. 'What seems to be the trouble?'

Making a great performance of lowering herself into a seat, Vi Ross turned to Iza to announce, 'A lady doctor. Fancy that eh?' before launching into a long-winded account of her ailments.

Iza watched the doctor's smile wilt until clenched teeth were all that was left of it. 'Pain, vomiting, excessive wind, constipation, diarrhoea. Anything more?' she cut in.

'There's a big lump down here.' Vi Ross clasped a baggy bulge resting on her lap.

'Up on there and we'll take a look-see. Can we get your skirts up?'

Iza laid her head back against the wall and drifted off above the current of her mother's tale of that dreadful confinement when she got ripped ragged. 'It was the fifth, or the sixth, live birth finished me off. But then ah had the one more. Or was it two? You lose count, don't you?'

'You have a hernia, Mrs Ross, inflammation of the small bowel and severe damage to the perineum. In fact, your equipment's in a sorry state. All treatable though. First things first, you need a hysterectomy.'

Iza helped her mother straighten her clothes. 'Can she get that done here?'

Ignoring her, the doctor addressed her mother. 'We'll get you in as soon as we can.'

Iza wanted to ask how much it would cost but couldn't bring herself to. The way she turned to her notes, the doctor made it clear she was done with them.

Out in Meadow Walk, sitting on a bench under a marbled blue and grey sky to eat their rolls, her mother started on about their St Leonard days when the boys used to go off to the Meadows to watch the football, how one time when she went to have a look the ball landed at her feet and she kicked it right across the field and straight in the goal. Iza shook her head, hugged her mother's arm, said they'd better call at the chemist and get back home to get her belongings carted upstairs.

Leaving her mother to tell the chemist all about her innards and what the lady doctor had to say, she nipped next door for matches and a *People's Friend* for her mum. Outside the newsagents a thickset woman, arms crossed over a wad of bosom, stood scowling at billboards that declared 'Militants call for support for printers' and 'Printers' strike ultimatum'.

'Shocking, eh?' The woman plainly expected Iza's

agreement. 'All these strikes when there's plenty folk would be glad of the work.'

'What would you know about it?' Iza brushed past her.

Before they reached the tram stop, Vi Ross stopped to look in a window at tea caddies decorated with pink elephants and a glossy black teapot with gold Chinese markings on a red lacquer tray. Behind them was a poster and pennant in green, white and gold.

'Can we get a cup of tea?'

'Ah've no money for tea.' The medicine had emptied her purse.

'Ah'll treat you,' said her mum.

'It's not a tea shop.'

'Tee ee ay.' Vi Ross pointed to a sign. 'That says tea where ah come from.'

Iza knew what was in there. She'd been in the Women's Freedom League shop when it first opened, one Saturday afternoon back in the early days of her marriage when she and Margaret still met up occasionally. Margaret usually had a collected, mindful way about her, but that day she seemed to have been put together in a hurry. Some famous suffrage woman who'd walked from Edinburgh to London with a petition was to be at the shop. Margaret was agitated, anxious not to miss her. Iza wasn't keen and didn't see the rush. Then, when the woman didn't show up and Iza said she'd be seeing to her blisters, Margaret was not inclined to take a joke.

Now, standing behind her mother, who'd stopped dead just inside the door, Iza spotted the woman who'd pinned the ribbon on her chest at the Amelia McLean meeting. Hands swimming through the air, Mrs Sinclair was greeting folk and directing affairs from behind a counter. When her eyes lighted on Vi Ross and Iza her hands halted in mid-air and her eyes squinted as she tried to place them.

Vi Ross was heading for a small corner table, but when a group of women, cutting and sewing ribbon badges, stopped talking to look up expectantly, she turned heel. Iza knew just what made her mum retreat. She'd got a wee taste of it at Mrs Sinclair's house, that slight tilt to a head and slight smile that told you something was expected of you but gave you no clues as to what that something might be.

'Come away, Mum,' Iza whispered.

'It was thon women's vote lot, wasn't it?' Outside, Iza's mum clasped her arm. 'Lucky escape. We could have got ourselves chained to a railing.'

'Don't be daft, Mum. They chain themselves to railings.'

'So how do they get the tea on or go to the cludgie, eh? You tell me that.'

Back home, Vi Ross was up the stair to Iza's house like a youngster. Iza got her installed in an armchair then fetched her clothes and bits and pieces from Rab and Jeannie's. Jeannie caught her at the door to hand her a quart whisky bottle saying, 'She'll be wanting this.'

'Where'll ah be sleeping?' Vi Ross had the air of an excited bairn.

'In the bedroom with me and the wee one. John sleeps in here.'

Her mother looked well pleased with that, but she had to spoil it. 'He's a bit funny, your man, eh? But then you're a funny one yourself so you make a fine pair.'

'What do you mean?'

Iza expected no answer and got none. What she got was a ramble about how her mother was too old to be seeing to bairns, how Jack wanted her to stay at his but that wife of his wouldn't have it, about how she'd quite like to stay at Violet's but her man was that stuck up. 'Ahnguss,' she minced, eyes raised to the ceiling. She took a dose of medicine, some sweet tea and oatmeal porridge then went to bed, worn out and sore from trekking up the town and the doctor's poking and prodding she said, which was no doubt true, though with Vi Ross there was no telling. Were Jack to appear, she might be up and dancing a jig.

Iza nipped round to Mrs Cossar's to fetch baby William then got stovies on, ready for John getting in from work. At first he made no comment about his mother-in-law staying, just nodded and buried himself in her *People's Friend*. But after tea and a smoke he said with an assurance that took Iza unawares, 'Your mother can have the set-in bed. Ah'll shift into the bedroom.' She simply nodded her agreement. John was generally willing, if not exactly happy, to go along with whatever arrangements she made. Once in a while though, like now, something got into him and he put his foot down.

Evening was upon them before John took his sealed pay packet from the mantelpiece and set it down. Made nervous by an alteration to their Saturday ritual, he clicked ragged fingernails on the table as he waited for Iza to sit down by him with a jotter and pencil. Just the one pay packet to open this week, what with Iza missing payday. Its absence made her nervy, but as always she'd done her sums and knew within a farthing how much would be in the packet she'd collect on Monday. John lifted his packet, shook it and pinched it to tear off a thin and even strip before pouring out coins. He counted them once – thirty-five shilling and fivepence, and again, thirty-five shillings and fivepence. Where Iza would normally do the same, she announced thirteen shillings and five pence halfpenny as she wrote it down and busied herself totting sums, knowing what John was thinking but willing him to keep his thoughts to himself. The strike levy meant her packet was three shillings short. Gas, laundry, messages, Mrs Cossar, the half-year's rent fund – she turned to the front of the jotter to check what she was already sure of – rent due November the fifteenth.

'How much have we put aside for the rent?'

'Two pounds, eighteen and fourpence. Just over half with over three months to go. We'll be fine.'

'We should put a bit more by in case the strike's on.'

'They say it won't come to it, but even if it does we'll be on full pay.'

John picked at a crumb lodged in a crack in the table. 'Says who?'

'They told us.'

'A likely story.'

John pocketed the two-and-six newspaper and tobacco money she handed him then to turned to fill in a pools coupon he'd got from a neighbour who worked in the brewery. Iza sat in curdling light making a poor job of mending a shirt collar, pricking her finger and getting blood spots on it. They were sitting in silence when, out of the blue, John said, 'Think ah'll go to the boxing. Your brother's in the ring the night. Ah bumped into him on mah way home.'

'Can ah come?' Iza's mother must have been up and standing by the bedroom door.

'You take the biscuit, Mum. You were at death's door and now you're wanting to go to the boxing.'

'Ah love a good fight.' Vi Ross was looking around for her coat. 'As long as Jack wins. Ah'd hate to see him get beat.'

But the something in John that put its foot down was still in him. 'Don't worry. You'll not be seeing him win or lose. There's a bed for you there,' he said, pointing to the set-in bed. And with just a wee pulled face Vi Ross climbed into bed. What a pair, Iza thought. Hard to make sense of either of them. John and Jack had never hit it off and boxing meant crowds, which John didn't like. But she was glad to have him away out, and, though she'd scarcely admit it to herself, away out to something manly at that, and her mother there to hear it.

She kept her back to him when he fumbled at her nightgown to stroke her thigh with a light touch that set her teeth on edge. She knew she could say she still wasn't ready after the birth, but she didn't. John's occasional pumping at her, clank of bones and kneading of flesh, was easier to bear than silence thickening in the room. His tentative approaches made it both easier and harder: easy to brush off, yet hard to dismiss. Long after John began to snore she lay awake, her mind hopping from Agnes's squat bulk to Margaret's tall stature. A grizzle from the crib reminded her she must mind to take new muslins to Mrs Cossar. And John was right about putting extra aside for the rent. She'd cut back on messages, though with her mother here there'd be an extra mouth to feed.

Though needing sleep, she was nowhere near it. Up out of bed and through in the other room where her mother, like her husband, was dead to the world, she clenched her shawl to her chin and, leaning on the draining board, watched how a full white moon glistened on wet roofs. As she stared, her mind's eye turned the glitter into her scrawny signature on the strike notice. Why had she signed? The question demanded attention. She'd keep her job, that's why. Grace would keep her job. But the thought didn't bring satisfaction. The comfort to be had from being at one with her work chums, with Lizzie and Agnes? That answer brought scant comfort. Far off, a foghorn sounded. Down below, cats wailed. She poured a cup of lukewarm water from the kettle and drank. It tasted brackish.

§§§§§§§§§

It is sometimes met with in women of
twenty; and the younger the individual
the more malignant is the disease.
Married life seems to have no effect as
regards the incidence of the disease,
but it often happens that a breast
which gave trouble during the period
of suckling becomes later the subject
of cancer;

As her eyes see a block of lines as a pattern of black and
white and she goes to make fine adjustments to spacing, her
right hand swings away from the case to feel her breasts.
Bags of lumps. How would you pick a tumour out of that?
What happens if you don't suckle, if you let them dry up?

Does that make matters worse? Her eyes run ahead of her.

> Later, the nutrition of this patch of
> skin may be so interfered with that it
> mortifies or breaks down and thus a
> cancerous ulcer is produced. This ulcer
> slowly spreads, and its floor is covered
> with a discharge in which septic
> micro-organisms undergo cultivation;
> in this way, the ulcer becomes highly
> offensive.

When, just the other day, Grace was setting an entry
on Malta fever she'd become convinced she'd got it, even
though it said goats' milk was the cause and as far as she
knew she'd never had a drop of the stuff. Whenever you
worked on a disease, Iza and Grace agreed, your mind
would tick each symptom. She sneaked another feel of her
breasts. 'For goodness sake,' she chided herself. 'You've no
more got breast cancer than you've got Malta fever.'

> As regards the value of radium in the
> treatment of cancer of the breast,
> the high expectations which were
> somewhat widely associated with this
> newly-found element early in 1909
> must be said to have been unjustified
> by any precise results.

Fixing her attention so as to shut out thoughts of
suckling and breasts, ulcers and tumours, she checks and

justifies her last line and eases the block of type into place. Hands over the case, empty stick ready for its next load, she glances up over the frames. There's Lizzie's mop and the tip of Agnes's brown bun down there. They've been giving her the cold shoulder since they had words in the yard. Well, that's their look-out, she decides. If they insist on acting like bairns in the playground there's nothing to be done about it. There's a mass meeting tonight. She won't be going. Mrs Cossar can't see to the bairn, her mother would at a push but it isn't worth the pushing, and, besides, she's had enough. Agnes and Lizzie are sure to be there, though, and when they hear Amelia McLean speak out they'll know for themselves they've shut their ears to the half of it, that it's not as simple as vote to strike with the men, keep your job, win improved conditions.

# –11–

Though she was greeted with grumbles – 'Ah couldn't get the washing done. Big beam-end at every sink,' or 'That bizzum from next door was wanting to borrow sugar again. Just a wee bit till Saturday, she says, holding out a bloody great bowl!' – still, these days Iza's heart lifted as she opened her door to enter a house with a presence in it. Tonight it smelled of beef-bone stock and onion and the greeting was, 'Your face is filthy dirty and you want to see to your hair. You look a right sight.' She gave her mother a poke of treacle toffee Mrs Cossar had made. She'd tried a bit herself but it had set her teeth on edge.

Nights were starting to draw in, to creep up, until one evening soon folk would find themselves lighting the mantle, striking a match to a fire and closing curtains to shut out the dark. When Iza sat to feed baby William with the bottle he felt like a hot dumpling. He'd been feverish today. Mrs Cossar had given him gripe water and kept him well wrapped. Just a wee chill, she thought. He likely senses winter coming on. Though her tender way with the baby didn't please Iza as much as she knew it should, she knew Mrs Cossar could be trusted. The wee lamb was certainly thriving, but right now he tossed his head back, wailed, wouldn't settle. Rather than try to put him down Iza cradled him, relaxing into a gentle rock while she and her mother ate their tea. They left plenty of broth in the pot for John. He was going straight from work to the mass meeting. 'See what they've got to say for themselves,' he'd said. The pub, the boxing and now a mass meeting. Fine, she thought. Her husband seemed to be more of a piece. Fatherhood might be making a man of him. Wincing at the sound of that in her head, she revised it to might suit him.

Baby asleep now, Iza and her mother sat dozing in dimming light to the sound of boots pounding pavements in the street below. Bellevue and Tanfield workers on their way to Free Gardiners Hall. For god'sake get it settled and done she muttered as the clomping faded to the point where she couldn't have caught up with them if she'd wanted to.

A few streets away trains still clattered and hooted in and out of the depot, but this street, this tenement, this house, fell quiet. While her mother sat cutting an old tartan wool skirt into strips to make a rug, Iza got down on hands and knees to sweep up threads from round her feet.

'Shift yourself,' she said.

'Don't you speak to your mother like that,' Vi Ross said, mock-severe.

Iza sat back on her haunches to look up with a fierce face on. 'Do you want us witched in the night?'

'Might liven things up round here.'

'True enough.'

'Ah once said that to your father and the look he gave me you'd think ah'd invited the devil in for a dance.'

'What, he took it serious?'

'A funny lot.' A flick up of her eyes and a squint of her mouth said the rest: folk from up north.

'Och, Mum, you say that about everyone. Have you ever been?'

'What, up north? Ah've been across to Fife. That's as far north as you'll get me.'

A rap-a-tap startled them. 'Oh, help mah bob, it's the witches come early,' Vi Ross keened.

They were sharing a laugh when Iza's wee brother William came in.

'Talk of the devil,' said their mother.

'We weren't talking about him.'

'Give me a chance. Ah was just about to. Come here and let me take a good look at you, son.'

William straightened his jacket pocket flaps, stood to attention, flicked his bunnet off and bowed low. Despite the summer, his face was powdery white. It was his night off and he'd thought to stop by a while, he said, but if he didn't pass muster he'd as soon be off to the Empire Palace to see the Great Lafayette, though he'd missed the start by now. When their mother wanted to know who the Great Lafayette was when he was at home, William showed as much as he told, pulling rabbits from a hat and yards of hanky-chain from his sleeve, tossing flaming torches in the air.

'How do you know if you've never seen him?'

'Everyone knows, Mum. Anyhow, ah *have* seen him. Twice.'

With her mum's rags put away they settled down at the table with a glass of port William had brought. He took coffee. William wasn't a drinker. He asked for a pack of cards, shuffled, spread them and had them pick one out then place it back in the deck. As he shuffled again then dealt face-up, he told them Jamie had called in the pub the other night, said to say he'd be down to see them soon. He was fine. He and Jessie had another one on the way.

William had a way of sailing through their mother's, 'His own mother and ah'm the last to know,' that didn't leave her behind to sulk but scooped her up and carried her along. She looked well pleased.

'How many's that?' She started to tot on her fingers. 'One, two, three.' Halting, she glanced at Iza with a grimace. 'Oh, and there's the big lassie.'

Now William picked out the cards they'd chosen, bowed for applause, then shuffled again. All the while he'd been stifling a cough but now it erupted. As he pulled a hanky from his pocket and held it to his mouth Iza saw what looked like blood.

'Is that...?'

William's warning look shut her mouth if not her disquiet. She'd get a word with him later, out of earshot of their mother. And, anyhow, after catching his breath and mopping a brow that looked clammy, he was off telling tales of wonders. They'd been up the Amazon, crossed the channel in an aeroplane with Louis Blériot, sat in the gardens and orchards of Ghazni and were just marvelling at ostrich eggs and tiger-skins found in some foreign tomb when Jack and Rab, then John and his brother Alex appeared, back from the meeting. Jack had a flagon of beer, Alex a bottle of whisky.

'Just come by to see how the best mother in the world's doing.' When Jack kissed the top of her head she tittered like a tickled bairn. 'And look who the cat's dragged in.' Jack had his fists up, shadow-boxing at William.

William smiled with that look of his that made you think he could see right through folk. In some ways William, the youngest, was like Jamie, the eldest. The pair of them never rose to it. But where Jamie sat well settled in his world, William seemed to sit on the edge of his, his eyes on somewhere beyond. If, as it had appeared to Iza when she was wee, the red crags that rose up behind their childhood home marked the edge of the known world, Jamie would sit at the foot with his back against a smooth boulder, whistling a tune, chewing on a grass stem; Jack would set straight off climbing, bristle at jagged rocks, start berating them; Rab would fashion some tool from a twig to poke out, examine and classify loose shards; Violet would try to gather everyone to climb together and, when that failed as it was bound to, would set out the picnic she'd thought to bring then join a family nearby to talk to a lassie her own age; William would conjure up an expeditionary force, and, before they knew it, he'd have disappeared. And Iza? She'd sit with Jamie a minute; humour Jack a minute; argue with Rab; take a quick look at Violet, then start to climb, get stuck half way up, perch for a while looking over rooftops, then make her way home wondering where William had got to and forgetting about the others.

While Rab, John and Alex stood about looking like stray sorts, Jack had their mother on her feet for a dance.

'You've had a drink, son,' she said.

'Aye, and ah'm not the only one, Mother.'

'You mind your tongue, son.' She had that dewy-eyed look that both Jack and drink brought on.

Jack turned to William. 'Are you not winching yet?'

'What, and get shackled like you? Not on your nelly.'

They were all starving. Iza boiled what rice she had to stretch out the remains of the broth. With a half loaf of bread it made scant helpings, but it filled a hole. While the men ate, she set to making semolina pudding, keeping an ear on the talk at the table.

'Did you hear yon Kelley and his, "Ah thought a deal was

done, but the men of Edinburgh took a different view"?'

'Too damned right we did.'

'So what are they saying?' She had to repeat it, louder, for them to take notice. It was Rab who answered.

'They're saying the strike is on.'

'Till they say it's off, that is.' Jack was up out his seat, breaking into 'The Grand Old Duke of York'. He tried to pull Rab up, failed, had William up, linking arms to march back and forth. 'He marched them up to the top of the hill and he marched them down again.' When William broke into a fit of coughing Jack slapped him on the back, saying, 'You want to get yourself fit. Look at you. You're like an old man.'

'Leave him be, you big bully,' Iza shouted.

'Huh. Would you listen to her? You should have been there the night, hen, bawling and shouting along with the other lassies. You get yourself up to next week's mass meeting and give them what for. Tell you what, you lot have got more balls than those pansies up on the platform the night. What a load of drivel.' Legs astride, chest puffed, hands clenching an invisible waistcoat, he launched into, 'If it comes to a fight – which, even yet, I do not anticipate – we are in a strong enough position to gain our object.'

'Aye. Supping at the masters' table.' John had been quiet till now. When he spoke, Iza saw how his brother Alex, clutching his spoon over an empty bowl, looked up at him admiringly, nodding slowly as though at words of great wisdom. Jack and Rab eyed John askance.

'Now, now. We need to put trust in our leaders or we'll get nowhere,' Rab said.

'Ah wouldn't trust them with mah granny's fanny.' Jack bent to kiss Vi Ross's forehead. 'Begging your pardon, Mother.'

Watching her mother beam up at him Iza did not feel the irritation she might have. She felt glad. Glad to see her mother happy, glad to have a house full of visitors, especially glad that her wee brother William was among them, though that cough was a real worry.

She started to say she minded years back Fred Henderson, Ballantyne's Father of the Chapel, telling her disputes usually got settled without strike action. We give a bit; they give bit, he'd told her. But she was talking to herself, because the men were on about football and boxing and a neighbour who was off to Australia that week. Saying he had to be off, William headed for the door, but before he reached it Jack had him by the arm and was off on '*He flies through the air with the greatest of ease, that daring young man on the flying trapeze,*' twirling William round the room before he managed to unhook his arm and, calling to Iza he'd be round soon, slipped away, taking the best part of Iza's gladness with him.

In a thickening fug of cigarette and pipe smoke, Jack poured and downed more beer, Vi Ross sank into herself and Rab and John stood either side of the fireplace like bookends, holding newspapers up to the lamp. Aware of Rab's eyes flicking from his newspaper to glower at her, she asked him, politely enough, was it not time he got home to his family. Folding and tucking his paper under his arm, he gave a curt nod and left.

Alex came to lend her a hand with the dishes and, curiosity aroused by the way he boosted John, she gave him her full attention. Having his own brother and not just hers by him would account for John acting more sure of himself. But there was more to it. And now, watching the way Alex's full-lipped mouth hung slightly ajar and his unveiled grey eyes drank from hers as she spoke, putting her in mind of baby William watching sunlight in tree branches, it dawned on her that Alex was slow. Older than John, much bigger than John, finer-looking some would say, Alex was slower than John, not the full shilling, and that made sense of John behaving in that sure way when his brother was around. And she discovered Alex was easy to talk to. His face was wide open as he listened. Invited to speak, he'd ponder a while before answering in a soothing, low voice. She just had to take time to listen and not be too fussed about what question got answered. He told her no, he'd never married though he'd like to. Aye, he stayed with his mum and his sister Christina who'd never wed, and his cousin Jean and her two bairns.

'And your dad?'

Alex's face fell. Like the sun blotted out, a wee cloud shaded his eyes. But the dark didn't linger. 'Mah cousin Jean's a widow,' he said. 'Her man got hit on the head by a girder at his work. She suffers, you know.'

'Aye, ah can imagine. A girder. What a dreadful thing to happen.'

'No, mah mother ah mean.'

Iza decided to change the subject. 'You should come and visit your nephew.'

'Ah haven't got a nephew. They're both lassies.'

'Ah mean our baby. William.'

'Ah'll come on Sunday and take him fishing.'

'He's a bit young for that yet, but we could take him down to the river, catch some frogs.'

Alex looked well pleased with that.

Jack had gone off to fetch more beer and now came back towing a work chum he'd found propped on a wall outside. More drink was downed. Talk grew gruffer. Staggering, Jack's chum muttered threats to a phantom antagonist.

John, who'd been keeping to the sidelines, came over to the sink where Alex still stood by Iza, threw an arm up over his shoulder and led him over to join the men.

'Mind out, ye big lout,' Jack bawled.

The lamp's glow on Iza's ivory puzzle box had caught Alex's eye and he'd stretched to the mantelpiece for it, shouldering Jack in the process. Seeing John about to loose his tongue, Iza strode across and lifted the box down for Alex. She showed him how the lid slid off, how the wafer-thin squares and triangles inside splintered and joined up again. All thumbs, Alex fumbled the box. It fell to the floor. He dropped on all fours to scrabble among feet to gather in pieces and, in the process, barged Jack and sent him staggering. 'For the love of God,' Jack yelled. But he was wasting his breath because, like a bairn after farthings thrown in a poor-oot, Alex was after what he'd spilt. As he lunged for a stray piece Jack grabbed his collar, mounted him, and, mock whipping, cried 'Gee-up cuddy!' Iza yelled at Jack to get off and leave him alone. Alex reared. Jack clattered to the floor. Next thing, Jack was up and at him with fists raised and John, face white and twisted, had hold of Jack's arm, yanking, and Jack swung and landed a fist on John's face.

In the hush of the wee hours Iza sat John down to swab his swelling cheek with witch hazel. She'd seen her brother out the door, dragging his work chum out onto the landing where, for all she knew, he was slumped still, and got Alex put up in her and John's bed. Her mother, who'd sat watching the whole affair like she was at the variety theatre, lay snoring in the set-in bed. Iza would have to shove her over, just like the old days.

§§§§§§§§§

> The harbour is accessible for vessels
> of 26 ft. draught and the city's leading
> industry is the shipment by water and
> by rail of fish (especially salmon) and
> of the products (largely lumber, wheat
> and fruits) of the rich Willamette and
> Columbia valley.

'Heh, Grace, fancy emigrating to the rich Willamette and Columbia valley? We can pick fruit. Fresh air and sun all day. Bite into a juicy orange straight off a tree.'

'And get stung by wasps and be on the lump all winter,' McWhirter calls.

'Miserable old sod.'

'Have they got peaches?' Grace called. 'Ah love a tin of peaches.'

'They've got everything by the sound of it.'

> The value of the exports in 1908 amounted to $16,652,850 and the value of imports to $2,937,513; the foreign trade is chiefly with Great Britain and its possessions, and with the Orient, where wheat and flour are exchanged for raw silk, tea and manila and other fibres. Portland is the principal manufacturing city of the state.

Short of dollar signs again. She waits for an apprentice to stop his blethering and fetch her a fresh supply. Complaints that the apprentices are slow when it comes to filling the lassies' cases, always seeing to the men's first, have got nowhere. Should have brought it up with the other grievances, she thinks. Seems a trivial matter, but it's not. It gives Struthers and his crew cause to say we're slow and not up to it.

The sight of the apprentice lad come with her sorts, printer's hat perched crooked on account of big, sticky-out lugs, melts her ill-temper. She stands back to let him fill her case, tells him to take more care, shoos him away with a playful cuff.

Lifting her setting stick and glancing at her manuscript, she ignores Struthers' voice in the background. But the voice is rising and before she can shut it out she hears the words 'strike break'. She pricks her ears. 'Ballantynes,' he's saying, and 'we bloody women' and 'rats'.

'What's he on about?' she hisses to Dougie Black.

'Trouble,' he calls back. 'Word is the We Women lot have said they'll rat on the strike.'

Iza gulps. Rat on the strike. It has a sickening sound to it. Just the other day she'd told herself that's what she'd do if it came to it. But could she do that?

A great weariness washes through her. These past few nights the baby's woken less. Last night just the once. But that seems to have made her all the more tired, as though her being's glimpsed the prospect of a full night's sleep and is reaching out to snatch it before it's due. She could sink to the sawdust-strewn floor, curl up and sleep.

# -12-

She sensed someone there before she saw her. A tall slip of a thing pressed to the wall at the foot of the stair, leg hinged as a prop like a brash lad.

'Mary? What are you doing here?'

The girl stepped forward. With a quick glance at the babe in Iza's arm, she took hold of the message bag in her other and set a foot on the first step.

'Ah came to see you.' She had a full, throaty voice for such a young lass, the voice of someone older than her fourteen years. And she had a steady gaze.

'Aye, ah see that.' Clutching bairn and bag, Iza set her eyes up the stair to avoid that gaze. After a moment of silence that felt like an age she let go of the bag and said, 'Well, you better come up.' When she added, 'Ah'm just in from mah work,' she well knew she was stating the obvious. At least ah called her by the right name was what she was thinking.

With Della-Mary following her, staying a few steps behind, Iza marvelled at how even in dim light she'd instantly recognised this girl who'd changed from a wee lassie to a near-woman since she last saw her. They mounted the stairs in silence.

Hand on the doorknob, Iza paused to pray that John wasn't home yet. Then she composed her face before turning to say, 'It's not a good time. Do your folks know you're here?'

'No.' The one wee word had challenge in it.

'Then maybe you should come back another time?'

'They won't expect me in from work till later.'

God, such assurance Iza thought. And yet. And yet there was something else in there. An accusation? Or am I imagining that? Expecting it?

'Right you are.' When Iza held the door open Della-Mary walked straight in.

Vi Ross was at the sink. She turned, mouth open to speak, but when she saw the girl she blinked, shut her mouth and turned away.

'We've got a visitor,' Iza announced. 'Jamie and Jessie's lassie. Your granddaughter.'

'Aye. Ah know who it is.' Vi Ross dried her hands and, with a squint smile in the girl's direction, moved to take the baby from Iza saying, 'Ah'll put him down for you'.

'It's all right. Ah'll do it.'

While she put the sleeping baby down the girl stood in the bedroom doorway watching.

'So where are you working?' Iza succeeded all too well in sounding matter-of-fact. With that tone of voice she knew she might as well have added, 'not that ah could care less.'

Without looking, Iza saw the girl's deep brown eyes soak everything up: the double bed, nice dresser, John's good jacket on a hanger, the crib and herself squatted over it, rocking. She glanced round. The girl's plain green dress was too short for her. She had fine shapely legs. Didn't get those from me, Iza thought. Have ah got a dress ah could give her? No. Maybe buy her a new one? No. That wouldn't do.

'Ah'm at Menzies. Envelope folding.'

Vi Ross had an ear out, of course she did, and she caught that.

'Me too. Ah was at Menzies,' she chirruped. 'It's a good job, eh?'

No reply to that, but Iza saw the girl's wry smile of distaste.

'Ah thought they had machines to do that now,' she said, glancing at the window to get a sense of the time. But these late summer evenings, light still dimmed slowly so you couldn't tell. It might be seven. It could be nine. She needed to get this girl out and away before John got in. But why? It struck her – why shouldn't her niece, her mother's granddaughter, pay a visit, even if she'd never done so before, at least not in a while, and never before on her own like this. A run-of-the-mill family visit. But she couldn't convince herself of that and when she moved to go to the front room and the girl didn't budge from the doorway so that she had to sidle by, her heart thumped in a fashion no other family visitor, not even Rab, could have brought on. When she joined her mother at the stove Della-Mary didn't follow but walked into the bedroom as if she belonged.

As Iza busied herself chopping onions and boiling rice, Vi Ross too went through to the bedroom. She could hear low voices but couldn't make out what they were saying. With a glance at the clock – John would be home any minute now but it was fine, she told herself, nothing untoward about a niece dropping by – she joined them. While Vi Ross sat on the bed leaning in, the girl sat on the floor rocking the crib. Watching them, Iza felt tears sting backs of her eyes. She sniffed them down.

'It's getting late. You best be getting off home, eh?' she said.

When the girl made no move Iza went to the front door, opened it and called out, 'Come on. Ah'll see you along the road.'

Soon as they were out on the landing Della-Mary piped up. Solemn and serious, she launched into what had the ring of rehearsed words.

'Ah know mah dad asked before, but ah wanted to ask you mahself. Ah want to get into the caseroom like you. A girl in our street who's at Ballantynes said they're not taking girls on. She told me they were about to shut girls out for good. Is that so?' There was no trace of wheedling in her voice. In fact, there was more of a demand in it.

'Some are saying that. Others say different. No new learner girls for the next five years.'

'But when ah told her mah aunt worked at Neills, she said she it might be different there, there might be an opening. So can you get me in?' She wore no hat, she had thick dark hair, and the way she tossed her head put you in mind of a frisky young cuddy. 'Please,' she added as an afterthought.

My, but she knows her own mind, Iza thought. She had a yen to ask the girl how she'd done at school, was she good at English, what about sums, did she like storybooks, but she bit her lip and kept the yen to herself. At the foot of the stair Iza stopped and turned. The girl was in no hurry. But, then, she seemed to be limping.

'Have you hurt yerself? Your leg?'

Della-Mary looked puzzled for a moment, then she looked down and waggled a foot. 'No. Ah was born like it.

Ankle a bit crooked. Mah granny says she had to pull me out the wrong way round, feet first.'

Iza clamped her lips to stop 'No. No she never' getting out of them. How come ah never knew about her ankle? How on earth did ah never notice?

Someone was coming in the stair door. Could be any of a dozen neighbours in from work. But it was John. Iza braced. Her husband, though, paid scant heed, just nodded and went by as though he always came upon Iza walking out with a daughter he knew nothing about.

'If you're still keen in five years time, ah'll see what ah can do,' were Iza's parting words.

Saying nothing, the girl looked at Iza steadily as though pinning her to her word before striding off.

Though it had lasted a scant half hour, Della-Mary's visit had seemed like an eternity. Or a second? Both at once. Later, when Iza had a moment to chew on it, she at first fretted about the caseroom business. She heard Margaret say, 'What if you'd had a girl?' So how about ah side with Margaret's lot? Would it help her daughter if she ratted on the strike if it came to it? But was she bound to help her daughter when she wasn't her daughter? Did she owe her? This girl with the look of her father! Nothing in particular. Not the nose or mouth or chin. Something of his colouring and a ghostly likeness that was clear as day to Iza. She certainly had his shapely legs. Poor thing, one of them crooked! And she had his eyes, though hers were more watchful than his had ever been. How she paid heed. Did she suspect? Know? Iza thought not. The girl gave the impression of someone who, had she known, would not have held her tongue.

§§§§§§§§§

There's an edgy clamour to the caseroom. Two apprentices get themselves sent off to the storeroom to clean formes, ears ringing, for bashing a trolley into a frame. Voices are raised at Charlie Dewar's frame where the overseer stands with a hand, half-way to being a fist, raised. Charlie, who's carrying on with his work regardless, seems to be having the best of it. Close by Iza, Dougie Black whistles a marching tune, drumming on the edge of a chase with strips of leading.

The enormous war loans raised by Japan in 1904, 1905, 1906 exemplified aptly the more modern methods of dealing with the disturbances to the money market which such operations produce. The loans were issued by

three banks, one of which was a
Japanese institution and represented
the Japanese government in the
operations connected with the various
loans.

Though she's got beyond railing against squeezing in
reduced point paras, still the sight of them patched about
the pages offends her. She'd like to be able to start from
scratch and make a proper job of it, but if there's no time,
there's no time.

Of the other two, one was a leading
London bank and the other the
principal British bank doing business in
China. These large loans were issued
with the minimum of disturbance to
the London money markets.

The overseer strides away into his box, but he's straight
out again and out the door. Up to the offices to confer. Iza
spots Agnes heading for Charlie Dewar's frame for a word;
she keeps her head down.

The Japanese not only applied for
treasury bills and bought them in the
market but they also took up some
of the exchequer bonds issued in
connexion with the South African
wars

What are the Japanese doing in South African wars? she wonders. John will likely know. If he gets beyond advertisements in the paper before nodding off, he'll turn to war reports and read out accounts of battles with what seems to Iza an unholy relish.

Before she sets her hands in motion she snatches a keek at a handbill she took this morning from an outstretched hand at the work's entrance, a hand that had her look at the face, a face that had been roused in her by close sight of Della-Mary's face. But this agitator was short, not tall, he was bunneted, not bare-headed, and he was a good bit older than Roddy Mac will be now, if he's still among the living.

'No to cheap labour. Make the masters pay.' And what's this? 'Fight for equal pay.' Chance would be a fine thing. The words echo though. Mr Scott. That's what he'd said. She'd been so struck by his claim that you could wed and have a bairn and stay at the case that it had slipped in her ears unheeded. But slip in it had. 'I've told Margaret you're wrong to dismiss the claim for equal pay. That's conceding the ground before you start. Demand equal pay.' Spoken as if it was so obvious it shouldn't need saying. All very well for you to say, Iza tells the handbill.

# -13-

The day's heat still hung in the air and a soft southerly breeze came as a blessing. She stopped to catch breath. Up ahead she could see the tail end of the great crowd of Bellevue and Tanfield printers stomping uphill into town. Half an hour earlier, babe in arms, she'd had to make her way against the flow. After saying he wouldn't be going, John had decided to attend the mass meeting after all, so a minder was needed. Her mum had made herself scarce, down to Jeannie's for company. Along the road to Mary Cossar's had been hard going, what with folk tumbling out of stair doors to fill the street and a voice in her head tugging her shoulder, whispering 'Don't go. Turn about. Go home and stay put till it's over.'

But, like slipping into a doorway when you're battling against a gale, a visit to the Cossar's turned out to be the very thing to silence the whisperer and ready her for what was ahead.

As she was handing her bundle over, Mr Cossar said, 'So you're off to the mass meeting. Ah've been following it in the paper. It's a hard one this, eh?'

Iza was about to say she had to rush, but Mr Cossar's tone gave her pause.

'Aye, it is at that. Ah don't know what's for the best,' she said. She sucked in air through gritted teeth and eyed the ceiling like the answer might be up there.

'Little wonder. Ah'm not so sure ah would know, not on this one.' Mr Cossar pulled out and patted a seat. 'Why don't you sit a minute?'

With a quick look from seat to door and back again, Iza sat down.

'So the women are divided into opposing camps?'

'Aye.'

'And which one are you with?' Soft eyes squinting at her, head atilt, he added, mildly, 'If you don't mind me asking.'

'Ah'm in the middle,' Iza said. 'Ah've signed the strike notice to support the men, but if we're striking to keep women from the caseroom then...' Her voice tailed off.

'Will it come to a strike?'

Again, though his question pulled her up short, Mr Cossar's soft tone invited honest reflection. Busy dreading the day Agnes and Lizzie would be picketing gates while Margaret and her chums walked to their frames, Iza had lost sight of something she knew perfectly well. There was no good reason to think it would come to a strike. The men give a bit; the masters give a bit; it's settled. Fred Henderson's words.

'Not if the deal's accepted tonight.'

'And what's the deal?'

'Ah don't know the details, but it's looking like no new learner lassies for five years and all the new Monotype machines to go to men.'

Tugging at an ear, Mr Cossar invited her to go on.

313

'The thing is, mah chum Margaret from Pauls works, they're mostly in the We Women movement, they say it'll be the end of female comps. They say we're being duped into supporting the men.'

'And do you think it'll be the end of female comps?'

Iza racked her brain. 'Ah really don't know the answer to that.'

'And do you think you're being duped?'

'No,' she said straight off. 'Ah've always known there were some wanted rid of us. You couldn't help but know. But not all of them. They are all bothered about us being cheap labour, though. And ah think they've got a strong case.'

'What about equal pay?'

Iza smiled. 'Just what mah chum's dad says. And the socialists on their handbills. And a Glasgow printer, a man, said it in a letter in the paper. They're right, aren't they? But it's never raised at work. Even the We Women lot rule it out.'

'That's a pity.'

In the moment's silence that followed Iza heard the quiet of the street and quickly stood up. 'Ah have to get going.' A quick smile for Mrs Cossar and the baby and she was at the door, Mr Cossar seeing her off.

'Listen to what's said and listen to your heart, and your guts. They'll tell you what's best,' he said.

Iza caught up as the last odds and ends of Bellevue and Tanfield printers turned a corner to join a great confluence of their fellows come down from St Leonards and up from Leith to proceed shoulder to shoulder, so tight across the broad street that hackney cabs were held up in side streets, occupants peering out of wee windows. To be part of such a great clatter of footfall and buzz of voices filled Iza with an unexpected rush of joy. As, slow-shuffling, she neared the hall she got stuck behind an old boy who'd propped himself on a railing to cough and trawl for breath. When the old boy looked round, Iza saw her father in him, face grey as a winter's sky, fear caused by tattered lungs pulsing in bloodshot eyes. She stood by the old boy's side to stop him from being buffeted until his breathing settled into a slow, regular heave.

In a postcard, Margaret had said she'd wait by the Assembly Room doors. Iza kept an eye out but was not sorry there was no hope of spotting Margaret, not in this solid swell cramming up stone steps and through gaping double doors and across a lobby, up a sweeping staircase and into a huge, high-ceilinged hall with its row upon row of full seats and bodies a dozen thick down the sides and rear, and its clamour of voices and smell of grease and damp wool. Swept down the central aisle, she was attempting to retreat to stand at the rear when Margaret's voice reached her. And there she was, on her feet in the middle of a row, behind a big cluster of green and white and gold-sashed women and another cluster in purple instead of gold, beckoning Iza to a seat she'd kept free. As Iza reluctantly made her way along the row, Lizzie's bright hair caught her eye. She and Agnes sat a row or two behind with a crowd of Bellevue women and men. Iza waved to them, then, keeping her eyes to the front of the hall, on four men and one women sitting at a long table on the platform in front of a draped Printing and Kindred Trades Federation banner with a red clasped-hands emblem, she took her seat. When Margaret leant in to whisper she shut her ears to concentrate on reading a sheet handed out by stewards at the doors. She'd not got past the heading, 'Summary of proposals', before the chairman raised his gavel and brought it down on the table.

He had to raise and bash it down a lot harder before voices sank and he could introduce Robert Allan, president of the Edinburgh Typographical Society.

After greeting all and sundry, nodding left and right and up to the balcony, Robert Allan paused, chin high, before launching into his speech. His voice was weighty and it carried.

'Forty year ago there was a general movement throughout the United Kingdom among organised workers for a reduction in the hours of labour. Edinburgh printerdom took part in that movement. Back in 1872—'

He got no further before his audience joined in, the Bellevue lot behind Iza contributing more than their fair share.

'Before we had the electric.'

'And we aw stayed in caves.'

Robert Allan raised his arms, palms forwards to pump the air for quiet. 'They asked their employers for a reduction from fifty-four to fifty hours.' A pause. 'They asked for a modest increase in rates.' A longer pause. 'The masters would give nothing. Not a minute less, not a penny more.' He raised his eyes to the ceiling. 'A strike took place and Edinburgh printerdom was badly beaten.' He studied the floor to let the weight of defeat sink in. His audience responded with a heavy silence peppered with coughs. 'After thirteen weeks they had to go back to work. And when they did, what did they find?' Here, Robert Allan made the mistake of pausing and spreading his hands as though inviting answers. He got them.

'Guillotines had been put to good use on the masters.'

'Somebody'd drunk their beer.'

The speaker cut off the barracking with sideways chops of his hand.

'They found females in the caseroom—' he called out.

Again, his few seconds' pause was soon filled.

'And it wisnae Lilly Llantry, more's the pity.'

'Or Florence Lawrence.'

'Shame. Shame.' The women to the sides and in front of Iza, Margaret included, were on their feet, stamping out their chant.

Iza stayed seated, eyes on the platform.

When the chairman raised his gavel, Robert Allan stayed him with a hand and a smile of enduring patience. He waited for the chant to end before shouting at the top of his voice, 'Edinburgh was the birthplace of female labour in the caseroom.' He must have known this would raise a barrage of cheers from the We Women crowd and an equal and opposite barrage of jeers and stamping of feet from a large part of the men, but he'd miscalculated its ferocity and, as the ruckus failed to subside, his smile dropped away. Cheeks sucked in as though he'd bitten a crab apple, he called with agitated flicks of a hand for the chairman to use his gavel. When he continued his speech, he'd lost the measure of his delivery and his voice had risen a few notches.

'The press recently and invidiously inculcated into the public mind that we wish to drive females out of the trade. We emphatically reject any such notion. I tell you now that as long as I am your president, female labour will remain in Edinburgh's caserooms.'

This had folk from all quarters jeering and hissing.

In front of Iza, a square-jawed woman wearing what looked like a bowler hat stood and turned to shout, 'Barefaced lies. These men mean to deny women a trade for which they are eminently suited.' Her green and white and purple-sashed bust heaved.

'And what business is it of yours?' a voice behind Iza

rang out. She didn't need to look round to know it was Lizzie's. 'You're no more a tradeswoman than ah'm a duchess.'

'Sisters,' the woman raised and spread her hands in a plea, 'can you not see how you're being used by the men?'

'Ah'll use you in a minute and you won't like it.'

Iza looked over her shoulder to see Agnes waving a clenched fist. Agnes was on her feet and wasn't about to stop. 'She's one of them that says, "If a printer on thirty-six bob a week took ten shillings less, but his daughters got fifteen shillings a week, we'd all be better off."' Hands on hips, head bobbing, Agnes cast her eyes round her audience. 'Ah mean, why don't we all work for nothing and be done with it, eh?'

As the chairman banged for order, Iza felt Margaret's eyes on her. She didn't respond. Responding would, she knew, involve sharing a raised-eyebrow tut, and she could not tut because Agnes was in the rights. Glueing her eyes on the proposal sheet, she read '(i) No new female learners until 30 June 1916.' She quickly scanned the rest. It said nothing about getting rid of existing women. She nudged Margaret and leant in to whisper, 'Read it, Margaret. Read what it says.'

'Of course they're not going to come right out and say it. Not those slippery customers,' Margaret said aloud, tossing her head towards the platform.

Margaret's scathing tone made Iza bristle and pull apart.

Poking his chin and tugging at his waistcoat, Robert Allan was shouting over voices still bubbling away in the hall. His first words were drowned out, but by raising his voice to the full he at last made himself heard. '...by making common cause with the men, as the best of the Neills' lassies are doing.'

Two rows in front, close by the Women's Freedom League cluster, a woman was on her feet. Head high, a hand raised to point at the platform, Amelia McLean put Iza in mind of a knight on a rearing steed, lance raised ready. She smiled to herself as an illustration and a name came to her. Prince Dobrotek from the Slav fairy tales!

'Aye, after being cajoled and threatened by you and your crew,' Amelia McLean challenged.

'Ah'll cajole you in a minute and you won't like it.'

When Agnes's voice boomed out behind her Iza's mind dredged up a name. The dwarf with the long beard. She blinked hard then looked up at the hall's sparkling chandeliers to dispel the image. 'Come magic horse with mane of gold, Come horse, oh come to me, Fly like the birds as you did of old, As flashes of lightning o'er land and sea,' she recited under her breath as, with a sweep of an outstretched hand, Amelia McLean addressed the women seated round her.

'Look at what the men demanded from the masters: the ultimate total elimination of women compositors from the trade. Only because the masters would not accede did they come up with this subterfuge, a pause in taking on learner lassies. Make no mistake. The tactics may have changed but the intentions have not.' She'd got the attention of all those around her and had those further off craning to see and hear, but now her voice was being drowned out by hisses and jeers.

'I implore you,' Amelia McLean pleaded, turning to the rows behind her. 'These men are not to be trusted.' She pointed to the platform with a straight, extended arm. 'They are duping you. They mean to be rid of us.'

'You're the one duped,' a man's snivelling voice called. 'Your head's got turned through supping tea with my Lady

Bountiful who wouldn't last five minutes in the vitiated atmosphere of a print works.' Sounds like Rab, Iza thought. She looked round but couldn't spot her brother. No sign of John or Jack either, though they were in here somewhere.

'They'd be doing us a favour if they got rid of you and you crew,' Agnes bawled at Amelia McLean.

Lowering her head and blocking her ears, Iza read the proposals. '(i) No new female learners until 30 June 1916; (ii) All new keyboards to male union labour for 5 years; (iii) 50% of upmaking and corrections of machine-set matter to male union labour; (iv) Remedial measures for betterment of linesmen; (v) All matters to be reconsidered in 5 years time.' Who knows what'll happen in the next five years, she thought. The world and all its doings might have ended by June 1916. If they'd just get on with the vote and let us all go home to our beds. Voices lapped at her ears like wavelets on the shore, some causing a rumble, others a hiss. When, every now and then, a voice rolled loose, she tried to block out the words and hear only the sound. Sounds like he's got a lump of hot potato in his gob; a countryman not long in the town, ink mixing with earth in his fingernails. Syrup's set her teeth on edge; she maybe needs a tooth pulled. He's swallowed broken glass; his throat must be red raw. Like a floorboard groaning, that one; not cheap deal though; a board of aged, oiled wood. A regular songbird, her; she'll have a pert wee mouth; must have a job getting a spoon in it. His nose has got blocked with porridge.

The word 'strike' penetrated Iza's musings. Different voice. Glaswegian? Iza looked up at the platform. The figures on it appeared to have shrunk since she last looked. Robert Allan was seated. A tall, square man stood in his place.

'Who's that?' she asked Margaret.

'Templeton of the Scottish Typographical Association.'

Head tilted back, Templeton seemed to eye the audience from a great distance. 'We hear it loudly proclaimed by opponents of our movement that the women having been in the trade for thirty-eight years it would be a great shame to turn them out. But we must bear in mind why the women were introduced. They were introduced while men were on strike.'

Amelia McLean was up and at it again. 'Now we hear the truth of it,' she called. 'The men brought our admittance into the caseroom upon themselves. And who was to blame for that? Not we women.' Cheered on by calls of 'Hear, hear' from those around her, she turned, arms outstretched, to address the hall. 'The men brought it upon themselves and now they want to make we women pay the price,' she boomed.

Iza was on the edge of her seat, all ears. 'Brought it upon themselves!' she spluttered. The old machineman at her dad's funeral flashed through her mind. Earlier, her dad coughing his lungs out. Earlier still, her sister Violet and baby William laid in a shabby old drawer. Blood boiling, she was on her feet before she knew it, shouting, 'Brought it on themselves! So you're saying our fathers set out to impoverish our families? How dare you!' She turned towards Agnes and Lizzie as she shouted, 'Shame. Shame,' a call that got taken up the length and breadth of the hall, stamped out with a thumping of boots on the floor. As the chant subsided and Iza sank to her seat, she saw that Margaret was looking at her open-mouthed.

'So working folk deserve all they get if they stand up for their own, eh?' Iza hissed. 'That's wrong, Margaret. They're wrong.'

After a fleeting glance, Margaret stared straight ahead, her neck stiff as a post. Studying her chum out of the corner of her eye, Iza saw distress in those pursed lips and hands clenched in her lap. She gripped and squeezed Margaret's arm, and felt her about to give, but just then a big hearty clap landed on her back and Agnes leant between them to say, 'That's mah girl. You tell them,' and Margaret tugged away.

Iza sank back into herself. Her head felt light. She closed her eyes, imagined herself out in the air, down at the Puddockie or, better still, up by the crags, whin in bloom. For an instant she almost sat with Roddy Mac by the Braid Burn, but her backside was back on its hard seat in the hall before it touched green grass. For what must have been a good half hour, though, she succeeded in filtering out all but odd snatches.

'... in association with our English brothers ...' Frog in his throat. Templeton? No. Shorter and bushier moustache and eyebrows. The other one on the platform.

'... English agitators meddling in Scots' business.' Voice like a meringue with a cherry on top.

'Common cause. Common cause.' Wee man with a round head on a short stump of neck.

'The memorial, nothing more, nothing less. That's what you lot wiz saying just two weeks ago. So, tell us, why have you turned round and taken less?' Stubby sausage fingers stabbing at the platform speaker.

'There is no sane reason for appointing negotiators if there's nothing to negotiate about. If we simply hand in our ultimatum, negotiations are at an end, superfluous.' Platform man sweeping away superfluous negotiators with flicks of a hand.

'The sooner the better. You can join us on the old heave-ho.' Scrawny neck, Adam's apple like a rubber ball in an old stocking.

'... lay down firmly, once and for all, that only the standard rate must be paid for all new work introduced into the Edinburgh printing trade.' Malted voice.

'Better to get the most we can with the prospect of peace and harmony than get the whole thing at the point of a bayonet and suffer years of persecution.' Robert Allan given up tugging his waistcoat to tweak his tie.

'Listening to you is persecution enough.' Highland lilt. Bunnet clasped to his chest, showing off a fine head of steel grey hair.

'The men state they have no objection to women's labour provided it is paid at the men's rate.' Not a yard away from Iza the bowler-hatted woman was up and turned about again. 'Another ruse on their part. Their talk of equal pay, we all know, is ludicrous.'

From somewhere near the back, a man's voice, Irish lilt, came slow and steady like a liner into harbour. 'Why so? The cotton trade has done that and it could be done in our trade.'

Iza turned her head and craned but couldn't catch sight of the speaker. Might have been, for all the world, Jim Connolly speaking. Mr Scott, Margaret's dad, might have said just that in his Lancashire accent. But the liner was halted by thumps of the gavel and an announcement that the proposals would now be put to the vote.

'First motion,' the chairman barked. 'All those in favour of rejecting, I say *rejecting*, the proposals, now show your hands.'

Margaret's arm went up along with Amelia McLean's and a solid patch around her as well as a smattering elsewhere in the hall.

Iza's stayed down. Her heart and guts didn't lift it.

'Second motion. All those in favour of accepting the proposals now show your hands.'

When Iza raised her hand in concert with the greater part of the hall she felt no exhilaration, but neither did she have any qualms.

'The second motion is carried,' the chairman announced.

When the lone woman on the platform now took centre stage, curiosity and a vestige of good manners won her a lull in a bout of hoots and cheers. Ellen Smith of the Independent Labour Party started by saying she'd not keep them long from their well-earned rest. 'The masters combine; labour must be organised. You have won a magnificent victory without the displacement of a single man or woman.'

'That has got to come later, and it will come. Females will be cleared from the caseroom.' A gangly man, long arms hinged to narrow shoulders, thrust his way down the central aisle and attempted to mount the platform. Failing, he turned to yell, 'It is not a vote of the trade. There's all and sundry in here voting.' He swept a hand round the hall. 'Lamplighters, scavengers, newsboys, the suffrage mob. Ballot, ballot,' he called, slamming his fist on the stage till the chant was taken up by a curious alliance of patches of men and Amelia McLean's We Women section.

Ellen Smith waited for silence then held it by launching into an account of how, three years earlier, while the wealth of empire flowed into British coffers, over sixteen thousand of her native Glaswegians, in Govan, were on the verge of starvation, brought to the brink of destitution. 'The masters will always try to keep the rewards of labour at its lowest.' She paused for boos and growls. 'And that is why the Edinburgh printers are right to defend the standard rate, why men and women are right to stand together.' She narrowed her eyes at murmurings breaking out, raised a fist and called, 'You have won a great victory because of organised workers handing in notices to strike work. Now you must extend the hand of fellowship to the women and teach them trade unionism.'

As applause rang round the hall, Robert Allan came forward to clench and raise Ellen Smith's hand and to use the moment to call out, 'I beg you to go back to your employment and see that you do nothing to cause the least heartburning inside the office.'

'We'll be giving you heartburn. Victory my backside. Bloody sell-out.' Iza looked about her. Sounded just like her brother Jack. Likely was her brother Jack, but she didn't catch sight of him.

'Absolutely ridiculous,' Robert Allan flapped. 'We have in the trade a difference of opinion. The settlement is not acceptable to all.'

'A rat's compromise,' was the last call heard loud and clear before all was drowned out in a great scraping of seats and scuffling of feet.

When Iza left her seat Margaret stayed put. Shuffling down the wide curved stairs, she glanced back, and for a moment she thought that was the red feather on Margaret's hat bobbing among a sea of hats and bunnets. But if it was there was no hope of waiting, for she was swept across the lobby and down stone steps, out through a funnel of arms thrusting handbills and newspapers, through a line of black-clad women holding placards and umbrellas and the green, white and gold Women's Freedom League banner and on past a cluster of working men holding a banner handmade from an old sheet declaring 40,000 shipbuilders locked out in Glasgow and Newcastle.

'Home rule mah backside. You lot couldn't run a tote,

let alone a country. Why should honest Scots working men support your Irish republican rabble? Go on, you tell me that.'

The voice rose from within a cluster of folk blocking the pavement. Iza knew that voice. She pushed her way through to where her brother Jack harangued two men with placards and pails. One of the two, tall, bareheaded, had his back to her. Coils of dark hair lapped a green flag draped round his shoulders. Iza's innards lurched.

She had a hand on Jack's arm and was tugging and saying, 'Come away out of it, Jack,' when the man turned. His flimsy shirt clung to a sunken chest. No. It couldn't be. He was as young as Roddy Mac and she had been all those years ago. It wasn't him. Letting out the breath she'd been holding, she let go of Jack and made to get free of the crowd, and as she did so she caught sight of a tall thin man on the edge of it. He stood near to a streetlamp, he was looking her way and it was him. He wore a charcoal derby hat and a good thick overcoat. He had a trim moustache. He was a bit stooped. But it was him. No mistaking. She barged her way out of the throng.

'Heh! Wee sister, wait for me.'

Paying no heed to Jack, she kept walking without looking back.

'To hell with your Connolly and Larkin. You want to get yourself a job of work,' Jack bawled over his shoulder as he reached her side and threw an arm over her shoulder. 'You know your trouble, hen? You can't take a joke. You shouldn't go taking it so serious. It's just a bit of fun.' He tugged her towards him in a hug that hurt.

'For goodness sake, Jack, why can't you leave it be?' Iza pulled free. Her head was swimming. Had her eyes played tricks on her?

Jack took hold of her arm, softer now, and slowed her down. He was serious. 'Ah know all about it,' he said with a nod over his shoulder. He tapped his cheek just below an eye. 'Ah was looking out for you when you were getting yourself mixed up with thon Irish rabble. Ah had a word.'

Iza had stopped short to stare at her brother, trying to take this in, when a chorus of voices swelled. Arm-in-arm, leaning forwards with heads down, a line of women came clomping along the road in a cross between a march and a skipping dance that was turning into a charge.

'Heh, Iza,' a voice from the line called out, and Agnes pulled free of it. She punched Iza's arm. 'Was that you getting in a scrap back there? We'll need to get you up to fighting weight, eh? Bit late, though. The battle's over and done. Come on, we might catch the chip shop open if we run.' She took hold of Iza's arm, but Iza held back.

'You go on. Ah'll see you the morn.'

Agnes got dragged away.

Iza turned to Jack. 'Leave me be, Jack.'

Jack questioned her with a glance back to where the agitators were packing up, the cluster around them down to a handful.

'Ah'm fine, Jack. Leave me alone. Ah'll wait a wee while and look out for John.' Her decided tone had him do her bidding.

And, standing well back on a doorstep, Iza scanned faces as the solid body of printers streaming by splintered into wee groups and pairs, wanting to spot John and take his arm and yet not wanting that at all. And the willing of her blood and breathing to cease their racing began to work, though her mind kept on at a gallop. Did Jack really do that? Did he, all those years ago, warn Roddy Mac off? He was certainly capable of it. But he was capable, too, of having her on. But if he did, what sort of man would take flight? No. He wouldn't have. It was Roddy Mac's calling, his cause, that took him off, wasn't it? Well, now it made no odds. She'd a husband and a baby boy to get home to. She refocused her eyes on a thinning stream of faces, just a trickle now. A hackney cab clipped by with a flash of purple, white and green inside. She had a frame in a caseroom to be at. And she had a chum, Margaret, to make amends with. That wouldn't be easy done. It'd take a while. Just a scattering of folk and lone voices echoing on stone walls now, and Roddy Mac was walking towards her and she, chin up, was not fleeing but standing her ground.

# -14-

'It's you, isn't it?'

'I should think so.' He lifted his hat and dipped his head.

He'd aged a lot. Though they were standing in a darkish spot, she could see his face was drawn, paler, and that his brown hair, still thick, was streaked with grey.

'Ah'm surprised you knew me.' She stayed on the step so she was nigh-on eye-to-eye with him.

'Of course I knew you.' He met her eyes for just a moment then looked over her shoulder at the closed door behind her.

'So, tell me, what became of you?'

He thought for a bit before saying, 'I became someone who thought of you a great deal.' Though he tried to lighten it, his voice was leaden.

'And when you weren't thinking of me?' she scoffed.

He faced her now. 'Oh, I was trying to be something I was not.' He attempted a grin but it didn't take.

'And what was that?' That failed grin made Iza erase some of the challenge in her voice. Though she was loath to linger here, she needed to know what he'd tried and failed to be.

'It's a long story.'

'Give me the abridged version,' she said.

He shuffled his feet. 'You first. Tell me what became of you.'

'Me?' she said. 'Och, ah've had an easy time of it.'

He quizzed her with a tilt of his head, but she didn't elaborate.

'Tell me about Dublin,' she said. 'The papers are full of this Home Rule business.'

'I might. If you'll come for a wee walk with me.'

Iza shook her head slowly, smiling in disbelief. 'Ah've no time for walks.'

'A drink?'

'Ah've given up the booze,' she said.

Eyeing this man steadily, she listened to her insides, feeling for a flush. There was none, at least not to speak of. But when he held out a hand in a plea, a longing for youth and the sight and smell of green grass, blue air and water burbling on brown stones washed through her. It came on so sudden and strong she gasped.

To let it pass, she looked away down the street. It was nigh-on empty. The Assembly Rooms' lights were out, though lamps by the entrance were still lit. On the steps the officials were shaking hands. They were climbing into a cab. The dispute was settled. That thought steadied her. She had her work, her frame to be at the morn's morn. That lifted her. She had a husband and a bairn to get home to. That thought alarmed her. Why? She raked her mind. Because she'd be taking home with her something that didn't belong was the answer that came to her. What? What would she be taking? The answer came like the thud of a dropped sack of coal. Della-Mary.

Roddy Mac had stayed silent, looking at her with his head cocked. Should she tell him? Maybe she should.

'Tell you what,' she said, 'you can walk me along to the corner. But no further. Not down the hill. Ah don't want you coming near Canonmills.'

As she stepped down he hooked an arm for her to take. She refused it.

'So why are you not in Dublin?'

'It didn't work out,' Roddy Mac said.

'So you didn't truly believe it? Common cause and all that.'

'Oh, I believed it. I still do.' He groaned. 'Truth is, I wasn't up to it. I didn't have the makings. Not enough...' He searched the dark sky for the word.

'Courage?' Iza offered. 'Loyalty?'

They were at the corner. Iza stopped and turned to him. 'Ah've learnt a thing or two about loyalty.'

He flinched.

'Still learning, mind. It's not so simple, is it?'

Roddy Mac went to take hold of her hands. She kept hers clasped at her back.

'I'm sorry I didn't treat you well.'

'Ah'm not talking about you,' Iza said. 'We were young. You owe me nothing. Ah'm talking about me.'

'What about you?'

'Nothing. Except ah have failings of mah own to live with. That's mah business though.' She made to leave but stopped.

'So tell me,' she said, 'what do you do with yourself? Working? Wed? Got bairns?'

She heard the accusation in her 'bairns'. He did not. She sensed the answer would be no. It was.

He raised his hat to scratch his head. 'I study. And I see to my mother. She's not well.'

'Well that's one thing we have in common. Bit old for a student, aren't you?'

A sheepish grin in answer to that.

'What about your father?'

'Never came back from India.'

'He's in India? What, in the army?' is what Iza said, but her thoughts were elsewhere. She'd realised with a jolt where her name for the girl, Della, had come from. Rodella. Roddy! How foolish. How stupid. The girl's name was Mary, she had a perfectly good father in Jamie and she was nothing to this man. And he would be told nothing of her. She would, though, find out something of the girl's true family, in case one day... She cut off the thought.

'My father was a judge. He'll be retired.'

Ah. So they are well-to-do, just like Violet said.

'He'll not be back. He's got another family over there. Never spoken of, of course.' Said like he'd sucked on something bitter.

Iza's raised eyebrows asked for more. When she got none she asked, 'So what's India like? You lived there?'

'I don't remember much. Crabs with big claws scuttling on a muddy riverbank. Green parrots. Getting into trouble for playing with a boy called Rajah.'

He was ready to say more but Iza had heard enough. Again, she made to leave and again she paused, though this time just for a moment.

'Did you ever meet mah brother, Jack? Ages ago. When we...'

Roddy Mac grimaced.

'Did he have words with you?'

'Not that I recall.'

'Ah'm going home now,' Iza said. 'Take good care of your mother. Cheerio.'

As she turned he quickly bent forward to kiss her forehead. She jerked back.

Down the hill to Canonmills she kept her eyes on the dark, distant hills of Fife. Above them, in a dirty purple sky, a clipping of silver moon had snagged on a strip of cloud. She was hurrying, but when she caught up with an old boy left behind by the others it was a relief to slow her pace to his and to take in deep breaths. Turned out to be the old boy she'd met earlier, before the meeting, and she was glad of his company. She asked what would become of their strike levy fund. Maybe they'd get their contributions back? He thought they might. That'd be grand, she said, what with the gas meter gobbling up money and a loaf of bread up to thruppence and her mum needing an operation.

'Aye,' the old boy said. 'We're settled.' Though they were walking downhill, he gasped for breath.

'Can you manage?'

'Aye, hen. Ah'll get there. Slowly does it.'

Leaving him behind Iza walked on past a silent Bellevue works, her mind on a pay packet that should be a bit fatter from now on, what with the improved conditions spoken of.

Mrs Cossar was surprised to see her. 'Your man came and fetched the wee one a good hour or more ago,' she said.

After standing a moment with a hand on the doorknob, Iza entered a silent house. Her mother was asleep. John stood by the stove. The kettle was on.

'Ah fetched the wee one.' He nodded towards the bedroom. 'He settled fine.' He came across to take her jacket and hang it on the door hook. 'Ah didn't stay,' he said. 'Too many in there. A terrible din.' He screwed his eyes and blinked hard.

Iza watched her husband make a pot of tea then stand with his back to her, gazing at the window's dark glass. 'Ah've seen them all go by,' he said. 'Ah wondered where you'd got to.' Like he was talking to someone beyond the glass, like she was still out there, she thought.

'Did you hear? It's settled. There'll be no strike.'

Though she felt an impulse to reach out and touch John, it wasn't strong enough to carry her across the few steps between them. The realisation that her lack was not just his loss but hers too brought on a deep sadness. Lack of what? Love's loosening was what came to mind, but since it made no sense she dismissed it. When she took the cup he held out and thanked him, he went back to gazing at the window. Fingers wrapped round the warm cup, she looked at his slight, still form. And it came to her. She and John enjoyed, if that was the word, a certain fellow feeling and familiarity. They shared a life that was, for the most part, amicable. But what they shared left them like a not-quite-matching pair of candleholders, forever set at far ends of the mantelpiece. And she knew she could not meet a need in this man, just as he did not meet a need in her. Perhaps that meant it was a fanciful need? Could there be such a thing? Was it, then, not a need but a mere fancy? Most likely it was. On that thought she went through to bed.

§§§§§§§§§

Upper and lower cases fresh-filled, floor swept and fresh sawdust dampened down by apprentices who, Iza notices, have attended to the women's side of the caseroom this morning with better grace. Rattles and clatters as rogue gusts of wind tug at a loose roof strut punctuate awakening clanks and taps and thuds. She adjusts the new combined stick and rule she's just getting the hang of and sets it down ready. When she goes to study hand-written inserts on proof pages, she blinks, takes off her spectacles to rub her eyes, breathes on the lenses and wipes them on her skirt.

'Ah'm off to Portugal,' she calls to Grace. 'How about you?'

"Parrots. Did you know the Oreopsittacus arfaki is the only parrot to have fourteen instead of twelve rectrices?'

'No ah did not. Astounding. Mah wee brother's got a parrot. Next time ah see him ah'll ask if he's counted its rectrices.'

Och. She must go and see William. See if his cough's better.

Passing Grace's frame on her way back from finding and fetching a letterboard tray from a great stack at the far wall, she says, 'Arfaki doesn't sound right. Should it not be Afraki?'

'Ah wondered that. Ah'll circle it.' Then Grace adds 'You can tell your brother he needs a tortoise-shell and ivory cage with silver wires. That's what the Romans kept their parrots in.'

'Ah'll tell him,' says Iza. 'Maybe he can pick one up down Leith.'

'Oh, and then they ate them. The parrots.'

'Aye, well, they'll have worked up a good appetite what with all that marching.' The thought of a good appetite has her stomach rumbling. She's hungry. 'I'm starving,' Margaret's voice says in her head. As she sets down her stick to take a bite of her piece without bothering to wipe her hands, the memory of weeks of licking lead from her fingers has her slowly shake her head. What a poor wee eejit she'd been.

# -15-

'Don't you go going in that pub. You'll get yourself molested. And tell him to come and see his mother. Oh, and get me a custard slice if the baker's still open,' were her mother's parting words.

By the time she got to Leith drizzle had congealed into thick, dank fog. Saturday afternoon and the Alan Breck was full to bursting, but there was no sign of her brother. A bald bloke rubbing a rag across the bar told her Willie hadn't been in for a week or so, had been on and off sick for a while now, he'd be at his lodgings. Iza made to leave as though she knew where these lodgings were, but there was nothing else for it but to admit to a stranger she didn't know where her wee brother stayed.

The lodgings were just a few twists and turn away from the pub. The stair door looked decent enough, if scruffier than she'd have liked, but upstairs landings got dirtier and dirtier. The top floor, where William lodged, had never seen a scrubbing brush. When she knocked and poked her head round the door, William, prone on a mattress on the floor, pulled himself up onto an elbow, tugged a maroon blanket over his singlet and attempted to smooth straggly hair.

'Where's your parrot?'

Iza didn't give a hoot about the parrot. It was shock at the state of this room, three mattresses and grimy bedding on the floor, a filthy bare window, had her blurt out something of no moment. The condition of her brother was as bad. His face glistened clammy white, his eyes spluttered like a stove when the gas meter's about to want feeding and his chest rattled like a faulty engine.

'He keeled over. Just as well. He'd chewed away the window frame. See there.' William raised himself to point. 'Landlady wasn't well pleased. Then the seaman gets back from Ceylon. Or was it Argentina? Anyhow, he accuses me of parrot murder. Mind you, ah think it was murder, chief suspect being him there.' He nodded to one of the other mattresses. 'Chief suspect, on account of my extraordinary powers of observation and deduction noticing him up in the night walking towards said parrot with his hands out saying, come here you wee bugger till ah wring your neck.'

William paid her no mind as she gathered up his few clothes from the floor, but when, on lifting his green velvet jacket, Iza uncovered a jotter, he sat up too quickly to take it from her and was doubled up by a volley of coughs. He gasped and worked at stifling another bout as he placed his jotter in amongst a stack of books in a crate by his mattress. She hung up the green jacket that had seen better days when William wore it to her wedding, years back.

'Have you had the doctor?'

'Who d'you think ah am? Andrew Carnegie?'

'They'll come from the dispensary.'

'They're all butchers. Fine if ah needed mah leg cutting

off, but mah legs are the best part of me. Look.' He waved
a skinny leg in the air.

'See these ah got from a seaman.' He spilled out a pack
of cards.

Iza sat down by him and admired pictures of carriages
on runners pulled through thick snow by prancing horses,
snow-covered firs and bears.

'Russian,' William said. 'These cards have been dealt
in a bar in Riga. Played for kopeks. Look. Black Balsam
stains.'

'Black Balsam?'

'Herbal liqueur. Bittersweet.'

Bittersweet was exactly how it felt to hear her brother
speak of far away lands he'd meant to visit.

'Ah'm going out to get you something to eat.'

'You can get me some wine.'

'Ah thought you didn't drink?'

'Medicinal. Just what the doctor would tell me to take,
and charge me five bob for the information.'

First off, she bought a new flannel singlet and a decent
blanket and jersey from a pile of used ones. Next, she got
a quart of milk and a bag of bread rolls. Then, in the Alan
Breck, she got the barman to fill a jug with barley broth
and she paid for broth and rolls to be taken to William's
lodgings every day till he got back to work. She was out
the door before she thought of the wine, but since her hands
were full, she left it.

Back at William's lodgings she bundled up laundry in
the stained blanket as William ate. He chewed, coughed,
chewed, eyes narrowed on her.

'You look to me like *you* could do with seeing a doctor,'
he said.

'Me?'

'Aye. You.'

'Nothing wrong with me that a good night's sleep won't cure.' She adopted a sprightly manner to lift the bundle, though in truth she wasn't so sure she had it in her to carry it home.

'Aye, well that'll be the joys of motherhood for you.'

'You'd make a great father,' she said. It came out of the blue but she meant it.

Her brother looked at her as though she'd made a joke that was so far from funny it was almost funny.

So that her mother wouldn't see the state of them, she dropped William's clothes off at the washhouse. She'd go back after tea. She'd have put them in to soak but there was no sink free. Back home, she told her mother William was in bed with a bad cold, that she'd go to see him after work during the coming week, that if he was was still sick she'd get a cab and bring him back here to stay till he was better.

'Will your man not mind?'

Seeing her mother strain to stop a grimace when she said 'your man', Iza gritted her teeth. 'No, Mother. He won't mind.'

Outside the sky was darkening. Nights closing in. Smoke rising from chimneys. Lamp and candlelight flickering in windows along the quiet street. Folk were at their tea, round their fires, having a smoke and a read of the paper, sending bairns off to their beds. A clatter from the railway depot rang through the air. When, earlier, she'd dropped William's clothes in the washhouse, she'd told herself it was wine stains on his blanket and singlet. But she'd not looked too close. Now, bent over a sink, soaping and scrubbing, she knew it was blood.

§§§§§§§§§

This is it then. Her last sheet of Ency Brit amends. And afterwards? No one seems to know. There's talk of lay-offs even though winter, their busiest season, is in sight. Chill mornings. Streetlamps spluttering of an evening. But, then, talk of lay-offs has stalked the works since the day she first entered the caseroom. Like turning to a blank page.

She's made space by reworking the whole of the revised Portugal Banking and Finance sections. So. Let's see. Three lines should do it. She lifts them to her stick to dismantle them, to break off a word at a time and pluck it to pieces, spelling it out as she drops each metal slither into its box.

> Constitution. The government is an hereditary and constitutional monarchy, based on the constitutional charter which was granted to King Pedro IV on the 29th of April 1826,

As soon as the comma's in its box, her fingers switch to plucking up to remake the lines.

> Constitution. Up to October 1910 the government was an hereditary and constitutional monarchy, based on the constitutional charter which was granted to King Pedro IV on the 29th of April 1826,

There now. One last sentence to slip in.

> The revolution of the 5th October 1910 brought the monarchy to an end and substituted republican government for it.

As she sets down her stick, wipes her hands and looks, bleary-eyed, at ranks of bowed heads, that stack of William's laundered clothes atop her dresser comes to mind. Should have been back before now, she tuts. Come Saturday she'll get down to Leith in the afternoon.

She hums to herself. At least she thinks it's to herself until Grace and Dougie Black take up the tune, and another and another – even miserable old McWhirter – join in. *He flies through the air with the greatest of ease* rises to the caseroom's pitched glass roof before dropping away.

Now a commotion draws attention. All over the caseroom necks crane. First one monotype then another stutters to a halt. Striding out of his box, the overseer's waving his arms as though he'll keep the machines in motion by sheer force of will. When the machine room's distant thuds shudder and cease, he rushes to the door. Handbells clang. Everyone downs tools to head for the nearest door. Those at the machine room end of the caseroom are blocked. After turning about, they stream out into the yard to the clatter of fire tenders' bells.

# -16-

Making his oil preparation, a machineman had set himself and the floor alight with his Bunsen burner. Whacking with their jackets, folk had managed to keep flames from reaching stacks of paper. The machineman's overalls were completely burned off him, but underneath he was just sooty and singed. A machine-feeder lassie who'd helped stifle the flames by walloping him with a jacket came off worst. Burns on her hands and arm. They were both sent home for the day.

Out in the yard all talk was of the incident. A machineman acted out the scene, hopping and spinning and swiping at his overalls. Another joined in, whacking the first with a sack, then another and another hopped and whacked until a good score were jigging, ringed by clapping bystanders. Now machinemen and feeder lassies and comps joined hands for a reel, spinning a circle while a lassie, thrust into the centre, leapt and twirled, hands on hips, and an outer circle clapped and stamped. Even if they looked up to see, they paid no mind to faces peering down from office windows.

When the work's hooter announced dinnertime, warehousemen and bindery hands came spilling into the yard. A few young bindery lassies ran to join the dance. But they were too late. Out of puff, the dancers were finding crates to perch on or a wall to lean on. Iza had contented herself with standing back to clap along to the jig and now, as she wove through groups dotted about the yard, catching snatches of blether, it struck her that no-one talked of the months' long dispute. No mention of last night's mass meeting. Not a word about the settlement. As though it had never happened, or had happened under a spell that, like the dancers, had run out of puff. Near the end of dinnertime, though, when, settled on a perch, she saw Agnes approach, she knew she meant to talk of it. And, right enough, as Iza budged along and Agnes sat, hands spread on splayed legs, she turned to say, 'So what decided you?' Her tone was uncommonly mild.

Iza chewed on it a moment and it tasted bitter. 'Her saying the men brought in on themselves. Ah pictured mah dad's face and it was like she'd slapped it. It even made me warm to mah brother who's dead set against us, and that's saying something. And they never once asked for equal pay. Ruled it out from the start. That was wrong.'

Agnes humphed at this last bit before saying, 'Your Ballantyne's chums were right, you know. The men want shot of us. Ah know that.'

Iza kept her eyes on a block of sky framed by roofs. The palest of pale blue with a trace of yellow, she thought. The sky looks further away today, she almost said.

'They knew they'd not get shot of us all in one go so they went for what they could get: a suspension of learner lassies.'

'So why...?' Iza turned her eyes onto Agnes's brown bun.

Agnes looked up. 'Ah also know that we had to throw our lot in with them. Ratting on them would have solved nothing. We'd all have lost out in the long run.'

Iza slowly nodded.

'Anyhow,' Agnes said, slapping her thighs, 'if they think they're getting the caseroom to themselves they've got another think coming. If lassies follow your lead, get wed, have bairns and stay on in the trade, they'll never get shot of us, will they?

'No, Agnes, they will not.'

Agnes stood up. 'Not unless we all drop down dead. And see me? Ah've no intention of doing that. And if they think they'll get the ban on learner lassies extended in five years' time they've got another think coming. We're not going to let that happen, are we?' She bent to clap Iza's back.

Iza got up. 'No, Agnes. We are not.' She wasn't wholly convinced, but right then it didn't matter. Five years. 1916. A long way off. Anything could happen. Anything.

# -17-

She'd stopped for a blether at the Cossars and was hurrying home when footsteps coming down towards her had her peer up the stair. A frail-looking figure stopped a couple of steps above her, blocking her way. Rab. How come she'd seen an old man when it was her brother?

'There you are.' Taking his spectacles off to rub his eyes, Rab sank to sit on a step. 'Jamie and Violet're at yours.' He looked up at her, blinking. His face looked fleshless, skin stretched over bone. 'William's passed away,' he said.

'Not William,' Iza said, as though correcting him. For a moment she was back on their St Leonard's stair with Violet announcing their father's death. 'Why do folk keep coming down stairs telling me these awful things?' ran through her mind as Rab's urgent voice called her back.

'Our wee brother, not your bairn.'

Iza gawped. Of course it's not the bairn. He's here in my arms, idiot. But did that make it better? She said nothing. When she tramped up the stair, Rab stayed put.

A lodger from William's room had come to the Alan Breck to tell the landlord; the landlord had told a workmate of Jamie's who was in for a pint; the workmate had gone straight to tell Jamie and Jamie had knocked off work. He'd got a doctor to register the death and he'd got William's body taken to his house. He'd tried to get a cab to carry him but it was against regulations; a workmate knew a cabbie who'd bend the rules for a bob but he was nowhere to be found; he'd got hold of a chum who drove a work's van. What sort of van, Iza asked. Delivery. Delivering what? Fittings and that, Jamie muttered, eyes on the floor.

'You could have told me,' Iza said.

'Ah'm telling you now,' Jamie said.

'You could have brought him here.'

'And leave Mum to deal with it till you got yourself home?' Jamie's voice was as close to scathing as she'd ever heard it.

Violet was comforting their mother. Now she laid off crooning, 'There, there,' and patting her back and came and held out her arms for Iza's baby.

'Ah'll put him down for you, eh?' Her eyes were full of concern and her voice was tender and Iza loved her for it, for knowing about her and William's special bond and not resenting it.

Rooted to a spot in the middle of the room, Iza let go of the baby.

Somber, but back to his amiable self, Jamie said he'd make funeral arrangements. Doubtless William wouldn't have kept up funeral club payments, but they'd all chip in.

'Can you get him brought here?' Iza said. 'Please?'

She worked her gums and spat on the kerosene iron she'd borrowed from Mrs Cossar, listening for its hiss and sizzle. Hot enough? Aye. She lifted and pressed William's shirt to her cheek. When she handed the shirt to her sister to have a sniff, Violet said, 'Lovely.' Last night Iza had taken a shirt and collar from the parcel of William's laundered clothes she'd never returned to him and had set them to soak overnight with a little bleach. This morning, eyes fixed on a trace of feathery ice slipping down the window pane, melted by steam from water heated on the stove, she'd mashed and rubbed the shirt until every last trace of stain had gone, and she'd scrubbed the collar until a rim of grime faded clean away. After she'd rinsed three times, the last with a splash of rose water, then used tongs to swirl the fabric round in starch mix, leaving the collar in a bit longer than the shirt, the idea of hanging them on the pulley to soak up porridge and broth vapours affronted her. But the powers above had been kind. Rain that had rained for days had stopped in the night and she'd hung the shirt and collar out in faint, glistening sun seeping through pale pink mist onto a back green spiked white with frost. Not two hours later, silver sun still low but grass turned to wet green curls, she'd pressed the shirt to her cheek and judged it perfectly damp.

As she ironed, Iza took glances at Violet who stood at the sink laundering William's jacket, spreading its green velvet over her palm to rub it patch by patch with a clothes brush. As she lifted the jacket up to her eyes to scratch at a spot with her nail, she nibbled her lower lip. Now she wetted a finger at the tap, rubbed, scratched some more, brushed, then held the jacket up to the window, tilting her head to squint at it. A sunbeam slanting through the window lit a peppering of red sequins in Violet's hair. She looks so pale and sad and lovely, Iza thought. Violet had suggested dyeing one of her husband Angus's jackets black, but she'd read Iza's face and quickly said, 'No, it should be his own one just as it is,' even though she couldn't quite hide the fact that William's green velvet affair pained her.

Iza smoothed the shirt over the board, lowered the iron to it, felt heat rise. As she leant in to press and wriggle over white cotton, back and forth until the smallest of creases vanished, she held in the corner of her eye the covered mound in the set-in bed that was her wee brother. Their mother had set a seat down to face the bed and there she sat in silence, back to the room, stroking the edge of the cover.

A pot of water set on the stove was nearing the boil and, chorus of works' dinnertime hooters sounding, Iza joined her sister to stand shoulder to shoulder by the sink, craning to watch comings and goings in the street below. The laying-out woman was due any minute. Not the one who'd delivered Iza's baby. She did most of the business round here, but not liking the thought of those cold eyes on her brother, Iza had found another. Violet took a bag of biscuits from her bag and though neither of them had any real appetite they both nibbled on one. Their mother took a look in the bag and shook her head.

When the knock on the door came, it startled them. While Violet helped prepare a basin of hot water, soap, cloths and towels, Iza went through to the bedroom and sat quiet, studying William's jotter. Jamie, Jack and Rab had cleared his belongings. Jack kept a belt with red beads woven into plaited leather. Violet had William's books for her boy. Iza kept the pack of Russian cards and a photograph of a steamer in dock, with William among folk on the quayside. You'd have had a job spotting him except someone had circled his head. The jotter had been among William's books. Violet had brought it for her, saying, 'Ah thought you should have this.'

On the cover William had written, 'Stories from Elsewhere by William Grant Ross.' He'd written 'Storys', but corrected it. A heading on the first page had read

'Travels of a Russian Frog', but this was crossed out and replaced by 'The Frog's Journey: an adventure in Russia, Scotland and America.' His round, childish hand, with a lot of crossings out, covered many pages. Folded in the back of the jotter was a page from a proof of the *Encyclopaedia Britannica* Iza had given him. As the laying-out woman pulled the cover from William and set to washing his body, Iza read to herself words he'd underlined on page 813: 'some are vocalic and soft – while a third set are harsh and guttural, the speaking of them (according to Payne) resembling coughing, barking and sneezing – gorgeous breech-clouts, cincture or short petticoats with women – flesh-eaters, cannibalism – Sioux, plains of the west, Shoshoni, interior basin.'

§§§§§§§§§

One by one, monotypes cease their clacking. One by one, figures leave frames to straighten, stretch, and, talking in soft tones, dawdle down the aisle and out the door. Far off, the machine room has fallen silent. Electric lamps fade and the caseroom is left in grey evening light. The lamp by Iza's frame casts a greenish glow. She peers at the jotter propped open on her copy holder. Charlie Dewar has cleared it with the overseer for her to stay on late to work on a private matter.

> The young, brown-eyed Fife miner lit the kerosene lamp and poured his last few drops of vodka into a tumbler. He'd bought the vodka from a Russian seaman at Methil docks. The miners were on strike, so every day he went

to the docks to ask for a day's work. Usually the answer was no, but today he had got a half day's work. He set down his tumbler, lifted his pen, and wrote in his journal:

"August 21st I was working on a steamer that was in the Dock discharging railway sleepers and saw a frog that had come with them (from Riga Russia). I got it in my pocket and let it away into a field."

Her brother William's script is littered with capital letters and his spelling is dreadful. She corrects as she goes.

Meanwhile, two days away from Methil by steamer a young lad entered a quayside inn in Riga. I never did find out the lad's name, but when he handed over his last few kopecks for a tumbler of vodka I noticed that his eyes were so deep brown they were almost black. Afloat on a sea of Russian and Latvian with a good spray of German, Finnish, Swedish, English, and also Chinese, the lad sat down in a corner alone. He'd had little work for a week and his belly was empty because the Scottish miners were on strike.

Grey light seeps down from the roof, softening the edges of the case and dimming the criss-cross compartments of sorts. Or is it her eyes dimming? No matter. So long as she can read her fingers go about their business.

Out into the night, windjammers, schooners, and steamers slept on the water like a herd of horses with waves sucking and slapping their flanks. The lamps of fishing boats flickering far out in the bay seemed to mirror the stars in a clear black sky.

Bedded down on his mat, the lad dreamed of the last stack of railway sleepers he'd helped to load onto a steamer bound for Methil and of the frog he'd placed in a crevice to stop it from being crushed. When the steamer chugged out of Riga harbour, the lad stood on the quayside watching it get smaller and smaller as it headed out to sea. There and then he determined that one day he would follow the frog

on a grand journey to Scotland and
from there to America.

She sets down her stick, clasps the leading front and
back, wriggles, clips the ends of the block of lines with
hinged middle fingers, swings the type to the galley, loosens
her grip to let the sorts settle then grips again to slide
them into place.

At the very same instant that the lad
watched the Riga steamer disappear
over the horizon, a young Souix lad
on the wild west plains of America
buckled up his beech-clout and went
to fetch his pinto pony.

She turns the page. Blank. Shall she set 'The end'? No.
She'll pull a galley proof, read and correct it, make up pages
and fold and stitch them. And give it back to William? Slip
it under his hand to be buried with him? No. She'll keep it
safe and when young William is old enough she'll read it to
him, tell him the brilliant uncle he's named after wrote it.
And when he says, "But it's not finished,' she'll say, 'No. He
never got to finish it. What do you think happens next?'

# -18-

When Iza's wee brother joined his father in Edinburgh Southern Cemetery it was lost on none of the family that for the youngest to go first was a cruel wrong. They carried this hurt with them to Canonmills, to Iza's house, for the funeral tea.

Among a few regulars from the Alan Breck to join the family, Old Tam made diverting company, as did a down-at-heel but well-spoken young man who turned out to be William's parrot-murdering fellow lodger. The pair of them related tales of William that painted him in a light not even Iza had seen him in. An eager ear they said, and remarkably knowledgeable, but modest with it, though Tam said William was quite taken with his nickname, the professor, full version being, 'Ask Professor Willie. He'll know.' And the way he could quiet a rowdy crew was a wonder to behold. Nothing to him, compared to most of the brawny customers, but, my, could he jibe and joke them into behaving themselves, spouting apt poetry he'd memorised, or even written. Some of it was fit to make hardened drinking men, never mind ladies, blush, mind.

'Aye, right enough, Willie should have been on the stage,' the fellow lodger said. 'He should have been famous.'

The family lapped this up, marvelling at a life of one of their own quite beyond and outside of them, and, too, grateful to the men for spreading some salve on sorrow.

Iza listened in as she collected empty plates, filled tumblers with beer and cups with tea, and wiped up crumbs. When old Tam fell silent and talk broke up into small pockets, she took in snatches and added the odd word as she circled the room.

'No, the lady doctor said she'd never seen anything like it. Big as a bag of tatties. And mah equipment, that's what she called it, mah equipment all to pot.' Jeannie and her mother were getting a full account of Vi Ross's innards. 'Ah've got to have an operation.' Iza heard both pride and fear in her mother's voice.

'If you add a wee drop of vinegar and heat it, not too hot, mind.' Iza had insisted her sister leave the serving and clearing to her, and now Violet sat talking to Jack's wife, Massie. Or, rather, sat listening. Massie could talk till the cows came home. As Iza went to take their empty cups Violet kept hold, rising and saying, 'Ah'll see to it.'

John, too, was lending a reluctant ear. Violet's man, Angus, was holding forth about the danger of the Irish Nationalists gaining enough seats in the forthcoming election to hold the balance of power. With a quick wince of a smile for John, Iza moved quickly on.

'True, we did not reach our objective, but we've taken steps towards it, and reach it we will.' Though he was fully aware that Iza was in earshot, Rab pretended he was not. He peered straight through her as she approached with full glasses. As he took a glass from Iza's hand, Jack, sitting by Rab's side, winked at her. 'What's that you were saying about the settlement?' Rab huffed and puffed. Iza thrust his beer at him so that he had to jerk back to clasp it. Then she took the full glass from Jack's hand, raised it and said, 'Cheers.' And when Rab spluttered, she leant to clink his glass, raising her voice to announce, 'To the settlement.' Jack laughed. And with what was close to a smile, Rab clinked her glass.

Jessie, who along with Jeannie and her mum, had suffered a dose of Vi Ross's ailments, had managed to escape and now she sat by her man, Jamie, talking under her breath so Iza couldn't catch what she was saying. The look on both her and Jamie's faces, though, told of a worry. Iza followed their eyes to a corner where the older bairns were gathered. As she'd circled the room, Iza had been aware of gaps in the family, the absence of two who belonged here. William, of course. But there was another. When the younger bairns had gone out to play, mouths stuffed with scones, the older ones had stayed put with the grown-ups. But Mary was not among them. Mary hadn't come.

'She's away out with her chums,' Jessie had said, making Iza aware of the searching glance she'd aimed over Jessie's shoulder as she and her family came in the door. 'Or so she says. She's a law unto herself, that one.' Iza had brushed this aside, but the relief Jessie's announcement had brought her was disturbing.

And now, at the sink washing dishes, she looked into her feelings. And she realised with a start that for a long while she'd told herself a tale so secret she'd kept it from herself. In this tale, her grown daughter came to her one evening when she was conveniently home alone. Sitting forward on her seat, facing Iza and looking into her eyes, the girl said she knew Iza was her mother. Her voice was tender. When Iza took hold of her hands, the girl pulled them away. So who is my father? she pleaded. And Iza fetched a newspaper clipping she'd hidden in the back of a dresser drawer, handed it to Mary and watched distress in her sallow face ease as she read a report of how a young Edinburgh man, Roddy Mac, had died bravely in some foreign place, fighting for a just cause. Then the girl reached out and took her hands and they shared a moment's silence. This nonsense, she realised, she'd let take shape and lodge in her. And the relief she'd felt at Mary's absence from her wee brother's funeral was relief at not having to face the girl now she knew the truth of it. The fleeting thought that her daughter's father's folks were well-off did not help. Money wasn't everything. Not by a long shot.

Someone was tugging at her.

'Ah said take the weight off,' her mother was saying, patting the seat beside her, empty now that Jeannie and her mother had escaped.

Preparing to offer comforting words, Iza sat down.

'It must be awful interesting, your job. Ah was top of the class, you know,' her mother said. 'Handwriting and reciting were mah favourites.'

Iza shook her head. This was a new one. It was welcome, though, and before her mother got off this track, she launched into, 'Aye. We've just finished off the *Encyclopaedia Britannica* eleventh edition. Twenty-seven volumes packed with information and diagrams and maps about everything under the sun.'

'When chapman billies leave the street,' Vi Ross sing-songed, ignoring Iza.

'It'll be printed and bound and on library shelves in a month or two.'

'And drouthy neebors, neebors meet; As...' Her mother had her eyes screwed shut in concentration.

'It'll be the last edition printed in Edinburgh. They're saying it's going to America.'

Mention of America caught Vi Ross's attention, but after a glance round the room to make sure none of her family had sailed off there, she was back tugging at her lower lip, mouthing, 'And drouthy neebors, neebors meet; As...'

'William'll know what comes next,' Iza said. Her heart lurched. 'Would have known,' she corrected, trying out the sound of it.

'Aye. Wee William.' Vi Ross's voice was full of sorrow, but it lifted as quick as it fell. 'He took after me, you know,' she said. 'Good company. Clever.'

'Mum. You take the biscuit.' Shaking her head, Iza patted her mother's knee.

When the room had emptied and John and her mother had gone to bed, Iza took down her ivory puzzle box and emptied the pieces onto the table. She slowly lifted each piece and fitted it. Where before she'd struggled, turning pieces this way and that, this time they all fitted straight off. She laid the box back on the mantelpiece, pulled on her coat and, leaving the sleeping household, walked along the street to the river.

The night was still, the sky deepest grey and nigh-on starless. By the reed-bed where puddocks spawned, she tried to picture William larking with bairns on a summer's day, but he wouldn't, he couldn't, come to her. Beyond the reeds dark water eased along so slowly it might not be moving at all. When she reached to pluck a sprig of bog myrtle, a nettle stung her palm. She clasped it to her mouth and sucked. But now, eyes grown accustomed to the dark, she saw dirty orange buds and she plucked a sprig, sniffed its sweet spice and threw it in the water. She'd liked to have watched it float away but the dark took it. Tears welled in her eyes, but they didn't fall. Reeds rustled. A tree creaked. When an owl swooped close by and a wee creature scurried by her feet, she turned for home.

The street was asleep: curtains drawn, lamps douted, candles snuffed. Nearing her stair door, Iza paused at Rab's ground-floor window, where a lamp's glow cast sepia patterns on dark curtains. Through a wee gap she made out her brother. Seated at the table, on his own, he was rubbing his eyes with the backs of clenched fists. When he ran a hand over the table to retrieve his specs, he must have knocked them to the floor, for now he bent to fumble round his feet. As he stood up, Iza thought she heard him groan, but with the window tight shut it must have been the ponderous way he moved that evoked the sound.

Slowly climbing the stairs, Iza, like her brother, rubbed her eyes, for now she was weeping. Weeping from relief that the dispute was settled and from sorrow that it had set folks at odds; because her wee brother, so full of promise, would never sail the seas; and because the girl who was and was not her daughter had stayed away today and she'd been glad of it because the girl's father, who'd got to her flesh, was a sorry specimen; and weeping, too, because in her heart of hearts she knew she could never care for the man she'd married as much as he likely deserved.

Outside her front door she stood a moment to wipe her nose and eyes with a sleeve. Then, hand on the knob, she told herself: in that house your husband, your mother, your baby son, live and breathe.

# Afterword

Rooted in the author's father's family history, The Caseroom is based on real events and features some actual historical characters. James Connolly, born and raised in Edinburgh, made an immeasurable contribution to the international labour movement. He was executed in the 1916 Easter Rising in Dublin. Compositor Amelia McLean fought bravely for women's rights.

The National Library of Scotland's print industry archives, which include Ballantyne's Chapel minute books and the 1872–3 strike minute book, and their newspaper collection, were a rich mine of primary sources. Siân Reynold's Britannica's Typesetters (1989, Edinburgh University Press), the one academic study of these events, was invaluable.